Kern loped up to the [...]
his teeth. One of the [...]
the dimming twilight and staggered back in sudden
fright. "Ymir! Ymir!"

Why the raider called upon the Vanir's chief god,
the legendary frost-giant who—legends said—once
grappled with Crom himself, Kern neither knew nor
cared. All that mattered was that he had only one man
left standing against him.

And that one hesitated as well, sword raised high,
confusion clouding his pale features. He struck
slowly, glancing his blow off Kern's upraised shield.

The Vanir wouldn't get a second chance. Kern's
broadsword bit into the raider's thigh, drawing a
bloody scar toward his groin and nicking something
important. Blood sprayed out in a warm jet to soak
Kern's kilt and splash streaming droplets across his
arms, his hands, his bare chest . . .

*Look for the next adventures
in the Legends of Kern series*

CIMMERIAN RAGE

SONGS OF VICTORY

*Millions of readers have enjoyed Robert E. Howard's
stories about Conan. Twelve thousand years ago, after
the sinking of Atlantis, there was an age undreamed of
when shining kingdoms lay spread across the world. This
was an age of magic, wars, and adventure, but above all
this was an age of heroes! The Age of Conan series features the tales of other legendary heroes in Hyboria.*

AGE OF
CONAN™
HYBORIAN ADVENTURES

LEGENDS OF KERN
Volume I

BLOOD OF WOLVES

Loren L. Coleman

ACE BOOKS, NEW YORK

THE BERKLEY PUBLISHING GROUP
Published by the Penguin Group
Penguin Group (USA) Inc.
375 Hudson Street, New York, New York 10014, USA
Penguin Group (Canada), 10 Alcorn Avenue, Toronto, Ontario M4V 3B2, Canada
(a division of Pearson Penguin Canada Inc.)
Penguin Books Ltd., 80 Strand, London WC2R 0RL, England
Penguin Group Ireland, 25 St. Stephen's Green, Dublin 2, Ireland (a division of Penguin Books Ltd.)
Penguin Group (Australia), 250 Camberwell Road, Camberwell, Victoria 3124, Australia
(a division of Pearson Australia Group Pty. Ltd.)
Penguin Books India Pvt. Ltd., 11 Community Centre, Panchsheel Park, New Delhi—110 017, India
Penguin Group (NZ), Cnr. Airborne and Rosedale Roads, Albany, Auckland 1310, New Zealand
(a division of Pearson New Zealand Ltd.)
Penguin Books (South Africa) (Pty.) Ltd., 24 Sturdee Avenue, Rosebank, Johannesburg 2196,
South Africa

Penguin Books Ltd., Registered Offices: 80 Strand, London WC2R 0RL, England

This is a work of fiction. Names, characters, places, and incidents either are the product of the author's imagination or are used fictitiously, and any resemblance to actual persons, living or dead, business establishments, events, or locales is entirely coincidental.

BLOOD OF WOLVES

An Ace Book / published by arrangement with Conan Properties International, LLC.

PRINTING HISTORY
Ace mass market edition / June 2005

Copyright © 2005 by Conan Properties International, LLC.
Cover art by Justin Sweet.
Cover design by Stefan Thulin.
Interior text design by Stacy Irwin.

ISBN: 0-441-01292-2

ACE
Ace Books are published by The Berkley Publishing Group,
a division of Penguin Group (USA) Inc.,
375 Hudson Street, New York, New York 10014.
ACE and the "A" design are trademarks belonging to Penguin Group (USA) Inc.

PRINTED IN THE UNITED STATES OF AMERICA

10 9 8 7 6 5 4 3 2 1

this book is dedicated to

Robert Howard

1906–1936

for the adventures and heroes he gave to us

Acknowledgments

Working in the universe of *Conan the Barbarian* has been one of the best writing jobs I've ever had. Not only did I get to work within Robert Howard's wonderful creation, I was allowed to create new iconic characters for people to enjoy. The best of both worlds. And for that, I'd like to thank the following people for helping me along the way:

Everyone at Conan Properties International for working with me on this book—Theodore Bergquist, Fredrik Malmberg, and Jeff Conner. Also Ginjer Buchanan, my new editor at Ace Books, with whom I've always wanted to work.

Don Maass, my agent. Dean Wesley Smith and Kristine Kathryn Rusch for their continuous support. And fellow barbarian Steve York, who agreed to read quickly and had many good comments.

Also a quick round of thanks to the usual suspects—Randall Bills, Herb Beas, and Oystein Tvedten, who are never too busy for one more research or "reading" question.

And finally, my family. My children—Talon, Conner, and Alexia, who put up with my (at times) odd behavior. Heather, my wife and my partner, who read every word and helped keep me at task on yet another insane deadline. I am also contractually obligated (by them) to mention my cats—Chaos, Ranger, and Rumor. And I suppose Loki, our neurotic border collie, deserves a quick nod as well.

Thank you.

SOUTHERN SEA

1

KERN WOLF-EYE'S BREATHING came in sharp huffs and thin, frozen wisps. Leather harness straps dug into his shoulders. He nodded Daol around a wattle-and-daub shack, steering clear of Gaud's trodden paths as the two clansmen kept the flat-bottomed sled, piled high with fresh-split logs and a pair of scrawny rabbits thrown on top, to a frosted patch of untrodden snow.

Icy crust broke underfoot. The old snow packed down with a dry, squelching sound that reminded Kern of stepping on dead fire coals.

Daol labored next to him even though the young hunter could have brought the rabbits back hours before. Both broad-shouldered Cimmerians leaned into the strain, counting the last hundred paces to the village lodge. Their final pull fell over a short downhill slope. Kern put the last of his strength into it, stomping through the snow crust.

The sled caught, hitched, then broke free into a short, fast glide that eased their burden for a few seconds. Too late, Kern realized the sled wouldn't stop in time. He and Daol scrambled to either side, pulling on their harnesses, but the heavy weight simply jerked them forward, and the sled hammered into the wood already stacked carefully under the lodge's overhanging eaves. There was a sharp crack from the sled, and the end pile of seasoned split-rounds collapsed in a slow-moving avalanche.

Daol massaged his shoulder, stared down at the tumbled wood.

"Have to carry some in, anyway," Kern said. He examined the front of the sled. One of the carefully sawn planks had split. "I'll get that fixed in the morning, before going out again."

He stood, kicked away snow clumping to his furlined boots. A bright patch behind the gray cloud cover warned the sun was close to the western Teeth, ready to slip behind the massive peak of Ben Morgh.

Kern looked back the way they'd come, at the crests of tall evergreens standing above straw-thatched roofs of Gaudic homes. Two leagues, he gauged. Maybe three. And they had beaten nightfall by an hour at least.

"Good pull." He thanked his friend. Daol had not been obliged to help, but the dark-haired hunter would not accept stronger praise.

"Kept me warm."

Still, Daol refused to meet Kern's eyes. He grabbed the rabbits by the thong binding their back legs together. They looked even scrawnier, dangling from the hunter's callused hands. Draping them over his left shoulder, he retrieved Kern's axe and his own bow and birch-bark quiver off the back of the sled.

"You'll drop off an armful of wood?"

He wasn't asking for himself. Kern nodded, setting the axe aside. "You will save Reave some meat?"

Daol's gray eyes flicked up, briefly, then he glanced

down at the rabbit hanging over his shoulder. "Hind-quarters. And any fat scraped off the pelt."

Nothing would go to waste. Especially with winter's stranglehold on Conall Valley pushing so deep into what should have been the beginning of spring. The fur would be cured, entrails boiled down into a fatty broth, and most of the meat stripped for the chieftain. Even the bones, often thrown to the dogs in summer's excess, would be ground up to mix in with oat meal.

If there was any oat meal left in Gaud.

"Find you tomorrow," Kern said. He snagged the carrying strap left hanging on the corner post of the small lodge. Nothing more than a pair of wide leather belts stitched together, with wooden handles sewn onto either end. Spreading it over cleared ground protected by the eaves, he piled wood onto the strap.

"Kern?"

Daol still stood near the back of the sled, wrapping his fur cloak tightly around him now that the warmth of exertion faded. A chill wind played with the hem of his cloak and stirred his knife-cut hair. He suddenly looked much younger than his eighteen summers. That same uncertainty that had marked him before he'd made his first kill in battle with Clan Galla. Daol's gray eyes searched the skies, the rush-laden rooftop, the side of the clan lodge. Anywhere but looking toward the man he called a friend.

"Do you believe Reave has a chance?" he finally asked.

A bold question, when their clan chieftain lay dying not twenty feet away. And why ask Kern? His support for Reave to eventually replace Burok Bear-slayer meant little, except some firewood and a few roots scavenged from a forgotten cave.

"By Crom, I hope he does," Kern answered. It was the best he could offer.

Daol nodded, then strode off toward the slaughter

pens on the south side of the village. He'd likely have the large lean-to and its bloodstained tables all to himself. No one had taken down a deer in weeks, and Kern knew the clan could not afford to slaughter any more of its small cattle herd.

Then again, how much longer could they afford to wait? Winter still refused to release its grip. The sun had turned in the sky on midwinter's day, but had yet to bring its warming touch back to Cimmeria. "Grimnir's curse," they called it, evoking the name of Vanaheim's great warrior-chief. Hardly a week went by without refugees traipsing through from a burned-out village or farmstead, all with that name on their lips. Grimnir the invincible. The immortal. The Great Devil.

Real or no, able to control the seasons or no, Conall Valley remained cloaked under winter's shroud. No new snow this night, Kern judged by the taste of the air, dry and raw, but no rain to hammer away the ice and no spring sun the next day either. So, more waiting.

In the meantime, Kern had his work to finish.

The village lodge wasn't large. Thirty feet to a side, and two small rooms off the back where the chieftain's family lived. The main room served as the clan's meeting hall, and as a place of refuge during attacks or severe storms that at times drove the folk of Clan Gaud into the common shelter for warmth and safety. In the winter, it was usually a place of stories and toasts around a blazing fire set on the hearth.

For the last few weeks, it had been instead a place of sickness and mourning.

Pinning the strap of split wood against the doorframe with one strong arm and the bulk of his weight, Kern slapped at the latch with his free hand and kicked open the heavy door. Regaining his grip on the wear-polished handles, he shouldered his way through the entry. The scent of corruption assailed him immediately, hidden under the scent of lye and smoked rushes.

It had a taste to it, like meat left to rot in a damp cellar. Wet and warm and putrid.

The lodge hall was warmer than outside, but not by much. Heavy, black bearskins hung from the rough-hewn rafters, forming a square tent around the center of the room, shielding the hearth and blocking in most of its warmth to keep the chieftain comfortable. Barren tables had been pushed up against the outside walls. Casks and kegs sat piled in the corners, too many of them empty as the clan rationed what little they had left from their autumn stores. Skewed benches and overturned stools, all empty save one where the chieftain's daughter worked.

Maev rose from her seat beneath one of the narrow windows, setting aside the dagger she'd been honing against a smooth stone. It joined a small pile of freshly sharpened blades, all glistening with a light touch of oil. Another half dozen small blades, each showing some rust from disuse, lay in a second, smaller pile.

Shutting the door with a solid shove, she cut the light down to a dimness challenged only by two un-shuttered windows and a small oil lamp hung near the doors.

Maev shared similar features with most of Clan Gaud's villagers. With most Cimmerians in fact. Like Daol she had coal black hair, ragged-cut below the shoulders where she simply hacked it off every month or so with a sharp edge. Her eyes were bright, sapphire blue, and her skin just a shade darker than fair.

Next to her, next to most of them, Kern was a pale reflection. His frosted blond mane, fairer even than the Nordheim tribes to the north. Such a light, ivory yellow to be almost white. The color of old frost. His pale, cold skin that never tanned, no matter how long he worked outdoors in the summer.

And the amber yellow eyes so few would look into. Night eyes.

Wolf eyes.

Maev had no problem meeting his gaze. Her strength did not allow her to bend under the hall's smothering presence. Searching Kern's face, her eyes blazed with a fierceness Kern often found disconcerting. Now he welcomed them for their defiant gleam. So many Gaudic villagers had given up, walking around with a defeated slump in their shoulders and attending the clan's daily needs with less and less energy. The harsh, unending winter sapped their strength, and Burok's injury corrupted their will as surely as the gangrene ate away at their chieftain's flesh.

She said nothing to him, measuring Kern the way one might size up a boar in the slaughter pens. The strap of wood grew heavy, and Kern's muscles ached with a dull throb, but he waited. For her approval or her denouncement, he wasn't certain.

Finally, she stepped around Kern and led him back to the hanging tent, drawing aside one of the heavy bearskins, allowing him to pass.

The scent of decay nearly throttled Kern as he stooped beneath the hanging skin. It burned into his sinuses and clawed with oily fingers at the back of his throat. He coughed once, then swallowed against the slick taste coating his tongue. He nodded at Jocund, the village healer, who hovered over the chieftain's exposed leg and glanced up only briefly.

A modest fire crackled and spit on the hearth, but it was still intensely hot within the curtain of bearskins. The shaggy walls trapped the heat most effectively. Kern set his strap of wood near the ever-needful pile, then fed the fire with a split-round, careful not to throw too many sparks. By the dancing light Burok's face held some color above his thick, black beard, but it was all a reflection of the licking flames. Kern saw past the false health, at the ashen pallor and the face drawn under weeks of pain and suffering.

Burok Bear-slayer grimaced, stared up at the ceiling where the covered smoke hole wept an occasional drop of moisture that fell sizzling into the fire's hot coals. He appeared even thinner today, skin pulled taut over angular cheekbones and yet too soft around the eyes.

"Easy, woman!"

The chieftain's voice was hoarse and angry, and he sounded very much like his namesake. A light sheen of sweat stood out on Jocund's forehead, creased with her decades of concern for the village and its people. Below her nose she had rubbed a glistening salve, likely to deaden the scent. She held a wooden peg in each hand. A fine wire stretched between them. In sharp sawing motions she stripped away more of the corrupted, gangrenous flesh which crept up toward the tourniquet.

Above the strap of leather more veins stood out, already swollen with infection. The healer had to know the leg, and the life, were beyond saving. Kern knew.

By the haunted look in Burok Bear-slayer's eyes, the chieftain obviously knew it as well.

All because of an accident. Stepping through a crust of snow and breaking his leg in a marmot hole. Kern had been there, heard it happen. The wet *snap* and hardly a grunt of pain to tell of it. And the bone splinter, sticking out through the skin. No one else had been close enough to signal, and certainly they couldn't call out just then for worry of Clan Taur.

"Get me home, Kern." That had been the chieftain's only order. He didn't call Kern "Wolf-Eye." He never had.

Ten miles on an improvised litter, in the face of a frigid, easterly wind, Kern dragged Burok back to Gaud with barely a stop to ease his flagging muscles. Another Gaudic warrior would never have made it. There were others stronger than Kern, more able with a sword or battle-axe, certainly, but none had his resistance to winter's touch. Even so, both men had frostbite waxing their cheeks when Kern staggered into the village, and the wound itself had frozen around the edges despite Kern's wrapping his own cloak about the village leader.

Without his aid, Burok would never have come home at all. But every day since, in the faces of those clan kin who looked on Kern, he saw that most wished it had been he injured.

And likely left to die.

"Need anything more?" Kern asked, settling the split log into a good rest, in the cradle of two burning rounds.

"New leg," the chieftain growled. His words slurred a bit with fever. "Good meat. Ability to piss on a tree, not'n some bucket my daughter empties f'r me."

"Peace and quiet." Jocund worried at the septic wound some more. She hid her grimace from the chieftain, but not from Kern. Didn't matter. He saw for himself it had turned from dry gangrene to a spoiled black. No poultice could cure it. Burok Bear-slayer wasn't long among the clan.

"Kern." The chieftain struggled up onto one elbow, face sweating with the effort. He squinted, as if having trouble focusing on the younger man's face. But no one else in the village had such pale hair. "You trekked toward t' Noose today?"

Three days ago, actually, but Kern nodded anyway. "To the foot of the Snowy River country."

A hand shot out from under a thick, woven blanket, grabbing Kern by the wrist. Burok's touch blazed with fever. "Saw? You saw?"

The older man shivered as Jocund loosened the tourniquet, letting blood seep from the fresh cuts and into a pile of stained rags. She nodded quickly at Kern to answer, wanting to keep her patient's mind—such as it was—on other things.

"Two fingers of ice on the lower ponds. No new

green on the alpines." The stunted evergreens would be first to show the coming of spring with fresh needles. "No elk sign. No tracks from the returning herds at all."

Driven far to the south by the harsh winter, they were unlikely to return until fresh shoots sprouted. But the village hoped.

Burok released Kern's wrist, settled back onto his straw mattress. Perhaps easing the tourniquet quieted him. Jocund refastened a tight bandage and her best poultice, smelling bitter and black and moist as the corrupted flesh beneath. The healer took her leave as quietly as she had worked.

The chieftain sighed. "Bad days ahead."

Very. Dried meats had given out the month before, and there were very few of autumn's roots left in the dry pits under the lodge. Hard bread and moldy oats and a few winter rabbits wouldn't keep the village alive for much longer. Clansfolk would be turned out of the village soon to fend for themselves, preserving what was left for the others. The old and the weak would be first cast out.

And Kern. A dying clan had no need for its outcast.

"No tracks. No tracks not good." The chieftain closed his eyes, shook his head with great deliberation. He opened one eye again. "None?"

Kern heard the lodge's main door open again, and close. He rocked back on his heels. "Only small game. And men. Not enough to be a Vanir raiding party," he promised, when Burok's eyes snapped alert.

"Scouts. Might be scouts. Following the mountain line. Tell . . . tell Cul."

Kern already had, though the self-named village "guardian" claimed to already know. Maybe so. Cul spent days roaming the countryside, well provisioned from Gaud's shrinking larders, scouting for Vanir. There was a great worry among many clan villages that the harsh winter would encourage more raiding. It had happened two years before, when winter lingered. That was not long after King Conan, newly crowned, pulled occupation troops back to Aquilonia trying to do well by his birthland.

The gesture came at just the wrong time. Unchecked, Vanir raiders—some led by the Great Devil himself—charged across Cimmeria in a frenzied bloodlust. Entire villages disappeared. Grimnir never made it as far as Gaud, but the Vanir warlord's reputation had been fierce and bloody.

Vanir raiders still attacked with impunity throughout Conall Valley and as far south as the forests of Murrogh. They did not take prisoners as the Cimmerian tribes did when raiding for sport or for "ransom." They took slaves. Worse, what they could not carry away as plunder they spoiled for those who remained.

There wasn't much left in Gaud for the raiders to claim, but that wouldn't stop them from destroying whatever remained.

The new wood caught fire, frozen pitch thawing and snapping with new life on the hearth. A green smoke scent told Kern that it hadn't aged well, but there wasn't much choice. The clan survived as best it could. He stoked the fire, hoping the flames would warm some life back into Burok's wounded leg. He stacked the strap of wood onto the pile, dusted bark and splinters into the climbing fire, and stood to leave.

Facing Cul, who stood at a break in the curtains, shoving aside the insulating blankets rather than stooping beneath.

Two summers Kern's senior, Cul stood only a finger's width over Kern's height but massed an extra stone's weight, easily. His dark hair fell back in a wavy crest, spilling around his shoulders in thick curls. He had the blue-gray eyes of a peregrine and a proud chin. Cul's war sword lay strapped across his back, cord-wound handle sticking up over his right shoulder. He looked ready to draw it on a moment's notice.

"Finished with your work, Wolf-Eye?"

Kern nodded.

"You can deliver a strap of wood to my hut, then."

He would not.

As boys, Cul had feared Kern's strangeness. As young men, he used it to disparage Kern and those few who befriended him. It had taken Daol and Reave working together to buy Kern some little peace. Kern remembered many nights, lying awake, hoping for a faster bear or a slippery rock to rid the village of his tormentor, no matter the loss to Gaud. How great a loss, of course, depended on whom you asked. Kern had heard Cul sneer at the Conan legends one fireside night, then compare his exploits with those of the Cimmerian-turned-king the next. Now, only Reave stood between Cul and the certainty of being Gaud's next chieftain.

So there would be no firewood. Not by his hand. Kern might not have much say in the clan, but he showed his support for Reave in whatever way he could. Cul would know for certain that someone else was ready to challenge if Kern did not do as bidden, and that person had Kern's loyalty if no one else's, but Kern had to think Cul already knew. The man was not stupid, more be the pity.

He almost told Cul nay to his face, in fact, to have it out in the open. But Burok Bear-slayer interrupted.

"Snowy River?"

Cul's gaze darted away, and the moment was lost. The warrior stepped fully into the tented room, puzzled at the outburst and at the clan's chieftain, who sat fully upright on his mattress. The furs Burok had been smothered in lay balled to either side. He looked almost normal, if one could ignore the scent of rotting death that hung over the tented room like a funeral shroud. His blue eyes—the same vibrant color he shared with his daughter, Maev—were clear and full of sudden strength.

"What were you doing as far east as the Snowy River lands?"

Dropping to one knee next to the chieftain's bedside, Kern wondered if a miracle had occurred. But the fever still burned in the man's flesh, warm enough to make the fire pale, and Burok's face was white as the blanket of snow outside. His speech, though, was clear, and there was real thought behind it.

"It was only three days' trek," Kern said, dismissing the leagues and the nights spent huddled in a thin bedroll. "I checked for herd sign, and ran our southern trapline on the way back."

"Too far, with this blasted winter hanging on. By Crom's stiff pike, Kern, Clan Taur was too far at half the distance."

Or not far enough, judging by the way Cul's expression soured at their chieftain's rallying strength. But Cul was not close enough to smell Burok's fetid breath, or see the cloudy film in the older man's eyes. Kern shrugged aside the caution.

Cul would not let it pass, however. "Clan Taur will not forget your daring for another generation," he said in rare praise of Burok's winter raid against the northern valley clan. "And Wolf-Eye does not fear winter. He's made a pact with it, after all."

That's what an elder had once said of him, anyway. That winter settled into Kern's bones as a child. His frost-tipped hair and amber eyes were proof enough for most. Even Kern's only friends, Daol and Reave, thought him a bit . . . odd. He felt chills under summer's strongest sun, yet could withstand the harshest storm with his cloak thrown wide and chest bared to the elements.

Another good reason to give Kern over into the care of the village foragers. His chances of accident were smaller than another man's, and it kept him busy and away from the village for most days.

"It was worth the trouble," Kern said simply, seeing his chieftain's newfound strength already beginning to sag. "Or would have been, if I had spotted sign."

Burok shook his head. "Too far. Never should have gone." But if he was talking about Kern's search for the herds or the chieftain's own bravado to conduct a midwinter raid for ransom, there was no telling. His rally was dying as fast as it had come on. And Kern was certain Maev would like to say good-bye to her father. He doubted the older man would last the night.

He grabbed the chieftain's shoulder. "Strength to you, Burok Bear-slayer."

Then he rose without so much as a nod or glance at Cul, grabbing his carry strap and ducking under the skins to find Maev already moving toward the sound of her father's voice.

He's strong, Kern wanted to tell her. But as usual, in Maev's presence he found himself struck dumb. He stood there, waiting for her to pass by, waiting to see if she'd say anything that recognized he existed. She did.

"It should be you," Maev said. Sharp and direct.

The first person in all of Clan Gaud to say it to his face, wishing him under death's watch rather than her father.

It was what Kern had come to expect. And they were the obvious words to carry with him out the door, and into Cimmeria's long, cold night.

2

HAMMERING ON THE door to Kern's hut shook him awake the next morning, batting aside his weary sleep and driving dull blades into his head. The door's leather-bound planks rattled together. Rafters trembled. The last of autumn's dust shook out of the overhead thatch.

Whoever it was had a heavy hand, and wasn't shy of using it.

Kern woke slowly, as he often did after a heavy day's work. Tiny shards of dimmest light peeked through cracks in the clay-daubed walls and ringed the smoke hole above like a faint halo, hardly stronger than the smoldering embers in his small, bedside fire pit. The Cimmerian growled a curse. Barely morning. The sun was not above the valley's eastern peaks. He stretched out beneath a coarse woolen blanket that scratched and itched at his chest, his legs, pulled up so tight the hem chafed around his neck. His muscles ached, he discovered, but not unpleasantly. Exposed to the hut's draft, though, his ears and the tip of his nose felt numbed. Frost in the air. He didn't need a window to know it.

More hammering, slow and methodical, like a battering ram.

Sucking in a deep lungful of brisk morning air, tasting the disturbed dust, Kern threw off his covers in one great sweep. His skin puckered immediately, tightening against the chill. He felt it most in his groin, behind the knees, and in his armpits. Grabbing his Cimmerian kilt—the heaviest one, dyed red with tribal sworls stitched into it and trimmed with the shaggy hide of a mountain ram—he wrapped it about him from abdomen to knees, belting it in place with a wide strap of leather and brassy gold buckle. Fur-trimmed boots yanked on next. Then a tattered leather poncho— lighter than his winter cloak, adequate for stomping around the village.

Also, when he took a swing at the person pounding his door, he wouldn't care if it got damaged.

Balling one hand into a meaty fist, he pounded his side of the door, once, in warning, then slid back the thin crossbar holding the ramshackle entry closed.

Yanking the door inward, he stepped forward and glared into Reave's brushy, black beard.

His friend stood a full hand's spread taller and had the shoulders of an ox; with his fur cloak wrapped about him, warding off the chill, at a distance he could easily be mistaken for one of Cimmeria's great black bears. He wore two gold hoops, taken off a Vanir raider he'd killed, one in each ear. His eyes were pale blue, like ice frozen over still ponds, yet they reflected more emotion than the usual Cimmerian bothered to show.

Now, Reave looked sorrowful, which was an uncertain expression on the Gaudic giant. One he was not used to wearing. Anger and annoyance fitted him better. Or laughter, around lodge fires and drinking games.

Kern could only think of one thing to bring Reave at his door so early.

Burok Bear-slayer.

He glanced down at Reave's hand, the one not held up to pound further for Kern's attention, and saw blood drying on thick fingers. And there were other villagers straggling by on the muddied, frozen path behind Reave, their forms little more than shadows in the dim light and the thin curtain of frosted fog draped across the village, all heading toward the lodge.

"Last night?" Kern asked.

Reave nodded silently.

Waving Reave ahead of him, Kern reached back into his cramped hut, grabbed a thin belt with a long knife sheathed in its scabbard. He strapped this on as he walked, settling it lower than his kilt belt and angling the knife over his left leg for easy reach. He caught up as the larger man waited for a trio of hobbled cattle to shuffle across the frozen path, released early from huts or homes where they had provided warmth through the night.

Cattle were wealth to the clan in more ways than milk and meat. Kern did not care for the way their bones showed so plainly under their hides.

"Daol went for his da," Reave said, finally breaking his silence as they began walking again. His voice was a deep rumble, as if it had been dredged up from great depths. "Cul roused most of the village. Saw you weren't 'round yet."

Of course Cul was beating down doors. The right doors. "You shouldn't be wasting your time on me."

Reave only shrugged.

Too late to make a difference regardless. At a quick glance, Kern saw the entire village had to be awake and gathered out front of the lodge. Men, women, and children. The elderly. Even Old Finn was up, hobbling forward on the forked branch he used as a crutch when his gout was bad. All were bundled in their cloaks and warmest blankets, standing a silent vigil, their breath rising above them in a halo of steam. A baby began to fuss, but was silenced when its mother pinched shut its nose, forcing it to choose between crying and breathing. Wailing babes had no place there.

Daol had already shoved his way toward the front with his father, Hydallan, who wore the peaked rabbit-fur hat his son had made him and so was easy to spot in the crowd of silhouettes. Reave bulled his way forward as well. Several villagers stepped aside for the strapping clansman. A few others, noticing Kern in his wake, shuffled away farther still.

Cul stood nearest the lodge doors, one of which was stained with several dozen bloody smears, dripping dark fingers toward the bottom edge. Kern did not miss the glance that shot from him to Reave and back again.

" 'Bout time, Wolf-Eye."

Drawing his knife in answer, Kern sliced quickly and cleanly across his palm, then sheathed the blade. He held Cul's gaze while letting a small pool of blood well up in his hand, then slapped it forward to smear the door, letting it mingle with the blood of Clan Gaud.

The last, apparently, as Cul quickly used his own knife to cut the leather bindings that held the door in place. Both Cul and Reave lifted it off the pivots to lay it flat inside the hall, over a pair of benches.

That was it. Their clan chieftain was dead. Burok Bear-slayer would be dressed, then stitched into a hide sack and laid out on the lodge door. On this he would eventually be carried east and then north, to be buried at the feet of the Eiglophians in the Field of the Chiefs, alongside the other great Cimmerian chieftains, in sight of Ben Morgh and the House of Crom.

But who would lead that passage, and when, was the decision for the new clan chieftain. Who would be selected that day.

The way in which Cul and Reave stared at one another, waiting for Burok to be prepared, Kern had no
doubt their minds were already on the Challenge.

BY NOON, EVERYONE had prepared.

Again the entire village turned out, this time to wit-
ness the selection of their new chieftain. Every clan and
village had its own custom, but common to most the
selection of a new clan head was an event to be celebrated. Different from their solemn procession that
morning, the Gaudic folk were louder now, even bois-
terous. They chatted. Some made sideline bets—for fa-
vors or chores or on their honor come summer. On a
warmer day, or in better times, a keg of ale would have
been broken open. Instead, they made do with mint
leaves steeped in boiled water and twice-baked bread
that had survived the wet and cold months of a Conall
Valley winter.

Chewing the tough crust with little enthusiasm and
less pleasure, Kern waited to see what the day brought.

Reave arrived in kilt and boots and not much else to
ward off the clammy touch of fog, which persisted past
morning. No cloak to snag or tangle with. Only a thick
matting of dark hair dressing his chest and his back.
The sword scar he'd taken the year before, raiding one
of the southern tribes, stood out waxy and pink across
his right shoulder. He still wore the large hoop earrings
in both ears, as Kern had suggested. They reminded
people that Reave had fought Vanir raiders, and survived, while Cul had only chased off a few scouts.

A few people cheered his arrival. More sent dark
looks.

The majority of the village went about their own
betting and boasting.

Kern met Reave near the Challenge Circle, an arena
staked out with poles festooned with somber strips cut

from bloodstained cloths and a bearskin from Burok's deathbed. He clasped his friend's right hand between both of his.

"Daol will be on the other side," he told the larger man. "He'll step in late, and try to wrestle one of Cul's supporters out of the circle."

Reave grunted, and blew a long draw of frosted breath out through clenched teeth.

"Expect the Tall-Wood brothers to come for you early. They work well as a team." The previous summer, in fact, they had outwrestled every match the village could put together.

A nod. And another grunt.

"By Crom, Reave, will you listen to me?" Kern grabbed his friend by the elbow, turning him around. "Cul's people are going to work together against you. You have to think faster than them."

"Thinking's nay my strong suit," the large man admitted. He punched Kern hard on the outside of the shoulder. "You think for me, Kern. I'll handle the Tall-Woods."

Blowing out an exasperated breath, Kern nodded. "They won't be looking for Daol come late and from behind them. When you see him, it's your best chance."

Any more advice was interrupted when Maev arrived, carrying a dagger that had belonged to her father. She held the hilt in her left hand, laid the blade across her right palm, which bore a crusted wound from the morning's bloodshed. No words were spoken as she walked into the Challenge Circle, looking neither right nor left to acknowledge or favor any one potential Challenger. Right to the arena's center she walked, then held up the dagger as she turned one time in place.

Kneeling, she drove the blade down into the frozen earth, sticking it two inches into the ground.

Then she retreated along the way she'd come, join-

ing a group of the village women, who waited in Jocund's company with bandages and splints and what
few herbs the healer had salvaged from her kit. Challenges were rarely bloody, but accidents happened.

Maev's leaving the Circle was all the men had been
waiting for. Two clansmen jumped in together . . . Brig
and Tabbot Tall-Wood. An older Challenger followed
them into the Circle—someone in the village pulling
for Reave, or thinking to make a stab on his own—but
the brothers grabbed each other by the wrist and
caught the older man across the throat, staggering him
backward as if having run into a tree limb.

He dropped to the ground outside of the Circle,
wheezing for breath but mainly unharmed.

The village cheered the first good challenge. There
wasn't a great deal of applause, but voices rose in support and defiance.

If it had been simply a mad rush for the dagger,
Kern believed the brothers—one of them—would easily have won. But Challengers remained in the Circle
until all opponents from the village had been faced
down or defeated. And with every new entry a clansman could reenter to oppose, though once cast out each
lost the right ever to pull the dagger from the ground.

Three other clansmen entered at about the same
time, two immediately falling on each other and the
third being set upon by the Tall-Woods. Then Reave—
who quickly tossed out a young pup with no business
in the Circle, without much more hurt than a bloodied
nose and kick in the seat—and finally Cul.

Cul kicked Wallach Graybeard square in the crotch
from behind. Kicked the veteran warrior again to roll
him from the arena.

When he did it, his eyes were on Reave.

Like metal to lodestone, the two favorites worried
less about the others involved and more for keeping a

wary eye on each other as they pulled closer and closer together.

Men had laughed at Reave's dealing with the ambitious teenager, winced and groaned at Cul's rough handling of Wallach. Kern took the challenge much more seriously, seeing his friend taking on all comers and being in no position to help. He grasped at the air in front of him, laying hands on imaginary opponents, ducking and weaving every punch or kick thrown at Reave, who battled like a northern Berserker unleashed on poor farmers.

The Tall-Woods rushed him right away, but Reave stopgapped them with hamlike fists into the sides of their heads, bashing the two together and dropping them like sacks of oat meal.

Reave had no time to drag them from the Circle, though, set upon by another of Cul's supporters. Meanwhile, Daol entered late and rapped Morne, one of Cul's most stalwart friends, on the back of the head, stunning the man and shoving him back over the boundary. Kern grinned savagely, and hoped, and yelled support for Reave to try and divert any attention from Daol.

Meanwhile the Tall-Woods shook themselves back to sensibility, staggering to their feet.

The taste of blood scratched at the back of Kern's throat as he quickly yelled himself hoarse, sucking back great breaths of frigid air. His pale skin puckered against the cold as he ripped away his poncho and stood bare-chested on the edge of the Circle. Watching Reave beset by two Challengers, and Daol being wrestled to the ground by a new man, he nearly jumped in himself.

He did not, though. Any man stepping forward had to be someone the clan would follow. His challenge would bring another half dozen warriors into the arena, and tradition or not, they would be ready to harm Kern as severely as possible. That wouldn't help Reave. It wouldn't help the clan.

Kern had done his best in Burok's memory by helping prepare Reave.

Unfortunately, his friend was a warrior born but not so much a leader. Daol, at least, had freed himself from his earlier tangle, and come up behind the Tall-Woods, putting Brig in a headlock. Cul tried crabbing over to help, but worried more about Reave, who now had eyes only for his chief rival. Kern winced as Reave ignored first one man—who smashed a two-handed fist into the side of his head—then a second, who threw himself around Reave's body, trying to stagger him backward.

Might as well have tried to uproot a tree. The massive Reave shrugged off both, but continued as well to ignore Daol, who fought toward Reave's side to lend a hand.

Cul and Reave swerved toward each other, catching another of Cul's friends between them. Cul shoved Dabin aside, and Reave continued him on his way with a kick into the stomach that folded Dabin over and rolled him from the Circle.

But before Reave laid hands on Cul, Tabbot Tall-Wood dodged around his brother and Daol, tackling Reave around the neck and dragging him down. Reave shed the smaller man with a violent clap against both ears, but then Cul was on him, wrapping a mighty arm around Reave's windpipe, choking the breath out of him while another man planted his knee into Reave's abdomen. And it was all over.

Brig Tall-Wood dashed Daol out of the Circle, hand beneath Daol's kilt and applying serious pressure, leaving Daol wincing on the ground and sickly pale. Together, Cul and the Tall-Woods manhandled Reave to one side of the Challenge Circle. Careful not to go to such extreme measures against one of the village's best warriors, Cul simply let the brothers carry Reave out of the arena with them, ridding himself of his strongest supporters as well as his only true rival.

No one else stood against Cul after that. Kern felt a sickening twist in his gut, watching Cul stare down a larger man, then throw a smaller Challenger out by the scruff of his neck.

And at that moment, Cul had the Circle to himself. Diving forward, he pulled the dagger from the ground, rolling back up to his feet with it held not for show, but ready in case any latecomers decided to challenge.

No one was so foolish. Not even Kern. Cul would have no choice but to gut anyone who opposed him.

Chieftains could not afford to let anyone challenge their authority.

Ever.

3

SNOWS RETURNED THAT night, mixing with sleet in the early morning but freezing hard on the ground again before next midday.

Trapped inside the village, most clansfolk gathered at the lodge and worked hard to scrub out the scent of sickness and death that had come with Burok's ailing. The old chieftain's body was stored in one of the empty dry pits under the lodge house. The burning scents of lye and alcohol slowly replaced decayed flesh and sour sweat. Fresh air, cold but clean, blasted in through the ruined doorway.

Kern wasn't sure when the whispers started, or who started them. The wary glances began around noon, at least by the time he noticed. Clansfolk eyeing their neighbors. All wondering whom Cul would favor and whom he would not. Many angry glances were shot out at the weather, as well, which had turned for the worse again. And at Kern, who always drew attention at such times. Several of his clan kin stared openly at him, as if discovering his odd presence for the first time. But no one held his amber gaze when he stared back.

The constant muttering, the shied glances, they set Kern on edge. His hands balled into fists when he wasn't working. He caught himself glancing over his shoulder far too often, feeling the prickling warmth of hostile eyes always on the back of his neck.

"The village can't take too much of this," Daol offered in a low voice, joining Kern and Reave as they kindled a small fire on the newly swept hearth.

Tiny fingers of flame guttered among wood shavings and dried moss. It smelled too green, but looked like it would catch regardless.

Kern fanned the fire with a flat hand, encouraging it. His mood had not improved, and his gaze flashed dangerously about the room. "You set a pot over flames, and don't watch it, it's going to boil over."

"You're nay the cheerful one," the normally quiet Reave said. But a smoldering anger burned behind his eyes as well.

Morning fare had been stale oat flat cakes sprinkled with bone meal. No cellars were opened at noon either, and people grumbled loudly. There were several uneasy looks at the too-small pile of casks stacked in one corner of the lodge.

Cul did not appear until near midday, arriving with Maev, wearing Burok's heavy bearskin cloak, trimmed in red fox and studded with iron tags. With the cloak's shoulders thrown back to bare his chest to the elements, he looked every inch the chieftain Burok had once been. He kept Maev nearby for the rest of the day, Kern noticed, or himself near Maev, anyway.

Kern also saw many villagers make a point of congratulating Cul on his victory in the Circle. Cul responded to most everyone, even Reave and Daol, though his answers were clipped short.

Those Cul ignored, or worse, spurned, quickly wor-

ried for their future in Clan Gaud. More than a few
fights broke out as Cul's favored lorded it over those on
the receiving end of such disdain. Daol quieted one argument before it got out of hand, trying to preserve a
fragile peace inside the clan, but mostly the fights
burned out on their own accord after heated words and
one or two thumps.

The worst, though, was when Old Finn limped up
without his crutch to blatantly offer Cul a water flask.
Finn's deep-wrinkled brow and long gray hair should
have afforded him greater respect. His life celebrated.
Few warriors lived to be so old, and in many Cimmerian clans an elder's advice carried as much sway as the
chieftain's word.

Cul wiped sweat from his brow with the back of his
hand, then turned his back on the older man.

For a moment, Kern thought the once-proud warrior
would strike at Cul. Instead, Old Finn slunk away like
a beaten mutt. No one looked in his direction.

No one save Kern.

Hard times, Burok had said. Yes, they were coming.

Cul barely waited for Finn to limp out of earshot.
"The clan comes first," he said, as if that explained
everything.

"Winter has not released its hold on Cimmeria, and
there isn't enough food. And now we must take Burok
Bear-slayer to the Field of the Chiefs at the foot of the
Eiglophians. We travel east, and then guide our way
north by the Snowy River country. It will be a hard
journey, but I will make it. Maev will come with me.
And Reave."

The large man looked surprised to be chosen, but
not Kern. A newly seated chieftain did not leave his
strongest rival behind. The Tall-Wood brothers would
ward the village for Cul, Kern silently bet with himself.

"I need a dozen strong backs for carrying, and some
young legs to run ahead as scouts." He smiled grimly

as a few of the village youths, barely more than boys, stepped forward to volunteer for the arduous trip.

"We leave tomorrow. Brig Tall-Wood and Tabbot will be your wardens. They will see to your safety. Those who are left behind."

He looked about with a severe gaze. The entire village held its breath.

"Those who are not cast out."

Kern caught the sudden slump in many shoulders as Cul made his promise to begin thinning Clan Gaud. Many, he saw, were resigned to it. Assuming—perhaps rightly—they would be among the first to go. Older clansfolk, like Finn. Those who knew their prime working years were behind them.

"It's too early," Kern spoke up, ignoring the sudden, wary glances Daol and Reave sent his way. He wasn't backing away from this fight. Gaud was all that Kern knew. Few who left the tribe ever survived. Fewer still thrived. Not every Cimmerian could be Conan. "We can all tighten our belts another notch."

"There is not enough food, Wolf-Eye. Burok should have culled the herd weeks ago. We all know that. The raid against Taurin cost us more than we gained. In the end, much more."

Rising to his feet, Kern met Cul's steely gaze with a determined one of his own. He swallowed dryly. "I still say we can survive as a village."

"And I know we cannot. It will take a great deal of provisioning to support us away from the village. The clan would die before I returned."

"Then do not go."

At Cul's side, Maev startled. Her dark look was full of sudden wariness. Cul also looked puzzled, not sure he heard correctly. "Not go?"

Kern nodded. "Stay in the village and let Burok Bear-slayer keep until the thaw. The dry pit will serve until the herds have returned and we can safely transport him over the eastern pass." It made perfect sense to him. Marshal your resources, and spend them in the sparest manner possible.

"Turn our backs on the traditions and customs that have served the clans since Crom walked the earth? Deny Burok his final rest?" Cul thundered his outrage. "I should have expected as much from you, Wolf-Eye. You've never belonged to Cimmeria, or to Clan Gaud, have you? You belong to the wolves and to winter!"

Kern turned his gaze to the assembled villagers. Few met his stare. Those who did glared back in open hostility. He had never felt his strangeness as clearly as he did at that moment. Cimmerians were not a superstitious lot by nature. Crom had created the Cimmerian people strong enough to handle the world on their own terms, after all. But each one, man and woman, had a breaking point.

"Burok knew what he was doing." He said this to Maev, wondering if she had Cul's ear as well as his prick. To Cul, "He thought we could make it."

Cul glared, stepping slightly in front of Maev as if protecting her. "Burok was wrong. The fever had him. And by Crom, Wolf-Eye, that is the last I will say on it!" Cul's voice thundered across the room, putting an end to the argument.

Everyone waited. Both Reave and Daol looked ready to stand in Kern's defense. Kern stared them down, keeping them to their seats by sheer willpower. He had known better, challenging the chieftain's first commands, and he would shoulder that cost alone. He had nothing to lose.

"Worried about your own future, aren't you, Kern?" It was a rare moment, Cul's use of Kern's given name. It sounded strange from his mouth. As strange as the grim smile that peaked up at the corners. "Well, you have a strong back and a good arm for wood if not for a sword. I think you have a chance."

"In fact," he spoke with some laughter in his voice, as if he'd just had a pleasing thought, "you'll be among those heading out tomorrow. That is decided." His voice turned dark and heavy again. "Now sit down."

The weight of the Gaudic chieftains rolled over Kern, pressing him back into his seat even though some spark of defiance encouraged him to continue arguing. His mind, though, told him it was done. Cul had bestowed favor upon him. To speak out again would appear selfish and shallow, and lessened the sacrifice given by those who would be forced to abandon the village, to look for life (if it was to be had) elsewhere.

"Take this night," Cul told the others. "Weigh your own worth, and be prepared for the morning.

"For it must be decided by then."

"HE'S REALLY GOING to run the mountain line in this weather." Kern shook his head. "It is a bad decision."

Daol shrugged. He prodded a small dung fire with the tip of his knife, stirring the flames to keep them lively and warm as fatty juices dripped down and hissed among glowing embers. The thatched home he shared with his father was at least three times as large as Kern's small hut, where his friend barely had room to lie down among his meager possessions. Here, at least, they sat in modest comfort.

"Leave off, Kern," he warned.

Smoke from the fire stung his eyes. He breathed in its sharp, green taste, and the scent of crisping flesh from the roasting chucker. The plump little birds were rare this time of year, but he had found three trapped by the morning sleet in a nearby thicket. Two for the clan. One for the hunter. Had to keep his strength up, after all.

"Still wrong," Kern muttered. He sat cross-legged

near the small fire pit, next to Hydallan, reaching a
hand out for warmth.

Daol saw him shiver even so, and wondered not for
the first time what it must be like to live with the frozen
touch of winter as your constant companion. If anyone
in the village accepted Kern's difference more easily
than Hydallan, who had shown Kern the skills of hunting and tracking in the years before his son came of an
age to be taught, it could only be Daol. Several years
younger than Kern's twenty-three summers, Daol had
looked up to Kern for quite some time before becoming truly aware of his friend's strangeness. And even he,
at times, caught himself looking sidelong at the pale
man, not understanding him.

He brushed dark hair out of his eyes, frowned, and
used his knife to saw at the long bangs. He threw the
hair into the fire, which gave off a quick, acrid stench.
"You tried," he said, trying to offer some comfort.

"Not hard enough. After old Finn was turned away
like that . . ." Kern trailed off, shaking his head.

Daol shrugged again, though less easy than before.
Perhaps Kern's ideas would have been better received if
spoken through Daol or Hydallan. The young hunter
wondered so at the time. But that might have put his father on Cul's chopping block. He'd felt relieved, truth
be told, when Kern stared him back into his seat. Kern
had been so completely certain he was already chosen
to be cast out and obviously feeling he had nothing to
lose.

Instead, he would be heading east, accompanying
Burok to the burial grounds of Cimmeria's greatest
chieftains while others paid the price in Gaud.

Hydallan shrugged, producing a pinch of hoarded
sage and crumbling it over the spitted bird. "Seen it several times, meself. Usually just one or two needs go. This
year?" He shrugged again.

"What else can we do?" Daol asked, turning the plump chucker. He did not mean for his question to be answered.

Kern considered it, though. "We fight."

"Against the clan chieftain?" Daol asked, stunned Kern would say it aloud. He glanced toward the door, half-expecting the Tall-Woods or Cul himself to kick it down.

"Nay," Kern said at once. It was obviously an automatic response, and rightly so. You did not raise your sword, or even your hand, against the chieftain. "But we don't lie down and die, either."

"Can't fight the weather," Hydallan said. An old Cimmerian adage. The elder man did not necessarily mean the lingering winter. Nodding slowly, he rested against his straw mattress, easing his back. His hands were not so strong anymore, and he had lost weight in the last year, but strength still pooled in the gray eyes he shared with his son.

Daol blew out a breath of exasperation. "Saw Cul posting guards on the dry pits and the lodge door." If they were going to talk about it, he was going to add in his own frustrations. "No food from the stores tonight. Worried that some might try to take it. When's the last time Burok posted guards?"

Kern remembered. "That spring when Reave kept hiding river catch in Bear-slayer's bedding. Shook us all awake every night for three nights running with his cursing." He couldn't help the smile. "Posted a guard at the lodge for a week after that."

The three men shared a short laugh. Daol pulled the roasted bird off the spit and tore it into pieces with strong fingers. He handed his father fully half, and split what was left with Kern. The meat sizzled, dripping fat onto the floor.

Kern held his other hand beneath it, catching the

juices, not caring if they scalded him. "Take a few days just to reach the Snowy River country," he said, thinking about the coming journey.

Hydallan grunted. "Imagine Daol will lead 'em over, or meself. I can still find the trails even under four foot a snow."

It was hardly a boast. Daol might have the keener bowshot, but he'd learned everything he knew about tracking and trailblazing from his father. Kern, too, had learned a lot at the side of the elder hunter, before being handed an axe, though the closest Kern now came to hunting was checking the clan traplines, looking for fish or small game caught in any of the snares set out every month.

"Three . . . four days north along the Snowy River. Then we'll pass close by the flats leading east to the Lake Lands." Kern balanced his portion of food in his hand, as if studying it. "Maybe their winter isn't as bad. We can trade for supplies, bring them back down."

"Mebbe their winter is even worse, and they'll be asking for ransom to let you pass by." Hydallan shook his head, crunched through some of the small, hollow bones. "Don't be borrowing from what ain't there, pup."

Kern nodded, accepting good advice when he heard it. Still, "A little luck, now and then, never hurts."

"Especially when you're rolling bones and looking for sixes." Daol licked his fingers and fished out a small bag with his gaming dice in it. Popular over drink, it also made winter nights pass a bit faster. "Up for a challenge?"

"Was earlier," Kern said. He laughed harshly, without a measure of humor in it. "Cul nearly tossed me out of the game. You two play. I don't much feel like it tonight." He rose, still cradling the uneaten chucker.

"You not gonna eat that, Kern?" Daol nodded at the cooling meat.

"Eat it on the way back," he promised, tripping the door latch and giving them both a nod against the night.

Daol watched his friend go, trading a glance with his father. Both had a good feel for Kern. Both called him friend.

And quite obviously to Daol, both were wondering why, of all times, did it feel that Kern had just lied.

THE SNOWS HAD stopped sometime after sundown. A small break in the valley's cloud cover let a half-moon smile down on the village of Gaud. It turned the snow a silvery white, and sparkled off the frost Kern breathed out as he moved away from the home of Hydallan and Daol.

He hated lying, but had not wanted them to feel he took their generosity lightly. It wasn't easy, what he'd decided. Kern's mouth watered for a taste of the chucker's browned skin. He resisted with only the greatest effort.

The small bird steamed, but not with as much enthusiasm as before. It cooled fast. Still warm, though, when Kern found the right hut on the east side of the small village. A strong light danced within, jumping shadows at the lower edge of the door and inside the hide-covered window slit.

"Burning up all his wood." Kern nodded. Might as well be comfortable for the night.

Old Finn answered Kern's soft knock. Slight and shriveled, the elderly man stared at Kern as if waiting to be mocked again.

Kern simply handed him the small portion of roasted bird, ignoring the complaints of his own stomach as he did it. Bad enough losing clan and kin. It was cruel of Cul to leave the village worrying over it through the night.

It was a long, cold walk back to his own hut. Kern spent it sucking every last drop of fat from his fingers and thinking on what their new chieftain might visit on the village the next morning.

4

KERN PACED HIS way slowly through the village, his fur-lined boots kicking through the light snow cover, stopping when he saw crusted handprints or a more recent, crimson smear.

On the door to the hut belonging to Gar and Fionna, a bloody swipe.

Two smears on the larger, ramshackle home, under which roof lived Reave's sister and brother-in-law, who had been caring for the husband's sickly parents.

Another, three huts farther along.

Daol and Hydallan passed him by, making their own rounds and their own count. Their gazes flat and empty.

Six, all told, by the time Kern threaded his way through Gaud and ended up near the lodge. By then he thought he could taste the blood, its metallic bite stinging at the back of his throat. Cul's words came back to him, echoing in his mind.

Weigh your own worth . . .

Many had, apparently. Six brave souls had decided to end their own suffering and ease their burden on clan and kin.

Kern rubbed a hand over his face, rough calluses burning against his freshly scraped cheeks, thinking he might still wake up from a terrible dream.

The lodge was a hive of activity, with people coming and going and several clansfolk looking excited to be off despite the solemn night. Others moved mechanically, wrapped up in their own silent mourning. Cul seemed extraordinarily pleased with himself. He oversaw preparations for a midmorning departure. Setting others to packing sacks and travel casks, and ordering the slaughter of one of the village oxen. A skinny cow that had stopped giving milk. Half her meat would be wrapped and taken along on the trek.

Maev was there as well, an arming sword belted at her narrow waist. She left provisioning to the others. On her order, Burok's body had been brought up from the dry pits and the door he was stretched upon fashioned as a litter with long poles strapped beneath it as handles. It could be dragged or carried as was convenient. For the moment it rested on the hauling sled Kern often used for wood gathering. A good idea for as long as the snow cover lasted.

Likely the entire way, given the look of the eastern mountains.

"Wolf-Eye," Cul called out, as Kern walked up. "You'll help pull the sled today."

Kern shrugged, accepting the order in turn. There had been no cruel glee in assigning him the work. Neither was there any vote of confidence in the clansman's strength, or honor, in being assigned the task of helping convey Bear-slayer's body to its final rest. It was simply handed out, almost beneath the new chieftain's notice. As if he had already forgotten Kern and the stand the other man had made the previous night. That it no longer mattered.

One clansman had not forgotten the previous evening, though.

Old Finn limped up to the lodge wearing his best winter gear, a bundle tied into his woolen blankets and hung over one shoulder, and a fresh-cut walking staff in one hand. The broadsword he once wielded alongside Burok Bear-slayer strapped proudly across his back. Except for his age, and favoring his right leg, he looked like a clansman ready for battle.

The activity quieted, then ground to a halt as the village's eldest warrior approached. Most had likely assumed him "released" in the night. Kern had noted the clean door on Finn's hut that morning, hoping it meant more than there was no one to mourn for him. Kern hadn't the heart to check for himself just then, faced with the other losses.

Now he wished he had.

Finn paused near Kern, just long enough to whisper, "Welcome at my fire anytime," then limped on.

Cul said nothing, watching the man's slow approach with something akin to amusement. No one doubted that Finn was quitting the village. He was certainly fitted for travel minus any decent provisioning of foodstuffs. None would be forthcoming. Cast out or quit of the clan, once outside, outside for good. His few personal items would be bundled up in the coarse gray blankets.

Finn did not bother stopping in front of the chieftain. He hobbled up to the remaining lodge door, taking an exaggerated interest in the lopsided entrance. He nodded at the open side, no doubt making his own farewell to Burok Bear-slayer.

Then he looked directly at Cul, back at the remaining door, and spat.

Swords rasped free of their sheaths as a few of Cul's supporters took the insult to their chieftain personally. Reave leaped in front of Morne, laying hold of his shoulder and straining against the man's anger with his own thick arms. Those farther away from the incident simply waited for Cul's order, or Reave's failing to hold Morne off.

"Let him go," Cul said, and Kern tensed to jump in at Reave's side.

But Cul had not said it to Reave, but to the others. He no longer appeared amused, but at least he did not seem murderously angry. Swords were homed. Those who would not drop their anger cut at Finn with nothing but glares.

Finn was no longer part of the clan. He was a traveler, moving on to another place.

South, Kern wanted to suggest. South as fast as Finn's legs could carry him, and hope he found a new clan to take him in or better weather and spring shoots. Cimmerians always went south, ever since the time of Conan, toward opportunities in the so-called civilized lands.

Which was likely why the pugnacious old man deliberately turned north, into the teeth of winter and the Nordheim realms.

And why Kern silently said his good-bye right then, as he had to six others that day. He did not expect to see Old Finn, alive, ever again.

THERE WERE MANY things Kern did not expect, in fact. Though when faced with them, there was little he could do but accept. It was a Cimmerian's way, after all. Fall down seven times, get up eight.

Strength. That was Crom's single blessing.

Hauling the sled with Burok's body on it tested Kern's physical strength, certainly. There was room

for only two clansmen in the leather harnesses, able to
pull without getting in each other's way, and Burok,
for all his wasting away toward the end, still was not a
small man. Daol worked the trail forward, so only
Reave spelled Kern on the one side of the sled though
never for too long. Kern knew the feel of the wide
leather straps. Was comfortable in them. He took the
harness again as soon as he worked out the strain that
knotted in his meaty calves or pulled at his back.

The first day remained shrouded in gray clouds,
threatening more snow. A few hardy birds flitted
about, chirping mournfully for the lack of forage. The
funeral party felt much the same, content with stale flat
cakes and dried tubers. They sustained a man, but did
not help him keep warm. Especially in the face of a
southern wind that blew down out of the distant
Eighlophian Mountains, carrying the frigid touch of
the Nordheim realms, Vanaheim and Asgard.

Grimnir's Breath, a traveling tinker had once called
such winds. For Kern, that had been the first time he'd
heard of the war chieftain's legendary—and certainly
exaggerated—powers, able to call upon the most severe
weather to aid his Vanir raiders.

The forest thickened up the farther they traveled
from the village, closing in during the second day at
places that would never be visited by Kern's axe.
There was an old feel to the land, where magnificent
oaks spread their limbs so wide they might have sheltered all of Gaud beneath the mighty branches of
a single tree, and an occasional sequoia—the rare
"watchtower" trees—towered overhead like Crom's own
plantings. Kern couldn't help staring at these, with
their bases easily five times as thick as he was tall, ice
caked inside the deep folds of their bark, and wonder
how anyone could think to take an ax to such awe-
inspiring titans.

Evidence of small game showed more clearly as well.

Kern spotted rabbit tracks and hunting fox, and the shuffling spread of snow that warned of a black bear early out of hibernation. Kern wondered if the long winter confused it, and might drive it toward clan villages.

There were also wolf tracks, but never enough to worry about a hunting pack. Stragglers and rogues, mostly. Outcasts. The party heard only one deep, challenging howl as a dire wolf marked his territory, but never saw sign of the beast. Kern did notice blood flecks trailing along one large set of tracks, guessed that the hunter had found a rabbit or marmot, and wished the animal luck.

Maev saw the tracks and blood spoor as well. Hand resting on the hilt of her sword, her measuring gaze left Kern feeling cold inside. Cold*er*.

The trail meandered east, entering hilly country and taking long turns around the steeper slopes. With no strong sun to guide them, the procession might easily have been lost if not for Daol's unerring sense of direction. For his part, Kern concentrated on putting one foot in front of the other, breathing in deeply when the harness relaxed, exhaling sharply as he leaned into the strain, calf muscles thrumming.

Downhill was no easier than uphill. He knew better than to let the flat-bottomed sled have its head, running ahead of them to smash itself against a tree or lightly dusted stone. Downhill was when the other hauler relaxed and Kern steered the sled by hauling against the harness leads.

Kern had already removed his winter cloak, folding it away and tucking it with his knife belt and blanket roll under one end of Burok's burial shroud. Head or feet, made no difference to the old chieftain anymore. Exertion flushed Kern's face a healthy pink, rare for him, and soon he shed his tattered poncho as well. While others bundled themselves up, a few pulling on hats or a rare set of gloves against the bite of the gusting wind, Kern struggled forward bare-chested and sweating. Never warm—the chill never left his bones—but his muscles had settled into that almost-pleasant dull ache that came with honest work.

It was almost with a shrug of reluctance, in fact, that he dropped the harness as Cul called for a second stop in the late afternoon.

The procession had just forded a wide creek, most keeping their feet dry by jumping stones. Kern and an older stalwart named Aodh shed their boots and waded over, carrying the sled and its burden between them. Aodh's salt-and-pepper moustache showed a hint of frost in the upper hairs, just below his nose. He huffed out great clouds of frostbitten vapor, more used to running the traplines than such demanding hauling; but he held up his end, never letting Burok come close to slipping off his funeral board.

The icy water numbed their feet, but dried and briskly rubbed, and back into their boots, they could have set off immediately.

Instead, Cul ordered a rest, sent lanky youths up- and downstream looking for Gaudic fishtraps, hoping to bolster their supplies. Morne, one of Cul's faster warriors, was sent running ahead to slow Daol, let him know of the unscheduled break. Then Cul went around the party, checking to see that most everyone was holding up well.

Kern rubbed his chest and arms down with a rough blanket, brushing them dry before the sweat iced up. He stomped around in a small circle, hammering life back into his feet, and glanced toward Reave. "Drink?"

Reave threw Kern a flask of mint-flavored water. The warm-leather taste of the skin was stronger than the crushed leaves, but Kern was in no mind to complain. Better than the raw metallic taste scratching at the back of his throat from gulping down the cold, dry air too fast.

"Think we'll reach Snowy River country by night?" Reave asked. He rarely had cause to travel out this far during the snows. Lacking Daol's natural sense of direction and distance, and Kern's experience in winter treks, it would be hard for him to judge how the party fared.

"Nay. We're actually slow-going with the sled and the pups along." The village youths held their own in stamina, but they just didn't have a man's stride yet. "Lucky to make it on the morrow."

"Saw pheasant feathers under branches a ways back. Got to be huddled up in the trees." Reave frowned at the height of the branches in some nearby elm. "Maybe Daol will catch a shot at some."

Kern remembered the scent of roasting chucker and the meaty taste of the grease from his fingers. His stomach growled an answer.

"Me, too," Reave said, as if Kern had spoken aloud. The large man's dry chuckle was good to hear.

Cul's call was not.

"Wolf-Eye. Kern!" He stood near the stream, one foot up on a boulder as he tightened down a boot strap, his war sword slung over his shoulder. Maev paused nearby, picking crumbs out of an oilcloth that had held dry biscuits. She had handed out food to everyone but Reave and Kern.

There were two biscuits sitting on the boulder next to Cul's foot.

Kern refused to be called to the chieftain's side like a dog. He turned toward Cul, though. Gaze steady and muscles tense, feeling the scourge of the other man's eyes rake over him.

"This stream is far enough," he said.

" 'Bout time," Reave muttered beneath his breath, but Kern knew right away that Cul did not mean to end his nearly continuous hauling of the sled. At least, not in the way his friend thought. A coldness hollowed out his guts.

"Six . . . seven," he said, remembering Old Finn. "Seven not enough for you?"

"Not about what is enough," Cul said. "About what makes the clan stronger. Your blood's no good. I said that last night."

"You said . . ." Kern began in a heated reply, then remembered.

Cul *had* said, hadn't he? *Heading out tomorrow . . .* but not necessarily coming back. Kern might make it, all right. *Outside the clan.*

A chill shook him that had nothing to do with the gusting wind. He glanced south, wondering how far he'd have to trek, how fast he'd have to run and for how long, to make the southern lands before winter claimed him forever.

Maev looked torn between what she wanted to say, duty to her father and to her chieftain. "We are burying Burok, Cul. Does this have to be now?"

"I want some distance on him before nightfall. This stream makes a good guide, and a boundary. Cross back over it at the risk of death, Wolf-Eye."

Maev hesitated, then shook her head and turned away from the men, back toward the stream. She obviously hadn't known.

Since the hands of three warriors were already on their sword hilts, Cul had warned a few of them this was coming. And he had sent Morne ahead to prevent Daol's appearance, leaving Reave—

"Nay!" Kern shouted, bracing one of his thick arms across Reave's chest before the larger man launched himself at the Gaudic chieftain. Reave hadn't thought to reach for the Cimmerian greatsword strapped across his back, fortunately. Though he looked ready to tear Cul apart with his bare hands.

"Don't do it," Kern whispered, having to lean in to

keep Reave from brushing him aside. "Not for me, Reave. He wants this. Wants you to try for him. Then you are banished as well."

Reave ran his tongue over chapped lips. His pale blue eyes raged with anger. "Never make it, Kern." His voice was rough, thick with emotion. "Nay food or fire. Three days to Clan Maran, if they'll have you . . . and they won't."

It was hard, listening to it come from a friend, but Reave was right. No one north of the thaw would want Kern near. His unsettling looks notwithstanding, there simply would not be food enough for an orphan.

"I might," Kern promised him. "I might. But you need to stay. For Daol and Hydallan. And Ros and her family."

Mention of his sister calmed Reave, cooling his warrior's blood. The giant man settled, but remained barely on the knife's edge of control. He seemed perfectly ready to leap in at Kern's side at a moment's notice, and fight for him. Cul had three solid backers, and at least one more of the small party who might fall in on his side. Many of the others actually looked torn over the decision. Aodh would not even meet Kern's lupine gaze, and neither would one of the younger warriors.

If Daol had been there, with his aim . . .

Any fantasy of actually standing against the odds, though, ended as Maev returned from the stream with a stoppered flask of water. She brushed by Cul, grabbing the biscuits off the smooth edge of the boulder and deftly tying both into the oilcloth she had cleared out earlier. Cul looked about to say something, but her quick glare silenced the new chieftain, who obviously wanted to keep peace with Burok's daughter and an important voice within the village.

Maev finished, then strode over and thrust the package into Kern's hands.

"Take it. Take it and go."

Water and food. He couldn't ask for much more. Kern tied the improvised sack onto his kilt's wide belt, then stepped over next to the sled. He considered trying to take one of the small hatchets, but he had no flint for a fire anyway. So he pulled on his poncho and clipped his winter cloak around his thick neck, letting the gray wolf's fur fall back off his shoulders. His knife he cinched below the wide kilt belt and his bedroll, tied with rope, went over his left shoulder.

The entire time he rarely took his eye off the southerly meandering stream, wondering how far he could run its distance.

Three days, he guessed. Maybe four. He'd have to keep running into the nights, if it turned wet. Better than sitting under the weather.

"Give him a weapon." Maev looked back at Cul.

Cul laughed, looked around the small clearing. Even the men who weren't solidly behind him reached a cautious hand toward their own swords. Cul shrugged. "Give him your own," he suggested.

Woman or not, no Cimmerian went unarmed by choice. Maev hesitated, and Kern shrugged off her concern. He would have felt more comfortable with an axe handle in his hand than the pommel of a sword anyway.

Maev shoved past him, to the side of her father's body. Drawing a small utility knife strapped to her leg, she bent over and sliced through the skin wrapping Burok Bear-slayer. Reaching inside, she grabbed and pulled free the chieftain's broadsword, the long, wide blade rasping free of its sheath. She threw it to Kern, who caught it awkwardly by the hilt.

With a wary eye on Cul, who glowered darkly at the gift, Kern tucked the blade carefully through his knife belt. He let it catch on the cross guard, holding it at his side without cutting through the thin strap.

He nodded his thanks to Maev, who glared him on

his way, and traded arm clasps with Reave. His friend's strength was impressive, certainly bruising Kern's arm. Which was when it truly struck at him: this would be their last moment. Once cast out from the clan, always cast out of the clan.

Not even Conan had tried returning to Clan Conarch. *That* would have been a tale.

"I can make it," Kern promised again.

"See that you do." His glacial blue eyes were heavy, holding his anger and his sorrow both. "Don't want your ghost haunting these woods. You're strange enough as is."

Kern smiled, pulling up one side of his mouth with effort. A longer delay robbed him of precious daylight, and would accomplish little more than a test of Cul's patience. With a final nod to his friend, he turned and jogged from the clearing, keeping a stone's throw from the stream as he headed south.

He let his anger fuel him for a hundred paces, then realizing how quickly it would burn him out, he settled back into an easy pace. If he hadn't, he might have missed the boy.

One of the youths Cul had sent foraging along the stream banks, hoping to find a basket-trap with fish in it. He had. His bony hands gripped the body of a silver trout, its head bloody and smashed in by a rock most likely. Kern nearly overlooked him, passing on the far side of a willow clump, then jogged back to halt the lad, who handed over the fish without thinking first what Kern might be doing jogging south with his bedroll and kit.

Tempting. Truly tempting. He'd had every intention of supplementing his meager provisions with the fish. He was outside the clan now. He had every right.

But then Maev hadn't had to send him away armed, either. Or with food Cul had already withheld.

Damn.

"I want you to listen carefully to me, boy." He crouched over until his wolflike eyes were scant inches away from the lad's. The youth swallowed hard, and nodded. "You give this directly to Maev. You hear? To no one else. You tell her I said so." He handed back the fish.

Frowning, the Gaudic youth took it and set off on his own jog back upstream. Kern watched him go, sparing the few seconds to make certain the boy knew what he was doing, then worked himself into an easy pace alongside the stream again. One foot in front of the other. One stride at a time eating away the distance between Gaudic lands and a new life, or not.

He didn't look back.

There was nothing for him behind.

5

HE DRANK HIS fill of fresh, sweet water that night, leaning over the ice-rimed stream bank to refill his skin again and again.

Saving the hard biscuits for morning in an effort to boost his strength for the long day ahead.

A gray mist, sparkling with hoarfrost, had rolled in during the night. It cloaked the countryside in a dismal veil, hiding the sun and drawing gooseflesh across his arms and his chest, leaving only the stream to guide him southward for as long as that lasted. The air smelled of new snow, but Kern refused to borrow trouble by worrying about it before the first flake had even made itself known.

Fall down seven times. Get up eight. That was the Cimmerian way.

No time for delay, Kern rubbed life into his arms and legs, breathed on the numb ends of his fingers and checked each one for frostbite. Rolling his winter cloak and woolen blankets around the broadsword, he kept out his tattered poncho, improvising a sling around the rest using his knife belt and a short length of rope. The shorter blade and sheath he simply tucked into the wide leather strap buckled around his heavy kilt.

Good for moving fast, and drawing fast if he spotted small game. But sign was scarce, with only the wide-spaced tracks of a large, running wolf showing that morning.

For several hours he jogged along, finally leaving the stream when it hooked back to the north. He had no choice now but to trust his own sense of direction. One pace after another hammering at the frozen ground; every step carrying him closer to new life, or to death.

He tried not to think of Reave. Or Daol, when the clan huntsman discovered what had happened at the fording.

He tried not to think of Maev. Or Cul.

Nothing worked. His thoughts and memories distracted him throughout the early morning.

One more reason he missed the wolf until it was upon him.

The beast came out of the frosted mist without warning, downwind and hidden by a dead bramble of gray, thorny stalks. A large animal. Eight hands across the shoulders and ten-stone weight at least. Slamming into his back, the dire wolf bore Kern to the ground with strong forepaws scrabbling at his tattered poncho and teeth snapping for the backs of his legs, looking to hobble him. Its prey.

Luckily, it seized upon the cloth-wrapped broadsword instead. Caught in the beast's powerful jaws, the thin belt strap Kern had used for a sling parted as if cut with a fine edge.

The dire wolf bounded back, dragging the gear with it, then realized what it had was not food and abandoned it, coming back at Kern low and fast. When it attacked, the wolf rose up partly on its hind legs, snarling savagely as it tried for an arm, a shoulder, the throat.

Kern barely had time to reach for his knife, still tucked into the broad leather strap fastened above his kilt. Instinctively, he kicked out hard, stomping the large wolf against its breastbone, hurling it back from him even as he fell farther away from his lost sword.

Rolling back into the snow, and over, Kern came to hands and feet quickly. Facing the wolf more on its own level.

The beast growled and snapped as it paced around Kern, taking better measure of its prey this time. It hunched low, shoulder muscles bunching under a bristling silver pelt. It was Kern's first good look at the animal. Before it had been a blur of silver fur and ivory teeth. He marked it now with the dark band of fur around its eyes, like a mask, and the snow-white left paw. A younger male. A rogue with no pack, obviously.

And a starving animal, he recognized. The bones of its shoulders and rib cage stood out as knobby bumps beneath the silver fur. Scrawnier than he would have expected, especially for how hard it had hit him, the wolf was certainly missing several stones from its autumn weight.

It would have to be driven by hunger to come at a man like this. Even in packs, wolves tended to shy away from people, and their readiness with swords and bows and fire. A knife, though, was poor defense against one of the forest's best hunters. The wolf seemed to recognize this, or was too hungry to care. Its yellow eyes did not hold anger or malice in them. Simply a strong will to survive.

It rushed Kern, low and furious. Kern made a stab for its throat. Missed, and scored a bloody wound off its shoulder instead. The wolf's head turned and bit at his arm, catching his elbow in its powerful jaws and shredding further the sleeve of his leather poncho. Gripping Kern solidly, it dragged him back, off-balance, and bit down.

Kern lost the knife as his arm spasmed, but not his senses. He balled up his left hand in a great fist and smashed it down on the bridge of the wolf's nose once . . . twice . . . The animal yelped, tried to shift its bite, and Kern yanked his arm free.

A few of its sharper canines scored bloody gashes down his forearm.

Red droplets spattered against the snow.

And when the wolf drove at him again, Kern grabbed two handfuls of fur and *heaved*.

Helping the wolf along the path of its own charge, Kern threw the animal a good seven or eight paces. Far enough for a rough landing. But the animal also lived by the Cimmerian way, apparently—fall down seven times, get up eight—as it scrambled right back to its feet and began to stalk Kern again.

In that brief respite, though, Kern had stripped his poncho overhead. As the wolf angled after him he retreated toward where his sword lay, wrapping the tattered leather in a thick sheath around his left arm. If he turned for the sword, the wolf would have him in an instant. Even to glance back, locating the precious bundle, was risky enough. He managed it in a kind of awkward shuffle, always keeping his body facing the large wolf, trying to locate his gear from the corner of his eye.

No time. The wolf wasn't waiting for Kern to even up the fight. Gathering itself, it snarled and leaped, jaws snapping once again for Kern's throat.

Kern stuffed his padded arm into the beast's open jaws, got his other hand into the scruff on its neck, and threw the animal back down at the frozen ground with his entire weight coming down atop it.

The beast yelped in confusion and pain and immediately wrestled to right itself, claws ripping at Kern's arms and chest. Dirty nails dug painful trenches into his skin, but pain would be the least of Kern's concerns if the animal freed itself and came at him again. That kind of contest could only end one way. So he rolled forward, pinning the wolf with more weight, shoving his arm harder into its jaws. He felt teeth work through the leather in places, digging into his flesh again.

And he pressed harder.

No sword. No knife. Not enough purchase to snap the beast's neck. Kern barely held the animal down. The wolf's fetid breath rank in his face, and the taste of blood at the back of his throat as his own breathing labored in the struggle.

He had only the same natural weapons as the wolf, and no choice but to use them. Shifting his weight across the wolf's shoulders, Kern thrust his face beneath that toothy muzzle and struggled to bite out the animal's throat. His teeth and jaw were not fashioned for such savage tearing. He chewed on coarse, rank fur and ropy muscle, searching for an artery or windpipe. The gamy, sweaty scent of the beast clogged his nose and throat.

The large wolf struggled desperately, howling and yelping, back feet kicking up a spray of snow and dirt as they fought for purchase. Front paws raked their nails again and again over Kern's chest. Yelling his own hoarse cry, Kern pressed forward with renewed strength, and bit down until he tasted blood.

And the wolf went completely still.

There was no thought that he'd killed the animal. Its flanks still rose and fell with labored breathing. Its breath misted in the cold, winter air. A shallow whine squeaked its way up from its chest.

A warm, rank stench rose around them as the wolf pissed on itself and Kern in one final attempt to humiliate itself in abject surrender.

Kern couldn't breathe. He raised his head from the

blood-matted fur, trying to clear the taste from his mouth without setting the animal back to its struggles. His face so very close to those powerful jaws, and its head, he stared into the yellow eye that so closely matched his own. The animal looked confused and frightened, its gaze turning vacant as Burok Bear-slayer's had been toward the end of his illness.

"If I let you up," Kern whispered, more to hear his own voice, to realize he was still alive, "you're going to come at me again."

The animal whined again. Yea or nay, there was no understanding it.

But Kern wasn't sure if he had the stamina or the strength left to fight the dire wolf on its own terms, holding it down and trying to rip out its throat with his own teeth. If he could manage it, he'd have meat enough to carry him through to the southern lands. If he failed, he knew the wolf wouldn't think twice before leaving him bloody and dying in the snow.

A battle of survivors. Of outcasts.

"By Crom, we aren't so different," he told the wolf, still spitting out the taste of blood and hair. "Let's see how much fight is left in either of us."

And Kern thrust himself away from the animal, rolling for his nearby blanket roll with his cloak and his sword tied up inside. Seizing one corner of the blanket, he tugged it violently to spin out his gear over the ground.

Grabbing for the broadsword's hilt.

Twisting around, preparing for the attack.

The wolf was gone.

Running back into the trees, favoring its right fore-leg and not looking back until it cleared the trunk of a fallen young elm. There it hunkered down with little more than its ears and eyes above the snow-dusted bole. Staring with an unblinking lupine gaze, alert for Kern's next move.

Bloodied and bruised, and utterly exhausted, Kern fell back on his own haunches and saluted the beast with a wave of his sword.

"Call it a draw," he said. And set about collecting his gear.

6

LACKING CLEAN CLOTH and any knowledge of forest herbs, Kern flushed the shallow cuts across his chest and arms with fresh water and left the wounds to cleanse and clot on their own. They bled freely at first, until his blood started to thicken. He hoped they might crust over quickly. But his rough trek overland reawakened the wounds every time his skin pulled tight across his chest or when his arms brushed against his body.

He left a blood spoor across the snow Daol could easily have followed.

Or any four-legged hunter.

Having tied cloak and poncho into his bedroll, Kern carried Burok's broadsword in his hand. A safeguard, in case the large wolf should make another charge at him. One pace after another. One league after the next. He saw the animal a few more times and always at a distance—a shadow in the morning fog. Tracking him by the scent of his blood, he guessed.

Too hungry to leave off. Too frightened, yet, to risk another attack.

Kern worried about the night, and what might happen then. So when he stumbled across the trail of a large party soon after midday, at first he considered it a favorable occurrence.

At first.

A large group, he reckoned. They had trampled the snow in a wide swath. Kern found enough clear boot prints to determine they were moving from southwest to northeast. Making for the Pass of Noose, maybe. Or just planning to follow the Snowy River country farther north.

That much made sense. It was the horse signs that confused him. Half a dozen of them: he counted by tracks through the ground cover of light snow. Good-sized animals, but hardly the long-haired draft horses that fared best in northern lands. Even then, Cimmerians rarely relied on such animals. Nordheimers, neither. Finicky beasts, in most clansmen's opinion. With healthy appetites and poor stamina. They couldn't climb cliff faces or move stealthily on the hunt. Horses also had the poor habit of breaking their legs in rough ground, and falling over dead if you pushed too hard. And if they ran off—or were taken in a raid—it was usually with half (or all) of your supplies strapped to their back.

And these were metal-shod, Kern noted, finding a good impression in the packed snow. That meant southerners. Nemedians, perhaps. Early in the year for a merchant caravan, and there was no sign of wagon tracks. Aquilonian soldiers, pushing back into Cimmeria? Had King Conan decided to extend a gauntleted hand into his birthland once again?

Kern stood on the trampled path, breath frosting before his eyes. The scent of winter freezing his sinuses closed. He looked south, and was lucky to make out the dim outlines of trees a hundred paces away. Though he knew what lay that direction. Forest and hills, then the snow-swept plains below Conall Valley, which finally gave way to Gunderland.

Three days. Maybe four. Running and covered in blood scent the entire way.

"I could make it," he whispered aloud, hearing the same promise he had made to Reave.

But if Aquilonia was resettling garrisons in Cimmeria again, then food and hope might not be far off. He scouted forward and found some horse dung, cold but not frozen through. Half a day. No more.

Kern's hopes surged, bringing a fresh burst of energy to his tired muscles, and he trekked after the horsemen's trail.

What surprised him when he found the slaughter was that he had not even considered Vanir raiders. In their frozen wastelands, they had less use for horseflesh than Cimmerians.

Except as food.

Fresh blood stained the snow red in a wide area. Where a crossbeam had been tied between two trees, for hanging the meat, ground cover had melted away entirely, turning the ground into a mess of red-stained muck and trampled entrails that smelled of bowels and the metallic scent of spilled blood. He found strips of hide, the castoffs too tattered or thinned for later curing. Definitely horse.

Ashes in the large cooking pit were cold and slightly damp. The trail led off again to the northeast. So the Vanir had stopped, slaughtered one of the animals (captured in the south) for food, and set off again. They would pass far to the east of Gaud.

But not the funeral host!

Kern stood next to the slaughter pit. He looked to the mountains northeast, then to the south, and finally back at the bloody scraps at his feet. He might salvage a handful of meat from the cast-off entrails, washing away the muck and twigs with the last of his fresh water. Even bits of hide, chewed slowly through the day, would lend him strength. He had everything here to help him reach the south. Everything but a bit of luck.

Turn his back. Look to his own safety and future. Leave behind the clan that had abandoned him.

Once cast out . . .

. . . *get up eight*.

By Crom, he'd not see his friends chained into a slave line or their heads set out on sharpened poles! Or Burok left to rot in the foothills below the Snowy River country!

Shaking dirt from a piece of hide, he sliced a small piece free and stuck it between his teeth. Worrying it free of any last trace of fat or meat. Sucking down the rancid oil that slicked the back of his mouth. A few more choice pieces he bundled up in the oilcloth sack that had held his biscuits. This he tied to his belt, for later.

And then Kern ran.

Northeast. After the Vanir.

KERN VERY NEARLY made it in time.

Premature twilight, brought with the heavy cloud cover and dense fog, stole over Conall Valley somewhere early of the sun being lost over the western mountain teeth. Still Kern struggled forward. League by league. His heart pounding. Lungs frost-scalded from breathing deep the cold air blowing down from the Snowy River country.

His wounds, scabbing over with a thick crust, complained with every touch as infection puffed their edges with red swelling. Staggering up against a thick alder, Kern rested with his head laid against the silver-gray bark, his breath coming in long, harsh pants.

He'd run the entire day away. Harder, even, in the last few hours, after the Vanir had crossed and begun to chase after another trail—the Gaudic funeral host. Kern's eyes, always his bane in Gaud, had no trouble focusing what little light was available, letting him find the paths and the trail sign of the Vanir's passing. And he had checked horse dung by touch and by scent. It had warmed over the course of his run, very slowly, but he was close. Close enough that a near pile of droppings continued to steam.

Closer than he thought, he discovered, as his ears pricked up to the sound of clashing metal.

He drew in a long, quiet breath, and held it. There it was again. A distant, sharp ringing. And shouts! Carried to him on the wind, though hardly more than a thought of raised voices. No words or way to identify who it was.

Then the horn; long and mournful. Like the zephyrs that blew down out of the Nordheim realms, shouting through the trees.

Kern shoved himself away from the alder, hands tearing at his blanket roll, stripping away the knife belt and woolen spread and his winter cloak and poncho as he ran. Leaving his items cast off along the trail. All but the heavy broadsword.

Staggering up a long, shallow slope, then sprinting down the far side.

Pausing to listen as the trail suddenly tangled into a knot of smaller paths, hearing a few hoarse shouts along a southern reach. Racing after them.

Nearly tripping over the body spread out in violent measure not another hundred paces along. One of the clan youths Cul had brought for foraging and for vanguard scouts. He had at least three sword wounds sliced across his upper arms, his body. His throat had been violently slashed open. The scent of blood was thick and cloying, and had sprayed over the snow in arcing jets.

"Cul!"

A shout from ahead. Not Reave or Daol. Definitely not Maev.

It was Morne. Bleeding from a shoulder wound. His back pressed up against a tall, snow-frosted cedar, blade held out warily before him to fend off the two flame-haired Vanir who struck at him from either side. Both raiders wore leather cuirasses studded with light strips of metal. Both had full beards and long braids swinging down their backs—common among the Vanir.

One of them, the nearer, wore a red cloak mantled with the silver fur of a wolf. He had a broadsword and shield. The other a war axe.

The ringing clash of steel against steel hid the sound of Kern's footfalls until nearly upon the raiders. It might have been a tremor in the ground that betrayed him. Perhaps the sound of a breaking twig or crunching snow.

Whatever the reason, the Vanir wielding sword and shield turned suddenly, bringing his blade around in a sharp, strong arc. Clashing with Kern's broadsword.

The blade vibrated painfully in his grip, his hands more used to the wooden haft of an axe than violent steel. But Kern hung on to it. His own slash was awkward and bounced off the other man's steel-faced shield.

A savage grin peeked out of a red, full beard. The raider knew he was not fighting an experienced swordsman.

Though the man had obviously forgotten Morne, who turned aside the other Vanir's chopping attack, then lunged forward to slash at the back of the first raider's leg. Hamstrung, the raider collapsed with a pain-filled bellow. Taking his sword with him.

Kern left him, circling around to the far side, where he and Morne could divide the attention of the second raider. Morne had more trouble deciding whom to swing at. His war sword thrust out left, then right. Hesitated.

"Move!" Kern yelled, shouldering in at the axe-swinging raider, throwing him against the cedar's thick trunk.

Morne leaped away from the sword-wielding Vanir, who lay on the ground. And away from the man with the axe as well. Without waiting to see how Kern fared, he sprinted away, still shouting for Cul.

Bouncing back off the bole of the tree, the raider sideswiped his heavy war axe at Kern. Thinking to parry, and Kern lost the blade as it was torn from his numb grasp. A shield, dropped by the first raider, lay nearby, and Kern dived for it. Came up with it just in time to deflect a bone-rattling chop at his shoulder.

Another chop, and another block. Then Kern moved inside, not letting the raider's greater reach work for him, and smashed the man in the nose with the shield's face. He heard cartilage crunch, and blood sprayed out over the metal surface of the shield.

The man staggered backward, one hand clasped over his broken nose.

Rather than waste more time, Kern quickly found his sword and left the two men there, struggling in the snow.

"Reave? Daol?"

Kern floundered through a snow-hidden bramble patch, feeling the wooden thorns cut at his exposed legs. He followed Morne's general direction, looking and listening, trying to draw in on another skirmish. He found the sled bearing Burok's body, overturned up against a pair of boulders. Then another of Cul's supporters not much farther along, lying in the snow, trying to hold in his entrails where they oozed out of a slit belly.

He staggered past two Vanir bodies, stretched out in death. One of them had bloody fingers wrapped around the sharpened edge of an arming sword. Like the kind a slight man might use. Or a woman.

"Maev!" Kern called out, bellowing at the top of his lungs.

"Kern? Kern!"

Reave's shout found him searching among the trees, looking for Burok's daughter. Kern hauled his shield and sword toward another copse, where Reave laid about him with his Cimmerian greatsword in giant, swinging arcs, holding back four men who circled him like wolves bringing a bear to ground.

Reave was as good as dead. Kern, too. For all of Reave's strength and skill, four raiders were easily a match for the two of them. They had to cut down the odds quickly. And without help . . .

Kern stopped in his tracks with the birth of a desperate idea. *Help!*

"This way." Kern looked back behind him, where he had found dead bodies and a dying Gaudic warrior. "I found more over here!"

As bluffs went, he thought it a good one. Reinforcements just over the snow-covered dale. No time to finish off these two barbarians. Run!

Instead, two Vanir men peeled away to confront Kern while two others stayed after Reave. Swords struck and danced. The raiders called encouragement to each other in their harsh, nasal language. In the dimming light, they weren't much more than shadows with gleaming steel in their hands and feral rage twisting their faces. Kern doubted he looked much different, from a distance.

But as he loped up, a snarl of defiance baring his teeth, one of the men got a good look at him by the dimming twilight and staggered back in sudden fright. "Ymir! Ymir!"

Why this raider called upon the Vanir's chief god, the legendary frost-giant who—legends said—once grappled with Crom himself, Kern neither knew nor cared. All that mattered was that he had only one man left standing against him.

And that one hesitated as well, sword raised high, confusion clouding his pale features. He struck slowly, glancing his blow off Kern's upraised shield.

The Vanir wouldn't get a second chance. Kern's broadsword bit into the raider's thigh, drawing a bloody scar toward his groin and nicking something important. Blood sprayed out in a warm jet to soak Kern's kilt and splash steaming droplets across his arms, his hands, his bare chest.

The raider's howl was angry and laced with pain. It gave the others pause. Reave took advantage of the distraction, leaping back, swinging his greatsword through a wide arc and taking the howling man's head off his shoulders. Blood fountained as the body toppled to the ground.

"We have them," Kern yelled, again calling to imaginary reinforcements. His muscles felt like lead weights, but he waved an arm overhead and forward anyway, as if calling them up.

Between the yammering raider who had fallen away from Kern to Reave's impressive strike, and the prospect of more Cimmerians running up in the dark, the three raiders decided to cut their losses. Dropping back into the night, they kept swords held before them. Then the Vanir horn sounded again in three sharp blasts, and they quickly turned for the trees and what companions of their own they might find.

"Where are . . . the others?" Reave asked, gazing back along Kern's approach. He, too, was trying to catch his breath. Then he seemed to realize who had just come to his aid, and wrapped the other man into a strong embrace. "You came back!"

"Obviously." Air whispered between Kern's lips as Reave crushed the breath from him. Wedging his newly won shield between himself and his friend, Kern asked, "Daol? Maev?"

Reave shook his head. He drove his greatsword point first into the ground and leaned heavily on the crossbar. "No idea. Started a running skirmish just after twilight, hoping to gain the pass before dark. But more of them slipped around front. Hit us from two sides." He wrenched his sword free of the earth. "What, by Crom's large orbs, are you doing here?"

It would take too long to explain just then. "Did Cul outlaw me from heading east?" he asked.

His friend considered that. "Nay."

"Then here I am," Kern said, with the ghost of a tired smile. Every muscle in his body vibrated with nervous energy, ready for action, but soon the adrenaline rush would sour, and he'd be left weak as a pup. If they were going to be any good to the others, they had to keep moving.

He hefted his shield up to cover one shoulder, and gestured with his sword ahead. "Now let's go tell him."

7

THE SURVIVORS HAD used weighty evergreen branches to sweep away most of the snow from within a small circle of trees. Those branches now crackled with forced enthusiasm on a medium-sized blaze set in the clearing's center, throwing angry, short-lived sparks into the night and piling up pungent smoke that tasted both warm and salty.

Kern squatted outside of the fire's warmth, barely within the flickering pale of its light. He wore his tattered poncho and winter cloak again, having recovered his castoffs after the battle. Broadsword strapped across his back. An abandoned war axe resting head down on the ground in front of him and both of his large hands wrapped tightly about the handle. Uncertain and angry gazes—at times both at once—always found him waiting. He might not be part of the clan any longer—once cast out, never returned—but he wasn't going to be easily run off either.

Though Cul looked ready to try at a moment's notice.

Cul's proud chin had a nasty cut slicing up toward the right corner of his mouth, and his hair, matted with blood, stuck against one side of his head. He paced with relentless energy and had a feral rage kindled in his eyes, matching the fire in intensity. The warrior in him no doubt wanted to chase after the raiders. The chieftain knew his duties better. And his debts.

"Share the fire, Wolf-Eye." His voice was little better than a harsh growl. "You've earned that, at least."

As any stranger would, who lent aid to the clan.

"That, 'n' more," Reave groused. The hulking giant and one of the women dug through what was left of the stores. His sword lay within an arm's reach, still bared and bloodstained.

Kern remained where he was, the rogue on the outside of the pack. He wanted no illusions in the way. And he didn't want some of these men at his back, either.

Twelve left. Twelve of the twenty who had started out from Gaud. He looked at the nearby sled, with Burok's body still waiting for its final rest at the Field of the Chiefs. Three more bodies lay stretched out on the cold ground next to the old chieftain. Jurga, one of Cul's most stalwart men. Oscur and Agh, both old enough to make the journey but too young to have stood against seasoned Vanir. Three dead, and four others missing.

And one exiled.

"Well?" Morne finally asked of Reave and Desagrena. He held a wad of bloodstained cloth against the wound in his shoulder.

Kern had already weighed the stores by eye, measuring them against the day's journey ahead to get up to the northern valley. And home. There wasn't enough. At least five packs had disappeared, along with the four missing. Along with Daol and Maev!

"Six, maybe eight days," Desa told them all, returning to the fire, shouldering her way between two of the men. She had a lithe body, not as hardy as most Cimmerians, but was known to be lightning quick and full of a summer storm's fury when angry.

"Not enough," Cul said, stating the obvious. He rubbed at his jaw, winced. "Morne, you will run for Gaud at first light. Bring back Croag, and Hydallan. And more from the winter stores."

And starve another four or five clansfolk before winter finally broke and spring allowed for new foraging? Kern rocked himself to his feet, dragging the heavy war axe with him. "And what about Daol?" All they had found was a broken hunting bow and a raider with an arrow through his neck. "Maev and the others?"

Cul stopped his pacing. "Weren't you here, Kern? Vanir! Two dozen at least."

"Seemed like more," Aodh said, hunched down on one side of the fire. He poked into the embers with a stick. A voice from the other side whispered, "Aye."

Two dozen could seem like more in twilight and fog, coming out of two directions. Cul shrugged it away. "Too many. We'd lose as many as we'd save going after them. If the raiders haven't already bled the life from them in sport."

To be fair, it looked like a hard admission for the new chieftain to make. No doubt thinking about Maev more than the rest. But, "You will order Hydallan to chase you along the Snowy River country while his son is tortured and dragged off to the northlands?" Kern shook his head. Yet the old man might do it. Clan before kin. Daol's father had shrugged aside the expulsion so easily, after all.

"By Crom, Wolf-Eye, that is exactly what I mean to do!" Cul stormed over toward him, hands grasping at the air. "And it is not your concern any longer! You are outside the clan. I no longer see you."

"Well I do!" Reave jumped to his feet, greatsword in

hand with its point dragging the ground behind him.
Six feet of naked blade. "Kern means to chase down
the raiders took Daol from us, then I'm with him."

In fact, Kern *had* made just that decision. Made it
when he started back to the north, in fact, chasing after
the raiders, intent on coming to the aid of his friends.
He would not leave Daol in their hands.

Nor would he allow Reave to sunder his standing in
the clan.

"Daol would not have you do this," he said, stepping up next to his friend, voice hoarse and low. A shift
in the breeze blew green smoke into Kern's face, stinging his eyes. "It's a fool's adventure, Reave. Let me do
what I can."

"Ten, maybe twelve raiders? You *might* need help."

Reave could never count. The Cimmerians had
taken a good measure in the fight, but not *that* good.
Cul had left two raiders for the crows come morning.
Reave another, though with Kern's help. Daol, apparently, a fourth. Maev, five. That left . . .

"Nineteen," he told Reave. "Or more."

"Settles it, then. Take at least the two of us."

"Three." At fireside, Aodh shoved the stick he'd
been prodding the coals with deep into the fire, stirring
up a swarm of waspish sparks. He brushed them away
from his face and stood abruptly. "I go as well."

Cul looked about to say something, but Aodh
jumped in first with a sharp tongue. "Burok Bear-
slayer was my chieftain eighteen years. I can nay abandon his daughter, then stand by his grave?"

Aodh was also an aging warrior, Kern saw, and
might also be wondering if he would be the next one
forcibly expelled from the clan.

So might Wallach Graybeard, whose hair was thinning on top and whose beard was shot through almost
fully with iron gray. Who also stepped forward. He
could not meet Cul's dark gaze, but he did nod once. "I

as well. Better to die a warrior than live in hunger and feeble age."

Not the best of omens, but Kern could hardly refuse the men to follow their own consciences. He looked from one face to the other, each one looking flushed in the firelight. Each one with a hard look of determination.

"And me."

The young voice wavered and broke, though from his age and not out of fear. The boy, Ehmish. The one who had taken back the large trout to Maev. He couldn't be more than fifteen summers. He also looked a touch scared, a hesitation in his dark eyes, but he stepped forward with one hand on the short knife belted at his waist.

"No," Kern said, shaking his head.

It was more than Ehmish's not being considered a man by clan standards—not until he made his first kill in battle. Every youth made his own decision when to join a war party. When to go looking for his manhood. But Kern knew Ehmish had no idea what he was getting himself into, life as an outcast. Chasing down Vanir raiders.

A short life, most likely.

"Show some sense, boy," Cul snapped, eyes blazing dangerously as his small group fractured. "You've got no business with the likes of him."

"Oscur was my friend. He saved my life by pushing me on ahead. I can hunt, and I can scout. And I go with Kern Wolf-Eye!"

Vengeance wasn't what Kern was looking for, and began to say as much. Reave, of all people, stopped him with a shake of his head. "Better short help than no help," he said of the youth.

"Would you call me 'short help' as well, Reave Oxheart?" Desagrena, stepping away from the fire. Her mocking tone made it sound like Reave might be the

child. One of the men reached out for her—Morne—
but she slapped his hand away with a stinging blow.
"No woman should be left with the Vanir. Better to kill
Maev than let her be taken."

At a loss, Reave could only shake his head again.
"Soon we'll be outnumbering the Vanir."

Not quite. No others stepped forward, and from the
suspicious and even hateful eyes that chased out from
the fireside, none would. Cul was left with seven strong
backs, though Morne had a wounded shoulder. Enough
to get Burok north. Maybe. If he borrowed more heavily from the village. And its stores.

"We'll take a wood hatchet," Kern said, speaking to
Reave but more for Cul's benefit. Giving him some
warning and room to object. Any fight that broke out
between the two camps would only leave both sides too
hurt to accomplish anything.

"Flint and stone and a handful of tinder. Our own
bedrolls and skins." He shook his own. Empty. Well,
snowmelt served almost as well. "We'll take enough
food for one good meal. We run down the raiders, and
recover our own stores, or we die trying."

By Kern's taking such a small bite out of what was
left, Cul would not have to raid so heavily into the village stockpile. More lives might be spared.

Not that Cul appeared ready to accept anything like
a compromise. His hands clenched, no doubt itching for
the cord-wound hilt of his sword. But not even the
chieftain could compel clansfolk to stay against their
will. He knew he didn't have the steel behind him—not
anymore—to prevent the others from taking more,
should they demand it.

"Take it and be damned," he growled. "Follow this
whelped creature from your village?" He glared at the
other man, dark gaze challenging Kern. "You *are* night-
born, Wolf-Eye, and you'll be the death of them all.
Take your spoils and chase off after the rest of the

raiders, then. But don't you ever cross my path again."
He ground each word between clenched teeth. "Not
ever."

Kern knew enough to take a victory, however mar-
ginal, when he could. He nodded. The others set to collecting their own gear quickly. Ehmish brought Kern
his bedroll. He slipped his improvised sling over one
shoulder and carried the battle-axe in his other hand,
gripping it at the balance point of the haft.

He couldn't help putting in a word of support for
the rest of his lost village. "Do right by them, Cul. Do
right by Burok."

"Winter take you, Wolf-Eye! I've never done otherwise."

Perhaps. To Kern, it hardly should matter anymore.
He breathed deep, tasting the warm flavor of the burning greenwood and the crisp freshness of the night air
both. The firelight danced around the clearing, casting
shadows into the craggy faces of those who stood or
crouched, watching him as they might a dangerous animal stalking the edge of the flames. He shuffled back
slowly, never dropping his lupine gaze until he had
stepped far enough away from the fire to taste it no
longer. Only a light scent remained, burned down into
his poncho and cloak, clinging to his frost blond hair.

Then he turned and trotted into the darkness with
the others stringing along behind.

"How long to camp?" Reave asked, moving up on
Kern's side.

"No camp. The Vanir won't get caught bedding
down so close to people they raided. In case we do come
after them. They'll move through the night. So will we."

"We can't see well enough to run through the dark."

Kern glanced sidelong at his friend. Even under the
fog-shrouded moon, he knew his eyes would be notice-
able. "I can," he reminded the other man.

Reave hesitated, then nodded. "Right." He shrugged

aside the concern as if it had meant nothing. "A man could wish for a few torches to light, though."

Next in line, Desa overheard. "Wouldn't if we could," she pointed out. "If they spot us coming, we're dead."

"We're dead anyway," Reave muttered. Not that such dark thoughts kept him from falling into line behind Kern.

Kern ducked a thin branch, which whipped at Reave's face instead. Trotting along, he looked for the trampled snow that would lead them after the Vanir. *See them coming . . .* Something about that idea sparked a thought in Kern's mind.

It was something else for him to chew on, as his pack ran through the rest of the long night.

8

MORNING BROUGHT BROKEN skies and an occasional glimpse of the sun, a welcome rest from the heavy overcast which usually socked in Conall Valley for the winter. A light breeze wandered around with very little interest. Crisp and fresh. Not the cold sweep that usually came down off the higher peaks. Optimistic thrushes and a few chuckers danced in the highest tree limbs, calling for spring, but still no new buds on the trees or new grass peeked up through the white blanket.

Sunlight, when it was there, glittered against the frost-crusted snow like a thousand tiny jewels. It brightened the harsh landscape and stabbed daggers into the eyes of the Gaudic rescue party whenever they looked too far ahead.

Head down. Eyes on the trail. Kern knew that to do otherwise risked snow blindness. Painful eye strain at the least. Still he shaded his brow more often than necessary to gaze ahead. Once he thought he caught glimpse of the dire wolf, still stalking his trail. Or *a* dire wolf, anyway. But he didn't worry with so many blades at his side. Instead, he searched for any sign of a Vanir rear guard.

Before the Vanir caught sign of them.

North and east the trail led them. Perhaps a touch more east than north, but the raiders held a fairly straight line of march right up to the foot of the Snowy River country. The white-capped highlands loomed very close, standing above sheer cliffs like clouds settled permanently over the mountains. A steady trail to follow, heading north. Also home to Clan Galla, the mountain nomads of Cimmeria, with their wild, primitive living.

The trail was fresh. By midday it showed signs that the raiders could not be far ahead. A quarter day? Less?

The strength of Kern's small group was beginning to wane, however, with lack of rest and food catching up with them while the raiders gorged on fresh horseflesh. Kern's meager scraps had been passed out, and the last strip of hide between his teeth all but chewed down into tattered leather.

Then the trail split into two.

At the site of a new rest camp, next to a blood-stained clearing. Even Kern, who had seen a similar slaughter the day before, also worried first for the lives of the captured Gaudic clansfolk upon seeing the scarlet-slashed ground. No bodies to be found, though, after running off a few black crows who protested with raucous caws. Just the stink of animal offal and the metallic taste of blood and the ransacked carcass of another horse. This one so hastily butchered that the Vanir had left large chunks of meat on the discarded bones and good strips of flesh and fat.

Did the raiders know they were pursued? Or were they merely wary of it?

No time for a fire, and Kern wouldn't risk the

smoke being seen even if there were. The ravenous pack fell on the gibbets and shards of horseflesh left behind. The meat had a bitter, gamy taste to it, but all of them had eaten worse. And less, which was often just as bad.

Ehmish called for the others before they had swallowed more than a few bites. Accustomed to wait for his elders, the youth had scouted a quick circle around the slaughter site. Silently, he pointed out the two separate trails leading away from the camp. One southeast, and the other suddenly turning hard into the north.

"Which one?" Aodh asked for the rest of them. He didn't speak aloud the common fear. If they chose wrong, and the prisoners had been taken a different direction, there would be no hope of rescue.

Reave frowned. "We follow them both?"

Kern shook his head. "We split up, and we might as well have not come this far together."

He ran alongside the southeast trail for a hundred paces, then did the same heading north. The crows watched him from the trees, commenting—or simply complaining—loudly. He wished for Daol's expertise in reading trail sign. Or Hydallan's. It looked to him as if the larger party, and the remaining horses, went north. Maybe a half dozen to ten had turned southeast.

Wallach nodded when he said as much. "Larger group went a-north, yea. Following a line along the Snowy River country." The man didn't know as much hunting lore as Daol or even Kern, but as a seasoned warrior he knew how to gauge the signs of men on the move. "Southern group traveling smaller and faster."

Someone had to choose. Everyone looked at everyone else. Eventually, they all looked at Kern.

"North," he said, sounding decisive. He didn't need them squabbling about it after. Handing a small cut of meat to Ehmish, swallowing another shard of uncooked horseflesh himself, he choked it down and swallowed against the taste of blood. "We go north. You don't move light or fast with prisoners." You especially didn't race for a difficult pass with such baggage in tow. It made sense to him.

Reave hesitated. "If you're wrong . . ."

"I'm not wrong."

He couldn't be. Too many lives depended on his decision.

He also did not point out his second line of reason. That the smaller force was likely setting up a second ambush, thinking to take another bite at Cul's host. Smaller this time; meant to hit, grab, and run rather than stand and fight. You didn't haul prisoners on such a task as that, either. Not even for sport.

They headed north. And by midday, caught their first sign of the Vanir raiders by daylight.

Kern had jogged ahead, with Ehmish not far behind. Farther back, Reave led the others. Kern's breath came ragged, and his throat tasted raw from exertion. His mind was beginning to narrow down, concentrating only on a point farther up the trail as fatigue finally claimed its due. The war axe in his hand weighed heavily, as did the broadsword across his back. He should have dropped the sword, but could not. It had been Burok Bear-slayer's. Nor could he part with the war axe, thinking he would show better skill with the chopping weapon than he had with the long blade.

Concentrating on such thoughts, however, he nearly missed the movement ahead, and might have given away the pursuit if he had.

Kern dropped down into the snow, rolling to one side to get behind the skeletal shrub of a red bellberry bush. He stared through brown branches and a few blackened leaves that clung stubbornly from the previous fall, and counted twelve . . . fifteen . . . eighteen shadows exposed on a ridgeline not a league distant.

Eighteen! Had the southern band circled back to meet them?

Then he realized that at least four of them had to be the prisoners. In fact, trying to gauge them at a distance, he picked out a line of six figures. One was shorter than the others (Daol?), and one looked a mite leaner (Maev?). They followed in single file, very close together. Roped or chained in a line.

"How many?" Ehmish whispered at Kern's side, causing him to jump. He had seen Kern roll away from the trail and approached so stealthily the man had not even felt him there until he spoke.

"Twelve," Kern decided, heart pounding. He pointed out the slave line to the youth. "Our kin," he said.

"Now what do we do?"

That was the question. One to which Kern had only the beginnings of a plan. He sent Ehmish back to warn Reave to slow up, letting the raiders move farther ahead of them, then waiting longer in case a rear guard had been left on the ridge to watch for pursuers. They took the time to eat what little food they had left, harboring their strength, then set after the Vanir more carefully this time, not wanting to draw attention to themselves until they were ready.

Reave was all for an all-out attack just after nightfall. "Ox," Desagrena muttered under her breath.

Aodh had a hunting bow and a handful of arrows. Kern carried the war axe. Every man and woman also carried a sword of some type. But it was the wood hatchet that Kern put to work first, cutting a long straight sapling and shedding its branches. Another hour's work, waiting for twilight to pass, let him cut a half dozen short handles. Without any rope, they used strips of cloth cut from Kern's blanket to fasten the handles to the sapling at intervals of one arm's length.

Desa cut small, tough strips from the horsehide they

had picked up. With these they tied bundles of twigs, dead brush, and tinder, and more woolen cloth around the end of each short pole. Crude torches that might burn for a handful of minutes if they were lucky.

Cimmerians did not count on luck.

Darkness was not absolute, not with the broken cloud cover. A waxing moon shed silver light over the white-blanketed land. After a day of welcoming back the sun, Kern cursed the poor conditions for a midnight raid. Against the silver-white pale of the snow, five fast-moving shadows were sure to be seen.

"Timing will be important," he told his small band of warriors. They crouched down over a piece of ground cleared of snow. Kern used the tip of his knife to dig his plan into the earth. He drew a rough circle for the Vanir campsite, then put a row of six small x's on the eastern side, between camp and the mountains.

Young Ehmish listened, wide-eyed, as his part in the action was explained.

"They will come for you quickly, and quietly as they can. Stay alert! We can't spare anyone just to guard your back. You have to decide on your own when to run, and you have to run fast and far." Kern caught the youth's gaze, held it. "Don't make me have to come back for you."

Ehmish nodded.

"That leaves the rest of us to take the Vanir campsite." He drew a small arrow on the southern side of the Vanir, and four circles on the western approach. "Nay telling how many will be left behind. Enough to guard the prisoners and defend the camp."

"Four, mebbe six, was me," Wallach Graybeard said, chewing on the long hairs of his moustache.

"So we might have an advantage." Kern nodded. He pointed at the arrow with the tip of his blade. "Aodh, you get a head start on the rest of us. Work your way within bowshot. Be ready to cause trouble and make sure you're not shooting Daol or one of the others full of arrows. You will also be closest to Ehmish, and it's your call if you need to go help him or come down after us." He waited until the other man caught his gaze, and the meaningful glance toward Ehmish, and nodded.

It was one thing to impress the boy with the seriousness of his part. It was quite another to abandon him out there.

Kern unstoppered his skin and drank a long pull from the leather-tasting snowmelt, swishing it around in his mouth as Hydallan had taught him long ago. Best way to take the edge off a thirst. Swallowed.

"We give Ehmish a few minutes to pull the raiders apart, Aodh the chance to stir up the camp, then we hit them hard as we can." He drew a line from the four small circles into the Vanir camp. "If you spot the slave line, and its rope, cut the line and throw someone your knife. Keep them with you! Remember, none of them know our plans or how we'll match up afterward."

Desagrena brushed locks of oily hair from her face, and nodded. "We grab what we can of their food stores and supplies, and we break away before the rest of the Vanir return. They will expect us to head back south." She lifted her gaze into the heavens, and found the Pole Star peeking out at the edge of a cloud. "We can do this, Kern Wolf-Eye."

"For our friends," Kern said gravely, "we don't have a choice."

EHMISH CERTAINLY DIDN'T have a choice. He'd given up that right when he'd stood up for Kern Wolf-Eye, against his chieftain, and volunteered to run north with the rest of them. After their kin.

After Maev.

A stupid fish. That's what it came back to. Kern giving him back the trout, which Ehmish had snagged from the basket-trap set in the stream's freezing waters. Telling the young man to give it directly to Maev. Ehmish knew there was something wrong then, with Kern heading south, but the strong gaze of Kern's wolflike eyes had held him, pressed in on him, and (to be honest) had basically frightened him into it.

Maev accepted the fish with sad eyes and a wry smile. If it was a joke, Ehmish hadn't seen it. What he had seen was that it was important to Burok Bear-slayer's daughter. Her approval of the gesture had certainly outweighed Cul's dark glower, and settled around Ehmish's shoulders like a mantle of armor.

Where was that armor now?

As the moon slipped behind a thick pile of clouds, the moment Kern had told him to wait for, Ehmish struck the flint he'd been given with the haft of his knife, chipping sparks into a small pile of tinder. When it caught, he quickly dipped one end of a small blanket strip into the brief flame.

Using the burning cloth to light all six torches, he touched off the tinder and twigs Desa had tied to the poles. Shouldering the sapling, feeling its weight press down into his shoulder, Ehmish balanced the long pole carefully to keep it from dipping down and snagging the ground. The bark was smooth except where the hatchet had skinned off a branch. Pitch, smelling of winter's slow-moving tar and fresh-cut wood, stained his hands. The torches crackled with lusty strength. He hadn't thought they would provide so much light. It suddenly felt as if every raider in the northern valley could see him. Ehmish's instincts told him to run. Far and fast, as Kern had told him. But that would come later.

Right now, his job was to draw the raiders out of their campsite, pretending to be the entire rescue party moving by torchlight.

He didn't feel like part of the rescue. He felt like a

large target. "Imagine what it will look like from the raider camp," Kern had told him, and he tried.

Much smaller than the raiders' campfire, which had been a small lick of orange flame in the distance before they scattered their embers for the night. Ehmish stared at the three torches burning in front of him, how they dipped and wavered as he staggered forward through the thinning forest. And three more behind. Six sparks of light, dripping ashes and glowing cinders. To the Vanir, they had to look tiny and distant, carried by six individual hands.

And Kern had imagined it all without the aid of any fire for comparison. Impressive. But Ehmish still felt as if he'd been stuck out on a shaky tree limb, trying to keep his balance over a very long fall.

He wondered if that was how it always felt, to be a man.

Not that he was one yet. Or was ever likely to be, with his mind wandering. It was nearly too late, in fact, by the time Ehmish sensed the raiders approaching. A glowing cinder landed on the back of his neck, stinging him just above the collar of his winter cloak. It sharpened his focus for a moment, and suddenly he felt the eyes on him from somewhere far out in the darkness. Kern had warned him . . . quiet and quick. But the torches were barely half-burned when he heard the first stick break in the stillness. Somewhere up ahead!

Was it time? Should he give it another moment? There were no more sounds to warn him. Ehmish knew he'd have to rely on his instincts. And every one of them screamed at him. *Run!*

As he'd been instructed, first the young man ducked down and back up, bouncing the long pole hard against his shoulder a few times, causing the torches to waver as the blanket ties loosened. One of them up front twisted over, falling to the ground. Looking like it had been doused against the snow. Close enough! Ehmish dumped over the entire contraption, putting the torch heads into the snow and making sure each one had hissed out its last breath of life.

Darkness plunged in, wrapping around him like a smothering blanket. His eyes had grown too used to the torchlight! Kern had warned him to squint, and stare at the ground more than the burning brands. He'd forgotten.

Shuffling to one side, eager to put some distance between himself and the raiders' attention, Ehmish tripped over a log half-buried in the blanket of light snow. It pitched him over, dropping him to hands and knees.

The frozen touch of the ground stung at his exposed fingers. Crawling forward, near panic, the young man cast about wildly for any sign of danger. Branches scraped at his knees and he smelled scorched snow from where the torches had fallen, but he heard no sign of movement and saw no shadows against the dark backdrop.

Think! It was Kern's voice in his head, taking hold and thrusting the panic aside. *What is going on right now?*

The raiders saw the lights doused. They would pause, going to ground in case their quarry had acted on impulse rather than out of fear. So they weren't moving either!

But they were in front of him. Behind him, too, likely. Ehmish was supposed to run east, but crashing blindly through the underbrush and snapping off dry branches was a good way to bring every one of them after him. Move carefully. Move quietly. Those were warrior's ways.

Fortunately for him, Ehmish was not a warrior. Yet.

With roars of challenge, the raiders suddenly leaped forward from hiding, crashing in from three sides. Ehmish stood and bolted east, the only way open to him. His eyes had adjusted enough that he avoided the dark pillars of the trees, though branches snagged at his cloak and whipped at his face. He ended up running with hands outstretched to protect his eyes.

But he wasn't going to outrun the Vanir, Ehmish realized. Especially as he was leaving them an easy trail to follow. He veered toward the thicker stands of trees, where the snow was thinner and would not tell his passage as easily. He considered climbing high, but somewhere he had heard how that was a natural instinct, and the first mistake an unseasoned man made. From a tree, there was nowhere left to go.

Always better to go down. For cover.

Over there! Where the trees thinned again, spreading out to create several small clearings. The snow was thicker on the ground, but so were a few patches of underbrush.

One hedgelike stand held up a large blanket of snow from the ground, leaving room beneath its branches for a small man to hide. Ehmish dodged in that direction, taking large, jumping strides to keep his footprints to a minimum. Then he grabbed up his cloak, wrapped it about him as best he could, and rolled under the tangle of branches.

Some of the suspended snow fell down on him, and Ehmish took inspiration from that. He reached out and swept long armfuls toward him, building a small wall that might hide his legs. Then, grabbing a thick branch, he shook the brush and brought more of the crusted snow down around him and on top of him.

Pulling the edge of his cloak over his head, he waited.

He waited while footsteps thundered against the frozen ground not a sword's stroke distant. Waited while the raiders called to each other in their flat, nasal language, all around him.

He waited until he heard the first wounded cry in the

distance, which would be Aodh and his bow, and longer while the Vanir shuffled around him, torn between pursuit and a return to camp. Ehmish waited until the forest was filled with the sounds of distant fighting, and the footfalls of the Vanir had all faded away.

And then he waited some more.

9

DODGING AROUND THE back side of a simple lean-to tent, hunched over, Kern stayed low to the ground. The sharp, ringing clash of steel against steel and grunts of exertion drew him around the corner at full speed.

He ducked under the lean-to's support rope. Raced into the clearing.

To nearly be trampled by a runaway horse.

The Vanir's entire camp boiled over with chaos. Warriors roared their battle cries or called out the appearance of a new threat. Prisoners yelled to be rescued. A pair of horses, freed from their tether lines by Desagrena, raced about inside the circle of trees and tents, trapped, frenzied. One bled from a cut along its left foreleg, bawling up a storm with its high-pitched cries.

Slipping around the flanks of the wounded animal, careful of its lashing hooves, Kern came at the blind side of a Vanir warrior battling Wallach Graybeard at the center of the raider camp. The two men circled around a large stone ring, inside which the embers of the raiders' fire still glowed a dull orange. The raider, a large man, belted with a metal cuirass and thick furs, wielding a bastard sword with furious energy, easily outmassed Wallach by several stone's weight.

Wallach kept his broadsword in the way of the Vanir's brutal chopping strokes, but wasn't able to strike back with anything more than halfhearted slashes before the raider was on him again.

Kern struck the man full-body on, shoving him away from Wallach. Tripping over the fire pit stones, the raider rolled through the burning embers with a cry of pain and rage. Kern went after him, circling the fire pit with the haft of his battle-axe gripped tightly in both hands. But when he struck at the raider, the red-haired warrior easily ducked the clumsy blow.

His second cut and a third did no better than slice the air again, though they kept the raider dancing among the live coals.

A return slash nicked Kern's wrist, stinging him, but he turned most of it against the axe's thick handle.

He jabbed the axe head at the raider, trying to hook him with the back side of the sharpened flange. An awkward motion, which missed. Surprisingly, Kern was finding the battle-axe hardly as comfortable as a wood axe would have felt in his hands.

Not that it mattered so much when Wallach leaped into the fire pit and laid the raider's flesh open just over his ribs. The Vanir hissed in pain, but did not drop his sword.

Wallach's next slash took the man's hand off at the wrist. Kern's sloppy overhead chop ended a howl of pain, cleaving through the man's head, wedging the axe's thick blade in the raider's skull.

The stench of crisped flesh and singed furs burned at the back of Kern's throat. He tried to pull his axe head loose, but only succeeded in dragging the raider's body half-out of the fire pit. His gorge threatening to rise, he placed a foot into the mess of blood and brain, ready to pry his weapon free. Then realized he wasn't having a great deal of luck with it regardless.

Dropping the haft in disgust, he reached back and freed Burok's broadsword. And from the strap over his left shoulder he unslung the small, bronzed-faced shield he'd salvaged from his last battle. With these he quickly chased after Wallach, who had run for the slave line.

Thin rope bound the five prisoners' wrists and hobbled their ankles together. A chain stretched from neck to neck, attached to thick leather collars that secured at the back. When Kern arrived, Wallach was sawing at Daol's bindings. The small man gasped in pain and relief as his hands were freed and circulation returned. He struggled with his collar, numb fingers fumbling with the clasp.

Swatting Daol's hands away, Kern worked it himself. A simple twist of a metal toggle, which popped through a riveted hole and the entire collar and chain fell away from Daol's neck.

Daol actually hugged the other man, grateful for his rescue.

"Thought you'd be dead in the snow," he said, voice hoarse and breaking from lack of water. "Where's Reave?"

Kern didn't know. Wallach did. "Saw him chased off by a pair of raiders. Two more went toward the horses, and Desa, but Aodh got one of them through the heart."

Daol paused over the collar of the next slave in line. A man with ebony skin and bright eyes, and very, very far from home to be trapped in Cimmeria. "How many'd you bring with you?" the young hunter asked, amazed to hear so many familiar names.

"Not enough if the other raiders make it back before we're done." Kern had looked over the line of prisoners and found the one missing. "Maev?" he asked, an icy fist punching him in the gut.

Daol startled as if stuck with a knife. "He took her." He cast about, trying to orient himself. "North end of camp. Other side of the hanging felt."

Kern had seen the makeshift wall, but had not been close enough to look behind it. Figured it to be the local trench. Had Maev been there, bound and gagged, the entire time? He drew the knife from his belt and tossed it to Daol.

"Find Reave or stay with Wallach. Grab whatever supplies you can." He set off at a sprint, glancing back only once. No sign of Aodh, who should have gone after Ehmish. Desa he noticed scavenging from among packs and slings on the south side of camp. "Gather them and get them out," he shouted back to Wallach.

He went for the hanging sheet of felt. It lay over a cord strung between two tall pine, on the north side of camp as Daol had said. Kern didn't bother running around, or trying to lift it as a raider lying in wait might guess. He swung the heavy broadsword up and around, slicing through the thick material, cleaving it nearly in half and forming a door in the privacy screen.

Then followed the sword through, ready to take a blow against his shield.

There was no one there. Just an abandoned bedroll and a large shaggy fur blanket no doubt come with the raider from Nordheim lands. A horned helm rested on a nearby branch, forgotten in his haste to leave. But he had taken Maev with him, or come back for her in the confusion in the camp. Which meant the other raiders might not be far behind.

"Grab and go," Kern yelled back over his shoulder, plunging after the two sets of tracks in the snow. Moonlight was strong enough to read the trail. "Go now!"

He should have grabbed a pack on his way through. Or returned for one, and maybe find Daol to help him track after the missing pair. He'd also left behind the battle-axe. Kern had his bedroll tied around the middle of his back and a few meager scraps of raw horseflesh wrapped in the oilskin. He had his sword and shield and not much else.

He wasn't turning back now.

His winter cloak streamed out behind him as he sprinted down a short, shallow slope, crashing through a light stand of brush at the bottom. He used his sword to clear a bit of tangle from in front of him, hacking at the skeletal branches as if he bore a machete and not a battle-quality weapon. Out through the far side, he saw the wide prints of the raider and the shuffling trail where Maev either stumbled along or was dragged.

Even if the raiders' leader had fled with the initial onslaught, he could not have better than a few moments' head start. And why drag along a prisoner? There was only one use Kern could think of for separating Maev out from the others, but not while running. Every ten paces, Kern had to make up time on them.

Then the moon slipped behind the clouds, and he was forced to slow or lose the trail altogether.

"Maev?" Kern called out loudly. He feared losing the trail, or slowing too much, against what the raider might do to her if she called back.

"Here! Over here!"

The shout did not come from too far away, around a small screen of scrub pine and hemlock. Again, rather than go around, Kern came through the evergreens with sword in front of him—to find Maev in torn clothing and a haunted look in her eyes, tugging uselessly on the rope that bound her collar to a tree. Her wrists were tied together, making it difficult to undo the knots. And, of course, she could not reach the clasp at the back of her neck.

She spun around as he crashed into the small clearing. "Kern! Kern he's—"

But Kern understood at once that Maev had been dragged along as bait and as a distraction at the same time. Staked out in the clearing to give the raider a chance to strike from behind. He dived off to his right, arms flailing, as the Vanir burst from cover with blood-stained bastard sword already stabbing for Kern's side.

It scored off Kern's shield, more by luck than design, turning the point away from his kidney.

Kern hit the frozen ground hard, losing his broadsword, rolled and came up with shield between him and his attacker. Expecting one of the flame-haired Vanir or a close cousin of Asgard with their fairer skin and golden hair.

A large man, certainly.

A ferocious warrior.

But not the frost white hair and beard that looked so much like one of the fabled snow bears of the far, far north.

Certainly not the yellow eyes Kern had only ever seen in a still pond's reflection.

The frost-haired man was huge, standing at least three handbreadths over Kern. With waxy-pale skin, he wore the leather cuirass banded with metal that was common among Vanir. And he used the bastard sword as easily as Kern might a knife. No wild, slashing attacks but with short, brutal stabs that went for Kern's heart, his face.

Rage twisted the raider's mouth into a feral snarl as he jabbed and struck.

Kern's shield took most of the damage. It was easier to handle than the heavy steel blade he retrieved from the ground. In a hand accustomed to its weight and grip, the broadsword was a solid weapon. Not as fearsome as a Cimmerian greatsword, perhaps, but few men other than Reave or perhaps this giant of a northerner could effectively wield such a length of edged metal.

Still, Kern flailed at the other man. Each weak thrust was turned aside or parried directly, the blow ringing down through the steel and up his arm. Several times it felt as if Kern had dislocated his shoulder, though he did not lose his grip on the sword again because without it, he and Maev were dead.

The northerner came at him again. And again. He had incredible strength, which did not seem to flag, while Kern was on his second day with little to no rest and very little to eat. Twice they came up body to body. Once Kern managed to slam the boss on his shield directly into the other man's face, laying his cheek open in a wide flap that showed the teeth behind.

The stream of curses he spit back at Kern were a heady mix of Nordheimir and Cimmerian.

The second time they pressed together, the Vanir worked his sword around the edge of Kern's shield. The shield's leather arm strap took most of the thrust, leaving Kern with a shallow slice up his forearm and holding on to the shield by the handle alone.

"What are you doing?" Maev cowered back against the tree as the fight pressed close. She had lost her cloak and her kilt. Only a long tunic protected her from the cold. "Kill it!"

Easier said than accomplished. "He isn't a tree, and this isn't a wood axe," Kern snapped back, circling at the edge of the clearing, keeping a wary eye on the frost-man.

Kern was doing the best he could for never being heavily trained as a warrior. Also, he had to admit, the northerner's similar features had him rattled. If the yellow eyes both men shared were of concern to the frost-man he did not show it at all, while Kern could not help wondering where this odd-colored man had come from.

And if there were others like him.

Another clash. Kern felt his arm growing slow behind the broadsword.

He couldn't last a great deal longer. As the giant man charged forward again, Kern whipped his shield up barely in time to stop the point of the bastard sword, which aimed right for his heart. He remembered the single-thrust wound that had killed Oscur, and knew this warrior was the one responsible. It had been a slaughter for the veteran raider, this strange northern warrior, not a battle. The youth had never stood a chance.

Rather than falling into despair, however, Kern banked the anger. Fanned it into a strong flame. He borrowed strength from it, letting it fuel his muscles as he brought his sword up and around in an overhead slash, chopping down at the raider's shoulders.

The Vanir got his own sword up on guard, and Kern hammered against it.

In fluid, swinging motions, Kern brought the broadsword around again, and again. All overhead swipes that arced down at the larger man. All relying on the practiced muscles he'd built while chopping wood.

Up. Around. Down.

Hacking away at the Vanir's defenses, trying to shatter the bastard sword or beat down the man's arm long enough to take him at the throat or the chest. Kern drove the warrior back step by step, until the last of his strength was nearly spent.

Then he lost his shield to a mighty swipe of the northerner's blade. The raider slammed forward, knocking Kern off-balance, shoving the Cimmerian back against the wide bole of a red cedar and pinning him against it. Kern's sword arm caught between the press of their bodies, trapped.

With numb fingers Kern clutched at the frost-man's wrist, holding off a finishing blow as the bastard sword wavered overhead. Then he felt a large hand wrap around his throat, beginning to *squeeze*.

The warrior's breath reeked of carrion. His yellow eyes smoldered with rage. He spit words at Kern, all in the nasal tongue shared by Nordheimers, but Kern did not need a translation.

He was going to die.

"Do something!" Maev yelled.

He couldn't work his sword free. If he'd had the training and the strength left, he might have snapped the blade up hard enough to gash open the raider's leg. Maybe into the groin. Kern was barely holding on to it as it was. The heavy blade pointed at the ground, and try as he might, Kern could do nothing except slap it weakly against the side of the raider's leg.

Gasping for breath, he felt his knees begin to buckle under the pull of the earth. Dragging him into darkness.

With everything he had left, Kern shoved *down*. Working his shoulder into the raider's chest, he put his full weight behind the thrust that speared his broadsword through the raider's foot, through flesh and the crunch of small bones, pinning the northerner to the earth.

A pain-filled roar filled Kern's ear, nearly deafening him. Kern sagged in the northerner's grip.

Then there was a stinging slap, and the raider jerked. The hand at Kern's throat lightened, and he twisted away with a diving roll that took him out of the bastard sword's reach. Cool, fresh air filled his lungs with new energy. He stagger-sprinted for Maev, intent on working her neck clasp free to give her the chance to run. Saw her staring back to one side, no longer interested in the fight.

That was when he remembered Maev's shout, and the stinging sound. A cut through the air that reminded Kern of hunting trips.

Maev had not shouted to him, but *for* him.

He spun back toward the raider. The frost-haired giant sagged forward, hugging the cedar's scaled trunk, sword still rammed through his foot, the gray-feathered end of an arrow sprouting from his back just below one shoulder blade.

The Vanir warrior tried to push himself back upright, levering his large hands beneath him, against the tree. Another arrow *thwapped* into his body, higher than the first. Then, as Kern watched, a third. Into the back of his neck. Finishing him.

It was an easy path to follow, turning back along the arrow's flight. A shadow stood just within the trees, reaching out into the moonlight with only his hands and a Vanir hunting bow visible. One last arrow nocked and ready. He lowered his weapon slowly, seeing it wouldn't be necessary.

Then, drawing the knife wedged under his belt, he stepped forward into the clearing and tossed the short blade to Kern, who caught it by the hilt.

Daol.

They met near Maev. Daol waited silently, eyes glancing away from her disheveled state while Kern cut through the rope at her neck, then carefully untoggled the clasp to rid her of the leather collar. She staggered away from the tree but did not fall, keeping what remained of her dignity. Checking on the northern warrior, she spit, then retrieved the broadsword for Kern and brought it back to him.

"If you're going to keep this," she said, "learn to use it." She thrust it back into his hands.

The men said nothing to her, letting Maev find her balance.

Daol glanced back the way they'd all come, searching the shadows. "I thought you might need some help," he said.

Kern nodded. He unfastened the bedroll roped at his back and retrieved Maev's arming sword, which he had wrapped into the middle. She took it without a glance or a word of thanks, belting it on over her tunic. With the sheath hanging down alongside pale legs puckered in new gooseflesh, Kern again became aware of how undressed Maev was and quickly doffed his winter cloak. She accepted that, too, wrapping it tightly about her.

Daol stepped back into the forest, picked up a pack where he had dropped it. "Food," he promised. "Flint and rope as well. I cleared out right ahead of the returning raiders. They were barking up a storm, trying to decide who to chase down and kill. But our kin all left on different paths, following horse trails it looked like."

Good. And if Aodh and Ehmish had evaded the first Vanir, they might have a chance as well.

"So is there a plan?" Maev asked, breaking her silence again. "Or do we stand here until the Vanir think to chase after their leader?" She nodded toward the dead body but made no reference to the northerner's strange looks. Though her eyes were guarded as she stared at Kern. Wary.

Kern nodded north toward the Pole Star, visible through a break in the dark, overhead clouds. "We meet up with the others," he said. "Then we get you home."

"Good enough." Maev began walking, striking out ahead with determined strides.

The men had no choice but to follow her. She made it nearly an hour before the adrenaline and her strength gave out completely, and she collapsed in the snow.

After that, Kern carried her.

10

SIX CLANSMEN, SOME with rescued prisoners in tow, trying to find each other in the dark and lonely stretches of Conall Valley had seemed a nightmare to consider. All of their familiar landmarks were to the south, the one direction they didn't dare go. Following the line of foothills below the Snowy River country always made for a good path, but there was that small raider band split off from the main group to worry about. If the Vanir turned away from Cul's party, or were on their way back after another successful raid, they would be doing the same.

Kern knew that his small band wouldn't have another full day's travel *and* another battle in them. He'd had to come up with something different.

Which was why he was going to head straight north on a run, holding it long enough for the Dragon to chase the Bear around the Pole Star about twice the breadth of a hand. Roughly an hour. Only then would he swing around to the west. Everyone else had fled the raider camp on some north or north-by-west path. They would hold that line for only a hand's turn of the constellations. After that, everyone made a slow turn. West, if they had traveled north. North, if by west.

Sooner or later they would cross his path and converge on a new campsite.

It would also put them in the vicinity of Clan Taur, if Kern's reckoning of distance and direction were holding. As a backup, the Gaudic clansfolk could rendezvous there. There would be no free handouts. No sympathy. But with Vanir raiders about, they could hope for a parley at least.

Maev slowed them down, of course, after her collapse. Some things were harder on a person than long runs and short, violent battles. She woke up after a time, recovered enough to struggle forward on her own. Slowly. She kept her silence throughout the long march, even when their small group broke through some underbrush to see a dire wolf outlined on a nearby hill, or later saw such an animal lurking near a sheltered dale.

If she noticed or thought it strange to see the beast stalking them, she gave no outward sign.

Daol raised his bow at one point, seeing a clean shot. Kern simply put a hand on the end of the arrow and pushed it toward the ground, shaking his head.

He had no explanation for himself or in answer to Daol's raised eyebrows. It was just that . . . if it was the same wolf he had fought and wrestled with, shooting the creature now would feel like he had betrayed it. If he was going to kill the wolf, he should have been willing to do so on its terms, with tooth and claw. He'd had that chance, and decided against it.

His friend let it go without an explanation. Maybe he sensed the connection.

Maybe he was simply too grateful to be alive and free that he wouldn't argue.

Finally, scouting out a protected vale, the three swept away a good clearing in the snow and had built up a fire for warmth by the time Desa, then Wallach, staggered in with supplies and the rest of the rescued prisoners. A few were content to drop onto a cleared section of ground, roll themselves into a blanket or muddied cloak, and fall asleep. Most stayed awake as Wallach produced a large shank of venison, and Kern quickly set strips of it to cooking on sticks propped up near the flames.

Soon the savory scent of cooking meat drifted out from the camp.

Kern believed it was the smell that finally brought in Reave, the slow-moving man leading in a wounded horse that he'd discovered along the way.

"Traveled a bit farther west than needs be," Reave said. "Cut back northeast to make up. Did a little sleepwalking, an' worried that I missed the tracks."

So he had crossed back and forth over a great run of territory before finally hitting someone's trail. The horse he had found only an hour back, already complaining of its broken leg. The animal was too weak to resist anymore, offering only a small neighing cry when it limped forward. Reave led it over to one side, hitched it to a nearby tree.

Then he dropped his heavy bulk at the fire's side, took a skewer of partially cooked meat for himself, and tore off a large, bloody bite.

More stories came out slowly. Few as boasts. Most simply retellings. Wallach and Daol both told theirs while setting up a slaughter pit for the wounded horse, putting the animal out of its misery and staking out more meat to be slow-cooked for preservation.

Daol, as it turned out, understood enough of the northern tongue to know the Vanir had been looking to join up with another raiding team. Coming across the funeral host seemed a bonus for them, and their frost-bearded leader had been upset to the point of raging when the initial attack cost them five warriors. Which was why he sent a small party back to regain their honor, including two wounded men who slowed down the entire band.

The northerners, Daol said, had called their leader *Ymirish*. The *blood of Ymir*. As if he might be descended from their frost-giant god. Talk degenerated to careful conversation regarding the yellow-eyed warrior with the pale, waxy skin and hair the color of old frost. Even Maev joined them long enough to confirm that it had been the northerners' leader who had taken her, and later kept her as spoils of battle. She shivered, holding her hands out to the fire. Then she wrapped herself tightly in Kern's cloak and left, bedding down at the outer edge of the cleared area, barely within the cast of flickering light.

Silence reigned. No one looked specifically at Kern, though he suspected there were many among the former prisoners especially who stole glances his way, comparing the two men.

In a small side pouch on his pack, Wallach found a small wrap of dried fruits, which he passed around. Kern chewed slowly on tough leather slices of sun-dried apple. They tasted musty, with only a hint of flavor, but still a welcome relief.

When another of the venison skewers finished roasting, he tore meat off and bounced it from one hand to the other as it cooled. It had a wonderful smoky taste, and occupied him for a time as the night deepened and others told halting tales of their captures, or parts in the rescue. It was then he noticed a pair of savage eyes shining out in the darkness, reflecting back the firelight. They hovered far enough back that the wolf was hard to find unless you were looking for it. Kern looked. Feeling generous, he went to the slaughter pit and found a pile of entrails that would only be left to rot and chucked them out into the darkness. They fell too close to the camp, though, and the wolf would not come for it.

"You pick your friends strangely," one of the rescued prisoners said, as Kern regained his place by the fire. The ebony-skinned fellow, who had sat quietly and listened, until now. He used the Aquilonian tongue. Haltingly, and with a thick accent, but clear enough for most Cimmerians to follow.

Kern glanced at Daol and Reave. "I think they would say that they're the ones with poor taste."

"Any man with friend who come to rescue him like you did . . . he not poor." That said, he turned back to the fire and continued to shred his food, bringing the meat up to his mouth in tiny slivers. Making it last.

Fewer than half of the troop remained awake by then. There weren't any stories left or much conversation to speak of. "So?" Daol was first to ask. "What do we do now?"

"You take Maev back to Gaud," Kern answered slowly, thinking through the next steps. He was amazed that any of them had survived this long, but where did they go from here? "You, Semie, and Fough." They were the other two captured with Daol and Maev. They were all still part of the clan.

"What about you?" Daol took in the other outcasts by eye.

Desa shrugged, poking into the fire with the tip of her knife, watching the end turn black. Reave and Wallach both looked to Kern.

"We cannot go back," Kern said. "Cul will have sent his runners back to the village, and the Tall-Woods will know we are all outcasts." Once outside the clan, always outside. That was custom and law. "I don't know if Cul will take in the other two we rescued." The dark-skinned man did not look up, either not understanding Cimmerian or not caring. "But they can be given enough food to have a chance at making the southern borderlands." Horseflesh and hard biscuits.

Daol chewed on that a moment. Then he shrugged. "I go where you go," he said simply.

Kern had expected the younger man's gratitude. But he also owed a thought to Daol's father. "Would Hydallan appreciate that decision?" he asked.

"He'd remind me . . . and you . . . that a man makes his own decisions, and he does not turn from his debts." He glanced at Reave, suddenly unsure. "We should have come for you when Cul cast you out."

There was no way to tell how deeply that hurt had sat inside his friends, festering. No doubt it would have caused them trouble with Cul before ever reaching the Field of the Chiefs.

Still, Kern remembered something Burok had spoken over a summer fire. "*Being* chieftain is easy," he said now, reaching back for the words. "Earning it. That's hard."

"Becoming king easy," the dark-skinned man said absently, as if correcting him. Obviously he did understand the Cimmerian language. Though he still spoke Aquilonian. "What you do as king, this hard." He saw everyone staring at him. "King Conan say that many years before your chieftain."

Silence, marred only by the crackling of the fire, was absolute. The strange man had the look of the fabled Black Kingdoms of the far, far south, but his tattered clothes and his language resembled the nearer "civilized" kingdoms. He chewed slowly, staring into the flames, oblivious to the quiet.

"You heard Conan speak?" Kern finally asked for the others. "As king?" Despite the black words most Cimmerian clans had for Conan, everyone hung on the man's answer.

"Aquilonia smaller than Shem," he said, glancing to either side. The whites of his eyes looked unnaturally bright in his dark face. So did his large teeth when he smiled, skinning back thin lips. "But not that small. King Conan's words, they written down in books I read."

Desa snorted. "Now he can read, too." Literacy was highly regarded among most clans, but not widely pursued. Hunting and tracking. Fighting and farming. Skills that kept you alive; those were the important ones.

"I can read," the man said. "And write. King Conan has many books about him. One I saw, it was about his challenge to the wizard, Zathrus. He had to order many men to their deaths. He knows they cannot win, but was necessary to tie wizard down in one place."

Clan before kin. Kern remembered the pair of Aquilonian soldiers who stopped to trade for meat last summer. What was it they had said? "You can take the barbarian out of Cimmeria, but you can't get Cimmeria out of the barbarian." They had laughed afterward. Around this fire, men and women nodded seriously.

Conan might have forgone his people, but not their ways. And Cul had forgone neither, in fact. He had done what he could for the clan. It didn't matter if others agreed, or it eventually set him apart from his kin. That was his life now.

In a way, it was also now something of Kern's life.

For his part in touching off the discussion, Daol didn't seem to care one way or another. "I still go with you."

"Same," Reave said.

Wallach Graybeard thought a moment, staring out in the dark, then nodded, tying his fate, for the moment, to Kern. Desagrena kept her own counsel but did not deny that she'd remain. When she had something to say, Kern had no doubt that she'd speak up. Silence was not among her faults.

Reave frowned, as if suddenly remembering something he'd forgotten to ask.

"So, where are we going?"

THERE HAD BEEN several ways Kern could respond to Reave's question. Spreading his woolen blanket over a thick pad of felt Daol had stolen from the Vanir camp, Kern thought about how he had answered.

"To look for Ehmish and Aodh if they don't show by morning."

It was the easiest answer to give. It satisfied Reave, simply in need of direction. It put off the harder questions that Daol or Desa might have asked, comforting them with an important fact. They would care for their own first.

No one would be left behind. Ever.

And the simple truth of the matter was Kern hadn't thought too much past that. There were several questions to answer regarding the northern man, and his appearance so similar to Kern's.

Where had he come from?

Were there others like him? Like Kern?

Leaving first watch in Desagrena's hands, with a rotation split among the four outcasts through the night, Kern decided to put off those questions till the next day, when he would be rested and thinking clearly.

Which might have been one reason he was shocked Maev had been thinking so much farther ahead. That, and her appearance at his bedside.

She wore his worn winter cloak, having never handed it back after Kern's battle with the frost-man, the Ymirish, bundling it around her as if afraid to show herself to anyone still awake. He couldn't say why, but she looked more vulnerable and yet more determined and strong than he had ever seen. She spread her own blanket next to his, then lay down with the cloak spread over her and slightly overlapping Kern's woolen cover.

As she bedded at his side, he noticed that she had removed her tunic and wore little else than a thin cotton shift.

"You'll freeze," Kern whispered harshly, not wanting to draw attention to her.

Maev shook her head, bedraggled hair whispering over one bared shoulder. "No," she said, slipping closer, tugging the hem of his blanket over her as well. "I won't."

He glanced around. Having chosen a place farthest from the campfire, to give one of the rescued prisoners a warmer place, Kern and Maev were half-cloaked in the night with barely a lick of flames from the dying fire to show against her bared skin, or glowing in his eyes. Only Desa remained obviously awake, perched on a nearby log with her back blatantly turned toward the couple.

Maev's hands closed on the large brass buckle that fastened the belt around Kern's heavy kilt. He had stripped off his poncho, never too worried about catching his death of a cold. He never suffered from exposure except in the most extreme circumstance. Now, here, Kern felt the chill touch of the night air very, very close. Just as he felt the heat Maev radiated, spilling into him where her fingers brushed against bare skin.

"You don't know what you're doing," Kern whispered, fastening his hands around her wrists. She froze, terrified, and he remembered that she had spent the last night and a day bound against her will. He released her.

"I know very well. You look like him. Same eyes. Similar coloring. No one would ever know the difference. *I'll* never know."

"Maev, you're going back to Gaud. Cul will be there. I will not."

But he hadn't understood. Not fully. "You think my

place in the village will be any more comfortable if I end up carrying a Vanir's get? That would be the only thing worse than what he did to me. I wouldn't want to live through it."

And by comparison, Kern read into it, lying with him would be a much easier fate to bear.

"I don't know . . ."

Maev found his hands, seized them in hers. "I do." She huddled close, and he could smell the sweat in her hair, the sweet taste of dried apple on her breath. Her mouth worked, but no sound came out for a moment as she fought for the right words. "Kern. I need this. Something to hedge against fate. The village knew you. You came back for us. They'd understand."

"No. They wouldn't."

"They'd accept. It's close enough."

Was it? Kern could see the logic behind her mad request, her need. A woman pressed into a corner by desperate circumstance. Worried about giving birth to a child with amber yellow eyes and white hair among a people that tended toward blue-gray and dark. If Kern's mother had been equally careful . . .

Vanir bastard or an outcast's son. The choices weren't in Maev's favor, or in favor for any child she might catch. But that was not exactly his decision to make. She was there. She knew what it would take to go on living among Clan Gaud. And so did he.

Maev seemed to sense his acceptance, moving in, pressing against him. Her hands opened the buckle, then pressed into the washboard muscles along his abdomen with urgent need.

She recoiled suddenly, as if struck. Kern thought it was the crusted scars across his body, his arms. Trophies from the tangle with the dire wolf, and a few sword cuts as well. But Maev had been a chieftain's daughter. Scars, even fresh ones, were no large matter to her. It was something else.

"You're . . . you're cold," she stammered. Not afraid. Not repulsed. She sounded only concerned, as if she might be the cause.

Kern nodded silently in the dark. "All my life," he said. Then reached for her and gathered her under his blanket.

11

TAKING THE LAST watch, Kern left Maev sleeping fitfully inside her own bedroll, his cloak draped over her. If Wallach had anything to say about Burok's daughter bedded down so close to Kern, if he noticed her bared shoulder peeking from beneath her cover, he said nothing. Just rolled himself into his own blanket for another hour's rest.

Kern fed the lingering embers a few more sticks, keeping flames burning under meat still staked over the fire pit. Then he took a turn around the campsite, walking with the same care he'd taken when hunting deer alongside Daol. He saw many drawn and haggard faces, looking tired even in sleep. Looking too thin.

He also saw tracks in the snow on the outskirts of camp, where the dire wolf had finally come during the night for the tripe tossed out to him. A blood trail dragged away, back into the safety of some nearby brush. There was no sign of the animal now, but Kern supposed it would be back.

Another mouth to feed.

Finding a good resting spot, leaning up against the silvery bark of a tall alder, Kern watched the skies lighten over the eastern mountain range. Gray cloud cover piled up over the valley again, threatening snow or sleet. A drenching rain would have pinned the small camp in place, but it would have been a welcome sign of spring's return. The clouds were too high, though. It looked to Kern as if the day would stay cold and dry.

But not uneventful.

Camp stirred awake slowly, with Wallach and Reave among the earliest to rise. Wallach found a camp skillet, and worked to make fresh flat cakes with meal and water, frying them in horse fat. Reave finished shaving any last meat off the hanging carcass. Without being asked, he left the guts that would not keep in a careful pile where the wolf would find them later.

The ebony-skinned man rose not long after. Stretched, and did some sitting-up exercises to warm his blood. Kern had finally learned his name. Nahud'r. Difficult to say, coming out something like *Nahudra* or *Nahuderr* from most of the Cimmerians. The man readily answered to either.

Finished with his stretches, he tore himself off a small piece of horseflesh while waiting for the flat cakes, then staggered outside of camp to relieve himself in the snow. A golden stream, just like any other man. Kern shook his head. What had he expected from a Shemite? Something dark and dry, like stories of the desert land?

Nahud'r took an extra moment, wandering around the southern edge of camp as if searching for something. He took some time facing east, offering some kind of prayer to the lightening gray sky, then turned abruptly and crossed back through camp near Kern's perch.

"Someone out there," he said softly, moving to a

few nearby bedrolls and lightly shaking others awake. Desagrena came up with her knife in hand, but stopped short of plunging it into the black man's throat.

Kern snapped alert at once, embarrassed that he'd not seen or heard an approach. He strode out to the edge of camp, peering into the gray and not bothering to hide his knowledge of the company. If they were raiders, they would attack. No amount of guile would prevent that now.

Instead, a trio of shadows detached themselves from the hillside that sloped down into the small vale. One waved an arm overhead, signaling an "all clear" sign that Kern recognized all too well. A quick, efficient slash. And a peaked cap on his head.

"Daol," Kern called, bringing the hunter to him. He gestured up the hill with a casual nod. "Run up there and bring your da down to camp, if you would."

Thrusting his bow and a pair of arrows into Kern's arms, the younger man set off with a sprint and a shout of happiness.

It was, Kern thought, one of the best sounds he'd heard in a long while.

OF COURSE, HYDALLAN was not prone to joyous reunions. Kern heard the elder tracker complaining all the way into camp. Chastising his son as if he were a youth of ten summers, and not nearly twice that age, for even thinking about leaving his weapon behind. For being captured to begin with. For dragging him away and tormenting his old bones with the cold and the long, forced march from Gaud.

Kern swore he saw Daol stifle a smile.

Hydallan stopped just long enough to brace Kern with a hand on each shoulder, and a nod of thanks. Then he walked over and kicked a spray of dirt over the smoldering fire. "Smelled that an hour away, we did."

Kern doubted it, but wasn't about to argue. "Fair enough," he said, accepting the light rebuke. "Have a bite?"

"Don't mind if'n we do."

With his long knife, Hydallan hacked off three chunks of meat and threw two of them to the clansmen who followed. Garret wasn't a surprise to see. A man nearly as old as Hydallan, and an old friend of the tracker. But the third man, looking sullen and trapped, was a shock.

Brig Tall-Wood.

The young warrior carried a pheasant by the feet, neck broken and flopping limply against his leg. He tossed it to Daol, refusing to meet the other man's eyes.

Kern wasn't going to let it go so easily. As everyone began to break their fast, he asked, "I thought you were watching the village?"

The young man shrugged. "Tabbot can handle that. Cul wanted to know if Maev'd been found."

"He sent you? Sent all of you?"

Hydallan snorted, having overheard. "Sent Brig, here, when Garret and I walked out on him. He can carry his own stubborn ass up to the northern ranges. Or he can plant himself until spring, like you said." He chewed silently for a moment. "Don't matter to me now, neither way."

Apparently, Cul and Morne had both returned to the village, ready to draft as many men as would be necessary to make the pass and continue with Burok Bear-slayer to the Field of the Chiefs. The story came out about the raiders, and Kern's return. And how Kern had gone against the clan to lead away more good men on a fool's mission.

"I think he was just angry for not going after you hisself," Hydallan said, speaking to Maev. "Which is why he unbent enough to throw Brig, here, in with us." He chewed. Swallowed. "We moved all day and most

of last night. Figured you all for the Snowy River country. Then we struck a few trails, all heading the same
direction, and thought we'd follow up. That dark fella,
he threw me for a turn. But still weren't sure you
weren't no Vanir camp until Kern showed that stark
mane o' his."

"Don't take that for certain, next time," Daol
warned his father. Though he held off mentioning anything more about the frost-man—the Ymirish—until
they had a moment alone.

"Not going to be much left to return home to, at this
pace." Reave glanced at Maev.

Kern shrugged aside Reave's comment. "Doesn't
matter. We still need to get the others back, and we
need to find Aodh and Ehmish." The entire camp had
assembled around him like a hunting pack around its
leader. As good a time as any. "Our fallback was always Taur. The village can't be more than half a day
at a good run." Hydallan looked up in the sky, considering, then nodded. Kern continued, singling out
the five former prisoners, excluding Daol, who had
made his choice to stay. "We can break up now, with
the five of you heading southwest, along Hydallan's
back track . . ."

Maev hesitated. Then, "I'd like to know the boy is
all right. We can head home through Taur." Her voice
grew stronger, more certain, as she mapped out a plan
for herself at least. "Refugees who came through over
the winter said they were well prepared for any raiders.
Maybe we can learn something."

Nodding, Kern continued. "And maybe we can pick
up some trail sign on the Vanir we ran across, or the
second raiding party they were going to meet. If they
are in the area, Clan Taur is a good target. It'll draw
them like metal shavings to a lodestone."

It was Brig who looked at him sidelong. "What are
you thinking, Wolf-Eye?"

"That we might track them. Hunt them. Catch the northerners with another nighttime attack." More gazes looked to Kern, and several had a hungry gleam in their eyes that he recognized. "After two years of their preying on Cimmeria, I wouldn't mind taking some back for ourselves."

To that, there was a chorus of answering nods. No matter what else separated Kern from the others, there was still a great deal of common ground. Which reminded him of his second reason.

"And I . . ." Kern almost didn't say, but they had the right to know. "I have a personal stake in this now."

And no one save perhaps Hydallan—either there or at the village—was likely to confirm what Kern suspected after last night. He doubted anyone knew for certain, if his own mother had half the brains and determination that Maev possessed. So his answers, if there were any to be had, lay elsewhere.

"Break camp," he ordered after an awkward silence, feeling uneasy at having to direct such a large and growing group.

They fell to work without complaint.

Wallach found Kern rolling up his own bedroll, using a short length of rope to make the sling that he'd use to carry it. "Lost your war axe back there, didn't you?" he asked, motioning Kern toward a small collection of salvaged gear.

No need to mention the how or why of it. Wallach had been there.

"It wasn't as comfortable in my hands as I thought it might be," Kern admitted. "Too large and awkward."

"Because you aren't trying to chop wood. It's meant to kill a man. Fast. Brutal." The veteran warrior might have a lot of gray shooting through his beard and what was left of his hair, but he had seen enough fighting over his four decades to know what he was talking about. "It's also meant for a bigger man. Like Reave."

Kern nodded. "My hand wasn't much more comfortable around the hilt of a broadsword. Maybe I should stick to throwing rocks." As humor, it fell very flat. Kern hadn't really meant to be funny. His lack in the previous night's battle worried him.

"Comfort comes with time. For now, work on muscle."

He bent to a small stack of weapons, all the extras after the others had taken their preferences. It was a short arming sword. Hardly better than a knife. The kind of weapon you gave one of the village youths when you knew he wasn't in danger of cutting off a finger through stupidity.

Holding it in one large hand, Kern thought the blade might snap just by staring at it. "You want me to use this?"

"If you hope to stand against a seasoned Vanir, you'll learn to use it fast. Skill will have to make up for brawn right now. Now listen." Wallach took the blade away from Kern. In his hand, it looked like a natural extension of his arm. "You don't slash with a short sword. You stab. Like this." He took a few sharp jabs at the air.

Kern took the weapon back, tried it out. Then took a hesitant cut. "It feels better to slash with it."

"Yes, but you are going to jab. All day. You keep that in one hand or the other, and practice. No putting it in the sheath." In fact, after a second's thought, Wallach took the sheath and belt and rolled it into his own bedroll, keeping it from Kern.

Kern stared at the blade. A bare arm's length of good, sharpened steel. So small and light next to what he remembered of Burok's sword. He took another few pokes with it. Shrugged, then rolled his broadsword into the blankets and felt pad to give the roll some weight.

"Divide up the load," he ordered. "Everyone shares the food. Everyone shares the weight."

There was a solid pack load for each. Even without the butchered horseflesh, his small band and the escaping prisoners had carried away more than a fair share of stores from the Vanir. Enough for weeks, if properly rationed. Adding Hydallen and the other two barely scratched into the supplies, and both Daol and his father were master hunters. They could provide.

But an hour on the trail, when asked quietly about Kern's parentage, Hydallan provided nothing more than a shrug and information most of which Kern already knew.

"Your ma came to us from another clan already with child. During a good summer, so Gaud accepted her. And she brought a gift of blue-iron weapons from the Broken Leg Lands. Cul's war sword . . . that's the only one left. The others were traded away over the years. Then she died somewhere near your ninth summer if'n I recall."

Close enough. Kern didn't remember for certain, but figured Hydallan had it within a year or two.

"If'n she told anyone, 'twasn't me." He shrugged. "Does it really matter at this point, pup?"

Kern didn't answer right away, thinking it through. He slashed at some brush with the arming sword as he continued his exercise. Seeing Wallach's baleful glare, he went back to stabbing with it instead. His wrist ached from holding the sword on a tight line, and he had blisters forming on his hand in the few places not callused hard from years of swinging an axe.

"It shouldn't," he finally admitted. "But right now it does." By Crom, that sounded like something a Hyperborean might say! Southlanders preferred to talk so much. Cimmerians acted. "I guess it feels like I should *do* something."

"This ain't enough for you?" Hydallan swept his gaze over the snowy hills. "Crom's pike, Kern. What do you consider an active day?"

Whatever it might be, they began to see signs around midmorning. At the first burned-out settlement.

Sitting on a shallow river, overlooking a slice of cleared land where oats or turnips might grow over summer, the ruins were little more than a foundation of stacked river rock and a few charred timbers that had been used once for framework. The smell of wet charcoal hung in the air. The river's quiet murmur was all that disturbed the silence.

Clearly the Vanir had been through here, though sometime before the last snowfall apparently. What fresh tracks they found were in singles and pairs, cutting through the woods, then—upon sight of the ruined home—quickly veering away again.

It wasn't long after that Daol spotted the greasy smear of black smoke in the sky. The way it fanned out, rising in a blanket rather than a stream, had them fearing a forest fire. Except it did not spread. Hydallan watched it carefully while everyone else checked weapons. He measured the wind and waited to see if the fire marched along with the northerly breeze. It did not.

"What kind of fire ignores the play of the winds?" Daol asked. He wasn't old enough to have seen this before.

Hydallan and Garret. Wallach Graybeard. They knew. Wallach curled fingers into his beard, giving it a quick tug. "A town fire," he said.

"Taur is burning."

Not all of it, as it turned out. Only a few huts and some lean-to sheds on the outskirts of the village proper. Enough to make the carnage visible for several leagues. A warning sign, and a draw to other raiders in the area.

Daol had found fresh sign of a large party of men, moving west by north, not long after spotting the distant smoke. Nahud'r, with eyes nearly as good as Daol's, picked up on smaller sign near another burned-out farm they hurriedly passed. A quick inspection found two children, a boy and a girl no more than seven or eight summers, hiding in a dry well under a dark blanket. Their parents, charred flesh and bone, lay half-buried in the ash of the hut.

Maev had taken charge of them, coaxing them up with water and honeycomb. Taking each by a hand, pulling them along, the clansfolk moved quickly onward.

Now, hunkered down in the tall grasses and brush that topped a tree-barren hill, Kern watched the fires spread. Thatched roofs burned bright and deadly every time a new one touched off from the heat or drifting sparks. Woven slats, which made up the structure of the walls, burned down through the clay mixture so common to wattle-and-daub. The smell of scorched mud spread with the ash and smoke.

It was not all wanton destruction. The raiders obviously had purpose behind them as they dug beneath large sheds for dry pits and chased panicked cattle along the village paths. A broad-shouldered ox evaded the noose thrown at it by one Vanir. It plunged into a hut and crashed out the other side through a thin wall. Tiring of chasing the powerful creature, two raiders unlimbered bows and stuck the ox with arrows until it finally keeled over.

There didn't seem to be more than a few dozen raiders storming around on the flats below, but then Taur was smaller than Gaud and a great deal more spread out. How many settlements and farms had the raiders burned out before laying siege to the main village?

"Too many," Kern said, watching the raiders loot homes and round up cattle.

Another small team broke cover behind the village, chasing down a man trapped outside the lodge's defenses. Blades rose and fell. The scream carried to the hillside as a far-off echo.

"They have the right idea, though." Maev crowded between Desa and Kern, having left the children on the other side of the hill with another Gaudic villager. She pointed out the waist-high breastwork of earth around the lodge where most of the village had taken refuge. A palisade of sharpened trunks stuck out at sharp angles. "It must have taken them weeks. Months."

On the other side of Kern, Reave squinted. "What's that tangle around the palisade? In between the poles?"

Daol had the better eyes. "Spears. Stuck every which way. And I'll bet they are all tied together with good leather."

It wasn't a fortress wall, but it worked much the same. Put six men inside with bows, and any Vanir trying to break through the barricade made an easy target.

Letting the Taurin clansfolk know they had help waiting outside their village would be just as hard. Kern's people could not hope to take on the Vanir by themselves, but to coordinate an assault meant getting someone close enough to the lodge, without getting stuck full of arrow shafts, that the Taurin might recognize and let through. Trust between clans was not a strong commodity.

"There has to be a way in."

Reave shook his head. "The raiders would have found it. They look like they want whatever's inside pretty bad."

"Food or prisoners," Daol agreed. "Maybe they—

Kern!" He pointed, spotting something through the smoke.

Somehow, Kern knew what he'd see, following Daol's stabbing finger. Something in the other man's voice. The way his entire body went rigid. Kern rubbed a knuckle into his smoke-stung eyes, massaging moisture back into them, and then he saw him.

Hard to miss, when you looked. The shock of white hair, which at a distance made the warrior look very old. But no aging warrior moved so spryly, or manhandled his own men like a bear pawing at cubs. This frost-man—another Ymirish—held a battle-axe very much like the one Kern had given up. Just as large and just as heavy. Only he pumped it overhead, exhorting his warriors, as if he were brushing away flies.

"Two of them?" Reave asked.

Kern supposed he should be grateful his friend hadn't said "Three?" the way Reave glanced over at him afterward.

"At least." Kern shrank back away from the crest of the hill, careful not to disturb the tall grasses too much and draw attention from below. Bringing his warriors in around him, he brushed aside the coincidence of another frost-man. "Whatever these Vanir are, they are not common raiders. But they bleed." Kern looked Maev in the eye. "They die." His gaze traveled the line. "This one is no different."

"But in order to make this work," Daol said, "we still have to get a message into the lodge. And we have to be able to hold the Vanir off while the Taurin decide. How are you going to do that?"

Kern glanced back up the hill. "I might be able to manage the second part of that," he said, playing it over in his head, hoping he had an idea worth chasing after.

"And the first part?" Daol asked, obviously not liking the sudden gleam in Kern's yellow eyes. He shifted uncomfortably. "How about getting a message to the Taurin?"

"That," Kern said, "will be your job."

12

DAOL LAY IN the snow at the trailing slope of a small hillock, tucked beneath the branches of a small evergreen bush. Trying his damnedest to present *small* as Vanir raiders ran past him, intent on their siege of Taur.

Snowmelt soaked Daol's heavy tunic a dark, wet brown. The skin on his forearms felt as if it were all but blistering under the cold burn that came with crawling several hundred paces over frozen ground, moving so slowly his blood began to thicken. He breathed shallowly, tasting the scent of burning thatch, worried about even the smallest cloud of frosted vapor drawing attention to his position.

"What was I thinking?" he whispered to himself, drawing a small measure of courage from the sound of his own voice.

He knew what he'd been thinking, though. The same as Kern, and the same as the others. That every minute spent working up a better plan, or even putting this one into effect, cost lives. Cimmerian lives. Kern had given Daol an hour to work his way down the side of the hill and a quarter of the way around the besieged village to get as close as he could to the lodge. Daol's father and three others had remained on-site, watching, ready to cover his retreat if the Vanir noticed him. The others, Daol hoped, had gotten their part ready during that time.

He'd find out very soon.

It was no consolation that if the plan failed, his friends would be just as dead. Which was why he had taken so much care in his trek down to the village border, using every trick he had learned in eight years of hunting and tracking. How to divide his weight evenly across his entire body and snap not one twig beneath him. How to breathe properly while moving, and choosing the right line of attack, which kept him hidden from casual eyes.

Daol had chosen to come at the lodge across from the wind, so any raiders near him would be staring into smoke whipped off the burning homes. If their eyes stung half as bad as his, it was a good choice.

"Far as I can go. Come on, Kern."

Moving with exquisite care, Daol slipped the bow off his shoulder and stashed it under the nearby brush. Then his short quiver of arrows. He felt naked without them, armed only with a long knife. But he couldn't take the chance that the Taurin would think him a threat. He gauged the distance to the front of the lodge. He might make it back in time, if he had to.

If he wasn't filled full of Taurin arrows on sight.

Daol never pulled his gaze away from the hilltop for too long, waiting for the signal. He saw some of the tall grasses moving up there from time to time, waving against the chill breeze or waving when there was no breeze at all. Every time, he checked the Vanir, to see if one of them had noticed.

Nothing. None of them expected an assault from behind. Cimmerians had spent the last several years fleeing before the raiders, who rarely attacked in the open unless they had an advantage in numbers.

The sign was not meant to be subtle. And in fact, it wasn't. Two dark shadows suddenly rose over the white-blanketed hillside, silhouetted against the light gray sky behind them. Extremely exposed. Among fifteen men and women, there were exactly two hunting bows other than Daol's. Hydallan and Brig Tall-Wood carried them. Now the two men drew back, sighted, and released.

Daol thought he could hear the healthy *thrum* of bowstrings even over the crackling noise of the village's burning huts and the shouts of the raiders. Might have been wishful thinking.

He knew he heard the sudden shout of pain as a raider fell with a long shaft stuck in his shoulder. The Vanir bounced back to his feet quickly enough, though, facing right back along the arrow's flight.

Four more shadows on the hillside, all waving swords overhead. There was some distant shouting in broken Nordheimir, none of it complimentary.

The two archers drew and released. Drew back again. Released.

Another shout of pain as an arrow in the third flight found its mark, stuck through a raider's leg. Others of Kern's small band showed themselves on the hilltop. From a distance, if Daol hadn't known better, it looked like a small group all straggling up in singles and pairs.

Easy meat for the raider band.

And there he was. The frost-haired Ymirish Daol had spotted from the hilltop, striding through a small knot of raiders. He stabbed the magnificent head of his war axe at the hillside.

"At them!" he shouted in Nordheimir. Daol knew

enough of the language to recognize that. "Bring me heads!"

Fully a dozen northerners peeled away from the siege to storm the hillside. As two more shadows popped up on the ridgeline, the Ymirish sent another handful of warriors, keeping a two-for-one edge while leaving about a dozen or more in the village proper to watch for any movement from the lodge.

No one watching the brush though. It was Daol's chance.

Exhaling sharply, Daol committed himself by rolling out from under the brush and jumping up quickly into a half-crouch run. His legs glided forward with the loping stride he could keep up for a day and a half. Easy. Smooth. He waited for the inevitable call of discovery.

He actually made it halfway, getting well between the lodge and the nearest raiders. It was the Taurin who gave him away, as an eager bowman inside the lodge defenses swiveled around to loose an arrow at him. The shaft dug into the ground barely half a step in front of Daol, and the young hunter sidestepped quickly to throw off any follow-up shot, waving his arms frantically overhead.

Several raiders had followed the shot as well, and now saw Daol running for the barricade. As they moved at him, roaring for his death, he burst into a sprint and shouted on his own behalf, "Friends! Taur! Help!" Everything Kern had told him to shout.

No further bowshots came from within the compound, but there was no movement at the front of the barricade either to open a break in the defenses. Daol checked over his shoulder, saw the Vanir just now struggling up the hillside, shields held up against the Gaudic archery . . . and several of the nearby raiders drawing down on him with heavy bows of their own.

The first long shaft whistled by his ear to *thunk*

deep into one of the sharpened poles stuck out from the lodge bulwark.

"Crom's hairy left orb," he shouted, "open up!"

The wind shifted slightly, blowing more of the ash and smoke directly over the lodge compound. That was all right. Daol saw the gate now. A drop-down door held on a pivot bar with a counterweight on the far side. It rose in and up, and was spiked with sharpened stakes easily the length of a man's arm. The Taurin let him approach it, but still it did not open.

Daol ran right up to the gate. He saw the outlines of people moving on the other side of the artificial bramble of spears and spikes and sharpened stakes, within the haze of smoke that lay over the compound. Upset low-ing, from cattle the Taurin had managed to pull into the lodge defenses with them, was all that answered him.

Continuing to shout for their aid, he pulled his knife and turned back toward the Vanir who had braved Taurin archers to come after him. One raider had a greatsword, swinging it overhead in wide deadly arcs. The others favored broadswords and shields.

He could have used a shield. Another arrow bit into the door, barely missing his right leg. He jumped back and forth erratically, spoiling the Vanir's aim, keeping a wary eye on the door, the advancing raiders, and the hillside where half of the frost-man's men had nearly gained the hilltop, ready to join blades against Kern's small group.

No longer so small, though, as another five silhouettes popped above the hilltop. Half of the line bent down now, digging at the earth, lifting one of the heavy logs they'd carried up earlier while Daol crept into position. Kern and Reave had led that work party on a short run away from the village, so the chopping would not be noticed. Rolling it over the hilltop, into place, had caused the waving grasses Daol had spotted.

"A sled defense," Kern had called it. But Daol hadn't picked up on the reference then.

Now, watching five of his clansfolk start down the hill, then *heaving* the log into the face of the raider charge, he got it. He was reminded of that last good day, before Burok's death and all that followed. When he and Kern had pulled the wood sled into Gaud.

The sharp, downhill slope that had sent the sled smashing into the end of the lodge woodpile.

The split-rounds tumbling off the end of the stack

Three raiders actually caught the thrown log right in the face, bowled back like pins in a stonethrow contest. The long trunk hit the ground unevenly and bounced back up, clipping another Vanir in the leg and sending him tumbling forward. It slowed everyone behind him, who had to wait and gauge the rolling log so they could swerve around or jump over it.

On the hilltop, six warriors bent down and wrestled up a second thick trunk. They began running down the hill with it as well.

That was the last Daol saw of the budding skirmish as the gate behind him swung in with violent speed, and rough hands reached out to drag him inside.

KERN HAD BEEN one of the first to climb over the hilltop after the initial volley loosed by Hydallan and Brig. He waved his arming sword overhead, feeling foolish at its light weight when Reave stood next to him brandishing a Cimmerian greatsword. He kept his shield up, covering himself from heart to head, looking over the tapered edge with his yellow eyes fixed more on Daol's run toward the lodge than the advancing raiders.

Now, he encouraged the Taurin. Come out now!

After the first trunk was thrown, rolling and bouncing down the hillside, Kern quickly slung his shield and rasped his sword home in the sheath Wallach had finally returned to him. Digging down near his feet, hands gripping the thick, scaly bark of the fresh-cut fir, Kern helped Reave and Nahud'r among others wrestle up the second of the two "rolling rams" they'd cut and shaped with hatchets and with swords.

"Forward!" Kern shouted, and stepped onto the downhill slope.

The Vanir were ready for the tactic this time. They slowed. A few retreated, reaching for bows to take the Gaudic warriors down before the thrown log made another shambles of their line.

"Hold," Kern shouted, as the entire team stumbled forward. He saw that more than half of the raiders had spread out so as not to be within the dangerous path. But a few had leaped forward, never considering a second such attack, and there were two others slowly picking themselves up after being knocked over by the first.

"Hold," he called again, buying them another few steps.

An arrow *thunked* home in the trunk right between Reave's heavily muscled arms. The large warrior stared down at it, cross-eyed and angry. Someone on the other end, whom Kern could not see, cried out in pain, and the log began to tip in that direction.

"Now!"

Kern curled his part of the log's weight up toward his chest, then pushed outward as if bowling for upright pins in a summer game. Throwing the massive trunk forward caused him to stumble and nearly fall.

Nahud'r did fall, though he tumbled around and bounced back to his feet lightly, as if he'd never missed a step.

They all unslung swords and shields and leaped after the rolling ram.

The fir trunk caught both of the shaken warriors up front with another full-force blow across the upper body. One took it in the face, leaving behind a bloody mess that matched his crimson braids. The other got his arm in the way, protecting his life for a moment. But the weight pinned him back against the earth again, shattering his arm. Several splinters and spurs poked out through his skin. Nahud'r went down on his knees, sliding through the mud-scarred snow and grass. He reversed the broadsword he held, holding it overhead like a giant dagger, then plunged it into the stricken Vanir, impaling him through the chest.

The raider breathed out blood-flecked foam and died. He was the first.

Kern took the second. No time to grab for his shield again, he ducked to one side and let the war sword of a staggering Vanir clash against the metal surface that protected his shoulder. He ducked the tip of a backhand slash aimed too high, then struck with the short arming sword, thinking all the while that he didn't have enough reach.

And was surprised when the pointed end slid in between the raider's ribs.

Shocked to the point of staring, fortunately Kern's muscles remembered enough to draw the blade free and immediately jab the weapon again at the Vanir. He pumped his arm twice . . . three times. The Vanir took piercing wounds through his ribs, in his shoulder, and finally through the throat as he pitched forward with a dying grunt.

The downhill charge had given Kern's warriors all the momentum they needed. As the raiders staggered up to meet them, they crashed through the thinned line and buried several Vanir under a swarm of flesh and sharp metal. There was a thundering against the ground, cries of rage and pain, and ringing steel as blades and shields met in full force.

Kern smashed one raider in the face with the boss on his shield, kicked him aside to Maev who had taken her place in the line of battle as any Cimmerian woman would be expected to do. She fought back to back with Desagrena, each woman sensing the other's movement and shifting to guard. Maev's arming sword flicked out like a striking snake, pinking the raider in the arm and leg, whittling him down a piece at a time. Then, charged by a fresh warrior, she spun around to face a new threat.

Desa rotated with her, broadsword flashing out, down, and around. Taking the Vanir's head.

The odds were not so uneven anymore. Numbers and raw strength hedged a bit on the side of the raiders, but the momentum of their charge and several heartening cries of "Cimmeria" lent the Gaudic survivors a natural edge. Kern traded sword strokes with a larger man, ducked back from the slashing edge of a bastard sword, and found again that his stabbing sword actually had better length than he would have thought. The difference was apparently in the angle of attack—a slashing sword was held so flat to its intended victim that there was not a huge advantage in reach.

They pressed back and forth, Kern retreating uphill, then pressing back down. He saw raider reinforcements shifting their way. Another dozen northerners. Scattered pairs and trios showed themselves from huts and from the far side of the lodge.

Two dozen. Maybe even three. More than he'd counted at first.

Too many.

Kern's breathing came pitched and ragged, and he tasted blood from a backhanded strike that had smashed the hilt of a broadsword into his mouth. Lucky it wasn't the bladed edge, he decided, spitting out the metallic taste and hammering away at a Vanir's shield. He caught himself using wide, overhead smashing strikes, then remembered his practice again. Short, stabbing strokes. He held to it, even when his muscles quivered to be let free to cut and slash.

Eventually he sneaked in past the other man's guard and laid his thigh open down to the bone. The flap of muscle lay down along the raider's leg, bleeding severely. The Vanir limped back, grinding his teeth in the pain, seeking escape.

Brig Tall-Wood gave it to him. Having waited farther up the hill with Hydallan, he and his hoarded arrows went to work with devastating effect. One took the wounded raider in the stomach.

The next shaft found his throat. The man dropped like a stone.

Staring past where the raider had stood a heartbeat before, Kern was left with a clear line of sight at the advancing frost-man, who obviously saw Kern as well. His yellow eyes read a moment of confusion before feral rage showed through. The raider led forward a fresh knot of Vanir, having been among the closest bands when Kern sprang his trap.

The Ymirish's battle-axe smashed Wallach's wooden buckler into kindling, and possibly broke the man's arm as well.

A back-slashing swing folded Roat, another of the Gaudic prisoners Kern had rescued, over the spiked flange. The clansman screamed as the flange tore out his intestines, spreading them over the ground like so much knotted rope.

"Close up," Kern yelled, calling his people together. "Form a circle. Protect the wounded!"

The Cimmerians staggered back together, some of them holding the flatter ground at the base of the hill, others shuffling along on the slope. Maev dragged Wallach back by the man's thinning hair. From his yells of complaint, he wasn't too badly wounded.

Desa was, with a long shallow cut bleeding down

the side of her ribs. As was the other Southlander rescued from the Vanir. A Brythunian with sandy brown
hair and the tattered robes of a noble, or maybe a very
successful merchant. All Kern knew about the man was
that his name was Prospero, and he wanted to go home
as soon as possible.

It wasn't looking likely, with a wicked gash bleeding
at his neck and a raider arrow stuck in his shoulder.
Nahud'r stood over the Brythunian, protecting him
from further injury, but two raiders pressed in, one
from each side.

Kern's pack of skirmishers pressed together in a
tight knot, bristling with pointed steel. On the slope
above, Brig Tall-Wood took two arrows in his side and
folded over as if struck by a huge fist. Hydallan rushed
to his aid, pulling him back up the hillside, away from
the raiders. An arrow stuck into the earth close to the
old man's head. Another stabbed near his leg, chasing
after him.

The Vanir raiders roared in challenge, and half of
them pressed forward with savage blows that rained
down on shields and sword edges.

The other half turned and set themselves in a line
against a Taurin charge.

Through the shifting wall of flame-haired Vanir and
the ash and smoke that hung over the village, Kern
caught a glimpse of the lodge and its open bulwarks. A
dozen swordsmen and pike-carrying women rushed
forward from their abandoned defenses, picking up
Vanir stragglers, smashing in behind the raiders' main
line.

The first Taurin was too eager, and came up against
the frost-haired leader of the raiders with no help and
nothing but a broadsword to protect him. The battle-
axe came around in a devastating arc, shattering the
sword and cleaving deep into the man's chest, knocking him back several paces.

The Ymirish jumped forward, grabbing the dying man by the hair. Chopped once. Twice. Severed his head, and threw it into the middle of the Taurin line.

Kern pushed forward, trying to reach the northern leader, but a pair of Vanir closed the gap and one nearly took Kern's head with a savage broadsword cut. But Reave staggered between Kern and his attacker, blood slick along his arm and staining his leather jerkin, greatsword held forward in a defensive gesture. Clashing steel rang out in sharp, clear tones.

The second raider, this one with red-golden hair that spoke of Aesir parentage, leaped in at Kern. The snarl in his eyes, though, was pure Vanaheim. He slashed with his war sword, the tip clipping the top of Kern's shield and barely missing his right eye. The raider drew back as if to come at Kern again. Then he twisted about as if shoved aside—a pair of arrows sprouting from the back of his shoulder.

Kern quickly sighted back along the path, and found the two archers, both men with bows at full arm's extension. One was Daol, looking grim-faced but determined as he stalked forward in the midst of the Taurin charge.

The other man was Aodh!

Slipping forward, low and fast, Kern's arming sword slid a glancing blow off the raider's ribs. The press of battle swept them apart right after. Kern stumbled over Wallach's outstretched legs, finding the aging warrior stretched out in a mire of snow and muck and blood. The side of his face was bruising a dark purplish color, but he still breathed. Kern got a hand beneath the man's shoulder and dragged him back just as the first horn call sounded across the battlefield.

The frost-man held a great horn to his lips, blowing in strident calls to his warriors. Like quicksilver the band of raiders shattered into pairs and trios, all trading a last few sword strokes or bites with their axes, then sprinting for the cover of nearby brush and forest. There were several clansmen within striking distance of the Vanir leader, but the frost-man kept a healthy knot of warriors around him, enough to make a direct press against him come with a steep price in blood.

The Taurin seemed just as satisfied to let the raiders go.

Kern's people were in no shape to pursue.

One man lay dying painfully, wrapped in his own intestines. Two others lay stretched over the ground with possible grave wounds, and several more limped by with hands clasped around arrow shafts or shallow cuts.

Reave shoved the point of his greatsword into the earth, then sank to his knees while breathing in huge gulps of air. His face was red with exertion, but his shoulder wound did not look too bad. More blood than injured flesh. Maev's scalp cut bled even worse but looked even better.

She wiped blood from her eyes, spit red phlegm into the snow, then set about helping the wounded where she could.

With the raiders quit of the battle and the village, Kern had a job to do as well. He limped over to where Roat lay. The Gaudic clansman grunted through clenched teeth stained red with flecks of bloody froth, still trying to hold his stomach in though both hands weren't enough to cover the ruin the battle-axe had made. A latrine stench boiled out of the steaming wound.

Roat was already dead. His body just hadn't caught up to the fact yet.

"Anything we can do?" Daol asked, dropping to one knee next to Kern and Roat, looking for a miracle. Maev and Aodh knelt next to Daol. Desa and Reave watched from their feet.

"Something," Kern said, searching the clansman's face.

Roat stared back, eyes wide and unseeing. Unable to talk, or do much other than lie there suffering, he at least heard and understood. He gasped, then nodded in sharp, shivering motions, holding back the screams of pain by sheer force of will.

Which was when Kern stabbed forward in one short, brutal stroke—taking his own man through the chest and heart. Pinning him to the earth. Finally giving him release from the pain.

13

TAUR DID NOT exactly celebrate the arrival of so many Gaudic warriors. No matter Kern's small band made it possible to break the violent siege of their village, their welcome remained cautious.

To be expected, from people who had known generations of skirmishes and raids between each other.

No more than three Gaudic warriors at a time were allowed inside the lodge defenses. Instead, a large, circular clearing was quickly staked out with poles dangling strips of decorated fur and braids of brightly dyed cloth. Rivalries and feuds were left outside, by tradition.

Women swept away the snow and built several good-sized fires for warmth and for cooking. Soon flat cakes and a small treasure trove of eggs were sizzling in melted fat, replacing the scent of ash and blood. Men carried long tables out from behind the barricade. And stools. Blankets and benches. More food from their dry pits, and fresh cuts of meat from cattle that had been killed in the raid. The Taurin were reluctant hosts, perhaps, but not unthankful for their rescue.

And Kern was just as grateful for their protection of two of his own.

Aodh and Ehmish found the amber-eyed man supervising at the makeshift surgery, worrying for the Gaudic wounded. The two had arrived just before the raiders hit, apparently. Ehmish blamed himself for that.

"I hid longer than I should have," the youth admitted. "Long after the raiders returned to camp. It was well past the Dragon's turn by the time I rolled out from my spiderhole where I hid, and only because I knew if they came back, they'd see me sure."

Aodh gestured northeast. "When I finally caught up, he was at the end of a dead run heading north. Too far, I'd say. We completely missed any sign of you as we bent around toward Taur. Saw some raiders chasing after their escaped horseflesh. I brought one down with an arrow." His face darkened. "Then as we got closer we began seeing the burned-out farms and hunting shacks. Bad sign, that. We pushed through to morning and talked our way into the village. The Vanir hit mebbe an hour or so later. A few Taurin wanted our throats cut as Vanir scouts."

"What changed their mind?" Daol asked.

There were two tables at the surgery, scrubbed down to fresh wood and set at the edge of the clearing where ash would not fall easily into open wounds. Daol and Maev worked together at one of them, washing wounds clean with melted snow.

They also had taken on the task of drawing arrows. Usually this involved Daol lying over a man's chest while Maev gave the shaft a good hard yank. One of the long-feathered shafts stuck into Brig Tall-Wood had a broadleaf head, however, and had to be pushed through. They all watched while Maev scored the shaft with a sharp knife, snapping it in two about a handbreadth above the wound.

Brig grunted through clenched teeth. Ehmish paled.

Aodh had seen such things before and barely noted the efforts. "We weren't the first of Gaud to come through here, apparently. They knew about our trouble, so's most of them leaned toward believing our story."

Only one other Gaudic had come north anywhere within the last several weeks that Kern knew about. "Old Finn. So he made it this far at least."

"And then headed off north, looking to sell his sword where the raiders might be more of a threat than the long winter."

Kern hadn't even considered trading on the threat of the Vanir up north when he'd been cast out. Not a bad idea. Maybe even a better one than heading south for so many long days, as he'd been planning.

When he said so aloud, Aodh nodded. "Apparently Finn was decently provisioned before he got here as well. Traded a marmot and a fox pelt for some meal, some flint and tinder."

Watching Maev preparing to push through the arrow, Kern frowned. "Traded . . ." Then he understood. He shook his head. "That old dog raided the clan's northern traplines for himself." Hard to blame him. In fact, Kern hoped he'd picked up enough food to see him through, wherever he was bound.

"Jackal," Brig spit, cursing Finn. If he felt the least bit sorry for the old man's predicament, he didn't show it.

"Here." Maev thrust the broken half of the shaft between Brig's teeth, giving him something to bite down on. "Keep quiet and work on that while we draw the head."

She also drafted Kern and Aodh to hold the clansman to the table, rolling him up just slightly so there was room for the head to pass through. She put a small block of wood against the shaft's broken end, and shoved once, hard.

The wounded man bucked, back arching up in pain, then kicking out at Aodh, who held his feet. His yell was muffled around his bite on the arrow shaft. Maev hurried around to the other side, grabbed the bloody head in a fold of leather, and yanked it all the way through. This time Brig did little more than breathe a heavy sigh.

Maev wasn't quite finished with him, however. At a nod, Desagrena brought over a hot iron she'd been tending in one of the fires. She slapped it into the wound on Brig's back, sealing the flesh against a deep infection. Brig lost the shaft between his teeth as he shouted through the pain. His entire body spasmed, and this time his kick worked free of Aodh's weight.

He stomped on the other man's shoulder, then his ear, kicking him away from the table.

Kern and Daol rolled over onto Brig, pinning him flat, while Desa slapped the hot iron against the front of the wound, then into the second arrow puncture as well. There wasn't a lot of fight left in him after that. When they let him up, Brig simply rolled away and dropped heavily to the ground, eager to be free of his torture. He lay there next to the table, pounding a fist into the cold earth until the pain subsided enough that he could stand on his own.

"He's lucky that broadleaf head didn't do much more than slice muscle and fat," Maev told Kern.

Brig climbed slowly to his feet. "If that's luck, by Crom, small wonder I fare poorly at dicing." He gave a choked laugh, and shoved himself away from the table. Trudging toward one of the fire pits, he stopped long enough to give Maev and Daol a nod of thanks and Aodh a wince of apology for the man's beet red ear.

With Kern, he simply traded a long, measuring stare.

By evening the dead were in the ground and by mid-morning of the following day the wounded had all been taken care of to the best of anyone's ability. Taur also had a healer, fortunately, and she worked as hard over Kern's people as she did over her own, sewing shut wounds and applying damp poultices that smelled caustic but immediately took the sting out of cuts and deadened bruises. She had spread a gray salve over the shallow cuts on Kern's chest and arms. It cooled the raw edges of his wounds and took a bit off his infection fever as well.

It was also her work that saved the life of the Brythunian. A merchant, as it turned out. Those had been his horses in the possession of the Vanir raiders. He didn't begrudge their loss, happy still to be alive after the last several days. But he was in no great shape for hard travel. The Taurin healer recommended a litter and far too much attention to his wounds than Kern's small band could give.

He also had little interest in hunting down the raiders, which was why it was determined to send him south to Gaud, with Maev and any others.

With many others, as it turned out.

Liam, the Taurin chieftain, brought more of his clan's rapidly depleting stores and twelve village elders with him to an evening meal shared with the Gaudic band. Liam Chieftain had more gray hair in his beard than Aodh, and diamond-hard eyes that had seen too much in his lifetime. He scraped his scalp bare, which was an uncommon custom in winter but not unknown. Bushy eyebrows and his ragged goatee more than made up for it.

He carried a ceremonial arming sword to the cleared area—nothing more than a token of resistance. Perhaps, Kern decided, the chieftain was simply trying to match Kern's own weapon. He didn't explain that he carried the arming sword by necessity, not as a courtesy to their host.

Kern also decided to leave Burok's broadsword wrapped up in his bedroll.

Talk had barely turned toward who would accompany Maev back to Gaud when the chieftain made his offer. "We can offer a limited amount of supplies—jerky and a few skins of ripe ale, dried vegetables—to those who are moving on. Consider it a ransom on the village."

Liam Chieftain opened a skin right then, in fact, and took a strong draught before handing it on to Kern, who drank. The ale was dark and tart, on the edge of turning after too long in storage, but it left a promise of summer on his lips. It also freed up his guard a bit, which in Cimmeria was not always a bad thing.

"That's not why we fought," he said. "We can take care of our own, Liam Chieftain."

The man shrugged. "A simple gift, then. Something to help you on your way." Again, the chieftain stressed the idea of the Gaudic warriors leaving. Soon.

"You wish to know when we are quit of Taur," Kern said. It was not a question.

"Yea. That is exactly what I wish to know, Kern Wolf-Eye." He glanced at nearby clansmen and kin. "We've known your looks on the face of Vanir raiders at least three other times this past year. Your appearance does not sit well with many here."

But other than having seen Ymirish come through, leading Vanir warriors, Liam Chieftain knew little else of the strange men. Kern nodded, then looked around the mix of Gaudic clansfolk and Taurin. As twilight darkened and fires glowed ruddy health on the faces turned toward him, he weighed his own choices against those of the others. "I plan to leave on the morrow," he promised the Taurin and informed his people at the same time. "First light."

Maev shifted in her position near Kern. "Those of us able to return back to Gaud will leave by midmorning. We have wounded to tend. Any extra blankets and food you can spare, we will accept."

"It shall be done," Liam promised. "Burok Bearslayer was a good chieftain and a good adversary. His midwinter raid against our cattle herd showed daring and cunning. Cimmeria needs strength such as Gaud shows."

That, and much more, Kern thought. Looking from chieftain to chieftain's daughter, Kern passed the skin to another warrior, then stared into the nearby fire. "You could both do better," he offered quietly, broaching an idea that rattled around inside his head. He glanced over, saw he had their attention.

"Gaud has great strength, yea. But Taur has shown itself to be strong in the way of planning and preparation." He nodded toward the protected lodge. "Your food stores are deep. Your defenses are strong."

Liam stuck his chin forward proudly, but his eyes held a wary cast. "What are you thinking, Wolf-Eye?"

"Looking at what you have done here, that both clans might survive and be stronger if they shared strength."

Liam stood abruptly. "What is ours is ours alone! It belongs to Taur."

"And how long could you hold off another Vanir war party? Next time they will not stop with a few huts, or a stable. Next time they will burn the rest of your village around your ears, Liam Chieftain. You do not have the warriors to stop them."

"Do not think we are so easy prey," the chieftain warned, his face flushing with anger. Still, he did not argue against his clan's current weakness.

"How many of your people have struggled south in

the last few weeks as raiders attack and burn and eat away at the strength of Taur?" Maev asked, standing. She angled her way past a few crouched warriors until she stood a good arm's length outside of Liam's reach. "If I see what Kern is proposing, he is not suggesting you give up anything. But that we trade. Our combined strength for food and defensive help."

Shifting about on a small camp stool, Kern pounced on the chieftain's hesitation. "Your clan is dying. The raiders know it, and they will come back."

The man scoffed. "How can you be so certain?"

A wolf howled out in the night, calling to distant kin or warning them away. Kern's wolf, he was willing to bet. He listened to its yelping call, letting it die into a distant echo before he fixed each Taurin with his own predator's stare. "Because that is what I would do."

That did not sit well with several, reminded only a moment ago how Kern resembled some leaders of the Vanir raiders. Many shifted uncomfortably in their seats. A few hands crept toward daggers, toward sword hilts.

Liam rubbed at the smooth side of his check, just along the hairline of his goatee, thinking.

"As would I," he finally admitted. "Crom curse me if I didn't. The village has lost too many, fled south. And we've lost more traipsing up to the northern skirmishes this year. The raiders are a plague, and we haven't the means to fight them alone anymore."

"Then stand with Gaud," Kern said. "Take your people south with everything they can carry. There is room. They will make room."

"You can promise this, Wolf-Eye? You are outcast."

"He is," Maev agreed. "But I am Burok Bear-slayer's daughter. Cul Chieftain must listen to me. If *I* leave Gaud, more would follow me here than would stay with him. They will accept you."

It was a dangerous commitment for Maev to make.

Kern saw Brig Tall-Wood start, ready to jump to his feet and defend Cul. His dark glower, though, and his lack of action argued that he did not necessarily disagree with Maev's promise. Of anyone, she likely could break Clan Gaud.

Maev's words had the desired effect. Liam Chieftain stood and considered, and finally nodded. "I will think on this," he promised Maev, then turned back to Kern. "But first, I will see you and your wolves away from Taur. At first light."

Kern held the chieftain's gaze a moment, then nodded.

But Maev frowned. "Where will you go?" she asked.

He did not hesitate. "I will head north and west."

"The raiders broke for the northern trails," Daol said, as if reminding his friend of something he should already know. He had tracked out away from the village for several hours and reported back the same information privately to Kern and to Liam Chieftain. Now he made it public. "A few scattered out on their own, but I saw signs that most followed in one large band." Following the Ymirish, he did not have to say.

"I intend to track them," Kern admitted, staring at Daol. He shifted his gaze to Liam. "I will hunt them." To Maev. "And I will kill them. If I can, I will draw the fighting from Conall Valley, away from our villages."

"How?" Maev asked, her voice tightly reined. "According to Liam Chieftain, the northern valley clans have failed to hold the raiders back all winter. What more can you do, Kern?"

"I will push over the western pass, into the Broken Leg Lands," he said. "If I must, I will take this fight all the way to Vanaheim itself."

Except for the crackling flames, silence reigned. Gazes roamed the fireside meeting as several clansmen took measure of one another, and of Kern's promise. He had not arrived at it lightly. Looking back, to the moment he had turned north after the Vanir raiders, this had been the path he'd chosen. For himself, and those who had come with him.

Reave simply shrugged. "Well, nay sense coming all this way for nothing," he said. He swigged the last of his ale, tossed the dregs into a nearby fire, which hissed and spit. Desa was only one step behind Reave in agreeing, nodding her support. Wallach, too.

Daol looked to his father, then accepted for the both of them. Hydallan couldn't help adding, "You'd be starving pups within a week without us along."

Ehmish glanced around, looking trapped. A young kit on its own for the first time, being forced to make a decision that could mean survival or death. To his credit, he hesitated barely more than a few seconds. "Better what I have now, here, than what I might find when I reach the southern borderlands." He shook his head, laughing silently. "I am nay Conan."

Aodh, too, continued to cast his lot with Kern. And Garret. Maev offered to take Nahud'r back to Gaud, but the Shemite demurred with a slow shake of his head. "There's nothing left for me in the south. I will go north."

Even more surprising was when Brig Tall-Wood offered to stay. "If you will have me," he said, barely able to meet Kern's unblinking gaze. "If you are serious about going after the Vanir and keeping Gaud safe."

There was more in the young man's request than that, and Kern knew a moment of suspicion. But having another experienced bowman along would be a fine advantage and outweighed his misgivings. He agreed.

He also saw a measure of relief and cunning both pass behind Brig Tall-Wood's eyes, and worried about it.

In the end, Kern kept his original five outcasts, another four from Gaud, and Nahud'r. And four warriors of Taur who followed Brig's promise to help defend their village by taking the battle after the Vanir.

Their volunteering surprised Liam Chieftain, who suddenly traded more serious looks with Kern and with Maev, feeling the weight of the moment. Two of Taur's finest warriors, Liam promised. And a strong woman who knew some herb lore and healing skill.

The fourth volunteer created something of a stir. A man of twenty-odd summers and something of a local favorite, given the sudden sharp buzz of conversation that swept the circle. Like his chieftain, Ossian also shaved his head clear. And the hilt of his broadsword had a comforting, well-worn look to it.

"You are certain?" was all Liam Chieftain asked.

"As certain as should you be, accepting the offer of Bear-slayer's daughter."

An outspoken man as well, then.

"Your pack swells," Liam said, guarding against any further question of the decision. He shrugged. "Perhaps you can accomplish something after all."

It wasn't the strongest vote of confidence, but Kern would take whatever well wishes he could get. By Crom, his people would need them by the time this was done.

If it were ever done.

SHE CAME TO him one last time that evening, after the Taurin returned to their lodge and the fires had died down to beds of dusky orange coals.

With so many empty huts in the village, most of Kern's band decided to carry a bit of fire inside. Kern chose an untouched lean-to where a last scattering of damp hay provided some cushion beneath his felt bedroll, and the slanted roof above kept away any chance of snow or showers. His breath came frosty with midnight's touch, and his skin puckered tight as if trying to conserve a warmth he had never felt. But he had spent worse nights, recently. And there were many such nights ahead.

Best to keep prepared for them.

Her footsteps, when he noticed them, came warily. As if she were still deciding. Or perhaps she simply searched for him, not knowing for certain where he'd gone. Kern sat up, woolen blanket scratching down his chest and pooling in his lap.

She stood just outside the lean-to, framed in a rare patch of moonlight, not much more than a silhouette. A blanket held in one hand. Still fully dressed in the new kilt and cloak traded from Clan Taur.

"You will really fight your way north?" Maev asked. She stepped under the roof, ducking beneath low crossbeams. "After the raiders?"

Kern watched her spread the blanket out next to him, folding it to overlap with his own. "After him," he said. Meaning the frost-man. "There's more to these Ymirish that I have to know."

"To the Broken Leg Lands."

It was as good a place to die as any. Better than some, in fact. Conan had come down from the Broken Leg territory. It seemed the place of many odd tales and heroic legends. Why not one more? "It has to be someplace."

Her touch was warm against his pale skin. Maev had also bathed earlier, and now she smelled only lightly of sweat and fire smoke.

Kern hungered for her. His body responded at the slightest touch. But he hesitated. "I thought we took care of this." There would never be any knowing, now, if she whelped a child. That had been the whole point, hadn't it?

"I guess that's for me to decide." She sounded only a touch sorrowful. And a bit angry as well. "Isn't it?"

Gathering Maev to him, his large hands encircling

her waist, Kern nodded as she suddenly bruised her lips against his. It was her decision. He had honored it the other night, and he could honor it now. And because she had already decided.

Any well wishes . . .

14

KERN'S DIRE WOLF and a freezing rain saw the small band of warriors off the next morning. Daol pointed the animal out, his hunter's eyes missing nothing even in the gray, wet, postdawn gloom. The wolf's silver-gray fur lay matted against its body. The animal looked utterly miserable. Rather than seek shelter under brush or a half-fallen tree or some rocky outcropping, it stood on the same crest of hilltop that Kern's warriors had fought from the day before, silent and still, watching. As if daring anyone to come after it. Or perhaps daring itself to approach closer to the village.

Some among the Taurin muttered uneasily, seeing the strange behavior in an animal that tended to avoid humans. The Gaudic warriors shrugged it away, used to its appearances. They were more concerned with the weather, which was obliterating the snow cover but would soon make for a cold, wet slog into the northern foothills of Conall Valley. Already the smell of mud was turning rank in the air.

A few good-byes were made. Not many. Maev would not look at Kern, busying herself with the large group heading south within a few hours. Liam Chieftain did not plan to empty out his village, not yet, but he would travel south with Maev to open a discussion with Cul. That much, at least, had been decided.

There were no marching orders. No big send-off. Packs were stuffed with food and drink, dry blankets wrapped in oilskin, and the assortment of miscellaneous gear that always followed people on the move. As the last tunic was pulled on and any final braces tied down, warriors began drifting to the northwest edge of the village, silently packing together.

With Kern's arrival the majority slowly traipsed off by twos and threes, spreading out along the muddy trail. Daol and Hydallan led, their experienced eyes searching out the best trails. Nearer the front than the back, Kern trudged behind Ossian and Nahud'r. Reave and Wallach and Desa paced them not far behind.

Those who had lingered too long in the village rushed to follow, bringing up the rear.

The Shemite, Kern saw, had wrapped a long woolen scarf around his head, laying it around his neck and over part of his face, then tying it into a kind of loose knot over his dark, curly hair. Only his eyes showed.

Good for blocking out the cold winds, Kern decided. And capping in the body's heat. Not so smart in a downpour of freezing rain, though, where you would spend most of the day with a wet cloth soaking your head. Maybe the man wasn't quite so educated as he claimed to be.

Civilization, it seemed, prepared one to live, but not to survive.

He reevaluated his opinion before ever losing sight of the village, however, when the black-skinned man cut a spreading branch from a winter-stunted maple. Producing a small oilskin cloth from inside his tunic, he draped it over the smaller branches in blanket fashion. This he held overhead, to the short-lived amusement of the others. Icy water beaded and ran down the cloth, dripped over the trailing edges. Some of it dampened his arms, and it did not protect the legs of his southern-style trousers at all, which were soon heavy and dark with rainwater. But it did keep his head mostly dry. And therefore warm.

Ossian gazed at the simple device as if it were a minor miracle. His head was fresh-shaven and his cheeks scraped bare, leaving only a simple goat's beard that matted with the rain. He resembled Liam Chieftain very closely. He dropped back a few paces, whispered to Kern, "Now why we never thinks of that?"

Kern wondered much the same thing. There were drawbacks, of course. Having to hold your arm up. Getting in the way of a sword or shield use. But for traveling, it still was not a bad idea.

"That a desert trick?" he called ahead, turning Nahud'r around. The Shemite walked backward with graceful, smaller steps. It let Kern and Ossian catch up.

"This a Nemedian tool. I learn my first springtime in Hanumar. But works well in desert, too, I think. Keep sun out of eyes, and off head. Like small tent you carry along."

Kern had never thought of the sun being a problem like the rain or the winds. Cimmeria did not suffer often from drought, and certainly never from excessive heat. It made the desert of Shem seem even more an alien place than told of in stories and lodge fire tales.

"Nemedia," Kern repeated. It was a Hyborian nation southeast of Cimmeria and the borderland kingdoms. "This is where you learned to read?"

"I learn to read, and to write, in Aquilonia." He saw Kern's obvious doubt and stopped by the trailside, kneeling down next to a pine tree under which a soft carpet of wet needles lay undisturbed. Kern and Ossian both paused as well, looking down at what the other man was about.

"A miracle occurred this day," the black-skinned man wrote, using his fingers to dig small diagrams in the bed of needles. He drew another line of characters beneath the first. "The sun has risen."

Ossian laughed. "The sun rises every day."

Nahud'r smiled, and glanced up at the rain-swollen sky. "Prove it," he challenged the clansman.

"Not have to proves it. Sun travels south in the fall, north in the spring. But it always rises. It always will rise."

It was sound reasoning, to Kern. Because it had always happened, it always would. But Nahud'r merely shook his head. "That a tenet of faith," he said. "And beginning of enlightenment. No matter what else happen, every day there is divine providence to follow."

Kern continued to stare at the characters. These weren't pictures as he knew them. Far as he could see, there was no way they corresponded with the story they told except by memorization. What each character spoke, and what they made as a whole. He waited while Reave and the others trudged by, glancing over but continuing on with one foot placed after another.

"Is that what you are doing here?" he asked finally. "Following divine *prov . . . dance*?" He stumbled over the last word, not sure what it meant, except that it sounded important.

"I was servant for nobleman's house. Took care of son as bodyguard and sometimes sent as message carrier." Nahud'r's gaze looked wide from Kern's, and he smoothed the bed of needles back over, erasing his work. "Was sent to Gunderland with boy, Pheros. He decides to inspect what left of Aquilonian garrisons in Cimmeria. I came."

"What happened?" Ossian asked, not noticing the man's blank stare.

Kern nodded. "The Vanir happened." He waited until Nahud'r looked back up from the ground. "Pheros?" Kern asked

"Is dead. Why there is nothing left for me in south. Why I go north."

As good a reason as any, Kern decided. He listened as a few others slogged past, their footsteps squelching in the softened trail. Icy fingers of water trickled past the neck of his tattered poncho, trailing down his spine. "Are you sure that is the only reason?"

"Why else would I be here?" Nahud'r asked.

Kern knelt next to the other man. His brow wrinkled as he thought hard to remember what he'd seen. With a less careful hand than Nahud'r, he reached down to the smoothed bed of pine needles and drew shaky characters in the soft spread. "A miracle occurred this day . . ." he said.

He only remembered the first line.

The dark man stared at Kern from between the folds wrapping about his face. His eyes gave nothing away as to what he was thinking. Then slowly he bowed, touching his forehead to the ground.

Rising in one smooth motion, Nahud'r and his tent cover fell back onto the trail and continued their pace.

Kern and Ossian followed.

NORTH AND WEST.

Always north and west.

The freezing rains continued, off and on. By nightfall of the second evening, most everyone had adopted some version of Nahud'r's method for keeping warmer if not completely dry. Oilcloths were scavenged from food wrappings. Most of the men simply tied the cloths over their heads, knotting them at the backs of their crowns. Desagrena rolled a large square of leather into a fat, shallow cone. Using a knife to pin the edges together, she set it carefully atop her head. All that showed beneath the brim was the lower half of her face and her long, oily locks of dark hair, but she obviously stayed much dryer.

Very few braved it out, and they looked more and more miserable as the day wore on.

The next day dawned under a cold, blue sky and a distant, uncaring sun that barely warmed the skin. Early in the morning they ran into their first sign of others on the path: a trio of clansmen who leaped for their swords when Daol and Wallach stumbled into their campsite. The two men were lucky to escape with their lives, falling back on safety in numbers.

The Cimmerians were from Clan Galla, near the top of the Snowy River country. Their hair, shaved into topknots, and the tattooed sworls spreading over their chests made it obvious. Finding themselves facing a larger band than they had thought to expect, they quickly dropped the points of their weapons.

Primitive, but hardly stupid.

They had thought Daol and Wallach to be northerners. Not an easy mistake to make, but then the Gallan often attacked first and thought about it after. They were heading toward the Broken Leg Lands themselves. Supposedly, Clan Cruaidh challenged the Vanir for the Pass of Blood, and would accept any warriors who could handle a sword.

Kern let them retreat to their camp. His only other choice was to put all three men to the sword. That served no one but the Vanir.

These weren't the only Cimmerians on the move, either. Daol and Hydallan tracked other warriors to camps. Farmers and families as well, burned out of their homes by raiders or starved out by the long winter, running for the south and the hope of spring. All had heard or carried similar rumors coming down out of the northwest.

Few of them would do more than trade a bit of news. Some asked for food, and Kern rationed out what they could spare with a careful eye toward their own needs. No one asked to follow along with Kern's pack. Fewer wanted to do much in the way of talking once they saw Kern. With his pale hair and yellow, lupine eyes, Kern would look out of place among any Cimmerian clan. But most of these men did not look surprised at his countenance, but rather fearful or angered. One grizzled farmer, carrying his best tools on his back and a naked arming sword in hand, spit at Kern's feet.

"Ymirish!"

Frost-man.

The farther north Kern chased after the raiders, the more Ymirish appeared to be known. Known, and feared and hated. More than one sword was drawn at Kern. Several times he shouted his own warriors back, not about to watch a clansman killed over a mistake. But it wore on him, hardening Kern against his own people, in fact, as they glanced more and more his way when they thought he wasn't looking. Wasn't aware.

Fortunately for everyone's building tempers, the roving pack surprised more than Cimmerians on the run or spoiling for their own fight. They found Vanir as well. Not many, but enough that by twilight of their fourth day they'd left half a dozen raiders stretched out over blood-soaked ground or propped against trees. Their horned helms always hung on branches stuck into the earth as a way to identify them to any who passed.

Four days.

Always heading north and west.

That was when the blizzard struck.

After a day of clear sky and a cloudless night, black

stormrunners built up thick and fast during the morning trek. Massing higher, until they seemed like a huge anvil ready to drop on Cimmeria.

Watching them pile up over the Valley's western Teeth, blocking out the massive summit of Ben Morgh, Kern thought at first they had a chance of outrunning the storm to Clan Cruaidh and pushed his team harder. He didn't care for the ground they moved through, knife-cut ravines so thick with trees and thorny brush that it was best to run the high ridges of broken, crumbling rock. But there they fought narrow trails over sheer cliffs, often slicked with ice or waterfall runoff. Bad ground. He didn't want his people trapped there under dark and snowfall.

They pushed forward at a healthy pace, jogging for hours at a stretch, slowing only when Daol or Hydallan or one of the others spotted sign, and they grew careful of an ambush. The winds picked up, gusting down from the heights with an icy touch that cut through furs and wool and leather. A frosted ground fog rolled down in patches biting with frozen teeth at their exposed legs and arms just as the first snow fell.

It came thicker and sharper after that. Dry snow, stinging the eyes as the wind whipped it horizontally. The storm clouds collapsed overhead, running out across the valley with incredible speed, pushed by the sudden, northwest zephyr. More snow and a thickening fog created a white haze that lowered visibility to a hundred paces. Then fifty.

It caught Kern's people in some desperate territory, halfway along a steep bluffside trail. Sparse brush and stunted trees in all directions. No protection from the winds unless they wanted to hunker down together with blankets wrapped over their heads. A plan that was on the bottom end of Kern's thoughts.

"What do you think?" Daol asked, moving back

along the line of struggling warriors, calling out to Kern. "Go to ground?"

Kern squinted into the horizontal blow. He saw another of the trickling streams they'd seen cutting at the dark clay all along this trailside. Again, noticed the lack of heavy vegetation. Nothing put down roots there. Not for long. "Bad area. If the storm turns to rain or sleet, we might see flooding or slides. Not safe."

"Up or down?"

Up meant trying to get above the water runs, but they'd be more at the mercy of the winds. Worse chance of frostbite. Down would find them looking for a sheltered cleft or a windbreak of heavy trees, but put them in greater danger if the snow gave way to sleet or rain. It also meant giving up on Cruaidh for at least another day.

"Down," Kern decided, cursing the weather. No storm like this had been seen so late in the year in his lifetime. Maybe not even in Hydallan's lifetime. But they had to deal with it. "I think this is going to pile up on us. We have to get out from under the wind first."

"Wind first," Daol agreed. "Da saw some lighter slopes ahead. We'll need to turn right at the next fork, then bear off toward a shallow vale you might be able to see from the scarp."

"I'll see it," Kern said. To his eyes, the gloom was really not so bad as a clear moonlit night. He needed only a few breaks in the snow flurries. "Right, and then bear for the vale."

Nodding, Daol grabbed Wallach as he stumbled by, turned the old man around, and sent him back along the rear line to hurry the rest, passing the same instructions. Kern and Daol hurried ahead, racing past Ossian and Nahud'r. Coming up behind Ashul, the Taurin who had trained with the village healer. She held her own, using a walking staff in each hand to help steady her footing.

But she stopped, right in front of Kern, tilting her head one way then another. Kern listened as well. The winds hammered at the thin line of warriors, howling its building strength. Bringing snatches of shouting, of cries.

Of sharp, clashing steel.

"Vanir!" Kern yelled, springing forward, ripping his arming sword free of its sheath and tossing his winter cloak back from his sword-arm shoulder. Ashul tossed her staves aside and came up with long daggers in each hand as Kern passed her.

With Daol and Ashul laboring to keep up, Kern sprinted forward, catching Brig Tall-Wood at the fork Daol had mentioned. Shoving the younger man ahead of him, they half ran and half staggered through the rushing storm. Brig glanced back repeatedly, as if making sure Kern was right behind him. A dangerous expression crossed his face, but Kern had no time to ask after it.

The snow swiped at Kern's face, stinging his eyes as he ran. Fifty paces. A hundred. Too far to be spread out. Had they missed a turn?

Then he heard shouting again—much closer this time. He led the others off the path, angling on a sharper downhill turn. Scraping through dwarf pine and basket cedar, they stumbled into a small depression that must have looked like a good campsite when Hydallan and Ehmish found it.

Except the Vanir had found it first.

There were three raiders, each armed with a broadsword of some fashion. One blade had a curved edge to it that flared out near the end to give it some good weight for slashing—not native to Cimmeria, though certainly the raider was putting it to good use.

Hydallan reached somewhere deep within his flagging strength, flailing about with his own broadsword as he battled back two of the raiders. Never going on the attack, but parrying strongly as they struck at him again and again. Ehmish, too, was struggling for his life, and giving a good measure with his arming sword.

But there wasn't a great deal of time left in either clansman, old or young.

Yelling a Gaudic war cry at the top of his lungs, Kern crashed into the battle with Daol, Ashul, and Brig not far behind. He shouldered one of Hydallan's attackers aside, sending the man sprawling.

His companion slashed a wicked backhand at Kern's throat, but it met his arming sword instead of soft flesh.

Slash. Guard. Thrust! Kern rammed six inches of bright steel into the Vanir's gut just as Brig Tall-Wood struck the edge of his broadsword deep into the raider's shoulder.

The northerner's cry died quickly, choked off in his throat. He collapsed in an unstrung pile.

The raider who had pressed at Ehmish now faced both Daol's and Ashul's more experienced swords as well. With a feral snarl, he feinted a quick chop at Ashul, then dived for some brush on the downhill side of the shallow depression. Ashul ran after him, daggers ready.

Kern spun about, back to back with Brig Tall-Wood, looking for the third attacker as they heard what they thought were the shouts of battle. But it was only Hydallan, cursing himself with a real gift.

"Walked right into it! Stupid old man. Of all the Crom-cursed, northern-frogging . . . Garret! Kern, Crom take you, where is Garret?"

"Never saw him," Brig answered for the both of them. "Just you two and the three raiders."

"Four. There were four!" Never one to waste time on regrets over action, Hydallan dropped his pack near a pile of Vanir supplies and launched himself at the edge of the brush. He swung his broadsword in great cleaving arcs, cutting an easier path.

Daol ran after his da without word or wonder. Ehmish looked ready to follow, but Kern grabbed him by the scruff and pointed him uptrail. "Find the others. Bring them after us." He gave the youth a shove.

Ashul was too far gone by then to chase after. Kern hoped she could hold her own. Doffing his own pack, he laid it over Brig's and unslung his shield. Both men plunged into a break in the scrub, looking for Garret in another direction than the two hunters. Within a moment they were stumbling blind through the growing blizzard.

The makeshift trail turned between two patches of dead, brown thornberry brush. Thorn tips snagged at Kern's cloak and his heavy kilt. Kern pulled himself free and stumbled forward a few more paces to where the path turned again. Brig fetched up against Kern on the corner, swiping at his eyes, which teared in the wind.

"This was a good idea," he shouted in Kern's ear.

Then he looked around, noticing that they were isolated by the storm and had no clear path back. He looked back at Kern, at the arming sword the other man wielded.

"What?" Kern asked. He glanced desperately to either side. "We can't stop now. Move!"

Brig hesitated, then nodded curtly. He moved on, blade naked in his hand, held at a half-guard position.

And a good thing it was, as a raider charged into him not a dozen steps later. The man wasn't as large as some of the others, but he was fast. And he swung the curved, slashing sword. Brig barely slid his sword in the way, catching the wide blade against his cross guard.

The Vanir stiff-armed Brig in the face, throwing him back. Would have had him too, if Kern hadn't leaped forward with his arming sword already slashing for the raider's throat.

The raider ducked back, but he needn't have bothered. Kern's sword sliced nothing but air, coming up short because he had slashed instead of stabbed! Again!

But when he tried to follow up with a short jab at the Vanir's ribs, the raider spun inside his reach and circled a heavily muscled arm around Kern's, trapping it.

Caught in an awkward dance, the Vanir brought his sword hilt straight down against Kern's forehead, bruising the Gaudic outcast right between the eyes. The only thing that worked out in Kern's favor, in fact, was the unwieldy sword the other man carried. It was no good as a close-in weapon. Kern ditched his shield and managed to get a hand on the Vanir's wrist, and the two shuffled around in lockstep, staggering several paces off to one side, then farther downhill, then . . .

Then the ground gave way beneath Kern's feet as the two struggling men hit a steep drop-off.

The raider lost his hold on Kern's arm. Kern kept his own death grip on the other man's wrist, though, pulling him along as they both half tumbled, half slid through more thornberry brush, then into one of the muddy creeks that bounced and ran down the bluff. Kern's feet shot out from under him, sitting him down roughly in the muddied, freezing water. The raider sprawled forward.

No time for niceties, Kern chopped at the other man, hacking several pounding strikes at his head, his shoulders. Nothing certain to be fatal, but he thought he hit bone at least once. A few heartbeats later, though, Kern hit another drop-off, and he lost his grip and his sword both.

He wouldn't remember much more than flashes of the next few moments. It was all white splashes of water, horizontal snow, and more scrapes and bruises than he could count.

Scrabbling through mud. Fighting for any kind of desperate handhold.

Feeling plants uproot under his weight, then tumbling . . . sliding . . . falling back into open space.

He hit hard, his breath hammered from him. Rolled through more light brush. It was a good thing there were no large trees or heavy rock outcroppings, because Kern certainly would have broken bones or caved his head in against one. He managed to turn the barrel roll into a slide, with cold, clammy muck raking up the back side of his kilt. This lasted only seconds before another short fall spun him around hard again. And again.

And again.

15

THERE WEREN'T MANY things more dangerous than being lost, alone, in a Cimmerian blizzard. Even if it should have been several weeks—a month—into springtime.

Wet from a trip down the splashing creek. No food. No blanket. Just a threadbare, half-soaked winter cloak and a tattered leather poncho. Kern's chances didn't look good.

He finally slid into a patch of brambles, the thorns catching him by cloak, kilt, and skin. At least it stopped his sliding fall before something larger, like a tree, halted it more abruptly. Detangling himself occupied several long and painful moments while the ends of his fingers turned numb from the wet and cold. His teeth chattered, which for him was a huge worry. He had to get moving quickly, to work off the chill.

After a few false starts, Kern realized that any attempt at an uphill climb—snow-blind, in the dark—

was futile. At best, he'd end up rolling right back down into the brambles.

He tried to gauge his bearings. Failed. The dry snow stung his eyes, and the wind drew away any possible shouts for rescue, or hearing any rescuers. He remembered Daol talking to him about bearing for a protected vale, and figured he had to be farther down than the hunter had thought. Heading north, then, might catch him up with the others. Or it might get him hopelessly lost.

What happened in a wolf pack, he wondered, when the leader didn't come back? Did the pack go looking? Or did it move on?

Survival first. He had to assume the others would find a safe place to bed down and wait out the storm. They'd look for him as soon as they could. He worried about his exposed position. Down inside the narrow cleft he had some shelter from the wind, but not much. Brig knew about where Kern had gone over the bluff slope, but the Gaudic warrior was far from Kern's strongest supporter and, even if he did make the effort, there was no guarantee he'd be able to find his way back to the trail *and* back to the right spot with help.

No good praying. Crom had already done more than his share in making the Cimmerians a strong and hardy race. No matter what Kern suspected about his parentage, that was what he believed. And when left to one's own strengths, one did not sit around debating it.

Fall down seven times. Get up eight.

North, then. Struggling along for the best footing he could find. Over the next while, he crawled switchback up an easier slope than the one he'd fallen down, then half slid down the back side.

The feel of the land, the way the ravine wall twisted back, Kern thought he might be turned more east than he'd like. Forging on, he planned a more circuitous route that would bend him back around toward Cruaidh and his warrior band. The whiteout conditions robbed him of any certainty, but at least he was moving. Without shelter, movement was the next best aid to staying alive. Kept him warm—or less cold anyway. And each step was one pace closer to help.

Pulling his fur-lined cloak up around his head, Kern used a dry edge to guard most of his face as he'd seen Nahud'r do with the woolen scarf. Arms tucked in next to his body, fingers curled on the inside of the makeshift cover. The best he could do to protect against frostbite.

The rest was simple exertion. One foot after another. Never slowing down so much the sweat began to freeze against his skin.

That was how Kern spent his first night. Stumbling through the blizzard.

Near morning, hoping to find a clear path and hoping more that he still worked his way northwest, Kern stumbled up against a sheer cliff face with no easy way around it. He did find a granite outcropping, though, forming a small hole where the snow had yet to do much more than brush dry flakes over the ground inside. Kern shook the ice and snow from his winter cloak of gray wolf fur, then hunched down and pulled it over him like the smallest tent. Curling into a tight ball, rocking forward, he wedged himself under the rocky protrusion.

The wind screamed at Kern, a frustrated howl of rage that he had managed to escape its grasp. Sharp edges dug into his back, his side, and soon his muscles ached with cramps. But he warmed. The deep, teeth-chattering cold he'd fought and wrestled with the entire night withdrew. It settled back into the familiar chill he'd lived with his entire life, which meant—he hoped—that he had a chance once more to survive.

Finally, he slept.

Day and night was the difference of a howling,

wind-raging darkness and a blinding, snow-chocked gloom. It felt as if winter, being pressed once again by spring, had lashed back with a vengeance, refusing to release its death grip. Suffering under the chokehold of Vanir raiders wasn't enough, apparently. The weather wanted to remake Cimmeria into an image of the Nordheim wastelands.

Kern peeked out from under his cloak when he woke the first time, then bundled the garment back over his face and drifted off again. His body knew enough to resist going back out into the storm now that he had decent shelter.

The second time, a cramping bladder forced him out momentarily. He could not roll back into his cloak fast enough, but by then he was fully awake and so took further stock in his situation.

Every joint ached with the cold and his tight, cramped position. When he tried shifting around, his bones protested with brittle pain. His refuge smelled of urine and the drying muck caked about his body from the sliding fall of the previous night. His mouth was parched. He dry-swallowed, and his throat scratched as if he were trying to force down wooden thorns.

A handful of snow melting in his mouth helped some. Hunger pangs would go unanswered, however.

Every scrap of food he'd carried had been tied down in his pack.

Kern spent the day coiled up in his stone nest, like a rock viper waiting for prey. He slept when he could. Counted heartbeats when he could not. And he stayed alive.

The wind tried to trick him out into its clutches, at times howling in his ears like attacking Vanir, at others bringing him choppy gusts that hinted at the shouts of his friends. Daol. Reave. Hydallan and even young Ehmish.

Maybe not Desa or Wallach. They were quiet with him.

Certainly not Brig Tall-Wood.

Kern thought quite a bit about Cul's man, in fact. He remembered the strange looks—the desperation and the cunning, both—and the way Brig had acted once the two found themselves alone on the trail, cloaked by the snowstorm. Kern hadn't thought much of it at the time, but now had nothing but lonely, dark hours in which to think. Brig was not outcast. He had been sent by Cul to see Maev home. Hadn't he? If so, why hadn't he gone back to Gaud with her? Why exile himself from clan and kin, to chase after Kern and the others?

Unless he wasn't finished with whatever else he'd been sent to do.

Like take vengeance for Cul against Kern Wolf-Eye?

An unsettling thought to sleep on, but sleep Kern did. And he woke somewhere before morning as the storm finally blew itself out. He listened. Head muffled beneath his cloak. Breathing through the long hairs of the ragged wolf pelt pressed into his face. He heard the dying gusts, sharper than the storm winds and still cutting with mountain chill, but losing the blizzard's primal rage.

Now, Kern decided. He had to get moving again while he could still rub life into his tired muscles and frozen joints. Peeking out at the thick, new carpet of snow that tapered into his hiding hole, he stared into the dark for another hour at least, still yelling at himself to get up, get moving, and to survive.

Always, to survive.

Kern crawled out with lethargic reluctance, then collapsed into the snow with severe muscle cramps. Kneading life back into the rock-hard flesh, he watched his breath frost before his eyes and decided to accept that as a positive sign he still lived. Cimmeria would not claim him yet.

Though it might if he did not find food or better shelter. Soon. And not easy tasks, either one.

Scaling the cliff face strained Kern's cramping muscles, but there was not a hillside or mountain scarp yet made that a Cimmerian could not master. Gaining the summit, however, he saw he had little to look forward to other than more of the same. Kern had lost himself inside a wrinkled fold of land that was more cleft and cliff than the usual hills and vales of Conall Valley. Badlands. Hard on the traveler, and what Daol had tried to help the band avoid by swinging them along the bluff Kern had fallen off. He'd wandered farther to the east than he'd thought in that first night.

Now he had to crawl his way back.

A frosted mist hung over the morning, making it impossible to find the sun except in the most vague sense of "east." Enough, he hoped, to keep him on a fair track north and west. Again, north and west. Kern watched for any sign of his friends, his warriors. Any sign of a trail toward Clan Cruaidh. The sparse blanket of snow made trail-hunting difficult, though he did find some evidence of life in marmot tracks and fox. And then the farther spread of prints belonging to a lone wolf.

"By Crom, not possible," he whispered aloud. Coincidence. Had to be.

He believed that, mostly, until shouldering his way past some reaching branches of basket cedar, finding himself staring across a bloody kill at the dire wolf he'd fought at the very start of his misadventure. The silver-furred animal had the same dark band around its yellow eyes. The same snow-white paw. It looked healthier, stronger. Well fed, with new flesh filling out beneath its thick, coarse pelt.

Its muzzle was red with fresh blood, and when it

growled at him, he could see flesh caught in between its canines.

The wolf had dug out a marmot, by the looks of the clearing. Disturbed snow and broken earth lay scattered about in clumps and sprays. The wolf had already chewed out the stocky rodent's soft belly, going for the warm guts first. Now it was in the middle of ripping off large hunks of hide and flesh.

Kern let the branch he was holding snap back behind him, and the savage animal jumped back as if suspecting a trap. It left the eviscerated rodent on the ground between them, though closer to it than to Kern. When it made to sneak forward and grab its kill, Kern took a few steps and shouted at the beast.

It dodged away, but only a few more paces, then sank its front quarters low against the ground as it snarled a warning.

"I took you down once," Kern reminded it, as if the animal understood him clearly. "I'll do it again." He jumped forward, thrusting his head at the wolf. Never flinching, which would have brought the animal at him that much faster.

The wolf skipped back again, still eager to reclaim its kill but not about to charge. Not yet. The feral gleam in its yellow eyes reminded Kern very much of the Ymirish he had seen, and fought. Maybe he had a kind of kinship with both, maybe with neither.

"If it were my choice, I'd rather it be with you," he admitted, keeping his voice level and never breaking eye contact. It didn't matter what he said, really, just how he said it. His own lupine gaze remained hard and steady. "Now I'm going to pick up that marmot, and you are going to let me."

He stooped quickly, reaching out without looking as he kept his amber gaze locked on the wolf. The animal bounced back to a safer distance. It began to circle Kern, who now had its prey in his large hands. Hands it might still remember. It stopped snapping and snarling, but it did not leave him.

Kern turned with it, watching for any wild rush. He brought out his knife and cut through the fur around the marmot's neck. Gripping the fur in one hand and digging into the rodent's breastbone with the other, he jerked once, violently, and shed the pelt. He tossed the hide out toward the dire wolf, though not directly at it. It watched with suspicion, then edged in and caught up the mess of fur and fat, carried it a short distance away before ripping at it with tooth and claw to rend it into swallow-sized chunks.

"What are you doing way up here?" Kern asked. He stripped away tiny slivers of meat and chewed them slowly before swallowing. They tasted salty from the blood. Better than horseflesh. Not as good as venison. "What are you searching for?"

It wasn't hard, really, to imagine what had pulled the wolf along his trail. Not once he thought it out. Kern had overpowered the animal, forcing it into submission. Wolves were territorial, true, but they were also conditioned to be subservient to the stronger male. When the leader of the pack moved, the entire pack moved. And if there was any doubt about the wolf's choice, certainly that had been forgotten once Kern led it to the first Vanir slaughter pit. He pictured the dire wolf licking up blood from the snow and muddied earth, finding the strips of hide and flesh he had missed. All along Kern's trail thereafter it had found more slaughter and fresh Vanir bodies that would be easy to tear into for a meal.

Survival. That was also the wolf's main concern. Follow the food.

"Still strange," he said, slicing the last flesh and fat he could from the carcass, then tossing the bones and gristle out into the snow. Not quite far enough. The wolf hesitated. Kern backed off a few paces, and gave it room to come for what was left of the marmot. "Any raider corpse left out would have fed you and the crows for a week."

The animal stared at him as if it expected something more. Something profound, perhaps. Like a long, lonely howl.

"Bah! Go on!" Kern stomped toward it, waving his arms. Running it off with the marmot carcass gripped in its jaws. "Got enough problems of my own," he muttered.

But from the top of the next hill, he looked back along his path with a touch of regret. "Thanks," he said. And meant it.

The wolf gave him several glimpses of itself throughout the day, always at the edge of Kern's sight, ghosting through the frosted mist like a shadow stalking his path. Occasionally Kern rounded some brush or came over a slight rise to see the animal much closer, though never again as close as when they had stared at each other over the fresh kill.

Somewhere in the late morning he quit being surprised at these glimpses. By midday he would call out a greeting to the wolf when he saw it. He named it Frostpaw, for the one white patch on its left front foot. And when he had a choice of turning south or north around a particularly steep bluff, spotting Frostpaw's tracks heading south was usually enough to convince him. As good a way to decide as any. Until finally Kern came upon a long, uphill slope where he saw the wolf pacing back and forth just short of its crest. It danced and lowered itself, then skipped to one side or the other again. Looking nervous. Trapped.

Kern came at the animal slowly, knowing better than to treat it as anything but a wild and dangerous creature. The dire wolf trotted away from him, toward the crest. Stopped. Reversed itself and paced in between Kern and its path. As Kern advanced, he pressed the wolf forward reluctantly. Then suddenly it broke away, bounding over the crest in four loping strides, leaving Kern behind. Wary, Kern followed, and soon saw what had bothered the wild creature so.

Cruaidh.

Or what was left of it.

16

CRUAIDH HAD BEEN the largest settlement in Conall's Valley, spread throughout a wide vale that opened up on the western side toward the Pass of Blood. The pass allowed for the only way into the Broken Leg Lands without traveling far to the south, around the Teeth and the massive rise of Ben Morgh. Because of this, Cruaidh controlled all trade through the valley and most of what went east toward the lake country as well. Merchants passed that way automatically. Nemedian craftsmen and Gunderland trappers. Aquilonian ambassadors. Soldiers.

Raiders.

Kern had never seen the settlement, but it had been described by enough summer travelers that he recognized what was left of it even through the lingering mists. A gentle river cut through the vale, passed over in several places by rough planks set between piles of stone that might have once formed sturdy bridges.

Cruaidh's tall palisade had been pulled down along

one side, burned on two others. Not a complete loss, but close enough. One watchtower had been toppled by chopping a supporting leg out from beneath it. Swinging from the crossbeams of another tower hung several ropes. Kern could easily imagine the bodies that had been left dangling, turning and swaying in the mountain winds. He counted dozens of ruined sheds, and torched homes once large enough to house two families, at least by the standards he knew in Gaud.

A wide field of disturbed earth on the northeast edge of the vale told Kern where the funeral fields had been dug. It looked large enough to plant every man, woman, and child of Gaud three times over. And there were still half a dozen open gravesites. One with mourners gathered around it. Two more with bodies lying nearby, sewn into blankets, waiting their turn.

It made him remember Burok Bear-slayer. He wondered if Cul ever got Bear-slayer north, to the Field of the Chiefs.

Frostpaw had paused a third of the way down the far side of the slope, pacing along the hillside as if held back by an invisible fence. He clearly was not going any farther. When Kern started down, the skittish wolf circled back and behind him, standing a silent vigil, watching the shadows of men and women drift about below.

Dozens, Kern guessed. Maybe a hundred. Not even half the number he expected from the valley's largest clan holding. He saw tents strung up against the palisade's remaining side and more staked over the frozen ground near the stream. Enough to house the numbers he could see, barely, until homes could be rebuilt.

The people moved about as if sleepwalking, at least until they noticed him. His white-blond hair drew immediate attention. The wolf sitting on the hill above him drew more. The hairs on the back of Kern's neck stood up alertly as dark mutterings caught up from behind him. He glanced from side to side, watching carefully for any sign of violence. His amber eyes set people back for a moment, but strength of numbers was on their side.

Before crossing the first plank bridge, he had picked up a small following of angry faces. Hands were on sword hilts and daggers.

Kern hurried on.

His feet thudded across a set of planks, rattling them together. The makeshift bridge bent a bit in the middle, but not so bad that he worried about another icy plunge. The scent of damp ash finally found him as he passed by the stone foundations of ruined homes. Kern did not dare pause, but his eyes missed no detail in passing. The charred edge to the beams looked sharp, no weathering, as if the fire had only recently burned out. But he had seen no smoke, and smelled no heat of flames in the air.

It had to have happened during the blizzard, then. Kern glanced into the surrounding hills. Had the people fled into the storm, to die of exposure? Or had they all stayed and died fighting?

Whatever the answer, there were still plenty of warm bodies left. Those not on burial detail scavenged through ruined homes and dug down into the bottom of cellar pits, searching for scraps of food. A few took stock of the ruined palisade, cutting out charred timbers and shaping new trees to replace them. Many people wore makeshift bandages, ripped from blankets, or showed raw, open wounds that had barely scabbed over with reddish brown crusts.

Waves of suspicion and fear washed over Kern as he pressed forward. A tangible presence. The crowd drew in closer behind him. Ahead, a line of clansfolk barred his way. Several stood with blades naked in their hands. His instincts told him to run, flee! Or draw a blade to protect himself. But a hunting knife would hardly be enough against the twenty or more bodies that surrounded him, penned him in like a sheep being corralled for slaughter. Their bloodshot eyes and drawn, haggard faces. They were a people at the end of their rope, but lacking the initial push to set upon him.

"What happened here?" Kern asked, finding his voice and glad to hear that it didn't break too badly from lack of good drinking water.

No one answered. A woman spit at him. Her eyes were dark and sunken, and the tips of her ears were white with frostbite.

Kern licked swollen, chapped lips. His gaze traveled from one nearby face to the next, searching for any sign of leadership among these people. "Was it during the storm?" He waited. "Was it the Vanir?"

A large hand fell on his shoulder, clamping down, half-turning him around.

"And then some," Reave said, a grim smile tucked away inside his brushy beard. He had twisted his dark hair into fine braids down both sides of his face. He also wore a second gold hoop in his left ear. A new trophy.

Ossian stood behind the large Gaud, his hair growing in as dark stubble. Both men had white, waxy patches of frostbite on their cheeks and the ends of their noses, but the damaged areas were well slathered with either oil or raw fat and looked like they'd heal fine.

Kern wanted to sag with relief, but he wouldn't turn an unguarded back on the crowd. "You're safe," he said.

"Safe." Ossian tested the word. Nodded. "Cold, tired, and shriveled—my balls might climb back out before summer's end—but safe, yea."

"Nay need for them anyways," Desagrena chided him, hauling Ehmish with her through the nearby crowd. And Ashul. And Wallach Graybeard.

The Cruaidhi shuffled uncertainly.

"Mogh lost the tips of two fingers," Ossian told him. Mogh was one of the Taurin. A dour-faced man who had yet to say more than a dozen words to Kern. "Frostbite. Poor fool never changed his grip on his sword."

Wallach nodded. "Spent hours on that bluff face, trying to reach you. With two raiders giving us trouble. Took some time, but Reave an' Daol wouldn't let go of the idea until the storm turned for the worse and we had to squat it out. Worked ourselves a bit closer the next day, during a few soft spots in the blizzard. You must ha' circled wider. We never tripped over you, and we've been here since late morn."

"All of you?" Kern asked.

He didn't have Reave's impressive height, but he could see far enough into the gathered Cruaidhi to find Daol and Brig working their way toward him. There was Hydallan, who waved forward Garret and Mogh as well. And Nahud'r, with his dark skin, Kern picked out the man while still a stone's throw away.

His band of warriors nearly matched the assembled Cruaidhi clansfolk now. They backed up a pace, then another, under Reave's glacial stare. They finally gave way completely as a trio of larger warriors carrying war swords, and a large man with a pike and tall shield shoved their way up from the rear.

"This the one?" the larger warrior asked. His cheeks were shaven to a blue-steel closeness. He had flinty gray eyes that did not seem ever to blink, and wore a fox's tail swinging from his wide leather belt.

"A little worse for wear and rough around the edges," Hydallan said. "But yea, that's the pup."

"They say you hunt the Vanir and the Ymirish," the Cruaidhi warrior said. "Though you've got the look of one yourself. Grimnir's touch."

"Grimnir?" Kern asked. He saw several nearby clansfolk make a sign against evil, even though Cimmerians were not, by nature, a superstitious lot. Those who did not still shuddered. A few suddenly found business elsewhere. "Was it him did this?" Kern asked Daol. The hunter would have all the latest rumors by then. "The Vanir warleader?"

"Weren't no warleader," one of the nearby Cruaidhi said. "Weren't no man, anyway." There was some grumbling agreement with that.

"A demon," said another man with a hunted, haunted cast in his eyes. "I saw him. During the blizzard. The face of a beast and eyes of golden fire. Like all Ymirish. Like *his*!"

He thrust the accusation at Kern with a wild jab, pointing his eyes out to the crowd. They swayed, ready to surge forward, held off only by the sudden forest of steel blades that surrounded Kern, protecting him. Nahud'r swept in between Kern and the three able-bodied warriors, wielding the flanged scimitar Kern had last seen in the hands of the Vanir on the mountainside. Brig was there, too, holding his own broadsword as well as Kern's arming sword and shield in his off-hand.

But when the Gaudic warrior tried to pass Kern the weapons he'd recovered off the mountainside, the large Cruaidhi swept his pike up in a strong arc to bat aside Nahud'r and thrust the shaft's blue-iron tip right at Kern's heart.

Kern barely had the time to feel surprised. He did feel the lance's tip poking through his leather poncho, just enough to break the skin. A trickle of warm blood dripped down his chest.

"Tell them to stand down," the Cruaidhi told Kern. He held the pike in strong hands, ready to thrust it home.

"Do it," the man promised, "or your blood spills first."

• • •

DESPITE THE COLD, Brig Tall-Wood felt warm. His face flushed. A trickle of sweat itched along his scalp, then burned down the side of his face in a slow-moving track, every muscle tightening for sudden violence when Gard Foehammer shoved his spear-tipped pike forward and all but impaled Kern Wolf-Eye on it.

Everyone else had met the large Cruaidhi earlier, before Wolf-Eye's arrival. Gard was the ranking warrior—the settlement's chief protector just now—and had seemed a fair-minded man as he shared a drink of heavy ale with Reave and Daol and Brig. Reminding Brig of Cul Chieftain, in a way. Strong. A leader of men. He was one of few Cruaidhi not dazed into a stupor by the late-season blizzard and Grimnir's savage assault. If anything, he seemed eager to take the fight right back to the Vanir war leader, and restless that he had been left with temporary care of the ruined settlement.

Gard had also listened with great interest as Daol and a few of the others recounted the tales of their adventure. Brig had felt a moment of unease, listening to the truth about Wolf-Eye's banishment and the way he had come back to lend his sword. Saw the Cruaidhi's opinion for Kern—for them all—rise a notch.

So he never suspected that Gard would turn on them so quickly.

It startled Brig, the pike flashing up and around, thrusting past his face close enough to feel the breeze of its passing. If he hadn't been half-turned toward the outcast leader to hand him back his sword and shield, in a position to see that Wolf-Eye still lived, Brig might have cut around with his broadsword out of reflex, and certainly Gard would have run his pike through Kern's chest, which would have pleased Cul most strongly, as Wolf-Eye would likely have been killed on the spot.

And Brig could have gone home.

Instead, Brig hesitated. His embarrassed flush came as much for his feeling of failure as it did the tension sweeping over the entire group. He had taken his eyes off a threat. Everything his grandfather and his da— even his brother and Cul, in their more generous moods—had taught him over twenty-one summers. All forgotten in a moment's distraction.

It could be him right then, impaled on the large warrior's pike; its tip of razor-sharp blue iron pierced through his back and sprouting out of his chest.

As it stood, he could not say for certain that having Kern held under the sharpened tip of the pike was any better. Brig could still force the situation. Swing on the other man, and count on Reave or Wallach backing him up in the confusion of violence. But it would be harder. Requiring a deliberate effort, embracing the very act he'd put off for so many days.

Also, Cul had commanded that Brig kill Kern Wolf-Eye himself.

Brig damned Cul Chieftain and damned Wolf-Eye as well! And damned himself, for that matter, for losing his nerve. He'd had the perfect chance during the battle for Taur. A stray arrow was all it would have taken. But it hadn't been in him, he discovered, to kill a man so cold-bloodedly, in the back while he defended others against Vanir warriors.

Then Hydallan went and helped save Brig's life, and the old man obviously thought well of Wolf-Eye despite the winter-tainted blood.

And Wolf-Eye had shown leadership. Compassion. Courage. Brig had to allow the outcast that much at least. Even in this situation, he had barely flinched when the long pike swept up to snag him right above the heart. His amber eyes stayed level and even, still the predator even when under the tip of the spear. He made no move away. Nothing aggressive.

He simply said, "Drop your blades." As if asking them to bring in wood or get the campfires started.

And damned if every Gaudic warrior and Taurin didn't obey.

Including him!

Brig turned where he could see both Wolf-Eye and Gard Foehammer. He pointed his broadsword at the ground, but kept a ready grip on it. Feeling a prickling sensation crawling out from the back of his neck as Wolf-Eye casually sheathed his own sword and slung his shield within the crook of his elbow.

"Whatever you are looking to do," he said to Foehammer, "decide and do it now."

Kern might as well have been talking to Brig. Decide! Either Brig believed in Cul Chieftain's order, or he did not. His brother had agreed. Why was it he hesitated?

And why did Gard Foehammer?

Kern licked a dry tongue over his cracked lips. With his cold-ravaged face, his amber, lupine gaze, he looked like a creature out of the blizzard. Like a wolf. Savage and strong.

"To answer your question," he said. "Yea. I hunt the Vanir. And the Ymirish. And they might well be my father's people." Brig saw how the admission hurt. A quick flash of pain behind those yellow, unblinking eyes. "But my mother was Cimmerian, by Crom, and so am I."

Brig never saw Gard relax, not for the span of a heartbeat. But Wolf-Eye must have read something in the other man's face. He reached up and pushed aside the spearpoint with a casual wave.

"Now. What is it you are wanting from me?" he asked.

Brig couldn't say, not for Gard or for himself. All he knew for certain, it was too late, again, for him to decide. To act.

And he wondered what it would cost him in the days ahead.

17

"THE FIRST ATTACK came just before light," Gard told Kern, pointing out the fire-ruined walls of the palisade. Walking a slow tour about the compound, Kern listened and studied everything the other man had to tell him. Nahud'r and Daol walked with them. Reave and a handful of the others trailing behind.

"Vanir. Don't know how many for sure, maybe a hundred. Enough to overrun our watch posts at the entrance to the pass, and keep word from getting back. They splashed burning pitch onto the timbers there, and there. Then they spread out into the settlement, slashing and burning."

"Those timbers look treated." They did, with a black, sticky substance that smelled of tar and should not have caught fire easily.

"Put flame to any wood long enough, it burns." Gard glowered. "We had our hands full with the raiders. Sent two hundred men outside the walls, pushing the raiders back toward Cottonmouth Creek there."

Two hundred men! Kern tried to imagine, failed. Two hundred was an army. Two hundred should have been able to handle so many raiders.

He said so aloud. Reave frowned, the expression building on his forehead like a pending avalanche, then slowly falling down over his entire face. Daol merely shook his head. They had both heard the tale already. The others listened silently. For some, it was their first time.

Ehmish glanced about nervously, as if recounting it might summon back the Vanir horde.

"Maybe we could have held them. Thrown them off. But that's when the second attack came at us. From the north. More raiders, and a dozen or more of these Ymirish who have been showing their faces over the last year." He glanced at Kern, no doubt noting again the similarities in face, in features. "We've seen their like several times. Put a few of their heads on the walls, in fact. But these ones were larger, even. Stronger. And had a sorcerer among them."

Gard turned the small group away from the ruined palisade and the first few homes, leading them along a trampled path to the northeast edge of town. But here Kern stopped.

"A sorcerer?"

Another Cruaidhi, one of Gard's men, nodded. "He made the snow come alive. Saw it myself, I did." He had a nervous way of jumping his gaze around, as if never quite sure whom to look at. "A long hump, rising out of the powder. Coiling around. Then it lifted up a head like a serpent, with diamond-bright eyes and fangs of icicles."

Everyone looked down into the trampled snow, as if expecting such a demon to live again. Kern did see a slick of blood and snow, refrozen into a pinkish sheet of ice. So many dead.

"I didn't see it rise," Gard said, "but I saw it die. Not before it killed seven of our finest warriors, though, including Alaric, the chieftain's son. Alaric put a javelin through its head, which slowed it down. But it got him in its coils and squeezed the life right out of him before it simply fell apart."

Raiders and Ymirish. Grimnir the undefeatable. And now a sorcerer's demon. Kern exhaled sharply his frustration. How was Cimmeria supposed to stand against this?

"By this time," Gard continued, pushing the group ahead of him, "the fortress palisade was burning, and we were in complete disarray. The settlement came alive, and many men and women rushed out to help. But already I was losing men to the storm. Some lost. A few run off and hiding. The wind picked up, and the snow cut at our eyes like blades.

"That was when he came."

Grimnir the invincible. The immortal. Champion of the northern gods. A terrifying man, he had to be—the rumors could hardly keep up. He grew larger every time Kern heard of him, and the wounds he'd taken and survived were legion.

Ehmish had heard many of them by now as well. "I hear you have to cut-off his head," the youth said, his voice breaking with the changes of age. "With a silver blade."

"Twelve foot tall and shoots fire from his eyes," Hydallan groused, making fun of the young man's gullibility. "Eats young Cimmerians for breakfast and lunch, I'll wager."

"Why not dinner?" Ehmish asked. Looking abashed, he tried to stand up for himself by taking a bite back at Hydallan. He should have known better.

"Not enough meat on their bones," the old man said,

not completely unkindly. Reaching out, he pinched the youth's arm.

Ehmish had good, lean muscle on him, but Hydallan managed to make it seem like skin and bones. Ossian and Aodh laughed. Their barks invited others to join in, though no one did.

Gard frowned, shaking his head.

"You don't believe the tales?" Kern asked.

"After seeing Cruaidh taken apart like this," the clansman said, "I don't know what to believe. I never got a good look at him myself. Most men I'd trust to tell me, who got close enough during the storm, are dead. Some sliced in half. Some crushed. A few had savage claw marks ripping out their throats. I came upon a good friend out in the darkness. His chest had been caved in. All he could say to me was, 'Monster. Monster.' And then he died."

The rest was short and severe. The burning fort. The destroyed homes. Men dying by handfuls and no clear leadership. The Cruaidhi war host broke and ran, grabbing their families if they could find them, and their thickest blankets, heading out into the storm. Gard and Sláine Longtooth, the chieftain, rallied a short line of defenders, but that broke under a Vanir push, and so the call went out to run. Run and hide, and live for the next day. They hoped.

"About half came back," Gard said, as they approached the burial grounds still being dug, filled, and covered. "The rest were lost to raiders or to the storm. We'll be finding bodies deep into summer, if summer ever comes."

"Raiding for food. Raiding for spoils. That I understand." Kern looked around again at the total wreckage visited on Cruaidh. "This, this is madness. You can shear a sheep many times. You can only slaughter it once. Why do this?"

"Punishment. It's the only thing Sláine Chieftain

and I could think of. We've been pushing warriors up through the pass all winter, trying to open the Breakneck to the Broken Leg Lands. Cruaidh needs trade. It can't survive without it. Too big. But the summer trade and autumn's were choked off with Vanir controlling the pass. We saw no blue iron coming down from Clans Conarch or Morgach. None of the late-winter grains they are able to grow on the other side of the Teeth. We need these things to survive the winter. So we tried to reopen the pass.

"And Grimnir came for us because of that."

"But . . ." Kern counted the surviving clansfolk by clumps. "Your army. You could not have lost two hundred men. You said half of them returned, but I see very few warriors left." And not enough gravesites to account for the rest.

"You do not see Sláine Longtooth here either. That is because the chieftain has our war host up inside the pass right now." If it were possible, the Cruaidhi warrior looked grimmer. "Our best men and women, and some we dragooned from nearby clans and communities. And more on their way. I've runners carrying a bloody spear to every village and farm within three days of here. Conall Valley must answer."

They would, Kern knew, if the bloody spear arrived. Smaller clans and villages were compelled. Clans of equal size or position to Cruaidh would send whatever force they were able to muster on short notice. It was custom, and law. Even long-standing feuds must be set aside to answer the greater threat.

Gaud and Taur, already hurt so drastically by raiders and the long winter, would have still sent warriors. But three days? Sláine Chieftain was obviously not willing to wait.

Kern drew in a deep breath, tasting damp ash on the air, and sweat. He would have given a great deal just then for a heated kettle of water, a skewer of venison—

horseflesh, even—and a dry shack where he could roll up inside his felt pad. But he sensed those things were not coming anytime soon. Besides the fact there wasn't a standing shack anywhere in the settlement, he sensed that they had finally arrived at the moment Gard had angled for since their short-lived standoff.

Stooping, Kern snagged an exposed rock and pitched it off to one side. The smell of overturned earth was very strong, so close to the burial field. "You want our aid in opening the pass," he guessed.

"I do. Any band to survive the trek you've been on is a force not to be taken lightly. Sláine Longtooth plans to clear the pass and hunt Grimnir into the Broken Leg Lands. He will need every last man."

Whether he knew it or not.

Somehow Kern felt those words hanging between them, unspoken. He glanced at Daol, at Desa, two of his more astute warriors. Daol's look was guarded, wary. Desagrena stared through long strands of oily hair with a look of outright disbelief on her face. They had picked up on it as well.

"Your chieftain decided not to wait for more warriors." Of course not. A thought dawned, bright and clear as fresh ice. "He wishes to avenge his son."

"He may not be thinking with the best mind," Gard admitted. "But make no mistake, he is a warrior born and has survived longer than any ten chieftains you could name. I don't know what more sixteen men can offer, but if there is a chance, I will take it."

"Fifteen," Kern said absently. Then, "It seems a strange request to come from a man who was ready to run me through with a pike."

"I have very few warriors left to me and fourscore clansfolk to protect. Your warriors had naked blades. I wanted no injuries, and no illusion as to who was in charge of Cruaidh."

Kern crossed arms over his thick chest. Every muscle

ached, but even though he knew Gard was tensed for action Kern felt he could get his shield around before the Cruaidhi ran him through with the pike he still carried. "You are here with only two warriors. You must be very certain of yourself, Gard Foehammer."

"Or very certain of you, Kern Wolf-Eye." The settlement's protector deliberately turned his back on Kern, walked between two graves, leaving fresh prints in the black soil. The scent of sour earth was strong. Like mud left standing too long without drying in the sun. Two men with shovels worked nearby at the hard-frozen earth.

A third man with his back to the small group, slight and bent with age, turned his hand at a pickaxe with surprising strength.

Gard looked back, shrugged. "You could kill me now, that is true. But you would not." His laugh had little humor in it. "Even if you tried, you could not hold Cruaidh with sixteen warriors."

"Fifteen . . . and how can you be so sure? From a few stories told by freezing outcasts wandering in out of the storm?" He glanced at Daol, at Reave. "Maybe they lied. Maybe we all lied."

There was something else going on. Something hidden. Kern sensed it, like a trap lying below the silky blanket of snow. His guard was up, as he stood amidst the burial fields and several open, unfilled graves.

But Gard had another purpose for bringing them out here, other than any implied threats. "The man who first talked of you had no reason to lie." He reached back, laying a hand on the shoulder of the man with the pickaxe. The bent frame stiffened, as if caught out. Slowly he turned.

"Any man who would give up a rare meal to a clansman cast out," Gard said, "would not stoop to betraying a clan in need."

Perhaps not. And Kern knew when he was beaten.

Old Finn stared across the head of his pickaxe, a sheen of honest sweat matting iron gray hair to his forehead. He looked leaner than when he'd left Gaud. Leaner, and tough as old leather. The light behind his milky blue eyes burned brightly.

Kern didn't bother with welcomes or recriminations. He simply offered his hand, and smiled when the old man took it with his own—the gnarled fingers still had surprising strength in them. Gard Foehammer had been right after all.

Sixteen.

18

NO MATTER HOW badly Gard Foehammer might have wanted to press Kern's small band after the Cruaidhi chieftain, Kern was physically spent and in need of at least some minor attention for frostbite. He didn't have the deep white patches of Reave or Ossian, or half the others in fact, but the edges of his ears and high over his cheekbones required treatment. If left alone, the dull, waxy patches would turn bone white, then gray. As gangrene set in, bits of flesh would eventually go black with dry rot.

Kern remembered Burok Bear-slayer, and his final days as the gangrene turned wet and septic. It was an end he'd rather avoid.

Ashul worked hard on some of Cruaidh's more desperately wounded, so it was Desagrena who volunteered to see to Kern that evening. No healer, she certainly lacked the caring touch of Jocund or the healer Kern had seen at Taur. But she knew how to dress a wound and care for frostbite. Pulling her dark, oily hair back from where it usually hung in her eyes, she inspected the frost patches on Kern's face. Poked at them with a sharp finger. Kern felt only a numb pressure.

"Could be worse," she said, poking harder, then pinching the skin until Kern finally yelped. "It's not too deep."

A good thing. The Gaudic woman might have gone for her dagger to probe any deeper into Kern's damaged flesh.

"She do this for you?" Kern asked Reave, who shared the cramped tent with him.

The large man nodded glumly, frowning as he remembered. "Yea. Though I think she pinched a mite harder."

"And you squealed twice as much," Desa shot back, her viperish temperament still in place.

She didn't go for her knives. Instead, she wrapped damp rags heated on an outside fire over the damage. Kern's ears stung painfully as blood returned to the cold-affected areas, settling eventually into a throbbing ache. He woke up to lessened pain the next morning. Also to Reave's elbow digging hard into his side.

Kern extracted himself carefully from the tangle of blankets and limbs. Before leaving the small tent he smeared horse fat over his cheeks to protect them from further damage and dabbed a bit on his cracked lips as well. For his ears he cut a long strip off his felt pad and tied it back around his head like a scarf, knotting it securely behind his neck and letting the ends trail down his back.

The mist had cleared overnight, but thick gray cloud cover overhead still muted the dawn to a murky gloom. Old Finn and Daol tended a small fire not too far away, readying it and a camp griddle for flat cakes. Ossian sat with them, stropping his knife against a leather strap, sharpening it.

Closer by the creekside, Ehmish, Aodh, and Mogh

did some sitting-up exercises to warm themselves. Kern joined them, and soon felt the chill in his bones loosen its grasp.

Loosen, but never let go.

"Three of Gard's runners returned late last night," Aodh said, grunting as he stretched down to reach for his toes. "A dozen warriors in tow. Each."

"That fast?"

He nodded. "I was up, coloring the creek, when the first arrived. Volunteered to help them make some cloth lean-tos for sleeping. Never quite finished as more bodies turned up during the next watch."

Ehmish nodded toward another area swept clear of snow. No tents. Just a small pile of packs and bedrolls, with a couple of large men sitting on them. "They came in this morning. Five men and women from Clan Maugh. Heard them talking. Said they didn't want to let the Cruaidhi have all the fun."

Maugh. Kern knew the settlement. High up north in the valley, about as close as one could crowd the Eighlophian Mountains without being snowed in for eight months of the year. Hard men and women. Gard was lucky to have them.

"What do you think?" Kern asked.

Aodh bent down, finishing some squat stretches. His old joints cracked and popped. "Maugh?" He chewed on the ends of his salt-and-pepper moustache a moment. "I don't like those fellows much, but they're impressive with a sword, I'll give 'em that."

"No," Kern shook his head, "that's not what I mean."

He nodded everyone back up toward the fire where Nahud'r had joined the others. The dark-skinned man threw Kern a rag torn from an old blanket. Kern blotted away his sweat before the morning air settled a chill on him, then passed the cloth to Ehmish. Brig Tall-Wood crawled out from under a shallow lean-to of planks laid up against the stone ruins of one of the old bridges, scratching himself, yawning.

Daol and Finn handed out flat cakes. Hot. Kern bounced his from one hand to the other, cooling it.

"What do you *think?*" he asked again. His question included everyone.

Silence. Then, "Hundred . . . hundred fifty men up in the pass? Another fifty ready to head off after them?" Mogh hawked and spit to one side. "I think we're suddenly small game in a large forest." It was the longest speech he'd yet to make in front of Kern.

Ossian shrugged, rubbed some animal fat over his head in a greasy smear. "We was heading toward the Broken Leg Lands anyways," he said, scraping a sharpened blade over his pate, slowly, in even, measured strokes. The thin smear of fat protected his skin, but was not enough to soften the stubble. It rasped dryly against the blade. "Fifteen men trying to sneak past or a few hundred forcing their way through—either way, we gets where we're going."

"Come too far to call it off now," Old Finn offered. "Not like I can go back, anyway."

Not like any of them could, in fact. Kern tore a piece of flat cake away and popped it in his mouth. It tasted of stale grease and oats, but it was warm and would fill the hollow growing in his stomach.

He stared west, into the cold haze that had settled over the rising Teeth of the mountains. The Pass of Blood lay in between his band and the Broken Leg Lands. So much of what they could and would do depended a great deal on what was happening up there in the mountains.

"Daol?" Kern asked.

But his friend was already wolfing down what remained of his own food, rising from a squat near the fire. "I know," he said, anticipating Kern's question. "I'll see what I can find out from Gard."

Not a great deal, as it turned out. Gard remained

busy seeing after newly arrived warriors and preparing them for the trek up into the mountains. He did admit to sending runners westward, to check on the chieftain's progress. None of them had yet to come back, which could mean the fighting went well, and they were pressing farther through the pass than anyone had expected.

Or badly. And the chieftain had need of every man who came along.

He would be getting them. By noon, another fifty warriors from outside Cruaidh had swelled the struggling settlement, which looked more like an armed camp now than the valley's largest village. Axes hammered in all directions, chopping firewood for dozens of fires. Swords were scraped against sharpening stones. Warriors tested themselves against one another in several makeshift arenas.

There were a few real clashes between clans with centuries-old feuds. The skirmishes usually ended at first blood before anyone truly got hurt, but even that did not bode well for clansmen assembled under the bloody spear.

"No strong chieftain here to hold them in check," Ossian complained. "They answered the call of Sláine Longtooth, not Gard Foehammer."

The best Gard could do, in fact, was let it be known from the start that he'd set his own warriors on any clansman who maimed or killed another inside Cruaidh. Kern was glad for that promise. He did not miss the glances of suspicion and outright hatred that followed him around the settlement.

Feeding the assembling war host was a larger problem than a few squabbles. Most brought with them enough for a few days . . . a week at best. An extended campaign over the western pass would take better supplies, though. The villagers were already on starvation diets, and several dozen clansfolk—men and women, young and old—volunteered to leave with the growing army to relieve pressure on the kin left behind or simply to get better rations for themselves.

Fortunately, nearby farms and villages were also scraping the bottom of their larders and dry pits for the last of their dried meats and autumn roots. A few scrawny packhorses, loaded with whatever scraps could be spared, were led into Cruaidh close to noon. The horses were butchered directly after being unloaded, their meat cooked and wrapped in oilskin for preservation. Bones were split open for their marrow, and boiled into a broth that everyone shared at the midday meal.

There wouldn't be much left in Cruaidh once the army departed.

That included people.

Kern expected a visit during the day, but did not bother sitting around to wait for it. When Gard Foehammer eventually searched him out, the Cruaidhi found Kern and his warriors exercising with some weapons practice near their temporary camp at the creek's side. Wallach Graybeard officiated, having taken on the role of training master. He'd set half of them trading strokes against one another. The other half he left to call out advice and encouragement and jeers.

Several were taking wagers for honor in the current sparring match between Kern and Reave, a mismatch if ever there was one. Reave's greatsword had twice Kern's reach. The shield Kern had taken from the Vanir evened the odds only somewhat, but each time he turned away an attack, it felt as if his arm might shatter.

Kern saw Gard amble up and ground his pike against the frozen earth, letting the spear lean back against his shoulder, crossing his arms over it, waiting patiently. Kern had no time for conversation. Sweating freely, trying to work his arming sword through

Reave's guard, he merely grunted in the Cruaidhi's direction, then thrust for Reave's ribs again, and again.

Each time he was turned away by a hard parry as Reave whipped the greatsword around in magnificent arcs.

"Speed," Wallach called out. "Speed versus strength."

Twice Kern slipped inside of Reave's reach, but both times the larger man kicked him away. Kern was learning to whittle the other man's defenses down, but slowly. Too slowly. The arming sword grew heavier with each passing moment.

Finally, taking advantage of Kern's flagging arm strength, Reave managed to slap the flat of his blade against Kern's sword arm. Kern stepped back, defeated, gasping for breath which came raw and cold. Several warriors cheered for Reave's display.

As did Kern. It had been a great display of skill, and he was happy to have the bruise rather than be missing an arm. Still gulping for air, he thrust his arming sword point first into the frozen earth, letting it stand on its own for the moment. He blotted the sweat from his face, careful to avoid smearing away the horse fat protecting his cheeks. He caught Gard's eye, and saw the village protector gauging him carefully. Rather than stand under the attention, he nodded and gestured him forward at Reave.

"Care to have a go?" he asked, getting control of his panting.

As good a way as any to break the awkward moment. And to be completely truthful, Kern was eager to see how the other man wielded his pike. It was a strange weapon of choice for a Cimmerian.

Gard hesitated barely for the span of a heartbeat. "Don't mind if I do," he said. Grasping the pike in both hands, he raised it overhead in salute and a limbering stretch. He left it up there as he moved forward into the training area, angling the spear's butt end back down at Reave, like the stinger of a wasp.

Wallach Graybeard smiled, then hid the expression behind his hand as he scratched into his thick, gray beard. He nodded Reave forward. Obviously, he wanted to see the pikeman in action as well. Reave shook a spray of sweat from his brow, his dark braids slapping across his face, then against the back of his neck. The Cimmerian greatsword came up in a half-guard position, ready to parry or thrust home.

And Gard suddenly leaped forward with his pike thrusting out, easily half-again the reach of Reave's sword, looking for the Gaudic warrior's heart.

Reave beat the pike aside, barely. Smashing aside Gard's next thrust, he spun inside, sword slapping at the Cruaidhi's legs. But Gard grounded his pike in the way and Reave barely missed tripping over it.

The spearman had a unique style about him, Kern recognized, treating the pike as much as a staff as he did a spear. Perfectly calm with batting aside a sword strike or rapping the polearm against an exposed knee or elbow. Forcing an opening where he suddenly thrust for the heart, or the throat, or the groin. Always for a critical injury.

For his part, Reave relied on the greater weight of his sword, trying to smash aside Gard's defense. When he jabbed, Gard retreated. When he slashed inside, Gard met him body to body or simply spun him away with an easy swipe.

Back and forth, with neither man giving the other an easy victory. Then, stumbling aside from another slashing attack, Reave took the butt end of the pike right over his left kidney. He staggered but did not fall. Stepped back. There was no disguising the amazement that showed brightly in his pale blue eyes. Clearly he had thought to win the match.

Massaging the bruise, he dropped his swordpoint toward the ground in salute. A few of the others tossed Reave some jeers, laughing. Reave gave them back a rude gesture.

"Very well done," Wallach said, a rare compliment from the veteran.

With a flourish, Gard reversed his pike and grounded the blue-iron point into the ground. Then he looked over at Kern. "Are you rested yet?" he asked, leaning his pike forward in challenge.

Kern, though, read that question in two different ways, and considered carefully how he would answer. "Near enough," he said, speaking for himself and for his small band of warriors. He smoothed a hand back over the sweat-damp scarf tied around his head, protecting his ears. "But if you're in a hurry . . ."

"It's not good, most times, to cool down so much." Gard picked up his pike and stretched it overhead again.

"I'll give you the best I have left." Kern reached down and pulled his arming sword from the ground. He scraped the tip against the side of his boot, cleaning off a small clump of earth. "It may not be much, though."

The Cruaidhi laughed. It was a warm sound, not mocking at all. "Said the man who played his arming blade against a greatsword. And held his own from what I saw." He looked at the short blade in Kern's hand. "Why not pick up a real piece of steel against me?"

Because Kern couldn't handle one half as well as the arming sword. And he'd also rather his opponent continue to underestimate him. "We make do with what we have," he said, and lunged forward.

The pike flashed out, batting his sword point aside. An answering thrust tagged the butt end of the spear against Kern's shield.

"We do at that."

Kern came at the match a bit differently than his

friend had, concentrating more on defense until he learned how to create an opening in Gard's defenses. He worked shield and sword together, always wary of the pike's reach and the skill the Cruaidhi had already demonstrated with it.

It caused the match to drag on, pushing back and forth without rest. Kern's infamy around the settlement and Gard's high profile attracted a few more spectators. And still more. More than a few times, Kern heard calls of "Run him through," and "Take him! Take him now!"

It focused the attention of the assembling army on him rather than the coming battle and the real enemy. And Kern's people were just as susceptible. A few shoves and hands going to the hilts of knives and swords promised that bloodshed was not too far off.

"Maybe you're right," Kern offered, as he and Gard Foehammer came up body to body. "Sooner rather than later."

The Cruaidhi put his shoulder into Kern's shield, shoving him back. "Today," he said through tight lips. He spun the pike overhead, smashing it down at Kern's shoulder.

Kern turned it with the flat of his arming sword. But his own lunge fell short. The pike's reach was harder to get inside than Reave's greatsword.

He shuffled forward, stabbing and jabbing, trying to force the larger man back a few paces. "You still think . . . this-is-a-good-idea?" His words fell out in a rush, spit with each quick, short thrust.

Gard adjusted his grip, holding the pike by its center and smashing first one end in, then the other, parrying each strike, then battering Kern backward with a bruise against his elbow, his shoulder, his hip.

"Doesn't matter what I think. Matters what I need."

"Matters what we all need," Kern corrected. He jabbed.

"Cruaidh!"

"The valley."

"Cimmeria!" they shouted at each other.

Kern had shifted from his defensive gambit to an all-out attack, reaching into his reserves to fight Gard to a standstill. Both men leaned into the battle, neither giving up a single step. Kern's sword and Gard's pike were a blur of clashing steel and cleft air. With that last shout they shoved forward with speartip and sword-point, Gard high and Kern low.

Both men froze.

Kern looked into the sharpened end of the pike, its tip less than a fist's width from his right eye. Somewhere along the way, Gard had reversed the polearm. What might have been a blackened eye had the other man slipped by so much as a heartbeat in his timing came very close instead to blinding Kern. But Gard appeared satisfied. A victorious gleam in his own eye.

Until Kern nudged him with the edge of his arming sword, and the Cruaidhi's dark blue eyes widened with surprise.

Kern's blade had sliced in between Gard's legs, hiking up the heavy kilt and laying an edge of cold steel up against his manhood. If Kern had not stopped in time, the Cruaidhi would have bled out quite painfully.

"We can call this one a draw," the protector said, his voice pitched low for Kern's ears only. Barely more than a whisper, in fact, as silence reigned around the circle of spectators. Everyone stunned by the final volley of blows and the sudden halt.

"No, we can't," Kern said.

He'd seen the dark looks gathering like a new storm around him and his warriors. Now, grudging respect for the skirmish was turning once again toward resentment and even fear. These men didn't need to be worrying about what lay ahead any more than they already were. Kern knew that.

So did Gard, though he waited for Kern to make the first move.

He did, skipping back and drawing his sword up for another thrust. Pulling it back a touch too far, giving Gard the opening.

Gard swatted aside the blade. Reversed the polearm in a sweeping motion that smashed the pike down across Kern's shoulder, sending a shock down his arm, knocking the sword from numbed fingers. He jabbed the spear's butt end into Kern's midsection after that, folding him over, and then brought the other end around to bash him across the back of the neck.

Kern dropped, and Gard buried the tip of the pike into the earth right next to Kern's neck.

Cheers and shouts broke out among the warriors not among Kern's small band. A few jostled the Gaudic and the Taurin, and Reave nearly hauled off at a nearby clansman. At the last second he caught Kern's eye, though, and the yellow-eyed man gave his friend a brief shake of his head. Then hinted at a smile before rolling back to hide his face against the ground, picking himself up slowly.

Gard stepped forward to help Kern back up. His pike still stuck in the earth, he got both hands under Kern's arms. "Two hours," he said. "I'll have them on the march in two hours."

Kern shook his head, clearing the sparks still going off in his brain. "We'll break and be gone in one, then."

"You will not march with the others?"

"I think it's more that they won't march with us. We'll scout forward."

"Run hard and fast then. And let Sláine Longtooth know that we come." Louder, shouting for the assembled warriors, Gard said, "We come to force the pass and carry this battle into the northwest lands. And just let Grimnir Stormbringer stand against us during the light of day!"

It was a challenge Kern would just have well preferred Gard not make. Standing amongst the ruins of once-strong Cruaidh, boasting of their eventual victory against the Vanir, it seemed a challenge almost worthy of the attention of the higher powers. Not that he worried about Crom. The Cimmerian's maker remained above such mortal concerns.

But Kern was beginning to wonder if the Vanir's gods played by those same rules.

19

THE HIGHER KERN'S small band marched up into the western Teeth, the deeper the blanket of snow. From the few inches dropped on Cruaidh by the freakish blizzard, it thickened to a good handbreadth, and then two.

Ehmish considered himself lucky that it didn't get so bad to reach above his fur-lined boots.

As luck went, there were worse ways to spend it.

The young man kept his cloak wrapped tight about him as the world slowly turned a stark white and gray. Swirling mists guarded the upper slopes, bringing line of sight down to half a league and casting the trees and brush into shadow. Boulders wore caps of frosted snow. The red clay from which the Pass of Blood took its name remained bandaged under a frozen blanket except where several hundred feet had traipsed the cover into a muddy, reddish slush. Sláine Longtooth couldn't have had much trouble tracking the Vanir war host back up the pass. And they had little trouble tracking Sláine Longtooth.

They merely had to follow the trail of bodies.

There weren't too many. Just enough to prove that the Vanir hadn't left their rear flank unguarded. One clansman left under a cairn of unearthed stones. Two more sewn into their blankets, and covered with a skin of bark shaved off some nearby trees. Ehmish left a whispered word of comfort with each of them, knowing how close he also had come to such an end.

To Longtooth's credit, there were more Vanir corpses littering the upper slopes and even one of the Ymirish as well. Those were not treated with much respect, propped up against a nearby rock or tree, left out for animals to gnaw on. Coming around one bend in the path, Ehmish saw the wolf, Frostpaw, digging entrails from a raider's belly.

Everyone paused almost with a common thought, giving the wolf a moment before they moved forward and chased it on ahead. None of them looked at Kern except Old Finn, who glanced around the entire party for a moment.

"Sure and I've seen stranger things," he said. His voice was dry as old leaves, but strong. "Things worse than sharing blood with a wolf."

Or with a raider.

Ehmish followed behind Kern, walking over his footsteps, staring at the odd-colored man's back. He could not see Kern's white-blond hair, currently covered by the woolen scarf knotted over the other man's head. Kern's wolflike eyes he didn't need to see—they stared at Ehmish from out of the darker corners of his mind. Glowing and savage. And strong. Like they could pull Ehmish apart, rending him so that Kern knew his every fear and shortcoming.

Was that why Ehmish followed Kern? Because the youth feared him? He wanted to believe it was something else. The same something that had caused him to step forward and volunteer to go after Maev and Daol and the others. To avenge Oscur. *That* had been a decision.

But there hadn't been many chances for decisions since then. Not really. Only a cold and blood-slick trail that chased into the northwest lands of Cimmeria. Closer to their own deaths, it seemed at times. And Ehmish had yet to make a kill, to prove his manhood in the eyes of his clan and kin. Most of what he'd done so far was run away. No doubt, though, that was about to change. He'd be seeing a lot of battle up close very, very soon.

So be it.

Ehmish shrugged away his fears and concerns, and concentrated instead on putting one foot after the other. Trudging upward. Careful and alert through the bottlenecks of the lower pass, tense, then stretching his muscles out in a loping run whenever the warriors gained a level or short downhill slope. It felt good. His breathing raw in his throat, tasting of fresh snow and smoke. Heartbeat strong in his own ears. Muscles barely aching with exertion.

Smoke?

"Listen!" Ehmish whispered hard and urgent, before he could think to say anything else. "I mean smell. Taste!"

He fetched up to a quick stop, causing those behind him to stagger out of line before they simply plowed him over. Ahead, Kern and Desagrena slowed, glancing back quizzically. But they stopped. Desa whistled for Daol, farther on.

Everyone stared at the younger man.

"Smoke. On the back of my tongue." He breathed in through an open mouth, pulling the cold air up into his sinuses. It was there. And it had a kind of acrid bite to it, like greenwood or pitch.

Most of the others shook their heads, but Brig Tall-Wood paused, nodded. "The boy's right. I can smell it, too."

Ehmish didn't care for being called "boy," especially when not more than a handful of years separated him from Tall-Wood. Lacking his first kill or not. He bristled, nearly bit back at the other man, but Kern's hand on his shoulder stilled him at once. He shot Brig a quiet glare instead.

If Kern could take being called "pup" by Hydallan, "boy" wasn't so bad. Was it?

Daol trotted back, moving with the long, flowing strides that ate up the ground with practiced ease. He had unlimbered his war bow, gripping it in his left hand. "You scent it, too?" he asked Kern.

"The boy," Kern said. "Ehmish."

Ehmish fumed. "It's green," he said, more for the sake of saying something than thinking it had any real bearing.

"There's been a few echoes, too," Daol said, confirming that they must be close to the trouble. "Dull ones. Distant. I'd say an hour."

An hour. Caught in between two armies, Ehmish wondered if Kern would wait for the reinforcements to catch up, or press on ahead. No runners had come back from the pass, he recalled. Maybe they were needed up ahead.

Maybe they were being slaughtered.

"Forward," Kern said, not taking much time. "At a run. If you have to fall off, catch up as soon as you can."

For some reason, Ehmish thought this last comment might be directed at him specifically. There were older men in the small group, true. Hard-bitten warriors, mostly, who had proven they could keep up a stiff pace for nearly two days. The women, Desa and Ashul.

Desa, at least, wouldn't give the men the satisfaction of dropping behind.

No, it was "the boy" they were worried about. Making exceptions for. And that raised Ehmish's ire more than the casual disregard usually shown him. He'd have to work that much harder to earn their respect, then. From all of them.

When Daol lit off, taking point as he normally did, Ehmish was next off the mark pacing the hunter with long, easy strides. Daol glanced back once, but did not say anything. He possibly ran a touch faster. And so did Ehmish.

He'd drop in his tracks before he fell behind.

For him, there could be no other decision.

A REAR GUARD challenged them before they were in sight of the battlefield, although by then they all heard it. The braying howl of large dogs and a hammering of axes into wood were the sounds that carried farthest.

The screams of wounded men were still distant echoes.

Two men showed themselves from behind a large boulder, both with well-beaten broadswords. A third stood and lay over the top of the rock with a Vanir war bow very much like the one Daol now carried, an arrow nocked and drawn back to his cheek. A child, no better than fourteen Kern guessed, sprinted away about fifty paces and waited inside a clump of snow-covered basket cedar.

To see if the new arrivals were friendly, or if the child had to run up and warn Sláine Longtooth to look to his back.

Kern approved of the way the guard took few chances with his people, dark hair or no. He averted his eyes and was glad for the scarf, which hid his frost blond hair. Better to give the small band a chance to explain. "Cruaidh!" he shouted out. Then, "Foehammer! Sent by Foehammer."

That name did the trick. The guard relaxed, slightly, and waved a few of them forward. Kern sent Daol and Reave, Ossian, Aodh, and Desa. He waited in a tight knot with the rest until Daol waved up the entire group.

"Kit will run us up toward Longtooth," he said, nodding at the young boy who had crawled out from behind the cedar clump. "It's ugly," he promised.

And it was. A killing field with the Vanir clearly in control. Kern's small band broke from the trees and saw the slaughter taking place as the Cimmerian force threw itself forward yet again.

The Vanir held a slope that dropped down into a shallow, wooded valley, framed on both sides by steep mountain cliffs covered in their winter white ice pack. The slope wasn't so good as to give the Cimmerians any edge, and right where the grade leveled out for a few hundred paces, the raiders had dug down through snow, ice, and earth to create a shallow trench. The trench was backed by what appeared to be a bulwark of glistening, dark icicles. It took Kern a moment to understand what he was seeing. When he did, his spirits fell.

"Branches," he said, finally recognizing how the structure had been built. He pointed it out to Ossian and Reave. "They stacked a wall of branches against a small hillock of stones and clay, then poured water over it. Snowmelt, most likely."

The water had frozen, filling up gaps between the thin wooden limbs and eventually spread out into an icy sheet. Creating a hard, unyielding wall with no good footing for climbing over. It gave the raiders and their mastiffs a good refuge.

The trench had been started days, weeks perhaps, before the assault on Cruaidh. It spoke of organization and planning.

Two things the attacking Cimmerians currently lacked.

As the small band of warriors watched, several dozen men streamed away from large bonfires set near the tree line, carrying burning logs and brands of bound evergreen boughs. Knots of swordsmen hurried behind them, with them, shields raised. War cries thundered within the valley and echoed back from the frozen cliffs. The mastiffs brayed and snarled, roving in a few loose packs on the other side of the wall, daring any Cimmerian to cross into their territory.

Bowmen protected the flanks of the assault with a few hasty shots directed at the raiders, but the Vanir had their archers as well and much greater reach with their curved war bows. Broadhead arrows scythed out in scattered volleys, searching for unprotected flesh, and finding it.

Four . . . five men dropped, letting their fiery bundles hiss into the snow as they clutched at pierced legs or stuck shoulders.

Most made it within a stone's throw of the bulwark, where they heaved their logs forward, trying to stack up enough burning material against the wall of iced-over branches to supposedly melt the barricade. The flames were already dying long before they arrived, though, and bouncing off the frozen earth usually doused whatever fire had stubbornly clung to the burning brands. They piled up over earlier, futile attempts.

A few of the swordsmen, blades naked in their hands, attempted to force their way over the icy wall. Some of them made it. Most were turned back with spears or walls of sharp steel thrust into their path. Those who managed to vault the wall were set upon by three or four raiders apiece. There couldn't be more than fifty Vanir holding the wall and ten . . . twenty of the massive dogs, but it was likely enough to hold back five times their number.

Or ten, counting the sorcerer.

Kern didn't see him right away, but he had to be there. There was a warning shouted by one Cimmerian, who quickly vanished in a flurry of snow that seemed to explode out of the ground and take him. Kern remembered Gard's description of the snow serpent, and when the demonic creature stretched itself back out, he saw the thick coils and glassy fangs of which Foehammer had spoken.

The body was thick as a man's torso, and easily five times as long. Kern couldn't make out its eyes, not at this distance, but the fangs were the length of his arming sword and apparently just as sharp. A second warrior, too slow drawing back, fell under the serpent's jaws. It struck twice. A third time. Each blow left long, bloody gashes across the warrior's body. The last one severed a leg.

"There," Nahud'r said, pointing.

Three men, standing an arrow shot back from the center of the wall. All three had the same frosted hair and thick, unruly beards. Kern didn't need to see their faces to know that each man looked upon the battlefield with yellow, wolflike eyes.

Sláine Longtooth agreed when Kern and Reave were finally taken to the chieftain. He'd heard of Kern Wolf-Eye from a runner sent out of Cruaidh. One of the several he'd never sent back. He searched Kern's face warily for deceit, but was glad for the report that Foehammer's reinforcements were not too far behind. Glad enough to speak with Kern, at any rate.

"Yea, one of 'em be the sorcerer. Or all three together." It didn't seem to matter much to him, one way or the other. "Haven't seen them separate in two days' time."

The chieftain spit blood. He'd taken part in the latest charge, and had come away with a spear shaft broken against his face. Two of his own had dragged him back to safety. His jaw was dark with a purple-black bruise. Now, reaching into his mouth, he grimaced and pulled, then tossed aside a tooth.

Even with the swelling and the blood leaking at the corner of his mouth, Sláine Longtooth was still an impressive man. His woolen tunic and heavy winter kilt were the green and brown of Clan Cruaidh, and both were strapped with leather and iron studs. He wore his winter cloak thrown back, falling down his back like an afterthought. It bunched over the chieftain's wide shoulders and hid neither the chieftain's muscular arms nor his powerful legs. Sixty years if a day, with gray stubble thick on his cheeks and chin and a wispy white tuft growing under his bottom lip, he had salt-and-pepper hair, and blue eyes washed out to the color of a summer sky haze.

He also had a fixation on going after the Vanir. Raiders, dogs, sorcerer, and all.

"Only the one snow demon, but it has taken its share of souls. Took Alaric back at Cruaidh. Here . . . Cron and Hess, and three others I don't know."

He paced between two of the large bonfires. Watching as work teams pulled heavily laden sleds out of the forest piled with short logs and split-rounds and plenty of branches to be bound into new brands. Angry red sparks swirled out as new wood was added to the nearest fire, but he brushed them away from his arms as if they hardly mattered.

"That's five of the twenty-seven . . . twenty-eight men dead since yesterday."

"Mebbe you should think about pulling back," Reave said, the large warrior showing uncharacteristic caution. "That thing out there, it's only the one problem. Even if you beat it, you're not over the wall."

"I can beat it," the chieftain said, folding his arms over a massive chest. "But first I have to beat that wall.

I've pulled their defense apart one piece at a time. And I've almost got it."

"You do?" Kern asked. Not that he had noticed. Looking now, even through the thickening mountain mists, he should have been able to see any breach in the icy coating. There was simply the damp pile of brush and logs stacking up near the one section, and the bulwark appeared just as strong there as anywhere.

"Of course it does," Longtooth growled when Kern pointed that out. "In fact, the wall's a bit thicker there than anywhere else. You think I'm trying to melt my way through?"

It had certainly appeared that way to Kern. *And likely to the Vanir as well!* No matter how futile the attempt, Kern had stopped analyzing the assault when he had seen the burning debris failing to do much more than sputter out in the snow and red clay muck.

"You're building a ramp," he said, looking at the piled logs and brush.

It wasn't pretty, but it would work. Even the chieftain's choice of throwing burning brands onto the pile made sense. They would cushion and bind up between the heavier logs, preventing them from slipping so much when his warriors began to climb over.

"Nay other way," Sláine Chieftain agreed. "We tried some simple ladders before, and that got a few men over. But that damned snow demon rushed by and smashed them like kindling. Trapped my men to be slaughtered."

"Why not mass them up now?" Reave asked. "You have enough of a ramp laid out. Each man with a log and some bramble, you can finish it up and pile them over the top before the Vanir can do much about it."

Kern saw the answer, though. "Archers. The Vanir have more of them and a better reach. They'd fill a massed assault full of arrows."

"Between the bowmen and that snow monster, it would be a terrible slaughter. I'd face any one of them down, but both at once is tricky. Which is why I plan to build the beginnings of three ramps, though it'll take me most of the night and another few dozen lives to do it." He kicked one of his warriors in the backside, hurrying the man toward a waiting sled. "Get that fire built up and ready some logs for another charge. We go before twilight. Move, you dogs. The Vanir are laughing at us, but not for much longer."

As plans went, it was workable. But at a very high cost. How many of the dozens dead—and several score wounded—would be among Kern's men? Two men? Three? And that was before the real battle was joined. If he had to choose from among his people, whom could Kern afford to lose?

Whom could he stand to lose?

"There has to be another way, Sláine Chieftain. You'll need every man you have on the other side of the mountains."

The older man glared. "There are plenty of other ways, but each one still requires I feed lives into the Vanir maw until I choke them on it. So unless you can get me a few dozen archers onto that wall without being slaughtered or you know another route through these Teeth that I don't, Wolf-Eye, we do things my way."

A not-unreasonable bargain. And one which Kern was willing to take the chieftain up on. He stood quietly alongside Reave a moment, studying the Cimmerian preparations and the Vanir defenses, working the problem through. Like Sláine Longtooth had said: one piece at a time.

"Sláine," Kern yelled out, counting up the teams that worked to feed the bonfires and stack new logs to the side, estimating how many remained in the forest. He gauged the slope down toward the wall. Was it steep enough? He thought it might be. "Sláine Chieftain," he called, getting the older man's attention again.

"How many archers?" he asked.

20

TWILIGHT CAME EARLY as the gray sky and mountain shadows piled up on the battlefield. More fires were set. Small ones, easy to kick out when the time came. A few warriors thrust their swords into beds of coals, warming the blades just enough that they could feel the heat spreading into the hilt. To keep fingers from numbing around cold metal.

It seemed like a good idea to Daol, who dug his broadsword into a fire pit, then promptly forgot it as he worked to string his war bow with a new cord.

Bending the curved bow against the ground, he marveled again at how the horn reinforcement made for such a pliable but strong weapon. He had to apply real weight to be able to slip the cord's loop over the top draw, then let up easy to make sure it did not jump out of the groove. That accomplished, he plucked at the cord a few times, checking it for a nice, taut sound, and inspected it by eye. No frays. No thinning. He dried the cord carefully with a strip of woolen cloth. Nothing could afford to go wrong. Though something would. It always did.

At least it wouldn't be his part.

"How do I let you talk me into these things?" he asked Kern, as his friend carefully set another thick skin of bark nearby.

Kern frowned. "I asked for volunteers," he reminded the younger man. Lowering his voice, he said, "I'd rather you and Hydallan weren't along, actually."

"But Brig Tall-Wood is fine by you?" Daol asked softly. His eyes searched over to another small campfire, where Brig was testing his hunting bow, preferring a familiar draw to the stronger Vanir war bow. "Oh, no." Daol shook his head. "When this goes bad, you're going to need someone to pull your ass from the fire."

"Thank you for the vote of confidence."

Nahud'r dumped an armful of arrows over a spread blanket. "A good plan," he said. The bright whites of his eyes and his strong teeth shone in the firelight. "Worthy of Conan."

Not in the fireside tales Daol had ever heard. Conan would have stalked the Vanir army by himself. Climbed one of the iced-over cliffs in the dark of night, carrying nothing more than his sword and his bow across his back. Come up from behind the raiders unaware, taking out the sorcerer first, then dealing out death with arrows that never missed.

Actually, that didn't sound half-bad. He asked Kern about it.

"Sláine Longtooth sent some warriors up the cliffs," Kern said.

Well, of course he had. Cimmerians had never seen a mountain they couldn't climb. Daol eyed the dark bluffs, nothing more than a looming presence in the building twilight. He could do it. "And?"

"The Vanir sent men up the back side slope, which

is a much easier climb. They threw rocks down on their heads."

Ah. Daol hadn't considered that. He glanced at the tall climb again. It *was* a long way to fall. "Well, then, this just has to work. Doesn't it?"

Kern was busy cutting careful holes in the long skin of bark, trying not to break the fragile sheet in half. The sheet was half as tall as the yellow-eyed leader, and easily as wide. "It will work," he promised.

So far, Kern had made good on all his promises. And Daol would never forget who had come for him when he was bound to a Vanir slave line. The same friend he had let run south on his own. He'd felt his father's disappointment very keenly just then, even though Hydallan could have had no way of knowing what had happened. Didn't matter that Kern convinced Reave to stay. A man lived with his own decisions, not the decisions of others.

Daol and Reave had promised each other—secretly, while resting up at Taur—they would never make that mistake again.

And so, "Tell me again," he said, stepping over next to where Kern worked. He kicked at the flat-bottomed sled lying nearby. "How can you steer these things?"

THERE WASN'T A great need to steer the sleds, Kern guessed. There were only nine of them, and it was a wide-open slope. No tree stumps or large boulders in the way (or to provide cover for the warriors who would charge after them). It seemed simple enough. Point the haulers downhill. Give them a good hard shove. Let the pull of the land do the rest.

But just in case, he had experimented within the woods to see how heavily each one could be loaded, and how to guide them in the right direction. It was a fairly crude process of dragging a foot on one side or the other, but it worked.

Mostly.

Now the small fires nearby had been banked down to orange, glowing coals. Enough for warmth. Not enough light to give away to the Vanir what they were doing. While Daol held his metal-scalded hand in a deep snowdrift, Kern explained it again to the assembled group. Sláine Longtooth watched with an uncertain eye as Kern showed the gathered archers and a few swordsmen how he wanted them to lie down on the flat-bottomed sleds.

The first man positioned himself with head toward the front, chest down and legs splayed such that they hung near either side. Two more clansmen, being careful, crouched down on hands and knees behind and over the top of the first man, gripping the first clansman by his kilt. Bows, quivers, and swords wrapped loosely in a blanket were laid on the first man's back and also held by the other two.

Then came the improvement Kern had borrowed from Nahud'r's Nemedian rain shield. Using the sheets of bark, two per sled, he improvised an overhead cover. The first tree skin was fastened to the nose of the sled and laid over the shoulders of the kneeling warriors. The second was spiked into place overlapping the first, and resting over the warriors' backs, like the shell of an armor-backed lizard.

"Our arrows," Sláine said, knocking hard against the makeshift shield, "would pierce right through this thin bark."

"Some would," Kern agreed, smearing fat over his cheeks and retying the woolen scarf over his head. The bark *had* sounded fairly thin under the chieftain's raw-boned knuckles. "But we use hunting arrows. Vanir like broadleaf shafts. They can't sink in as far."

"You know what it is that you're doing."

Kern shrugged. "I'll be the first to know if I don't." Because he'd be first man on the first sled.

At least, that had been the plan.

The sled's stacking surface was pitted and gouged, and full of splinters that scraped Kern's arms and jabbed at him through the rents in his tattered leather poncho. The planks felt cold against the bare skin on his arms, his legs, like ice. There wasn't much of an edge to grab on to, so Kern splayed his hands flat on the forward area, gripping as best he could.

Daol and Brig crouched over him, balancing their bows and the weight of three swords on the small of Kern's back, then Kern's shield on top of those. Hydallan would ride on a separate sled, with one of Sláine's best archers and the man with the silver-chased sword whom the chieftain trusted to deal with the snow serpent.

The bark skins were laid over them, leaving just enough room under the forward edge that Kern could make out the distant shadow that was the ice wall.

Reave crouched down at the front of the sled. "You can see okay?"

Kern's mouth was dry and his tongue felt twice as thick as normal. But he could nod.

"We'll be right behind you. Don't go getting in too much of a hurry, yea?"

"Just try not to trip over that great blade of yours," Kern said, finding his voice again. His muscles quivered in anticipation.

Reave snorted, "No need to be jealous. It's not the length of the blade that matters, but how you use it."

Kern laughed, shortly but warmly. "Go howl! Thick-headed ox. Desa! Get this man where he belongs."

Reave didn't wait for the viperish woman to drag him away (likely by his braided locks). With a slap against the side of the bark skin, he thrust himself back to his feet and moved to the back of the sled, ready to push.

There was no gauging the other sleds from his position, so Kern waited with muscles trembling for action and the bitter taste of adrenaline drying the back of his throat. It wasn't until Sláine Longtooth called out "Ready," that Kern even had an idea that they were about to shove away. Within minutes, he guessed.

Much sooner, as it happened. The chieftain must have simply glanced over his line, made a few last checks, then given the nod. "Go," he ordered. "Send them!"

Kern braced for the shove, thinking that Reave and Nahud'r would simply brace themselves against the back of the sled and get it started with a mighty push. He heard the grunts of exertion coming from either side of him first, felt more than saw the other sleds begin to move.

There was a clap and a rubbing sound behind him. In his mind, Kern pictured Reave rubbing his hands together, bending down patiently with Nahud'r to get their hands fastened on the back of the sled, bracing themselves, and then—finally!—pushing forward with slow, strong steps.

The sled began to move, rasping over snow crust that bore the weight of the three men fairly easily.

Faster. Stronger. Gliding forward with greater and greater ease. To either side, Kern saw the nearby sleds about even with his, a few arm's lengths between each. It didn't seem like so much room anymore.

Smooth and slippery, the sled charged forward.

Kern heard the footfalls behind him, felt their hammering thuds through the sled's planks, and knew that Reave and Nahud'r were running for all they were worth, keeping the sled at speed. There were stumbling falls all around them as the running warriors finally lost balance or were outraced by the sled's natural tendency to pick up speed.

Reave, Kern felt certain, lost it first, staggering into a lopsided run, then crashing down onto the snow-covered slope. Nahud'r lasted another few steps, and managed a slight shove at the end that jumped Kern forward, almost catching them up fully with the racing sleds to either side.

The wind cut at his ears.

A spray of snow sliced up from the forward edge of each side. It smelled of fresh ice and dull, damp clay.

Kern ran a tongue across his chapped lips, squinting into the wind and gloom to try and see how they fared. His sled hit a rough patch of snow, and it shook hard. Then another. It sounded like stones scraping along the underside of the sled, loud and dangerous in Kern's ears.

"By Crom," Brig Tall-Wood said, packing into that all the same recriminations Daol had voiced earlier.

The next patch nearly shook Brig loose as the sled bucked and slewed sideways for a few long heartbeats. Kern leaned in the other direction and dug his left foot into the snow, feeling a hard, icy rough scraping against his toes. He knew then what it was. Knew without having to see it. Snow and mud, churned into frozen slush by Sláine's repeated attacks against the Vanir wall.

The sled turned, but not easily. Kern jammed his foot into the snow and ice even harder. They came within a few handbreadths of the racing warriors on Kern's right before veering away.

Elsewhere, a sled of warriors was not so fortunate. They shouted as their sled began to wander, and Kern heard the first man bail off before there was any impact of wood against wood. But that came soon. A sick, crunching sound that reminded him of smashing into the woodpile back in Gaud. At least one more body hit the earth nearby. Several others yelled in anger and not a little fear, but Kern didn't think any of the sleds over-turned. At least, he hoped not.

There were other shouts in the deepening twilight. Calls of surprise and alarm in the Vanir tongue. Challenging roars from behind them, as Sláine Longtooth's war host charged forward.

Squinting forward, Kern saw the watch fires behind the wall blaze up with new strength as raiders fed brittle evergreen boughs to the flames.

The first arrow shaft didn't whistle past for another few heartbeats. It was another five or ten lengths before a broadhead *thunked* into the barkskin shield laid over their backs. Daol shouted an exclamation, then, "All right. I'm okay."

The sled jostled them as it bounced over some uneven snow, then it leveled out over a long, rough slide leading up to the Vanir line. The blanket was worse there, chewed down to bare earth in a few places. The sleds skipped over these with grinding scrapes and violent shaking. Kern all but gave up trying to control the sled's direction. They wavered over the field, bumping and grinding against the neighboring sleds. Slowing, finally, but still too fast to bail off without worries of breaking a bow, or a bone. Too late to think about . . .

Too fast!

Kern's eyes widened as he saw the dark shadow of the wall approaching fast. Though barely more than chest high it looked very tall and very, very hard from the back of the fast-gliding sled. Kern saw a darker stain against the wall, not too far off to his right, which would be the piled logs and brush from earlier attacks. And around this was more iced-over slush and bare earth and *the ditch*—

"Hang on!" Kern had time to call out, and then the sled pitched nose down into the shallow trench that the Vanir raiders had dug across the slope.

The front edge dug into frozen ground and the entire sled stopped hard, throwing the warriors forward. Kern slid across the rough planking. He managed to get one arm in between his face and the bark shield before he smashed the tree skin in between his face and the icy wall. Splinters gouged deeply into his forearm, cutting long, shallow wounds. His head glanced off ice as strong as steel, but what lit off the sparks at the edges of his vision was when his shield slid up his back and cracked him behind the crown.

Kern didn't stay down for more than a few pounding heartbeats.

Rolling to one side, he disentangled himself from Brig Tall-Wood and the two bows which, remarkably, still appeared to be in good shape. The blanket with their swords wrapped inside lay nearby. A grab for one corner and a quick yank spun the blades over the ground in a clatter and clash of metal.

Snatching up his arming sword, Kern then hunted for his shield as Daol and Brig scrambled for the handfuls of arrow shafts littering the ground around them. It wasn't hard to find, resting on the front edge of the sled where his head had been a moment before, lying under a broken chunk of bark.

Bloodied, bruised but still whole, Kern staggered up to a crouch, staying low on the wall as warriors sprinted for his position near the makeshift ramp. Kern counted seven sleds scattered along the middle of the wall, most of them having crashed into the bulwark as he had. Another sled lay overturned about twenty paces back toward the slope, and a dark stain that might have been the last sat halfway up the slope, right about where Sláine and his war host came charging with their burning brush and charred logs and enough sharpened steel to put the fear of Crom into these northerners.

They had to hold long enough for the others to reach them. Had to keep the Vanir archers from turning the mass charge into a deadly gauntlet.

Picking themselves up from the wreckage, clansmen grabbed for weapons and shields and began to run toward Kern and the makeshift ramp. Some carried swords, and a branch or armload of brush picked up off the ground. Most of them carried bows in hand and arrows in their teeth, spitting out one shaft after another.

Nock-draw-*loose!*

A Vanir warrior shouted out in pain.

It wasn't as one-sided as the Cimmerians would have hoped, though. Right now, in fact, the swiftness of their arrival was all the advanced team had in their favor. The odds were stacked heavily against them. Arrows sliced through the twilight gloom, shattering against shields, searching for unprotected flesh and finding it.

Kern saw one archer pitch backward with a shaft through his throat, the broadhead tip sticking out near his spine.

Another man staggered forward with two shafts sprouting from his shoulder, and another in the meat of his calf muscle.

But as near as Kern could tell, in the building dark and the confusion of shouts and dying groans, Sláine's plan was working. With nearly two dozen archers grouped together, able to claim some protection from the bulwark, a few men could do a lot of damage and keep the raiders from concentrating fire on the onrushing war host. A man would drop here and there, wounded more often than dead, and never in the numbers they would have lost with three or four more feints to build up piles of wood as siege ramps. A handful of lives, spent to breach the wall. Once the main body of Sláine's host arrived, they would form the anvil.

And Gard's reinforcements would be the hammer.

The second wave broke cover from above with hearty yells and the thunder of another hundred pair of feet rushing down the battered slope. These were fresh arms and sharpened blades, saved back for a moment to prevent such an easy stream of bodies that the raiders could not help but turn their full attention on the charging army.

Now there were three targets for the raiders to worry about, and pressure eased along the forward line. Kern waited, crouched with shield ready, for his chance to lend a hand. As a Vanir leaned up over the bulwark, almost right over his position, Kern rose up and thrust his sword through the man's neck. A warm jet of blood gushed over his fingers, making the hilt slippery. The raider pitched back, gargling with a wet fury, drowning in his own blood.

"We have them," Brig yelled over, bloodlust thick in his voice. A stream of blood washed down over his face from a cut scalp, but he didn't seem to notice. His bow-string sang as he drew back and loosed again, and again. "By Crom," he said, "we have them."

It looked that way to Kern as well. But he had forgotten the Ymirish sorcerer.

And the snow serpent.

A high-pitched cry of pain lanced through the battle calls and shouts, dragging Kern around with his arming sword and shield held ready. Low to the ground and not a stone's throw away, a large body coiled up and around, brushing aside a nearby archer, falling over another man and pinning him to the ground. Where the serpent's head reared up, higher than the bulwark, the Vanir's blazing fires on the far side threw red-and-orange glints into its faceted eyes and along its deadly icicle fangs.

And caught in those fangs, the long spikes digging painfully through his stomach, was the same man Kern had seen struggling forward earlier with three arrows already stuck in him. A swordsman. *The* swordsman, in fact. The one Sláine Longtooth had counted on to bring down the snow serpent.

Who, with one final throat-rattling scream, died in the jaws of the monster.

21

BRIG TALL-WOOD LOOSED his arrow with a casual release that belied the knot twisting up his guts. With every whisper of a Vanir shaft narrowly passing him, sparing his life for another few heartbeats, that knot dug deeper. Tensing for the moment when a broadhead slammed into him again.

Would knock him over, setting his body afire.

As it had in Taur.

He'd been thinking about that moment more and more, ever since stepping forward when Sláine Long-tooth began hand-selecting archers for the assault. The Cruaidhi chieftain hadn't said a thing to him, but nodded to Kern instead. As if Wolf-Eye was anything to Brig other than the man he was supposed to kill. Under *his* chieftain's orders.

But rather than think about Cul—or Tabbot or the others back in Gaud knuckling under this hard, harsh winter—and how he would accomplish his task, finally, he remembered the arrows that had knocked him to the snow-covered hillside, bleeding the life from him in droplets and dribbles. He remembered how Hydallan had come to his aid, the old man leaving himself vulnerable as the others formed a tight knot around Kern Wolf-Eye and the rest of the wounded. And how Wolf-Eye stood his ground, protecting Aodh and Maev— protecting him as well!—until the Taurin came to their aid in the battle.

This time would be different, Brig had promised himself. He put himself back into danger specifically to have his chance at the band's outcast leader. The chaos of battle. An arrow just a little off its mark. That's all it would take.

Though it was still so hard to forget. And had grown harder every day, he found, as Wolf-Eye did his best by the people who had chosen to follow him into exile. There was no promise of easier times. Not much promise of anything except another battle, and another chance to strike back at the Vanir who gutted Cimmeria with their raids and their slave-taking.

On that, Wolf-Eye delivered.

Spitting out his last arrow from where he had gripped it between his teeth, Brig nocked it in the simple hunting bow most Cimmerians preferred and drew back with long-practiced ease. He shoved all distractions to the dark corners of his mind, as his father had taught him to do long ago.

The knot in his gut.

The crawling flush that spread over his scalp.

The bellowing war cries, the choked screams of wounded men; they coiled around the back of his mind like some kind of dark, Stygian serpent that Nahud'r could probably spin another tale about. But they did not cause him to so much as flinch when it came time to draw a bead and let fly.

His mouth and throat were painfully raw, tasting of blood from his bitten tongue. A sharp spasm twinged at the back of his neck. Both picked up in the wreck Wolf-Eye had made of the sled.

Pushed back. Set aside.

He couldn't shank an arrow—he believed—any more than he could forget to breathe. His muscles simply wouldn't forget. Maybe he was not quite as fast as Daol, who thrummed off shot after shot with the Vanir war bow he'd picked up, but smooth enough.

There!—he found a Vanir running along the other side of the wall. Like a dark ghost in the twilight's gloom and frosted mist that clung to the mountains like a burial shroud. Nothing more than head and broad shoulders slipping along above the icy barricade. A good steady pace . . .

Lead him by half a stride. Both eyes open with one sighting over the arrow's pointed tip.

Draw in a calm, steadying breath, and *loose*—without holding his breath in or exhaling in such a rush of anticipation that he jerked the shot.

The arrow flew true, taking the raider in the shoulder or the neck. He tumbled to one side, went down hard with a bellow of pain and rage. He did not rise again though Brig guessed the northerner was alive and still dangerous, just hurting and maybe a bit smarter about rising above the protection of the bulwark.

Bending down, Brig scavenged the ground for an unbroken shaft. He found a piece of the shattered bark skin they had worn for armor on the sled's run. Sticking partly through it was a broadhead shaft. He pushed it through the bark and ripped it free, wincing as he remembered Maev pushing an arrow through his side in a similar fashion.

He also recalled Daol on the downslope run, saying that everything was all right. But even in the growing darkness, Brig saw the smear of blood over the broadhead's tip.

Which was how he came to search out the other man just in time to see him limping for Wolf-Eye's side.

Just in time to see the serpent rise up from the snow, with a clansman impaled on its fangs, turning those diamond-glittering eyes on Kern.

There were two waves of clan warriors bearing down on the wall now, the first rank carrying the brush and logs that would form a good pile to scale over the icy bulwark. But the leading rush of swordsmen was still too far away. They would overwhelm the demonic creature eventually. But not before it claimed Gaudic lives.

Brig acted. He slapped the broadhead-tipped shaft against his bow and fumbled the cord into the notch. Drew back with a hard yank that bent the simple hunting bow nearly in half. Then he waited. Waited for the monster to drop the body, and strike. Waited for its mouth to be exposed, and he might send the heavy shaft straight down its gullet.

Waited, holding his breath.

Daol's first shaft skewered the serpent an arm's length below its head, smashing in and through as if he'd shot nothing more substantial than a child's snow sculpture. His second, fired so fast that Brig found it hard to believe they came from the same man, did the same. A puff of white crystalline snow showered out in a jet, like blood, but only the one quick burst each time.

The serpent shook the helpless warrior one last time in its jaws, as one of the Vanir's mastiffs might terrorize a small rodent, and flung him aside to strike at Daol and Kern.

Brig loosed his arrow with a violent exhale and a jerk. Spoiling his draw. He felt the shaft scrape heavily along the side of his bow, kicking the point out too far. *Knew* he'd shanked it, even before the arrow wobbled out on a short erratic flight that missed the serpent's throat and pierced its jaw instead. The shaft stuck fast, and the serpent hissed its fury like the howling winds of a blizzard—a long, cold banshee wail.

Then it clamped down, and the arrow shattered between icy fangs.

Out of arrows, Daol had thrown aside the war bow for his broadsword, but it was Wolf-Eye who leaped in front of the jaws of the snow serpent, thrusting his shield forward. The monster's head smashed at him, knocking him back and nearly knocking him over. Wolf-Eye stumbled into Daol, who slashed around in a sidelong arc and bit into the serpent's neck.

The monster lashed back with its blunt-nosed head, snapping at him, but Daol was too quick, jumping back and pulling his arm out of reach. He circled right, Wolf-Eye left, dividing the monster's attention.

Not enough to distract it from a third man, who vaulted up from behind and swung for the back of the creature's neck. The serpent's large body hunched up, knocking the man back with a coil like a hand swatting a summer fly. It dropped that coil over the prostrate man, gathering him into a deadly embrace. Squeezing the life from him as bones cracked and frothy blood jetted out his nose and mouth.

Scrambling around on hands and knees, Brig kept one eye on the fight as he searched for more arrows. He found a couple of flight-arrow shafts, smashed into kindling. And a Vanir broadhead missing two feathers.

Then he saw another broadhead, intact, stuck in the ground only a few arm's lengths in front of him. He dived forward, snatched it out of the ground, and rolled up to his knees with the arrow sliding home. Raising the tip up the long, sinuous body. Searching for the head.

The monster already had Kern Wolf-Eye!

The serpent had shuffled its first victim farther back in its coils, still squeezing as the dying man flailed with sword and fist. A second coil wrapped around Wolf-Eye, lifting him clear of the ground. The outcast had lost his shield, and his sword arm was trapped in between his body and the serpent. He braced his free hand up between the demonic monster's fangs, against the forward edge of its mouth, holding back those deadly icicles. Pressing and straining—holding off against inevitable death.

This was Brig's chance!

Bringing the tip in line with the back of Wolf-Eye's neck, the young Tall-Wood saw it in his mind. The poor lighting. The struggle between serpent and Cimmerians. In the haste of battle, who could blame him if an arrow went slightly off its mark?

It would be a mistake of a handbreadth. A few fingers, perhaps.

Now or never. He couldn't let the demonic creature solve the problem for him. Besides, Wolf-Eye had an arm wedged between life and death. Hydallan and two Cruaidhi archers ran up from behind, sticking the back of the monster's body with arrows. Daol charged in at the fore, swinging short, careful swipes at the serpent's lower neck, wary of Kern's dangling feet.

There was still a chance that Wolf-Eye would free himself.

. . . and Cul had ordered . . .

It was right in front of him. Here. Now. Kern Wolf-Eye's life, balanced on the tip of Brig's arrow. Just a release away. The singing *thrum* of a released cord . . .

. . . shooting a man in the back . . .

He let slip one finger, his "safety," drawing on the cord with the pads of only two fingers now. Breathing slow and easy.

. . . cowardly . . .

"Shoot!" Daol yelled, glancing back once to see Brig frozen in his spot, one knee down in the snow and bowstring drawn back to his cheek.

He was trying to, by Crom! Loose one fatal arrow and he could go home. Kill Kern Wolf-Eye. And Daol, who would fall under the serpent's coils next, and perhaps Hydallan who ran up after his son . . .

"Be strong," he whispered, gauging the depth of his commitment. Pushing himself toward the edge. "Be strong."

Brig sighted along the shaft, both eyes open. Checked his target, waited . . . waited . . .

"Strong."

Loose.

IT HAD TO be the head.

The head, or just behind it.

Before leaping in front of Daol, Kern remembered that Gard Foehammer said the first snow serpent had been killed after Alaric Chieftain's-Son skewered its head with a pike. Sláine Longtooth's warriors also discovered that the monster was vulnerable only in certain areas, or when a coil hardened enough to wrap about a man.

Or to silver. But the one sword the small war host had scrounged up with inlaid silver was lost now in the dark and the struggle, thrown clear when the chieftain's warrior had been snatched into the monster's jaws.

Kern took the first battering strike against his shield. It was like being struck with a maul. The shock slammed through his entire body, and it felt as if his arm might be broken. Bruised to the bone, certainly.

He and Daol split around either side, swords thrusting into the snapping jaws, jumping back from its snaring coils. Several times Kern brushed aside strikes, turning them with his shield. Close enough to feel the bitter cold radiating from the demon. To see the scales sculpted into the beast's white body. Its cries of frustration and rage were far more like savage howls than a serpent's hiss, and a carrion reek rode its breath. A smell Kern remembered. Wet gangrene.

The serpent took a third man. One Kern did not know. And when he leaped to the man's defense, hoping to jar the monster hard enough to throw that warrior clear, the serpent took him as well.

A glancing blow from its head ripped his shield from numbed fingers.

His arming sword bit only through soft snow, slicing out a spray of white powder.

Then his blade suddenly struck into hardened snowflesh as the body turned rigid. The shock nearly jerked the weapon from Kern's hand. He held on, but it pulled him forward, off-balance.

He felt the thick body snare him, looping around and pulling him into the serpent's deadly embrace. It trapped his sword up against his chest, the edge of the arming sword lying in close to Kern's own neck, its point thrusting just above his right shoulder. He slipped his naked shield arm free just before a crushing weight settled around his chest, and a good thing, too, as he managed to get it up against the serpent's jaw before those glittering fangs sliced into him.

It was a contest Kern was bound to lose. His strength waned quickly, holding the monster's head away from his exposed throat and upper chest. He felt scales rasping against his bare skin. Smelled the dank, cold breath this demonic creature had brought with it from whatever frozen abyss it had been summoned.

"Shoot!" Daol yelled.

Kern couldn't tell who Daol yelled for, but he did feel his friend working with careful sword strokes down near his exposed legs. The coils shifted around his body, and he worked his sword up a scant measure. Then a bit more.

If the creature hadn't been wrapped around another

man, finishing him off first, Kern would already be dead. As it was, he could barely breathe, and he heard the pounding of his own blood in his ears. Loud and pulsing. But if he had a moment longer, just enough to work his sword free . . .

Which was when the arrow struck.

He felt the hot breath of its passing as it whispered past his ear, and a sharp stinging pain he later discovered was the shaft's broadleaf head slicing along the inside crook of his elbow. It was a shot made with Crom's own eye. Threading the needle between his neck and his arm, plunging hard into the serpent's open mouth.

Kern felt the deep shudder of pain that lanced through the monster, nearly suffocating him as the coils constricted for the span of a handful of heartbeats. A rasping cry belched foul, frostbitten air into Kern's face.

Then it loosened its deadly grip. Enough to let Kern Wolf-Eye free his sword arm, spearing the blade forward even as he began to slip free, sliding down toward the frozen ground. The point of the arming sword rammed up beneath the serpent's lower jaw, then into the upper as well, pinning its mouth closed as Kern added a third "fang" between the other two.

He fell faster, legs crumpling as he hit the ground, dropping him into an untidy pile as breath rushed back in to fill his lungs. The serpent lashed about with its head and beat at the earth with thick coils. One spasm knocked Daol back hard. Another smashed Kern flat into the hardened earth, pressing down on him with new weight as the serpent's death throes piled it up over the top of him.

Just when he thought the pounding would never stop, the serpent's weight collapsed into nothing more than a small avalanche of snow. It fell over Kern like a smothering blanket, but one he kicked himself out of quickly enough with the helping hands of Daol and Brig Tall-Wood.

Daol had a bruise darkening beneath his left eye and a trickle of blood drawing a line from the corner of his mouth down to his chin. But relief showed clearly on his face.

Brig looked as if he had taken the beating under the serpent's coils rather than Kern. Haunted eyes. A weary slump in his shoulders and unsteady on his feet. Face taut against the pain, not wanting to show weakness.

"What is it?" Kern asked, gasping for breath.

Hydallan led a handful of archers forward, surrounding the trio crouching alongside the small snowdrift. Most turned their attention back to the bulwark's crumbling defense. Arrows lanced out into the night, adding cries of pain to the howls of loss for the snow serpent.

The first of Sláine's warriors also arrived, carrying short logs and armfuls of brush, rushing forward to throw their burdens up against the icy wall. A few did not wait for the pile to grow tall enough to climb, and simply leaped for the top of the bulwark and slipped over to the other side. The growls of mastiffs and yelps of canine pain soon joined with clashing steel as the battle breached the icy wall.

"What?" Kern asked again, shuffling about in the snow, searching for his sword and shield. He found the first and abandoned the second.

Brig Tall-Wood finally shrugged. "Just don't do that again," he said.

The makeshift ramp had grown up half the side of the bulwark. Slipping his bow back over one shoulder, Brig drew his broadsword and clambered up the pile just as Reave, Nahud'r, and Ossian all pounded up, winded, blades naked in their hand.

"Don't do what?" Reave asked between laboring pants.

Daol reached over and struck a fist against the larger man's chest. "Worry about it later," he said, and shouldered him toward the woodpile.

Nahud'r and Ossian helped Kern struggle back to his feet, and the three of them followed. Hydallan, Aodh, Garret, Ehmish, and Mogh staggered in by singles and pairs, adding to the growing knot of warriors that swarmed up Sláine's ramp and dropped over to the far side with blades ready, thirsty for Vanir blood. Brig, Daol, and Reave waited, a small island in the growing sea of chaos. Old Finn dropped in behind them, cursing as he slammed a knee against the hard ground.

"Others are right behind me," he let Kern know.

Reave had already claimed another head. Ossian and Ashul split aside only for a moment, dealing death to a wounded Vanir who had thought to hide behind a snowdrift.

Another raider tried skulking along the wall of ice. But when Desagrena came over the wall farther along, falling against him, his secret was spilled. The raider threw Desa down and pounced on her, driving his sword like a huge dagger. The blade missed as Desa shifted her weight, throwing the man off her chest. He would not get a second try.

Several men had run to Desa's aid, but Ehmish was faster. He bowled over the beefy raider, using a running start against the Vanir's greater weight. As the man tumbled over and struggled back to his feet, the youth whipped his arming sword up to rake its edge along the raider's throat. The Vanir fell back. Ehmish finished the job with a sharp stab into his chest.

Desa led the panting, wide-eyed Ehmish back to the others. Reave clubbed the young man on the back. There was nothing else to be said about it, and no time if there were.

"We stay together," Kern said, his voice hard and strong. "Shields up front to worry the archers. We take them two to their one when we can. No wounded is left behind alone, but other than that we don't stop. I want that sorcerer."

His warriors growled back an agreement, and the pack charged forward with a hundred Cimmerian clansmen streaming around them in all directions.

But most of those fanned out to either side, clustered by village and clan, running the wall as they struck down beast and raider. It was Kern's small band that speared forward, out into the open, charging into the throat of the Vanir maw with Daol and Brig working each side with bow and arrow, Reave with his greatsword out in front and Kern not half a step behind.

The others ran up on their backs, forming a tight wedge that blasted through the shaky raider defenses.

The Ymirish sorcerer and his two frost-bearded companions never stood a chance. Kern's pack ran them down like snarling, savage wolves after wounded game. By then, Daol and Brig were out of arrows, replacing their bows in hand with sword hilts. The trio of Ymirish turned to fight, with two warriors obviously protecting one among their number who hesitated in the back.

With no time or strength left for another snow serpent, apparently, the sorcerer still was not quite finished. The snow erupted in between the two groups, slashing at the Cimmerians like a thousand, tiny ice-wasps, stinging and bedeviling the attacking clansmen. A few stumbled back, or off to one side, temporarily blinded.

Reave fell face forward, having borne the brunt of the assault, and Kern had no choice but to run up his backside. He and Ossian and Nahud'r were first through the small, blinding storm.

The two frost-haired warriors in front of them carried broadsword and a warhammer. Nahud'r dived at the first of the two, Ossian the second, knocking them aside so that Kern could thrust his way between them with arming sword held high and search for Grimnir's sorcerer.

The tall Ymirish held a long dagger and scourge, flailing about to keep Kern off him while holding the blade for any body-to-body charge. He stood bare-chested to the frigid air, his chest painted or tattooed with large, demonic yellow eyes. Like the false eyes of a serpent's hood. A pair of silver bracers flashed at each wrist. His snarl was feral and full of white, white teeth.

He cursed in Nordheimir, and Cimmerian. Calling down the wrath of winter and of Ymir onto Kern.

"Too late," Kern said in broken Nordheimir, drawing near.

The sorcerer's feral eyes glowed in the darkness. As, Kern knew, did his own. The other man stared openly, as shocked to recognize Kern's features as Kern had been the first time he'd met one of Grimnir's frost-men.

It was enough of an opening. Kern pushed forward, ducking the scourge's barbed tails as he stabbed with his arming sword. Its tip punched through the sorcerer's breastbone, right between the raging eyes painted to either side. He drove forward, ramming the full length of his short blade through the other man. Propping him up as the strength fled his face, his arms.

Letting him fall back only when Kern felt certain the other man had lost his grip on life.

And of the sorcerer's two wardens, it was all over by the time Kern turned back. His pack of outcasts had swarmed over them, blades rising and falling, slicing, thrusting. Staining the snowfall red. Within a handful of heartbeats, all three of the great northerners lay stretched out over the frozen ground. By the shouts behind them, around them, Kern knew the other Cimmerians all claimed similar victories.

The pass was open.

22

THE BROKEN LEG Lands were supposed to be some of the most treacherous ground in Cimmeria, and, dropping down out of the mountain pass, Kern quickly saw why. Worse than the badlands where his group of warriors had been caught in the blizzard, the high plateau country was cut apart by narrow canyons and sharp-edged bluffs that fell hundreds of feet onto piles of boulders and white-water rapids.

A good challenge for raiding and cattle-taking during the best of times.

A hard land for chasing down a Vanir war party while still in the grips of winter.

Kern's small band of warriors stood at the bridge-head of a giant stone arch that crossed one of the deeper cuts. More than a ravine, Kern decided, but not quite a canyon. Below the ledge on which the warriors waited, white water smashed among dark rocks, raging down the cut and toward the plateau. To his left and right were long, frozen cascades of ice. Snowmelt that hadn't made the long drop to the broken water.

Come spring, these frozen waterfalls would drop with a brisk chatter, brushing the sides of the cliffs with frothy white splashes. Now they gleamed dull and gray, daring any Cimmerian to try his hand at climbing down the near side.

Not that the northern side offered much more. Less ice. Steeper drops between a few narrow ledges. A few ancient dwarf pine clung stubbornly to the opposite face, gnarled and twisted as they fought for sunlight and soil within the narrow cracks splitting the pale, red rock. The stone arch crossing wasn't more than two arm's lengths wide, and slicked with snow and ice. Room enough for one man at a time to cross.

Sláine had been first, of course. Now he led the early-crossers down the opposite side of the cut, finding a few narrow switchback trails but mostly climbing down near-vertical drops with nothing better than a crack in the rock face or roots of dwarf pine for a handhold.

Kern watched, crouched at the edge of the drop-off, a stiff breeze tugging at his bone blond hair. A clump of dwarf pine grew out of some cracks in the cliff face below him. Leaning out, he'd spotted a chucker nest woven between two branches with early eggs peeking out beneath a tangle of brown moss and wet black leaves. With Reave as an anchor Kern swung a large hand down into the nest, fishing up a clutch of red-speckled eggs. Five of them.

He tossed one egg to the four nearest of his warriors and cracked the top off the fifth for himself. Slurping the milky contents straight from the shell, which tasted rather flat and slid down his throat in one quick dollop.

Dropping the shell's crumbs over the cliff, Kern ignored the shrill protests of the chuckers, which had returned to find their nest plundered. As still as a craggy rock thrust from the cliff side, he counted the men and women spread out along the opposite face, the handful currently traipsing over the arch ducking low beneath the wind, then estimated the numbers still waiting for their turn to cross.

"Fewer," he said aloud.

A hundred. Maybe a few dozen more.

In the afterglow of victory, and without the constant threat of a Vanir attack, Sláine Longtooth had lost some of his control over the small war host not long after crossing the wintered pass. Around every outcropping, over every sharp-edged ridge, Kern noticed more Cimmerian warriors slipping away in tight knots and old allegiances.

Forgetting the common need that brought them together back in Cruaidh. Looking toward their own honor and the needs of their home villages first as the custom of the bloody spear lost its sway.

"Of course they do," Aodh said when Kern remarked on it. The older man stood brazenly at the edge of the cliff's plunge, letting the wind toy with his short, ragged-cut hair and the hem of his heavy winter kilt. He reached up to stroke the salt-and-pepper moustache he liked so much, now being joined by salt-and-pepper stubble from the beard growing in. "So did we."

Several of the others nodded. Reave and Desa. Garret. Brig Tall-Wood stood mute.

Ossian hawked and spit over the edge, then nodded up the cleft where a trio of Cimmerian warriors had split away from the main group and worked their way in another direction. "Sláine promises them revenge for the Vanir raids. What they needs is cattle, and wives. And blue iron."

The Taurin still scraped his head clean every morning, but Kern noticed that he had braided a few silver rings into his long goat's beard. Taken from fingers of the Vanir dead back inside the pass. Nahud'r wore a new cloak, as did Mogh and Doon. Ehmish, too, had claimed spoils from the battle, tying a silver-chased broadsword over his narrow shoulders.

Not even Kern had been immune. As well as the bracers, taken off the wrists of the dead sorcerer, he'd found a pair of metal greaves backed by good mountain goat wool. Anything to guard against the inevitable sword's edge.

Everyone wanted something.

"What is it *you* really want, Ossian? A few more trinkets to take home? Cattle for your chieftain?"

Ossian paused a moment, then, "For my father," he admitted for the first time.

Kin, easily, Kern had figured. But father and son? Ossian had left behind his clan, and possibly his claim on the chieftain's position once his father died. Likely he'd meant every word back in Taur, that it was a quest worth chasing for its own sake. But the personal reason . . .

"Why? What draws you on with us, then?"

The warrior gave it a moment of serious thought, looking out over the deadly drop. His smile, when it came, was grim and hungry at the same time. Like a starving wolf moving in at his prey. "A story worth telling around a campfire," he said at last.

Desa laughed. "In your old age?" she asked, not bothering to hide her mocking tones. "None of us will live that long."

Probably true. Wallach Graybeard and Hydallan were unusual for their collection of gray hairs and time-weathered faces. And in larger villages, Old Finn would have been looked upon as a respected elder to have survived so many years and so many battles. Larger villages with more food to afford such a luxury.

If Finn still harbored a grudge over the expulsion, it didn't tell on his face. "At my age, most men are already dead. So I figure I'm ahead on that score. I'll settle for my next campfire."

For his part, Ossian simply shrugged aside the prospect of violent death. His leg was bandaged heavily around the knee where a sword slash had laid it open down to the bone; but he hadn't let it slow him, or the group, down. "Something my sons will remember then," he said. "And tell to their sons."

Mogh, with the dour outlook Kern recognized as the man's habit, simply shook his head. "It will be told as a tale of Conan if anything."

The assertion made Daol laugh and even brought a thin smile to Kern's face as well. There could be worse endings, he supposed, than being added to the legends of Conan. Rising, stepping back from the edge of the cliff, he clapped Ossian on the back and steered the other man toward the bridgehead.

"Like the time Conan guested at Taur," he said, "and the Vanir came, led by a frost-bearded giant of a northern man. Conan led the charge from the bulwark gate, his broadsword striking out to the left and right, driving the Vanir before him."

Ossian *had* been there at the fore, in fact, cleaving his way toward the Ymirish who had escaped before the Taurin and Guadic warriors could fall on him together, dragging him down.

Kern left out his own contribution to that battle, of course. Conan rarely needed help.

But Ossian simply looked back with a measure of reluctant envy. "More like Conan's battle at the Pass of Blood, where he beat the Vanir in a sled-bound charge at their icy palisade walls, then wrestled the demonic serpent summoned by a Ymirish sorcerer."

Startled by the praise, Kern nearly slipped as he put his first foot on the stone arch. Before being outcast, his greatest adventure had been fending off young bucks from other villages and clans eager to make a name for themselves without inviting a long-standing feud. It seemed wrong for Ossian to twist events around in such a way, simplifying them to make it sound impressive. More impressive than it had actually been, when Kern had simply been part of the charge and had needed saving from the monstrous snow serpent. Daol and Hydallan and Brig Tall-Wood especially had been instrumental in that.

As he had determined earlier, Conan rarely needed help.

But Reave found the idea particularly amusing. "I like it," he said, following Nahud'r and Kern and Ossian onto the stone arch. He laughed a gut-splitting roar that carried into the deep cut as a long, drawn-out echo. A few warriors up ahead glanced back with frowns darkening their craggy faces, but no one was going to make an issue of it with a large man carrying a Cimmerian greatsword.

Especially while they traversed a slippery ledge over a raging river.

Reave didn't seem to notice. He stomped along with all the determination and confidence he brought to most situations. "Conan of Gaud," he said. "Hey, Nahud'r. What can you do with *that?*"

The Shemite walked with his sword out and gripped in both hands, one on the hilt and the other pinching the end of the scimitar's great, sweeping blade. He held it flat before him, using it as a kind of counterbalance to keep himself level. The trailing ends of the cloth he wrapped about his head and lower face fluttered in the breeze, pulled over his right shoulder.

"Conan and his adventure with snow serpent of Ymirish? When snow, it stuck so thick to Conan's hair he look blond? A great sled he constructed, able to hold ten men. Ten of best men that Cruaidh provide. He pull it himself, straining against harness to deliver warriors to foot of palisade of ice."

To hear Nahud'r retell the battle—a battle Kern had been in only two days before—it might as well have been a different land and a different time. The ice-rimed bulwark grew to twelve feet in height, formed by a sorcery similar to that which would be used to create the great snow demon. Most men, gazing into the palisade's thick depth, lost their souls to the deep, blue ice.

Putting one foot in front of the other, almost careless of the hundred-foot drop into a river of crashing water and black, sharp rocks, Nahud'r spun the tale out as easily as any he had told of Conan as warrior or Conan as king. Kern shook his head, following the tale and the arch of stone, not realizing until he reached the far side that he had never once looked down. Never once worried for the drop.

He also noticed on the far side how a few of the other warriors, from Cruaidh and its surrounding farmsteads, looked at him, as if they suddenly believed the new tale of what had happened. The fantastic battle with the serpent lasted much longer, and involved a great deal more swordplay in its retelling. And there was no saving arrow to strike the first blow.

There was only Conan, testing his strength against the demon-summoned creature.

Reave stomped off the arch, followed by Daol and Ossian. All three smiled grimly, and nodded, as if playing the new tale through their minds and finding it worthy. Brig looked over at Kern, and offered a hesitant shrug.

"That's not the way it happened," Kern said to the young Tall-Wood.

Brig shrugged again. "That will hardly matter around the campfires tonight."

No, it wouldn't. And the story would change and grow with any retelling. And to be honest, none of that mattered very much to Kern. He sought answers, not the trappings of a legend. Especially the legends of Conan. Not for himself. Because there was one thing the stories and tall tales had in common that he wanted no part of.

That in the end, most everyone, including the great Cimmerian's friends, often died.

IF KERN NEEDED a reminder of the potential cost of his pursuit of the Vanir raiders, it was made very apparent the next day as the war host traipsed farther out of the mountains and saw signs of a land under siege.

The day dawned with a bright, cold sun peering down between breaks in the cloud cover. Glimpses of blue sky carried the hint of a possible spring and raised a lot of spirits, including Kern's own, for a time. Broken ground sliced by deep cuts gave way to wide, snow-covered bluffs overlooking deep glens and chattering rivers. The war host spread out in a long line as they stepped up their pace, eating up ground with long strides and frequent runs for leagues at a time. There were some scattered marching chants, and the warriors shared charcoal sticks as they rubbed eyeblack on their cheekbones to cut down on the snow glare.

The chants died away when, that morning, they passed two farmsteads burned down to their foundations and the dry pits plundered.

Nothing lived. In a custom more Cimmerian than Nordheim, the heads of the families had been left outside on poles. There were no cattle, and no chicks left scratching beneath the trees. Bones and ruined hides and feathers were all that was left to be scavenged.

"A plague of locusts," Nahud'r whispered.

No idea what locusts were, Kern nodded nonetheless. The name sounded right. Harsh and mean.

Soon it became a common sight to see a slaughter post set up near trailside, with pieces of cattle carcass or sheep strung up for quick-and-dirty butchering. Midday, they ran through what remained of a small village. The Vanir raiders had laid it to waste, with huts and homes battered down or burned. The chieftain's lodge still stood on a tall mound at the center of the destroyed village, which seemed unusual until Sláine Longtooth sent men to look inside. They came back stone-faced, with new fury burning in their eyes.

The Cruaidhi chieftain ordered every man and woman through the lodge then, and Kern led his people forward when it came time for their turn. The lodge smelled of death. It hit Kern before he ever set foot near the thick oak doors. The stink of rotted flesh and open bowels. It left a rancid taste at the back of his throat.

Breathing shallowly, Kern ducked in through the door with Desagrena and Ehmish. The young man turned and fled without much more than a glance, fighting for his pride not to lose what he had swallowed at his last meal. Desa stared a good long while, her pinched face blank to what she was feeling inside. When she left, she drew her dagger and sliced a shallow cut across her palm, then smeared it against the door of the lodge as a sign that someone, at least, mourned what had happened there.

Bodies had been decapitated, and stacked like cordwood against the walls. Thrown there naked, or wearing only the tattered rags not worth taking as plunder. Several dozen. Their heads had been tied into the rafters by their hair or spiked there through an ear. Men and women. Youths. Children.

Everyone but the village chieftain, Kern guessed, if that was the brawny man pinned to the far wall with a spear through his gut and daggers driven through both shoulders and deep into the wood behind.

The condition of the bodies told Kern that this had happened some time ago. But though smaller than the Cruaidh, the destruction visited on this village was more severe. It spoke of more than punishment, even. It felt personal.

And Kern had no doubt that the Nordheim war leader, Grimnir, had been there to see it done.

23

THE WAR HOST found a few stray cattle as they traveled farther into the new territory and left behind the broken ground for tall stands of scale-barked pine and secluded glens. Enough to keep them well fed, and after the ruins they had visited there was no talk of claiming the cattle and simply heading back to Conall Valley.

Kern had no desire to turn back now, regardless. He had vowed to see it through to the end, wherever that took him. And the others never once questioned him.

Sláine Longtooth split strong forces out from his main army, spreading them out in several directions while his main army moved north and west toward the old mines near Clan Conarch. It was a dangerous decision to make among the clansfolk, but a necessary one if they wanted to strike at Grimnir's trail as soon as possible. Kern's small band wasn't told to go or to stay. Sláine seemed willing to let Kern lead them where he might. After a moment of thought, he pushed his peo-

ple ahead of the main army as a vanguard force, wanting to see what was ahead of them, to plan as necessary
for whatever that might be.

Fortunately, it wasn't all death and desolation. The
raider presence was known to be much stronger in the
northwest because this was the path they took to infest
the rest of Cimmeria with their marauding bands. But
many villages of the Broken Leg Lands continued to
survive and even thrive in the shadow of Grimnir's
looming presence. Which surprised Kern, in a way. He
had begun to expect they would find nothing but ruins
and a few rumors of survivors eking out an existence as
high up into the snow line as they could hide.

Before the end of that day, though, they came upon
a second village, one protected by a tall timber palisade and a number of thinly disguised pitfalls. There
were men and women moving behind the walls, Kern
felt certain. He sensed the eyes upon him and his warriors. But no one called out to them with a greeting or
challenge, and Reave's bellowed hails went unanswered.

Hydallan and Old Finn, Kern saw, kept an uneasy eye
on a nearby bluff that overlooked the shaded glen and the
fortified village. "What?" he asked the elder warriors.

Both men looked to each other, then to Kern. "Can't
say for certain," Finn said for the both of them. "If'n it
were me, though, I'd have archers or spearmen up on
that ridge. Best way to know someone's coming."

Kern scrounged a piece of overcooked meat from a
sack tied at his belt and chewed it thoughtfully for a
moment. The flavor was dark and smoky, and the flesh
tough between his teeth. That would make it last. He
nodded at the wall.

"Daol and Ehmish. See if they'll let you approach."

Ehmish frowned. "Why us?" he asked.

Desa did not let Kern answer. "Because Daol is too

quick to be shot with an arrow," she said, "and you're too skinny to waste an arrow on. Now go!"

A few of the men laughed at Ehmish's bruised expression, but Kern let it ride. The young had no luxury anymore for childish arguments. He'd have to come to understand that.

Whether he did or did not, there was no misunderstanding the arrow that came sailing out from behind the palisade. It landed about ten paces short of the two before they had closed half the distance to the palisade walls. Daol said something Kern could not quite catch, and both he and Ehmish beat a hasty retreat.

There was no laughing at the younger man this time. Daol walked right up to Kern, shrugged. "Nay," was all he said.

Still no one had shown themselves. Not even when sighting the arrow shot. This village was clear in its intention to stay isolated. Kern shrugged his frustration aside.

"Then we leave them for Sláine Chieftain, though I doubt he'll spend much time here either. Let's hope that the next village isn't jumping at shadows as well."

But they wouldn't find another village that day, and camp that night was very quiet. Aodh, given first watch, jumped at several noises that turned out to be little more than the wind rubbing some nearby branches together, or dropping a late cone out of a pine tree. After some grumbling and a few good-natured threats, everyone settled down into their bedrolls or crouched at the small fire pit with its dying embers.

Brig drew his blanket over his shoulders, like a second cloak, and crowded in between Desa and Ossian. He kept glancing across the pit at Kern, who stared back with a calm patience while he threw tiny twigs onto the coals. After a moment, one of the twigs would burst into fire and cast a flickering light around the small gathering. The guttering flame glinted off the rings in Ossian's beard and also shone in the bright whites of Nahud'r's eyes.

There was no story that night and very little talk. Ossian dug some mint leaves out of his pack and crushed them into water heated over the embers, drinking a pale tea. Kern chewed on the crust of some journeybread, hoarded from the supplies they had taken on at Cruaidh.

"Something," Brig began, then lapsed into silence again. Thinking through what he wanted to say. "You asked Ossian yestermorn, about what he wanted."

Kern nodded. "I did." He paused. "And you want to know now what *I* want from all this, Brig Tall-Wood? My path hasn't changed since Taur. I am looking for answers."

Answers as to who he was, and where he was likely to find a life now that Gaud had turned him away.

"Do you think you will find any?"

"Nay. Not really. I think I have decided that my father was a northerner, no matter how much I might wish otherwise. But I didn't need to force the Pass of Blood to discover that." Another twig. Another bright flare. "I knew it in the shadow of the Snowy River country."

"Then why?"

Kern felt the eyes on him. Ehmish hovering at the edge of the fire. Ossian and Desa across from him. Nahud'r on his right. This was important to more than just Brig, apparently. But with the young Tall-Wood, there seemed to be something personal driving his question. Something dark, which Kern had suspected from the strange looks he caught on Brig's face from time to time.

Was he still Cul's man? Could Kern ever really trust him?

"I look at what we have accomplished together," he

said, "and it amazes me. Tomorrow is another day we will spend outside of the clan. Without a home. We can spend it squatting in a cave and waiting out the winter, or running south for the lands beyond Crom's favor. Or we can spend it *doing* something. I prefer to *do*, rather than hiding or running." He thought about that a moment, and nodded to himself.

It was as good an answer as any.

"And if you find what you are looking for?" Brig asked. "What then? Try to go back? Challenge Cul's decision . . . challenge him as chieftain now that you have proven your own worth?"

Desa shifted as if readying herself to launch at Tall-Wood. Something in his tone, both dangerous and challenging. Kern heard it as well. Heard it, and knew Brig touched a deep, sore spot.

"What about you?" he asked. "Would you go home?" He saw the younger man's hesitation and the guarded look that shielded his eyes all of a sudden. "If there was the one thing you could look at and say, *There. That is it for me.* Would you then go back to Gaud?"

Brig stood abruptly. The younger man was not small, as wide across the shoulders as his brother or any man in the small band of warriors save perhaps Reave. Kern readied himself for an attack or a challenge. Whatever ate away at Brig Tall-Wood was very close to the surface. Kern couldn't say why he felt it was so, but his instincts warned him to be wary.

"That is the question, isn't it?" And surprising Kern, he stepped back from the fire and the small group, pulling away once again. Brig found a piece of cleared ground and rolled himself into his blanket and cloak for the night.

Another twig flared brightly for a moment, and Kern stared at the others in turn as each one drifted away for their bedrolls and what sleep they could grab before morning. Only Aodh remained up, on watch, circling at the edge of camp and decidedly not looking at Kern until the outcast leader rose for his own roll of felt and the blankets of his bedroll.

Then Aodh stopped and waved Kern over.

He thought that Aodh might want to make some comment on Brig. Instead, the other man tugged at his long moustache, and whispered, "Listen."

"More branches?" Kern asked, in no mood for another wild chase into the night.

But he closed his eyes anyway and reached out for the night with his other senses. The smell of the campfire was down to a weak telltale of ash and smoke. The night air tasted of snow, but the scattered clouds made a fresh fall unlikely. But other than a few hissing pops from the embers and some loud snores as Reave sucked at the cold, crisp air, Kern heard nothing.

Until it moved again. A shuffling, careful step, then a pause.

And then another hesitant step.

Aodh nodded out into the dark. "There," he said, pointing with his chin.

It took Kern's eyes a moment to find the shadow as it moved carefully among the nearby trees. A glint of moonlight fell through the broken clouds, and he caught an amber glare from two small yellow coals.

"Not possible," Kern breathed out softly. Except that it was. Frostpaw. "He chased us over that stone arch?"

He had, or found another way, and had struck Kern's trail again on this side of the valley Teeth. That spoke of more than a desire for food. More than a need for basic survival. It bordered on loyalty, or at least a need for kinship.

"We all have our reasons," Aodh said, answering the unasked question. "And Brig can't be any more dangerous than reining in a starving dire wolf."

Kern was not so certain of that. The wolf had attacked him out of hunger and need. The desperations eating away at Brig Tall-Wood, Kern felt certain, were not so easy to define. And they bore careful watch. Because one should never turn their back on a wild animal.

Another good reason that Kern had watches through the night, and none of them would be Brig Tall-Wood.

Regardless, the night passed without further incident. Kern rolled out of his felt blanket at first light, greeting the overcast day with a few stretches to work the kinks and the deep cold out of his muscles. Others joined him, Ossian and Wallach, and while they began to sweat freely so fast, the chill of winter's touch faded slowly with him.

Frostpaw made two appearances while the war party broke camp, hovering farther back now that light betrayed the wolf's position. Mogh was the first to remark on it, though certainly not the first to notice.

"That ain't normal," he said, with a glower in the wolf's direction. As if startled by the glance, the wolf turned and bolted for the cover of some tall pine.

"What is these days?" Kern asked. Settling his shield over one shoulder and his pack over another, he nodded Daol and Hydallan ahead of him, then struck out again for the long day's hike.

Midday found two more burned farmsteads, and another the raiders had somehow missed. It stood farther back from the trail, granted, and was partially hidden behind a stand of thorny acacia. No clansmen, though, and no livestock. There were signs of recent life, tracks in the snow and ashes on the hearth, but nothing else.

"Dead or fled," Desa said.

Garret nodded. "Or hiding nearby. We could search for 'em."

"We move on," Kern decided. "Where there are farms, there will be a village nearby."

He proved to be right. Just the other side of the next bluff, in fact, where a stream they chanced across splashed quickly down a narrow cut, then wound underside of a mammoth cliff overhang. The stone of the overhang was wet black streaked with rusts and yellows, and appeared alive with smoke. It dripped and splashed a constant light rain over ground suddenly devoid of snow, with several nearby fields sprouting enough greens that one might think for a second that spring had broken through in an eye blink.

The air smelled of minerals and metal. Sulfurous. Not so bad as rotten eggs, but heavy enough to burn inside Kern's sinuses.

Ossian called it first. He recognized the scent. "Hot springs," he said.

Not smoke, then, but steam. Warming the air with a moist, mineral touch that lay over the village like a blanket. The stream pooled in several places before it bent wide around the first of the visible huts and the charred ruins where others had once stood. It continued past palisade walls, behind which more steam rose no doubt from more hidden hot springs.

Because of their location or simply from what they had to protect, these people had been far more industrious in their defense. Digging enough rock out of the nearby bluff face to build a thick wall, on top of which they had planted sharpened timbers lashed together with bands of metal as well as leather ties. With the palisade joining on both ends to a steep rock face, it would take a large raiding party to even think of cracking such a defense.

Clearly the local clansmen had learned a great deal, caught between marauding Picts from the lowlands and Vanir from the north.

Kern pushed Daol ahead to find a good path down among the lower hills. Ehmish and Hydallan went with him. It was on a lower ridge where Ehmish discovered a funeral mound of dead bodies, half-buried in snow and left to rot. The aftermath of a large battle that had taken place the previous summer, certainly. They were Picts mostly. Swarthy skin gone slightly gray with death. Bodies painted in tribal patterns, and wearing little else but the loincloths favored by the lowland savages. A few heads had been set up on pikes, as trophies or as warnings. Or both.

Kern saw that there were quite a few Vanir heads near the end of the line. In fact, one could see in the scattered death masks where the Picts had stopped their late-summer attacks and the Vanir raiders had stepped up their own. The freshest heads were all northerners, taken over the long winter as raiders pushed for food and shelter and the slaves they needed to work their northern mines.

There was even a fairly recent Ymirish, with frost blond beard and hair. His yellow eyes stared blankly now, but Kern imagined he still saw a primal rage glinting in them.

Down in the glen, an alarm bell rang as someone finally sighted Kern's small band. Cimmerian clansfolk ran to front their wall, grabbing up whatever weapons were close by and waiting to see what manner of invader had come at them. They didn't hide from the challenge as had the previous village. They seemed to welcome it, in fact.

Kern did not rush into the situation. He circled his people around, letting them be seen, looking for a good path of approach while the clan chieftain no doubt summoned his elders and his best warriors. Give them time to feel safe, Kern hoped, and they would be less apt to strike out of fear or habit.

It worked. When Kern's men stayed out of bowshot, the local chieftain sent out a small band of warriors to challenge them directly. Faces carried the same deep-lined, craggy look that Reave had gotten from his mother, a native of Clan Conarch. Any one of them might be a distant relation of the tall Gaudic warrior. Kern saw more than one of his warriors frown in Reave's direction, but they were quick glances, with eyes snapping back to the fore right quick and hands never far from the grasp of weapons. These did not look the part of beaten men and women. They carried their heads up and their eyes blazed a fierce challenge.

The single woman in the group was as tall and strapping as any of the men, and she wore a feral snarl on her lips that reminded Kern, in a way, of the smaller but no less fierce Desagrena.

"Valleymen," the tall woman said, in about the same way one would spit out a piece of gristly meat.

She had blue eyes the dark, shaded color of an autumn twilight, and her raven-glistening hair was tied up in a knot on top of her head. She carried a spear in one hand and a war sword across her back. Her frown built up in slow measure, wrinkling in the corners of her eyes first, and then in the thin, flat line of her mouth.

"But not more Cruaidhi," she said. "Not Clan Maugh either."

Which gave Kern some idea of the warriors loosed in the Broken Leg Lands who had already passed this direction.

"You are the wolf-eyed one," she said at last, and the tip of her spear dropped a fraction. "I am Ros-Crana. I thought the story hard to believe, a Ymirish who is not of Nordheim and Grimnir's personal worshippers. You are of Gaud?"

"We are," Kern admitted, slightly taken aback by what this woman already knew. And also that the men obviously deferred to her. Crom's ancient blessing on Cimmeria gave many women as great a strength as the men, but few followed the warrior's path intentionally. "Of Gaud and of Taur, and lands to the south," he said, giving Nahud'r a nod.

Ros-Crana dropped the spear to her side, holding it loosely now. Kern had no doubt that she could whip it back to a guarded position in less than a heartbeat. "Then you may approach and speak with Narach Chieftain, who has also heard of you."

Kern eyed the well-manned defenses with a wary glance. "Strong walls and many tall warriors," he said by way of compliment. "I would ask your chieftain to meet me outside of his keep." Well outside of those walls, in fact.

But she bridled at this, obviously taking a measure of offense. "My word is your safety, Wolf-Eye. If it is not good enough for you, turn around and go back to your valley. Otherwise, you may advance as far as the gate." She held her spear up across her body in a warding gesture. "But you will not be allowed inside the walls."

There was something important in that distinction, to her at least. Kern thought to ask why, but there was no need. She told him in her next breath.

"If Grimnir comes for you here, we will not stand between you."

24

THE SUN WAS setting into the Pictish wilderness in the near west when Kern brought Sláine Longtooth back to the village. There were no shadows stretched over the ground, not with winter clouds filtering the sun's light to a stark overhead gray, but there was no mistaking the cold touch of coming twilight.

Clansfolk continued their work in and around the glen. If anything, their pace seemed to increase as dark approached. Animals were brought in from a day of sparse forage, and always there were homes to rebuild. A few women continued to tend fields of early greens that survived under the steaming rain falling off the cliff overhang. A line of tall youths packed carrying straps of sharp, head-sized rocks through the palisade, adding to a large pile that could be glimpsed through the narrow gate, and smaller children used flat-edged stones to scrape the outline of new pitfalls into the ground.

Longtooth nodded his approval at the industrious work. "What was its name again?" he asked.

"Callaugh," Kern reminded the elder man. Kern had also learned that it was the area's strongpoint. "Much as Cruaidh is the stopgap for any force coming into Conall's Valley through the Pass of Blood, any large war host moving north must pass within a half day's travel of here."

Its location, and its hot springs steaming against the bluff, made it an important village to Clan Conarch. Important enough for the Vanir to test its walls regularly. The funeral mounds (there had been more than just the one) and several dozen Vanir heads on pikes proved to Kern that the raiders had had no easy time of it.

Also, that these Callaughnan warriors were not to be taken lightly.

Sláine Longtooth agreed. But he'd also had no choice but to follow behind Kern as he led the core of his small army north.

With Ros-Crana and Narach Chieftain already aware of their presence, Kern had seen immediately that the Cruaidhi chieftain must strike a bargain with Callaugh or risk an attack from behind even as he hunted the Vanir. At his suggestion the two chieftains agreed to a meeting under the walls of Callaugh's keep. Longtooth was allowed a guard of no more than two fists of men. Ten in all. All weapons would be truce-bonded. Sword and dagger hilts tied to sheaths or belts with a strong leather cord. Bows unstrung. Spearpoints wrapped in a leather sheath.

Kern cinched his arming sword in place with a strong knot. He'd already been under those walls once. He knew it would not do to anger Callaugh further in the face of what Sláine Longtooth was likely to demand.

A few clansmen hauling in armfuls of wood looked

over at their arrival, faces dark, craggy, and glowering. Gard Foehammer glanced left then right as he rode at his chieftain's side, carrying a bearing spear with Clan Cruaidh's fox-tail totem on it.

"Sure and this is a good idea?" he asked out of the side of his mouth.

Kern hoped, but couldn't say for certain.

The sulfurous steam that wafted over the village made most clansfolk into shadows and could hide any number of plans to ambush the small envoy. But it simply wasn't in the nature of most Cimmerians to strike against their word. If they had to kill, they killed openly. And why lie at all? Crom had gifted them the strength to face the truth.

Still it was just good precaution that Longtooth directed Gard to carry the bearing spear. Kern knew from testing the other man's ability with a war pike, Gard could strip the sheath of his spear tip (or simply thrust through it) in less than a heartbeat. If things went badly, Clan Cruaidh would not fall without drawing blood.

Ros-Crana met them at the lower slope with a trio of warriors also carrying sheathed long spears and bonded broadswords. Longtooth and Foehammer studied her with something approaching cautious respect. After only a few minutes in her company, Kern had not been so surprised to learn that she was war leader for the village. Narach Chieftain, as it turned out, was her younger brother.

This was information he had passed along, of course.

Ros-Crana did not waste time, gesturing the small party, which included Kern as well as Daol, Reave, Desa, and Ossian, ahead of her. Sláine Chieftain had brought four of his own strongest warriors. It made for a good-sized force.

Coming under the shadow of the fortified walls,

Kern saw their construction make an impression on
Sláine Longtooth equal to the one it had first made on
him. Not only was the rock base a good three arm's
lengths thick, it was cemented together with "mud and
mill-crushed stone, and resists even the best battering
ram our own warriors could test against it." Ros-
Crana hadn't bothered hiding her savage grin. Rising
through the middle of the wall, the timber palisade was
held together with sharp spikes as well as being banded
in metal at two different heights. The sharpened top of
every fifth pole was missing, leaving a murder-hole
where an archer could lean out for a quick bowshot, or
for a strong man to pitch a rock down on the heads of
any attackers.

The wall sealed off the glen's two gentle slopes, relying on the steep bluff face to prevent a massed attack
otherwise. There was room enough for the local cattle
herd and fowl to shelter inside the keep, and lean-tos
for fodder and emergency shelter. Not every home
could be squeezed into such a space, however, and
leave room. There were several dozen wattle-and-daub
huts and a few timber-constructed great homes clustered together outside the palisade in small, isolated
neighborhoods with clear, open space in between them.

Grouped by family or friendships was Kern's guess.
With the wide spaces in between to form a stretch of
murder ground—any raiders who took one section of
the village would have to cross through that open area
to reach a second neighborhood.

Clearly, this idea had been of concern in the past.
The evidence of Vanir raids was clear. Newly raised
shacks and huts sat next to the burned-out husks of
older construction. Stone walls with fresh mud cement
replaced portions of walls torn down under duress.
Burned and brittle twigs cracked underfoot.

The valley clansfolk marched past a round-walled
hut made of quarried stone. Three men were busy

rethatching its roof, tying bundles of rushes and hay in place with bark-weave rope. A simple enough task to bother three grown men. Kern saw at once how these warriors could form a bottleneck behind him, trapping the small delegation. Each man, he noticed, had a sword tied to his belt. Though they didn't look too nervous or too worried, yet, with the valley clansfolk accompanied by Ros-Crana.

The six warriors guarding Narach Chieftain glared back with a great deal more suspicion.

The small Callaughnan party waited within bowshot of the palisade walls, within a circle of flame-bearing torches. Two camp stools had been set out at the center of the arena. Next to one a bearing spear had been planted in the ground, decorated with strips of blue and gray cloth and the skull of a mountain lion, which was Clan Conarch's totem. An elderly man with a white cast smearing one eye and white hairs coming in thick over his temples walked around the cleared circle, sprinkling powder from a muslin sack over every torch. The flames burned blue for a moment, then green. Then settled into a tinted yellow that burned away more of the lingering wisps of steam and cast a cleaner, brighter light than any normal brand. His task accomplished, the shaman stepped to his chieftain's side.

If a person hadn't known better, or hadn't seen the elder man set at a task rather than calmly waiting, that person might have assumed the elder man was chieftain over Callaugh rather than Narach's shaman. In fact, Narach Chieftain was much younger than any of his warriors. Younger than Daol or very close of an age. But he obviously commanded the respect of the older and larger warriors, which was not to say the younger man was small. Not of Reave's height and oxlike shoulders, but easily several fingers taller than Kern and built for his stature. He had a young man's casual grace and the lean muscles of a veteran warrior. His face held deep lines, his features craggy as were so many clansmen of Clan Conarch and the northwest region.

It made him look older than his years, though his eyes were as clear and bright as any Kern had ever seen.

"So you are the one they speak of," Narach had said at their first meeting, crossing arms over a thick chest bared to the cold. A cape of spotted mountain lion fur richly trimmed in white fox had hung from his neck and over both shoulders, as it did again.

"That would depend on what they say," Kern had answered carefully. Assuming nothing but the tallest tales had made it there ahead of them.

It was the shaman who responded. "The wolf-eyed outcast from Gaud, who hunts the Ymirish and challenges Grimnir himself. They say you have already defeated a snow serpent and one of the yellow-eyed sorcerers of the north."

"Mostly," Kern admitted. Modesty had not prevented him from agreeing to the basic truths. "Though the details are exaggerated I am certain."

Narach shrugged. "I would agree, if our tales had come from others among the valleymen who have stopped by here and traded Vanir weapons for food. But we first had these stories from captured Vanir." The chieftain nodded to one of his other men. "Ask Colin."

"Is true," a horse-faced warrior agreed with his chieftain. "We ambushed a small band coming back over the Pass of Blood a week ago. The Ymirish, he escaped us in a blizzard that quickly rolled eastward. We traded quick deaths to the raiders we captured in exchange for news out of the valley."

Meaning they tortured the Vanir, in repayment for several years of cruelty and murder, and finally cut their throats when they had heard enough.

Cimmerian justice wasn't easy, but it could be merciful. After a fashion.

Sláine Longtooth heard all of this as well, while he sat in one of two camp chairs brought out for the chieftains. Nothing more than a thick flat of leather stretched over the spread limbs of a tripod, it allowed the two men to sit while their warriors and advisors stood behind. Gard Foehammer stood closest, bearing spear holding the fox's tail over Longtooth's shoulder. Sláine traded what sounded to Kern like mostly accurate information concerning the destruction of Cruaidh.

Kern and his people sat through the retelling of both stories, quiet and concerned for where the talks might lead.

Narach nodded Colin back into line. "We learned that several raiding parties were ambushed this side of the Snowy River country, and that this Ymirish saw defeat at the village of Taur. We did not believe half of what he said, claiming that several dozen villages all rallied against them. But to admit defeat was enough."

It was Longtooth who first looked to Kern.

"So the Ymirish you fought against at Taur still lives. And he did not join in the assault on Cruaidh."

Kern had come to the same conclusion. "Though he must have passed Grimnir's war party on his path back to the Broken Leg Lands."

"Sent back in disgrace?" Ros-Crana asked of those who had fought against him.

Desa shook her head, oily locks swaying over her eyes. "An impressive fighter, that one. A head again taller than the one Kern described leading the raiders we met near the Pass of Noose. You do not set aside such a man so easily." For some reason, this last comment made Reave shift about uncomfortably.

Ros-Crana frowned, doubtful. But Kern considered it. Accepting a skin passed over to him from Ros-Crana, he took a swig. Dark ale, thick enough to stand a dagger in. He nearly choked on the strong drink, expecting something much lighter. He coughed back a gasp, feeling the alcohol burn up into his sinuses. A strong aftertaste of root ginger, added to a cask after brewing, clung to his tongue. He washed it away with a second draught. Then a third. Passed the skin along to Reave.

"I have to agree," he finally answered. "There must be another answer here." He frowned, remembering. "If Ossian had not led forward the Taurin fighters, and we hadn't outnumbered him two to his one . . ."

"If, if, if." Longtooth waved a hand, his patience wearing thin. "We all know now what *has* happened. What we do next, I care about."

"You have done enough. Grimnir's wrath will come swiftly." Narach glanced at the nearby cliffs, as if expecting the northern warlord to suddenly appear. When he turned his attention back to Longtooth, his eyes hardened. "Keep this one nearby"—he nodded at Kern—"and the demon will find you."

It was the second time they had implied a personal grudge between Kern and the legendary war leader. Sláine Longtooth scoffed. "This Grimnir may be a savage fighter, but he is no god, to know everything that has happened."

"He will know of the defeat you handed his followers in the Pass," Narach bit back quickly. "That will be enough."

Many Vanir had staggered west ahead of Longtooth's war host. Not everyone was stopped. A few stragglers always slipped past. One raiding party had been too large to risk intercepting, though it hurt Narach to watch a slave line of twenty clansmen being hauled north.

"Twenty?" Longtooth growled. If they had swarmed down from the mountains, likely the slave line was made up from many of his people. "I would not leave one man in the hands of those animals."

"That is an easy decision for you to make, Sláine

Chieftain." Ros-Crana balled her large hands into raw-boned fists. "Would you have still tried forcing the Pass of Blood, knowing now what Grimnir would visit on Cruaidh?"

"No one knows the future," Kern said, seeing Long-tooth's fury building around a toothy snarl. "It does no one any good to worry about what might have been. It simply is."

"It was not an easy decision," Narach promised, bridling at the implied rebuke to his honor. "There were risks I had to weigh against the good of the clan."

The Callaughnan shaman nodded slowly at his chieftain's words. "They had a sorcerer," he said. "You can tell by the dark clouds that lower themselves in the sky when they pass. Killing one of these men always invites the wrath of Grimnir."

Which was why Kern was supposedly a marked man. He had been the one to thrust a sword through a sorcerer's heart in the pass. The men of Callaugh knew of that as well.

"How?" Sláine Longtooth asked, biting off the word with a soured expression. Though Kern already had it reasoned out. And he was mostly right.

"Warriors from Clan Maugh passed by yester-morn." Ros-Crana spoke through clenched teeth. "They challenged for a small treasure of blue-iron weapons." And Narach had put them up against some silver Vanir bracers and a torc with a single, large ruby set in the center. Spoils from the battle for the pass. "The Snowy River warriors put down two of my best, one of them for good."

They had also told a fascinating tale of Kern's battle against the snow serpent that sounded a great deal like the one Nahud'r had spun out while walking over the stone arch two days before.

"No matter." Longtooth dismissed the tale and the Callaughnan's caution all at once. "We hunt the Vanir, as they have hunted us for two years and more. If Grimnir wishes to come out from under the cover of his blizzard, we will see how mortal he truly is."

"I cannot help you there. I have never come up against him myself." Narach's craggy face hardened into a dark mask. Obviously, this was a hard bone to swallow.

"I can tell you I've set some of my best warriors at Grimnir over the years when Conarch has called for aid. At first, I fully expected them to bring back the head of the Vanir war leader. This leader of the Ymirish. As more lives were fed into the maw, however, I merely waited for news that he had fallen to *anyone*. This year, I have hoped for even one of those warriors to return. None of them ever has. All Callaugh gets back are demands for more warriors, more weapons, and rumors of the beast-leader who will not die."

The rest sounded very familiar to Kern, and to Longtooth as well no doubt, who had experienced the northerner's savagery firsthand. A hulking demon with eyes of golden fire and the strength of five men. No, ten. Immortal and unbeatable. The Vanir told similar tales of Grimir's prowess and powers.

It was the trappings of legend. It was hard to fight against a legend.

But Sláine Longtooth seemed determined to try.

"We have not fought our way over the pass for nothing," he promised, fists clenched and barely held still where they rested against either leg. He rocked forward on his camp stool. "I tell you now, Narach Chieftain, I will not be pushed back to my valley by tales and superstitions. Grimnir is a living warrior. He can bleed, and he can be killed."

"Not by your likes, valleyman. If it were possible, a man or woman of Conarch would have accomplished this by now."

"Conarch!" Sláine spit the name aside as he might a

slug of soured ale. "Always so full of yourselves. Conan's birthclan. But Conan is gone, is he not? He left his people for Aquilonia. What has he done for us since but send foreign soldiers to 'tame' Cimmeria's villages? Weak-willed children who run at the first sign of snow or the scent of spilled blood. A traitor to Cimmeria."

Narach rose slowly to a half crouch, hands grasping at his sides as if wanting to reach for the blue-iron war sword tied to his thick leather belt. "Aquilonia maintains still an ambassador at Conarch. It was their *eng-in-eers* who designed our walls." The Cimmerian stumbled over the foreign word, but it did not hold back his pride in the accomplishment.

Longtooth had risen along with Narach, keeping on equal footing. "So while you stay locked away safe in Callaugh, in Conarch, you allow the Broken Leg Lands to become a door to the rest of Cimmeria. The Vanir do little more than scrape the mud off their feet against you as they march through to murder and raid *my* valley and beyond!"

"So you now speak for the entire valley?"

"Better than your speaking Grimnir praises!"

Watching the anger rise between the two prideful men, Kern knew before long they would come to blows. No Cimmerian stood up to such a rage of insults for long. Simpler warriors would already have broken the peace bonds to have at each other. Chieftains, apparently, enjoyed a bit more control. Or simply used the extra moment to rile their warriors up to the point of bloodlust.

Even Daol, the man Kern counted on for a level head when battle rage took everyone else, looked ready to reach for his blade. Kern thumped him hard against the shoulder. Turned and pounded a heavy fist against Reave's chest as well, drawing a glare and a question lurking deep in the larger man's glacial blue eyes.

Then Kern stepped away from the gathering, refusing to participate any longer and making that fact known in the simplest way possible.

He walked out on it.

Both chieftains stared after his affront. He felt their gazes boring into the back of his neck. Neither one spoke. It was Gard who found his voice first. "Kern!" he shouted. He asked for Longtooth, "Where are you going, Wolf-Eye?"

Kern paused, looked back over his shoulder. He stood near one of the torches that marked the clearing, and a cutting breeze whipped the bright fire close to his shoulder. It smelled unnatural. Acrid and sharp instead of the dull, oily flavor of a regular torch. From whatever the shaman had sprinkled over the brand, he guessed.

He saw that Daol and Reave followed only a few steps behind, and Desa and Ossian after them. His warriors had already fanned out to form a guard at his back, severing him from Sláine Longtooth and Narach Chieftain.

"I have not marched my warriors over a wintered land to spend their lives for your pride, Sláine Longtooth. Nor to avenge your son." That rocked back the Cruaidhi chieftain as if slapped.

"We're here for Gaud, and for Taur. And for ourselves. And if our path is not to be with you, we'll find our own way. And you"—Kern looked to Narach and Ros-Crana, taking brother and sister in together—"you can remain locked behind these walls, or you can strike at the hand that chokes our land and enslaves our people. It's your choice. It's been your choice for better than two years now."

"So what will you do?" the female war leader asked. "Where do you go from here, Wolf-Eye?"

"North," Kern said at once. "The trails all lead north. Grimnir is the head of the Vanir serpent. Strike off the head, and the body dies. I'll chase him through

the Eiglophian Mountains and into the frozen wastelands of Nordheim if I must."

"Snow and ice and storms are what you're likely to
find, Wolf-Eye." But Narach's voice was thoughtful.
"How do you hope to find Grimnir?"

Turning away from the leaders, stepping through the
ring of fire and acrid smoke and yanking free the cord
of leather that peace-bonded his arming sword to its
sheath, he gave the chieftain of Callaugh back his own
words.

"He'll find me," Kern promised.

"I'll make certain of it."

25

IT HAD BEEN a good run, Ehmish decided. A short, but full, life.

Slung over Reave's shoulder like a canvas sack of turnip roots, the young man bit down hard on the insides of his cheeks to keep from crying out as every hard, jostling step, every breath, sent new flames of fiery pain ripping out from his wound, burning through his entire body.

Blood soaked his slashed tunic, slick and warm between the fingers of his left hand as he tried to pull the flesh closed over exposed ribs. Two ribs shifted under the pressure, lighting up his left side with bright agony, his breath shallow and rapid through the torture.

"Crom, give me strength," he whispered, voice ragged in his own ears.

Then he wished he hadn't. Crom did not listen to weak men. His favor had given the Cimmerians everything they needed to survive the oft-harsh northern lands. Cunning and strength, and the will to face everything a hard life might throw at them.

That strength still allowed him to hold on to his blade, the broadsword he'd traded up for after the battle in the Pass of Blood. The fingers of his right hand locked around its hilt as if it were a lifeline tossed down a cliff face to him. His muscles trembled with strain as he held the flat of the sword pressed against Reave's back, careful not to let the point fall downward to slice at the back of the running man's legs. His cunning and his will kept him silent in the gathered darkness, chewing on the meat inside his cheeks, tasting the salty bloodflow and swallowing it back rather than give away their position with even one inadvertent cry.

To ask for more gainsaid those gifts.

Crom had at least seen to it that Ehmish would die a man, and not a boy in the eyes of his friends. His kin.

Beneath him, Reave seemed to sense the young man's regret. He tightened his grip across Ehmish's back. "Sure and you'll be fine." His whisper was loud and strong, despite having run a good league with twelve stones' weight on his back. His earrings jangled together with each heavy step. "Hold on, Ehmish. Hold on."

The mournful horns of the Vanir blasted around them, deep and long as they shattered the night. Calls of fury that echoed off the cliff face at their right. Ran among the trees behind them and moving forward of their path on the left. A single answering blast directly ahead!

"Penned!"

This from Desagrena, who paced closest to Reave in the bedraggled line of warriors. Desa had her broadsword naked in one hand, and carried Reave's Cimmerian greatsword by a leather strap wrapped around the balance point of its blade in the other.

Harsh, bellowing breaths, the squelch of disturbed

snow, and the thudding of booted feet against hard, rocky ground were all that answered.

Shadows jumped and danced all around Ehmish. He counted five . . . six others by the cloud-dimmed moonlight. Mogh and Ashul on Reave's left. Old Finn right behind, limping as he ran. A glancing blow with a spear shaft swelled his gout-inflamed knee like a knotted oak branch. Desa. And Aodh and Brig Tall-Wood just beyond her. Brig helped Aodh, letting the older warrior lean on his shoulder for support, Aodh favoring a sprained ankle. Brig held his own right arm in tight against his body, stemming the blood where he'd taken a gash along the inside length.

Ehmish could not count those who ran ahead of the pack. Kern, he knew, led the way. And he thought the rest were still alive as well. Battered and bloodied, certainly, but alive.

How many of them would see morning, that remained to be seen.

It had taken two days for the Vanir raiders to realize there was a wolf in their midst. A wolf who walked upright and led a bloodthirsty pack. Leaving Callaugh behind, Kern's wolves had moved north, slowly, in a weaving line that staggered from glen to vale to mountainside camp, searching for the flame-haired Vanir and their Ymirish allies. Finding them. Setting on them in a series of short, bloody ambushes that left an easy trail for Sláine Longtooth and Narach Chieftain to follow and sent ahead a message that the raiders were now the ones being hunted. The small band of warriors collected small scars and snow blisters, and a great deal of battle spoils in weapons, food, and gear.

That day's target had been a slave encampment near the old Conarch mines. Daol and Brig, with their sharper eyes, had scouted it out in the waning twilight. They counted half a dozen fresh heads set up on pikes. Local clansmen, or one of the smaller groups that had broken away from Longtooth's war host. Not that it mattered, as dead was dead.

They also witnessed the arrival of reinforcements. Raiders staggering in by pairs and small knots. And a Ymirish to lead them. The invaders were organizing, coming together, recognizing the threat in their midst.

And it had been Ehmish's job, again, to pull them apart long enough for Kern's ambush to work.

Reave stumbled down a short, fast slope, nearly tripping over some loose stones. He sank to his knees too fast, and spilled Ehmish forward among icy snow and hardscrabble rock. The young man grunted in a sharp exhale as he bounced against his left side, ribs afire.

"Easy, easy!" Desa snapped at Reave, dropping down at Ehmish's side and rolling him back to his right. "Clumsy ox!"

And Kern was there, bending down on one knee to get a new look at the wound. His yellow eyes gleamed in the dark, as if trapping what little moonlight filtered through the uneven clouds overhead. "It's bad," he promised Ehmish, watching the younger man bleed out over the hard, snow-covered ground. "But you can survive it if you hold on a bit longer."

"I'm fine," Ehmish grunted through teeth clenched so hard his jaw hurt. He swallowed against the metallic taste of blood. Setting his face into a grim mask, he applied more pressure to his hurt. There were rough patches chipped into the sharp-edged bones that pressed against his fingers. The wound ran from the outside of his left breast carving down toward his hip, flaying skin and muscle away from the protective cage of ribs.

Ashul checked the wound again. Clucked. "Lucky he didn't slip a blade between those ribs, by Crom."

Looking for anything to take his mind off the pain, Ehmish glanced around. Saw the yawning darkness of a cave opened up in the nearby mountainside. They had reached one of the old Conarch mines. A good, defensive position.

Ehmish glanced back up at their leader. "Get them out of this, Kern."

Raider horns sounded again, coming from all sides. Some were distant. Others, much closer. The way they bounced off the cliffs and sharp slopes, mixing together into a long, deep, mournful wail, it sounded to Ehmish as if the entire countryside had risen against them.

To others as well.

"Woken the whole north," Wallach Graybeard said, tugging at the thick, coarse hair under his chin. "Must be more campsites nearby than we thought."

Another blast from the horns. This time a wolf's howl answered them, driven to a distracted fury by the disturbance in the night. Ehmish did not doubt it was Frostpaw. No one did.

Kern nodded as if answering the creature. "We make our stand here. We have good cover, and we can retreat into the cave if needs be. If they come at us in small knots, we pull them down quickly and easily."

"And if they comes at us all at once?" Ossian asked.

Kern shrugged, his shoulders hunching and falling beneath his threadbare winter cloak. "Not so easy," he said.

While Ehmish watched, and winced as Desagrena used long strips of leather to tie a thick fold of clean muslin over his wound, Kern and the others set about making "spiderholes." That was what Ehmish himself had named them, and Kern adopted the term without argument. They were the younger man's idea, after all, wrenched out of the harrowing flight he'd made when luring the raiders from that first camp so long ago. Then, he had slipped down and rolled himself under some low-hanging brush, shaking snow over himself to blend in better with the ground cover. This time they were made with blankets and skins anchored against the ground on one side with a few large rocks. A man lay on the earth, with the cover draped over him, then was camouflaged with scoops of snow and a fallen branch or skin of bark.

He called them spiderholes because the idea reminded him of the trapping spiders, which dug out of the earth during the summer and autumn. Large as a robin, they were, with long, spindly forward legs for grabbing and shorter, stronger back legs for digging.

Dig a hole, prop a leaf or twig in the way, and wait for prey to come traipsing by. Then, *out!* Snare and sting them, and haul the catch back down into the underground lair for weeks of slow eating.

As Desa and Nahud'r helped Ehmish back to his feet, half-carrying him to the entrance of the nearby mine, he watched Kern and half of the troop burrow down into their spiderholes, blades in their fists, ready to come springing out on the attack. Everyone else grabbed some cover behind a boulder or small pile of hardscrabble tailings. They would wait and spring on the Vanir after the trap had been sprung.

That's how it should have happened.

Of course, Ehmish shouldn't have gotten himself wounded. Should never have been trapped in the situation he'd found himself in this evening. A little bad luck and one rushed decision had spoiled it all. He and Doon and Desa had been set to stir up the raider camp and draw the Vanir out so the rest of Kern's pack could fall on the main site and free the slaves. That they'd accomplished, with Desa sniping at the raiders with bow and arrow while Ehmish and Doon both used slings to slap small bullets into flesh.

One sentry killed, and several men around a campfire wounded before the Vanir charged into the night. The three of them split apart then, running for their own spiderholes, which had been set up earlier.

Ehmish's was right back along the trail where trampled snow made it impossible to tell his tracks from those of men who had passed by earlier. A stick held up one side of the snow-covered blanket, like a feeble tent just waiting to collapse. He lay in a prepared trough, grabbed the edge of the blanket, and simply rolled it over him in a quick turn, drawing along the snow's weight and its camouflage.

Then he simply had to wait it out, for the attack on the campsite to draw back the raiders, who would meet (as planned) Kern's ready warriors.

But there had been more Vanir camped nearby than Daol or Brig had found. And Ehmish had come scuttling out from his spiderhole too early, as a half dozen raiders ran back to join the growing fracas. Two of them set on him with a lust for blood, hammering at his defense while the rest charged onward.

He kept the broadsword in front of him for a moment. Maybe two. Then one raider slipped a blade inside Ehmish's reach to slice deep and long and painfully down his side . . . turning the blade in . . .

Trying to slip it beneath his rib cage and a thrust for his vitals.

Aodh and Reave saved him, having come to his shouts and warnings even as the entire plan fell apart. Most of the slaves, when set loose, had been too enamored of their freedom to bother with anything more than grabbing a weapon and charging off into the night. A few hesitated, looking for vengeance or simply recognizing the safety in numbers. But they weren't used to fighting as a group, and they straggled out into a loose wall that was the first to fall under the swords of the returning Vanir.

After that it was break away into the night. And running . . . running . . . Shouts and horns chasing after them. The sound of feet scraping against—

—the cavern floor!

Ehmish startled, coming back from the fevered

drowse he had begun to slip into with a hand clasped over his mouth and strong arms pulling him over to the wall of the cave. His side lit up with new fire, expelling the weariness which had nearly claimed him until . . . until . . .

Again, a distant echo of feet slipping against scrabble rock and smooth-worn stone. People moving deeper inside the cave.

And voices. Flat and nasal, whispering words that Ehmish almost recognized. He did not speak the northern tongues, but he had heard Vanir curses enough of late to recognize them when he heard them.

No one had bothered to check the cave for side passages or signs of life.

No one had had time.

Nahud'r held Ehmish against the cavern wall, his lean-muscled arms pulling the young man into the darkest corner, where they lay still and silent. Desa was gone, having returned to the others. Except for the scuffle and soft whispers echoing to them, silence reigned. Ehmish heard nothing from outside, but imagined the Vanir were getting close, close.

Now he understood the caution implied in the dark man's embrace. A shouted warning might bring the raiders outside running, crashing in among their companions.

But not to shout meant letting more warriors in at their backs, where they were not expecting trouble.

Light flickered back inside the cave's ultimate darkness, casting a few stray shadows before going out. Candlelight, Ehmish guessed. His breathing was rapid and shallow, panting like a dog through the pain. He hoped that the others had caught a glimpse of the light. That it hadn't been buried too far back from the mine's entrance.

No sign of the others. No call of help. It was Ehmish and Nahud'r. The young Gaudic still had his silver-chased broadsword, never having released his death grip on the wire-wound handle. He guessed that the dark-skinned Shemite still had his scimitar within reach.

But there were many, many Vanir. More than Ehmish would have thought, creeping up through the old mine. He felt their presence in the rock now, and heard the scuffs and shuffles of many feet. The shadows swirled and shifted deeper into the cavern, and he counted four . . . five . . . six men moving up on them. Nahud'r brushed his fingers lightly over Ehmish's eyes, and the young man understood without having to be told. He squinted, reducing any gleam off the whites of his eyes down to the barest speck possible.

He saw the shadow of movement as the first Vanir warrior stepped past them, moving for the entrance with naked blade held in front of him and teeth bared in a feral grin. Then the second. The third. That was when Ehmish made his decision.

That was when he realized that it had been his decision all along, to be a part of these men and women. These warriors. Every time he had stepped forward. Every league he'd run alongside them. Those had all been choices. Kern and the others, they had stood by him because he had done the same for them. And he did so now.

He broke free of Nahud'r's grip, rolling back into the main cavern with his broadsword already thrusting up from the floor, toward a raider's unprotected belly.

Warmth gushed over his sword, his hand. Slick and foul, with a latrine scent that promised a deep gut wound. The man's scream of pain thundered in the cavern's close quarters. It echoed up and down the cave's length and no doubt bellowed forth from the entrance like the roar of a wounded dragon.

No time to think about the sharp pain he'd reawakened in his side, or the new trickles of blood that spread down over his hip. There was only his sword, lashing out and biting at flesh, and the raiders who stood all around him, confused by the sudden loosing of a beast among them. A wolf!

One of Kern's wolves.

THE DARKNESS OF the spiderhole was absolute. Kern waited, facedown in the slush and the cold, sharp-edged hardscrabble that tailed out from the nearby mine, smothered beneath the felt mat Daol had drawn across him. The weight of snow across his back and legs pressed down with a firm hand. His poncho protected him from a great deal of abuse, but here and there a sharp rock dug past the tattered leather, and snowmelt trickled inside, drawing icy lines against his chest.

His breath quickly turned the air close—warm and humid. It drew out the smells trapped by the felt. The rank odor of the Vanir who had rolled himself inside the mat for who knew how many nights. His own sweat—and yea—blood, too. Even the scent of he and Maev, together, still lingered after all this time. Though perhaps that was wishful thinking on his part. And deep down, beneath the odors of use, was still the musky, wild smell of animal. Mountain goat or mammoth. Something that could never be washed or aired out of the tangle of woolen hair.

The blasts of Vanir horns were muffled to his ears, but growing closer still. The strength of their calls promised him that. He couldn't tell from which direction, but assumed every way but east, where the mountain cliffs would make passage difficult.

Let them come in staggered numbers. That was Kern's only desire. A pair at a time. Knots of three or four. Given that, his pack of hunters could pull down the raiders without suffering loss of life or even injury.

It was the way of the pack, and it served Kern's warriors well. The pack would always be stronger than a few rogue predators.

There were shouts by then. Hard as they were to grasp through the layers of snow and cloth, they sounded confused, and still full of pain. Perhaps Kern's warriors had hurt the raiders more deeply than they'd thought. The mournful blasts tapered off in number, though the few that remained became more strident. Excited.

Then nothing.

Silence descended. If the Vanir were still out there, they had to be close. Very close. Creeping up on the old mine site, perhaps expecting another ambush. Or planning one of their own.

As heartbeats counted off long, painful moments, Kern began to imagine the stealth of a raider, moving cautiously as he came down one of the paths so clearly marked by the footprints of his warriors. Spear or broadsword held ready. Shield tucked in close to protect his heart and throat.

There! They spotted the unnatural hillocks beneath the snow and knew them for what they were! Did that one move? Even just a little? A sharp breath, or a quick adjustment against the prodding of a sharp stone, that's all it would take.

The flame-haired Vanir, tossing his long braid back over one shoulder, waving down the Ymirish who also trod so close by and pointing out the deception. Kern's mouth dried with the sudden, bitter taste of adrenaline.

More warriors creeping forward now, careful of any betraying sound. Coming up with one or two men to each mound. Weapons drawn back for quick, deadly thrusts.

The spiderholes turned into burial shrouds for Kern and half his people.

A loose stone tumbled nearby, and a heavy thud

sounded near Kern's head as someone dropped down from the mound of old tailings.

Rolling back against the mat, Kern furled it beneath him as he freed his sword arm first. A handful of snow fell into his face. He shook clear with a violent toss of his head. In time to see the tall shadow standing over him with a javelin or pike held carefully across his body, whipping the long shaft around as Kern sprang his trap before the other man was able to deal death so easily.

His arming sword thrust for the other warrior's vitals, but the pike's wooden haft knocked his point aside at the last second. A return thrust nearly pinned Kern to the ground, but he turned it with the flat of his blade and rolled into the man's feet, trying to throw him off-balance as he whipped the blade up to slash at the man's exposed chest.

And stopped as he recognized the kilt, of all things, as the heavy woolen wrap common to Cimmeria. Not a banded or studded leather skirt at all. Not what his enemy would wear.

Not with the fox's tail of Cruaidh dangling down from his belt.

What Gard Foehammer recognized to stay his own thrust Kern couldn't be certain. But suddenly the two warriors both halted, both in midstrike. The nearby ground erupted as more warriors flung themselves out of their spiderholes. Kern hissed a sharp "Hold!" to his warriors before someone made the same mistake he almost had.

More of his hunters dropped down from nearby trees or ducked out from behind boulders or scrub. Kern rose carefully to his feet, wondering at Gard's arrival. And that of his clansmen, as several Cruaidhi gathered behind him, weapons naked and already stained with blood.

"The horns?" Kern said.

"Unholy noise," Gard said as if agreeing. "We ran right up their backsides without hardly a whisper of alarm." He shook his head. "You've set a hard pace to match, Kern Wolf-Eye."

The man might have said more, but that was when the wounded bellow of a great beast rolled out of the nearby cavern. Then came the ringing clash of steel against steel, and more shouts of pain and Nordheimir curses.

"Ehmish!" Kern shouted. And with one mind his troop rushed for the abandoned mine entrance.

Desa was closest, having concealed herself near the yawning black after helping carry the youth inside. She disappeared inside, briefly, then came stumbling back out into the silvery gray cast of moonlight with a large man wrapped around her, trying to club her unconscious with the haft of his broadsword.

Desa folded, but not from weakness. She rolled down onto the ground, pulling the shaggy-haired Vanir with her. Planting a foot into his gut and rolling him up and over the top to bowl him into Wallach Graybeard and Hydallan. Their swords rose and fell, rose and fell, hacking mercilessly at the stunned warrior. Kern caught up with Reave and Daol as Desa staggered back to her feet, and the six of them rushed forward.

Then Kern pulled them up short as the shouts and clashes of steel ceased as abruptly—and as shocking to those outside—as they began.

They waited, as if not daring to rush in blindly. Desa had been fortunate the Vanir raider hadn't run her through as she chased into the darkness. The silence that yawned out from the dark entrance promised them that the danger, however it had turned out for the men Kern had left inside, was over.

Two men, as it turned out. Nahud'r had remained a moment longer with Ehmish, and now came out with the younger leaning heavily into his shoulder, limping

and weak, but still on his feet. Ehmish's face was
twisted into a mask of pain and fury, made all the more
frightening with the splatter of blood that painted one
side of his face red and speckled the other with dabs
and dollops.

"We should have checked the cavern," was all that
Kern could think to say.

Ehmish grinned back at him. Blood stained his teeth
as well, and he spit the taste to one side. "Yea. We
should have," he said.

Then he tumbled forward from Nahud'r's grasp,
into Kern's arms.

Kern lowered the young man to the ground, shouting his people back as they crowded in. He shoved a
few of them who got in his way while he felt for life at
Ehmish's neck. A thready heartbeat. Too fast and too
weak, but still there.

"Let me," a papery-thin voice whispered in Kern's
ear.

A strong, liver-spotted hand grabbed Kern by the elbow and lifted him away from the fallen warrior. It
wasn't the strength that pulled him aside, though, but
the confidence in the grip. Kern stared into the other
man's face, and looked past the cast that smeared
across the right eye. Callaugh's shaman knew what he
was about, and it radiated from him in the same way
Kern had seen in healer and war leaders alike. He bent
over Ehmish, already digging into one of the many
muslin sacks tied to his side.

The appearance of the older man, though, raised
many questions for Kern. He looked back to Gard,
who had now been joined by Sláine Longtooth and
Ros-Crana, who held the severed head of a Ymirish by
his long, frost blond braid. And dozens of warriors
mixed together between Cruaidhi and Callaughnan.
Kern did not see him, but he heard Narach Chieftain
haranguing a troop farther back into the darkness.

"Both of you?" he asked, scarcely believing it. If he'd had to be rescued, having it be by the leaders of two strong villages seemed too good to be true.

"You made it hard to resist," Ros-Crana said. She hefted her trophy, letting blood and gore drip from the neck to spatter into the snow and slush around her feet. "The entire Crom-cursed land is stirred up behind you. And ahead. You've painted a target that no one could refuse."

A victorious chill washed through Kern as he read into her words, her tone. Something in the way she spoke. "No one?" he asked.

Sláine Longtooth crossed arms over his chest, stared off into the night as if already looking at the next battle. "Finally," he promised. "After all this way and so many lives."

Kern did not doubt that Longtooth thought of his fallen son, Alaric, first among them.

It was Gard Foehammer, though, who finally gave him a straight answer. Perhaps he thought of the many lives lost at Cruaidh, and again over the Pass of Blood. But he was a warrior born, and knew how to keep his target in sight once it fell beneath his gaze. "Grimnir, Kern." The protector of Cruaidh reversed his pike, jabbing it point down into the frozen earth. As if driving the finishing blow into his enemy. "He's drawn together his war host near Conarch.

"You've lured out the great beast himself."

26

A CLINGING FOG, damp and cold, cloaked the following morning. It rolled over the Cimmerian encampment before dawn, cutting visibility down to not much better than a stone's throw. Draping shadows over the warriors who slept or sat quietly, or walked about alone as they prepared themselves for the coming day.

Kern shook himself into action slowly, with heavy deliberation. The eve before Ros-Crana had promised they were but a short march away from Conarch, and the promise of battle had kept Kern awake most of the night. Back against a tree and huddled beneath his blanket, staring into the dark and cold as his breath plumed before him. Hearing Frostpaw's strong howl as the wolf patrolled the edge of the encampment. Watching the change of sentries.

Not caring so much what the battle would bring to him, but suddenly at ease that his long march seemed to be over.

For better or worse.

There was no call to assemble. No order to move for Conarch. Men and women simply started moving about with more direction, more energy. They drifted off in clumps and clusters. Kern checked on Ehmish—alive, but one of those being left behind that day among other wounded—and kicked a few of his own men awake. Then he set about preparing. Pulling his tattered poncho overhead and belting the iron-shod greaves around his legs. The heavy broadsword of Burok Bear-slayer he strapped across his back. Arming sword at his side, its sheath tied around his wide, leather belt opposite of his long hunting knife. Winter cloak draped over his shoulders, with its tattered roll of wolf's fur matted and filthy.

His extra weapons and the foodstuff he carried went into his blanket roll, tied with a few lengths of braided horsehair, then a long leather cord he slung over his shoulder. Kern slung back his new shield as well, then squatted near a dead fire pit as he watched the rest of his warriors gather to him.

Nahud'r rolled out of his bedroll with scimitar already naked in his hand. Finding a good whetting stone, he set to sharpening the curved length in long, rasping strokes. Aodh and Doon passed around shanks of dried beef and crusty flatbread. Old Finn rose cursing his stiff joints and the damp chill.

Reave and Desagrena arrived together, Kern saw. From a semisecluded patch of stunted cedar. Her acid glance burned Kern's cheeks with a touch of blood. Then she nodded sharply and turned to bash a fist against Reave's shoulder. "Watch his back, Ox-heart."

Reave swatted her on the ass as she went for her gear.

"Ox-heart?" Kern asked his friend, as Daol and Hydallan stumbled out of their bedrolls and readied themselves.

Daol's ears perked up, and he eyed Reave with his gray hawk's eyes.

"Yea, well." The large man shrugged. The gold hoops in his ears jangled together. "That was nay the part that interested her before."

The three men all managed tight grins, but not at Desa's expense. What wasn't being said was actually the more important. For the moment they were simply friends and could have been back in Gaud discussing the hunting or the prospects of a summer raid. And when they suddenly nodded at one another and turned north in tight step, no one even thought to step between them. Kern's warriors simply formed a heavy fist around them as the pack thrust themselves to the fore of the march.

For better or worse.

They would see the day through together.

EVEN FROSTPAW DARED show himself closer to the assembled war host than Kern would have thought, waiting out in the trees. Sometimes running ahead of them as if eager to hunt with the pack, or trailing behind to pick up scraps from their passing.

Kern worked his sword arm through the exercises Wallach Graybeard had taught him before Taur. Jab, block, and lunge. The swordplay and the march quickly loosened his muscles, but, down deep in his bones where not even summer's high sun ever reached him, winter remained Kern's constant companion. Even as the army rose up above the fog, tracing the edge of a high, peaked bluff and looking into a clear sky devoid of clouds, Kern shivered and mopped away a cold sweat only.

He caught more than one in his band casting longing glances south and east. Where the early-morning sun peeked over the western Teeth of Conall Valley.

Home.

But Hydallan, Kern saw, tasted the air with short,

ferretlike bites. Like his son, the aged tracker and hunter knew the tastes and smells of Cimmeria. Senses as keen as any wolf's.

"Smoke," he said, glancing down into the dirty gray fog that socked in the lower valleys and glens.

The wisps that tore loose of the heavy blanket were dark and sooty, and obvious once the older man pointed them out. Ros-Crana didn't waste any time when called up to the front of the march, nodding as Hydallan pointed out to her what her own nose had already told.

Conarch was burning.

If there were any doubts, the stragglers confirmed it as they came across first a displaced family, carrying their children to high ground and safety, then some few warriors sent on a dead run to call for aid from the nearby villages. Surprised to find a war host of Cimmerian warriors already on their way, the warriors quickly folded themselves into the ranks and let word spread that Grimnir had stormed down from the ice caverns of the nearby mountains, calling together a host of raiders and Ymirish warriors and sorcerers. They had struck at Conarch first, determined to set the Cimmerians back on their heels before raiding south for Callaugh, and the great war chief of the north had called down mighty beasts. Creatures of great strength, and others that struck out of the fog with lightning reflexes and sharp claws.

The tales grew in the telling, and rather than worry over them, Kern pressed his people harder, faster, kicking through the icy crust of snow, ready to come to grips with this terrible legend.

Eager for the end.

The trail widened as it turned down toward Broken Leg Lands and Clan Conarch, dropping toward a narrow bluff that overlooked the deeper glen. Rock outcroppings chewed their way up from the ground like

teeth through meat. The snow made footing treacherous, always hiding a loose stone or a small hole where
a leg could be snapped like dry kindling. In some areas,
the snow had drifted up in knee-high piles.

The fog slowly burned away under the pale sun,
thinning even as the war host descended into it again.
The curtain swallowed them back up, reducing the rising sun to nothing more than a dim light in the sky and
the Cimmerian warriors to ghosts among the shadows
of rocky mounds and sparse trees. Soon, there was no
trail at all. Simply a wide slope down which they
pushed toward the besieged village. Without being ordered, Kern's people stepped up to a brisk walk, then
an easy jog. Behind them, the Cimmerian war host
fanned out into two lines. Valleymen on the left.
Callaughnan and their allies on the right.

And ahead, a wild, banshee trumpeting and the
mournful blasts of Vanir horns rolled together to wail
like demons loosed over the land as the two armies drew
together. More stragglers fell back onto the army's position, seeking a new strong line, drawing the Vanir after
them and away from the village stronghold. Swordsmen
and archers. Pike-bearing guardsmen. Shield maidens.

A fist of Aquilonian lancers rode up on their war-
horses, wheeling around Kern's small band with their
long lances lowered and faces wary beneath conical
helms. They didn't recognize the Cimmerians, that was
certain, but they also knew that Kern's people were no
Vanir.

Kern gave them a heartbeat's pause, until Ros-
Crana ran forward to wave them aside. "With us," she
called to the Aquilonians. "Wolf-Eye!"

It was enough for them. The leader of the trio raised
the tip of his lance in salute, and they reined their
mounts in next to Kern's pack. Kern saw a few uneasy
glances, and heard one man say to his captain,
"Wolves."

"From Conan's *em-bass-y* to Clan Conarch," Ros-Crana told Kern, falling back toward her own people as they shook out into a ragged battle line. The Aquilonian word sounded strange in her mouth, but Kern took its meaning to be something like a gift of men.

More yells and shouts from the thinning fog. The slope lessened, running down onto the bluff's small plateau. There Frostpaw discovered the first Vanir, the wolf jumping through a sheaf of winter-dry brush and flushing the raider out from his own spiderhole. The animal growled and snarled, rolling out of the brush and in a pile of fur and leather and steel.

Snapping jaws tasted blood as the Vanir howled in pain. He kicked out with one foot and dazed the large animal enough to scramble back to his feet, sword raised overhead and ready to smash his blade through the wolf's skull.

An arrow took the raider in the chest, right through his breastbone.

Brig Tall-Wood lowered his hunting bow, having beat Daol to the mark by mere heartbeats. "Wouldn't do to have them claim first blood on us," was all he said.

Not that it would be much longer.

There were sounds of battle reaching them now, with clashing steel and the calls and cries of warriors in the grips of bloodlust. An arrow flew out of the gray curtain raised before them, at random no doubt, and stuck into the earth not far from the Aquilonian horsemen. A horse reared, but its rider clung to its large back without being thrown.

Kern slowed his people from their trot back to a walk, then to a stop as a large shadow moved through the gloom at them. At first he thought it was another of the large granite rock columns that stood out like petrified trees on some ancient dry wash. But this one moved. And when it lifted its head, there was another banshee wailing of trumpets and horns. Lithe shadows patrolled around its feet, blending into the fog, moving with a hunter's grace.

One of the smaller shadows leaped forward, suddenly revealing itself. A saber-toothed cat. White as the snowy pelt of an ermine.

The snarling yelp of Kern's dire wolf rose up alongside the cat's high-pitched, savage scream. The saber-tooth had found Frostpaw trapped between the two armies, and now the two creatures fought their own prelude to the battle to come. They dodged and slashed at each other, and the Cimmerian advance stalled, waiting as the larger shadow lumbered out from the gray curtain and made itself known.

A mammoth, covered in ropes of shaggy, coarse hair and strong as ten oxen. It plowed forward with a large form astride its neck, raising weapons overhead in challenge. A giant form. A true beast that walked upright, like a demon with blazing eyes of golden fire. The tales had not been so tall, after all.

At last, Grimnir stood revealed.

Giant-kin!

Frost-giant. One of the legendary true sons of Ymir. Easily half again as large as a regular man, with a thick hide the color of old, rotten snow and heavily muscled arms that could tear a warrior in two. His eyes did spark like yellow fire out of a face more bestial than human.

But this was no mindless creature of the deep, deep north. There was intelligence there, and purpose in the way he held his weapons. He raised a warhammer overhead with his right hand. In his other, he wielded a battle-axe one-handed and pointed it at the Cimmerian line.

"Crom's blood," Brig Tall-Wood said aloud.

From deeper in the gray swirls and sworls of fog, more shadows suddenly darkened into distinct outline as a large host of Vanir raiders massed to either side of the wooly mammoth. Large burly men, with dark, flame-red hair or the more golden touch of captured sons from Asgard, almost all with thick beards, which helped protect faces from the harder, icy winds of the Nordheim wastes. They wore full tunics and kilts banded with leather and studded with tiny metal spikes. Shaggy cloaks made from goat's wool, and metal caps with the horns of any number of beasts.

And Ymirish. Grimnir's faithful. A dozen . . . two! Two dozen. Frost-haired and heavy, deep-set features, with the same yellow eyes Kern knew from staring into summer ponds or silver-polished steel. They came to battle bare-chested to the elements. Some of them handled large mastiffs, being held back at the moment while waiting for the snow-cats to draw aside after killing Frostpaw. Others pumped weapons overhead, encouraging the Vanir.

Two of these frost-bearded men hunched together near the mammoth's side. Crom take Kern if the shadows and the fog didn't congeal around them to form a dark, heavy band. An unnatural appearance that twisted a small rope of fear somewhere deep within the mind. Each had two large orbs tattooed over his chest. Too far to make out detail, Kern already knew. Glowing, feral eyes.

Sorcerers.

And these weren't Grimnir's only warriors. The sounds of a heavy battle could still be heard far behind, as a rear guard held more of Clan Conarch's warriors back from the bluff. There had to be scores more lurking within the snow and fog. Hundreds.

Grimnir had drawn together a war host capable of hammering the Cimmerians back over the mountains. And beyond.

27

GRIMNIR ROARED A throaty challenge. His frost-giant's voice carried like the rumble of an avalanche, or the crack and deep growl of a calving glacier. The mammoth pulled back its long snout and trumpeted a new blast, echoing its master.

Horns brayed, and the large canines barked and growled to be released.

Cimmerian warriors all along the ragged line shouted back in defiance. Some shook their own weapons overhead. Others hiked up their kilts to waggle at the raiders, insulting the northerners' manhood.

By the handful and by the dozen, voices took up the roar. Kern shouted his own throat raw.

Reave unslung his bedroll and tossed it behind as so many were doing along the line, dropping their packs and shedding weight for battle. He unhooked his giant greatsword, and raised it in front of him.

Daol stuck arrows point first into the snow-blanketed ground, and put another three between his teeth.

"Let them come at us," Kern called to his warriors, and any ears that were close enough and open to his words.

There wouldn't be much chance for fancy plans or surprises this day. Once the fighting began, only strength would out. Kern unslung his shield and gripped it in his off-sword hand. Rather than worry about the short reach of his arming sword, he drew forth Burok's broadsword. The weight was unfamiliar in his hand but felt good regardless.

"Wait for them. Wait!"

But farther down a few of Ros-Crana's warriors had charged out in front, swords held overhead as they ran at the raider line. Not to be outdone, more than a handful of Sláine Longtooth's men also broke away for brave and heroic charges.

Brave and heroic deaths. Kern grabbed Ashul, who had jumped forward thinking a general attack was being sent. A scant few heartbeats later, a serpent rose up from the snow and slammed into the Callaughnan.

Two men, gripped in rolling coils. A third fell to the demonic serpent's icicle fangs.

Cruaidhi warriors fared no better. As if brought to life, a patch of the thinning fog suddenly lashed out with sharp, soot-stained tendrils, flailing at the fistful of men. Two of them reeled away, screaming in sudden agony, hands clawing at blistered faces. They stumbled and fell as if struck blind, then thrashed upon the snowy carpet, dying.

Three others made it through, and were swallowed up by a pack of mastiffs and Ymirish bearing war swords. The dogs tore at legs and gut. Blades rose and fell and slashed angrily at the remaining trio.

One Cimmerian managed to take two of the great-shouldered mastiffs and a Ymirish with him, splattering new blood over white snow.

The others fell without any enemy souls preceding them into death.

The insult was more than most could bear. As if released by Crom's own hand, the Cimmerians stormed forward in a sudden rage that their brave—if foolish—companions had been slaughtered so easily. Cruaidhi or Callaughnan or Conarch, did not matter. They bellowed their dismay and their challenge, and surged forward in the same kind of haphazard charge Kern had witnessed over the Pass of Blood. No order or thought. Anger and haste sufficed, and Crom's will to reach their enemy and throw them down just as easily.

The Vanir broke into a forward charge as well. Some Ymirish moved across the line, bolstering thin pockets. Others grouped around the war mammoth as their monstrous leader slid down to earth. Grimnir towered above all but the mammoth, which he sent stampeding forward.

No choice now. "Take them," Kern ordered, breaking into a loping run that crossed the snow with ease.

He angled toward one side, thinking to help Frostpaw before the large wolf was brought down by a pair of cats, but the animal was more cagey than that. Throwing off one saber-tooth's attack, the large wolf savaged one cat's foreleg with a strong jawful of sharp canines, then bolted. Trapped between the two war hosts, however, it was all the wolf could do to dodge back and forth, snarling its fury and building bloodlust.

Kern let the animal alone.

Running. Feet pounding the earth in cold, dull thunder. Behind him, Kern heard the violent *thrum* of taut bowstrings released together. Long shafts whispered overhead through the fog and taint of woodsmoke. Then spiked down among the raider line to drop two men back to the ground.

Battle cries varied up and down the line. Calls of *Callaugh!* and *Cruaidh!* dominated, but there were a few voices close to Kern screaming out *Gaud!* and *Taur!* as well. Unable to think of any village as home anymore, his lips parted and he bellowed "Crom!" for himself, and for Cimmeria.

The Vanir had archers as well, and most of them with the stronger war bows that allowed for faster, flatter shots. Kern saw a group bear down in the direction of his small pack.

"Shields!" he warned, and barely in time. He thrust his own up as they released, and two hammerlike blows slammed into its metal facing.

Ossian turned another shaft. Reave took a glancing shot, and the blood flowed freely as it cut deeply where his bull neck met his shoulder, but the shaft passed by to stick in the wood facing of Nahud'r's small buckler.

Without breaking stride, the dark-skinned Shemite simply sliced his scimitar over the face of his shield, snapping off the shaft before it fouled him in close combat.

Closer. Fur-lined boots kicking up snow and arrows whispering quiet death between the two lines. The horsemen of Aquilonia charged past Kern's warriors, just in time to put themselves between the Cimmerians and a close fist of flame-haired Vanir. Their lances scythed through the tight knot, and, when they rode on, there weren't more than two left standing.

Reave took one head. Ossian and Nahud'r the other.

That bought Kern's people time to close on their enemy and to still be in one solid knot as the two lines crashed together with all the force of a hammer striking an anvil. At that moment, Cimmerian war cries matched the Vanir horns and curses.

Then bodies slammed into each other, and swords fell against edge, shield, and flesh.

A riot of shouts, strikes, and screams.

The sheer momentum of the charging armies drove deep wedges into both sides. Warriors ducked and dodged. They ran over lightly defended patches and flowed around knots of stronger defense like white water breaking over sharp rocks. Kern's pack was a certain breakwater, smashing aside the Vanir line as the entire group hammered forward. Reave led, his greatsword swinging in deadly arcs, with Ossian nearly at his side. Kern and Nahud'r and Desa charged after. The others ran at their backs and sluiced the northern raiders away to either side as the pack staggered forward, slowing but never stopping. Not until two flame-haired warriors challenged Reave with tall shields and pikes.

Suddenly, Kern's pack was surrounded by Vanir. From all four sides the northerners came at them, jabbing and slashing with reckless courage. Their nasal language called down the curses of Ymir, god of the north, and Grimnir, whose terrible name was invoked about as often.

A large man rushed at Kern with a wild yell of "Oathbreaker!" There was no mistaking his sense of betrayal, finding a man colored as a Ymirish fighting on the side of Cimmeria. Kern thrust his broadsword ahead rather than slashing with it, adding reach to the blade. Sliding it past a Vanir shield and between two ribs.

The other man screamed in fury and agony, and tried to hammer Kern away with the war sword he swung overhead like an axe.

Kern raised his shield, letting the awkward blow hammer at him rather than pulling away. He took a firm grasp on the cord-wound hilt and *twisted*, spreading the blade between ribs and coring out a mortal wound.

Blood burst from the raider's mouth in a froth that covered a gargling howl, spitting warm flecks into

Kern's face. Kern jumped back, bringing his sword out. Bumped into Reave's side and wedging himself back to back against Reave and Nahud'r as the three men formed a smaller island of safety and sanity amidst the growing chaos.

Wallach Graybeard formed another, hauling in Old Finn and Doon and Mogh, fighting to link up with Kern. Ashul, Aodh, and Desa fought not too far away, using their combined strength to protect each other and pull down larger enemies.

Behind them all, Daol and the other archers fired the last of their arrows, and were finally taking to sword. They seemed far, far away.

There was no longer any order to the battle. Grimnir reaved through the enemy line with powerful strokes that sent men tumbling aside broken or bleeding. The snow-cats had returned to their master's side as well, and struck out with claws and teeth where men charged at the giant-kin's back.

The mammoth pounded forward, now guided by a small knot of frost-haired Ymirish warriors and one of the sorcerers, who cast before them that same wall of dark slashing mists that had blinded and blistered the Cruaidhi. The mammoth was the other strong point in the raider line. The creature shrugged aside arrows and swords, and few lances had the thrust to penetrate its thick hide.

Kern thought he saw Gard Foehammer working his way toward beast and northern brothers, and wished the man Crom's own strength.

Closer, the battle fared well. The smell of blood and bowels rose over the battlefield, and the snow had been stained red in many places. And though they bled, none of Kern's people were down yet.

Beating off another attacker's charge, Kern turned him into Reave and the greatsword's deadly reach. Then a horse screamed nearby as a lance punched through its chest. Its rider was thrown back, a jumble of tangled chain mail and leather straps and broken lance. The Aquilonian hit the ground hard, and the dying beast fell across his legs, pinning him to the ground.

Stupid, useless animals.

Kern did it without thinking, leaping for the fallen man's side as he would protect one of his own. He saw a raider staggering around the flailing beast's other side, intent on finishing off the downed soldier, who was slow to crawl back to his feet. Kern would not see any ally cut down so easily as that. Conan's man or not, that argument mattered little to Kern.

What surprised him was when a bare-chested Ymirish also ran forward, and slipped in at Kern's side!

Kern's vision dimmed and his eyes stung to tears, as if he'd been brushed across the face with the smoke of a greenwood fire. The smell was of hoarfrost, though, and it thickened at the back of his throat, closing off his breathing. Time slowed as he and the frost-haired follower of Grimnir pushed forward together. It wasn't the first time another warrior had glanced at Kern's coloring, and looked past his Cimmerian garb to see a threat from the north. It was one of the few times that a Ymirish had made such a mistake though, too intent on a victim to see the danger until far too late.

Black spots swam before Kern's eyes, and his lungs pounded, as if he'd forgotten how to breathe. Nothing wrong with his arm, however. He circled around in a spinning slash, chopping the broadsword right into the back of the large northerner's neck.

A set of yellow eyes glanced over for the space of a heartbeat, confusion reigning. He died without realizing the mistake he had made, staring into Kern's pitiless gaze.

Shouts of triumph and a bellowing roar of angry

displeasure assaulted the battlefield. Chants of "The serpent! The serpent is destroyed!"

The Cimmerian calls drew Kern's attention to a spot on the bluff edge not far away where three men slowly dug their way out of a small mound of snow. Two of them had blood leaking from their noses, their ears. The third dropped a heartbeat later from long gashes torn into his chest and neck.

Kern staggered forward as if suddenly released from a dark grip, coming astride of the fallen Aquilonian, who was barely back to his hands and knees with the thick chain mail slowing him down so. The fire-headed Vanir paused, shocked into a moment's hesitation. Kern thrust the broadsword through the other man's neck. Blood fountained down the length of the blade and splashed warmly over Kern's fingers. He pulled it free, then nearly whipped it around at Desa's neck as she elbowed him in the side.

"That's two of those bastards!" she said, and her normally waspish face was bright with bloodthirsty delight.

She helped the struggling Aquilonian back to his feet. His companions were wheeling their own mounts around, coming back to his aid.

Two. The events were so closely tied—Ymirish and serpent—that Kern could not fail to make the connection. He shook the last of the haze from his mind, and glanced around. Saw the patchy fog around him— stained dark and sooty—dissipate on a final breeze.

Almost he caught a glimpse of bright, springtime blue overhead.

Kern glanced at his feet. The frost-man had fallen on his side, and he toed the body over with a sharp kick. Two golden, blazing eyes stared back from the man's bared chest. A sorcerer! Kern had taken the head of another of Grimnir's cruel cadre.

And the northern leader knew it. Had felt it some-how. Roared still his anger and displeasure. Desa grabbed Kern by the shoulder and spun him around, pointing him at the danger.

Grimnir, hacking and beating his way through the Cimmerian war host.

Driving straight for Kern!

"Sure and you had to get that one's attention," Reave called back, slinging gore from his blade over the ruined snow.

Nahud'r and Aodh pulled in at Reave's side, but left room for Kern as well. Aodh's left arm hung useless at his side, blood sheeting down from a deep shoulder wound. He carried Ehmish's silver-chased blade in his good hand, having borrowed it for the day's battle.

Desa and Ossian also tightened up ranks, holding off a trio of raiders with blocking cuts and a lot of shield work, buying the pack time. Kern drew from their strength, their support. He hefted Burok Bear-slayer's sword, adjusting his weakening, blood-slicked grip.

"To the end," he called.

Reave was first to back him. "To the end!"

The end the others all whispered or shouted, or they simply nodded their promises. It seemed as if a deter-mined futility had settled in over them all, which was fine with Kern. In the face of desperate battle, what more was there?

Nahud'r gripped Kern on the shoulder. "A miracle occurred this day," he said.

Kern smiled grimly. Nodded. Then he brandished the broadsword and, with a violent yell, charged for-ward into the face of Grimnir's steady advance.

His wolves ran at his heels, snarling and snapping.

28

BLOOD SANG IN Daol's ears, and he tasted its iron scent on the air. Calls and battle cries hammered into his head, raising his own bloodlust even as his bowstring *thrummed* and swift death flew out on the late-morning breezes.

He recoiled just the once when he heard the crash of war hosts meeting in the center of the small plateau. Shattering bucklers and dented helms and steel ringing against edged steel. Wounded cries. Rage-filled shouts.

A fading scream as some unlucky warrior was flung off the edge of the nearby bluff to fall down through the heavy fog enshrouding Broken Leg Glenn.

Another arrow. And another.

Daol had felt the separation when Kern and Reave and the rest of the small band charged forward, leaving him, his father, and Brig Tall-Wood behind to volley arrows at the onrushing horde. Had felt it like a warm cloak being pulled from his shoulders, leaving him exposed to the dank and the dark.

Not a great deal of time to worry about such things. As fast as he could pluck arrows from the ground in front of him, Daol strung them, drew back to his cheek, sighted along the polished shaft, and drew in a steadying breath—*loose!*—and the arrow was away. Then the next.

And the next.

Hydallan and Brig worked as hard as he to feather the Vanir line with gray shafts and piercing heads. Here and there a man stumbled, went down, and was trampled by companions. More often their arrows bit into wooden targets or shattered against upraised, metal-shod shields. But it was something. Enough to soften the blow against Kern's charge.

If he could, Daol knew that he'd also have put himself right in front of his friend, facing down any swordsman who dared approach. Not out of gratitude for his rescue or for their longtime friendship, either. Not anymore. That might have been the case a few days back, or even a few weeks back when Daol had seen his capture by the raiders to be a just reward for his weakness in abandoning his friend. Nothing Kern could have done after that would have lost Daol's support. Not even Kern's determination to throw them after the Vanir.

Taur and Cruaidh and the Pass of Blood.

Callaugh and their series of hard, fast strikes over the Broken Leg Lands.

No. Not for friendship. It went beyond that. Daol couldn't say exactly when it happened—after the battle for the Pass, certainly before the meeting of chieftains at Callaugh—but it had. He'd realized it as he turned to follow Kern from the circle of torches there, ready to fight and die if Ros-Crana or Narach Chieftain threatened them. He realized it again now, plying the skies with arrows and always—always!—keeping one eye on Kern.

He'd begun to believe in the legend.

"Out!" Brig called, lowering his bow and drawing his sword. Hydallan did the same.

Daol still had a trio of shafts clenched in his teeth, but he mirrored the others. The battle had spread out from two shattered lines into a wide field of hard knots and solo contests. A group of raiders might band together for short, vicious assaults, then shatter like quicksilver as a heavy fist of Cimmerians pulled together to strike back. The tide of battle ebbed and flowed, washing over the snow-shrouded battlefield from the rising slopes to the cliff edge that dropped down onto Clan Conarch.

A few Vanir swordsmen had broken free to run loose behind the lines and Daol used one of his final arrows to put a metal head right into the gut of one raider who pressed too close.

"Getting friendly," Hydallan said, ducking a vicious slash by another raider and opening up the northerner's belly like overripe fruit with a single, efficient slash from his broadsword. He waved the younger men forward, after the rest of their band. Forcing themselves into the thicker part of the fighting.

Daol agreed, especially as it seemed that only Kern and Ros-Crana seemed to hold strong islands amidst the seas of blood and fortune. He saw the raven-haired war leader off to their far right, keeping a line of pikemen in good order as they set a defensive wall of glistening steel that no Vanir had yet broken. Kern did not operate so rigidly, Daol judged. His people simply knew how to respond as one, as if guided by a single will. They worked together, rather than in competition or out of blind courage.

Which also made them a target.

"Grimnir!" Brig shouted, seeing the danger at the same time as Daol.

While the sun rose, thinning the patchwork fog, Daol had lost sight of Grimnir. Or had forgotten him on purpose rather than worry about the terrible giant-kin. His ferocious visage was enough to strike fear even into the hearts of Crom's favored. The bestial face. A titan's strength that flattened men before him. His eyes of blazing fire, which reminded Daol of Kern except for the murderous rage that smoldered within.

Now Grimnir waded through the battle with the same care a man might take fording a young stream. Battling his way toward Kern and the rest of the valley pack.

"Worse, I'm thinking." Hydallan waved his blade toward the eastern side of the field, where the mammoth had trampled along, swatting and stomping over Cimmerian lives.

The great beast had a dozen arrows or more sticking out of its back, its neck. But it moved with fresh strength as it turned and stormed back toward its master, called by Grimnir's challenging roars or by some arcane sense. A trio of Ymirish flanked the beast on one side, and a dozen or more Vanir. An unstoppable force, pointed right at Kern's small bastion, putting them inside a slowly squeezing vise with it on the one side and Grimnir the other.

"I've got this," Brig called back over one shoulder, taking a step in the direction of the mammoth's path of rampage. Sword in one hand. Bow in the other. "Get to Wolf-Eye," he said.

Daol grabbed him by the elbow, pulling him along another few paces with him and Hydallan. "We all go," he said, talking through clenched teeth and around the arrow shafts in his mouth. "Kern ordered us together."

There wasn't time for a conversation. There was hardly time to draw breath in between threats. But Brig Tall-Wood spun around to face Daol, turning his back on the fighting as he shook his arm free of the younger man's grip.

"Then it won't be the first time I've ignored a command from my chieftain." The outburst was as surprising to Brig as it was to Daol. The fact that the other man even named Kern a chieftain seemed a hard admission for him to make.

"I stay away, and Cul has no chance to reach him." He shook his head before Daol could ask. "No time to argue. I need to do this, Daol. For me and for him." He shouldered the other man aside then, setting off into a hard sprint. "Get to Kern! Go!"

What else was there to do? Daol barely had time to spit out one of his last two arrows. Notch, draw, and *loose* at Brig Tall-Wood's back.

Taking a Vanir spearman in the side, just beneath the armpit, before he could run Brig through with his long shaft.

"Let him go," Hydallan said, kicking a body free of his sword. "A man makes his own choices. Always."

He did. And Daol knew his choice had been made already. He and his father ran forward, splitting apart from Brig's path as they raced after Kern and tried to get there before Grimnir. Before the northern force rallied to their living god.

Before their outcast chieftain was lost to them all.

KERN WATCHED AS Grimnir and a troop of his largest warriors bore down on Kern's small band with the savage fury of Ymir's legend. The outcast's mouth dried with the bitter taste of adrenaline and no little fear as the giant-kin stomped forward with a brutal swagger that dared all to cross his path. Those who did rarely lasted long. One-handing the battle-axe or smashing at raised shields with the warhammer, Grimnir reigned brutally over the blood-spattered snow and hard rock.

"Ymirish!" he bellowed. And then, "Gorge! Rend!" Not only did several more frost-haired warriors rally, but the white-pelted saber-tooths hauled themselves away from nearby fights as if jerked on the end of invisible tethers. Frostpaw snapped at the heels of one, giving chase, but shied away from a Vanir's sword when the raider suddenly blocked its path.

The large cats bounded to their master's side. And the next warrior who stood in their way, they both leaped at her. One sank teeth deep into her leg. The other into a shoulder, bearing her to the ground and working its back claws to eviscerate the hapless woman's bowels.

The animals left her screaming and dying, innards strung out and glistening against pink snow.

Forming into a thick wedge with Grimnir at its head, the juggernaut trampled forward over the lives of strong clansmen. A small fist of Cruaidhi hammered at one side, splitting off a few northern swordsmen. And a javelin flashed through the few remaining tendrils of fog to skewer a Ymirish through the chest, knocking him back and pinning him to the earth like a beetle fastened to a fisherman's barbed hook.

Hardly enough to dent the mob. Certainly not enough to slow it. Several dozen raiders with blood staining their blades and fury glowing in their eyes bore down. Too many for Kern's small band to hold off. Too many to stand against longer than a few sword strokes.

But Kern raised his blade defiantly, as did the others around him. Reave and Nahud'r. Ossian, Finn, Mogh, and Aodh. And the Aquilonian horseman, with his saber and a small shield held at the ready. Kern had almost forgotten about the Aquilonian.

Fortunately for them all, the southerner's comrades-in-arms had not.

Wheeling horses around with lances thrusting out and strong arms driving their points, they saved the wolf pack from taking the brunt of Grimnir's charge. Like avenging demons, they hammered into the side of

the mob, driving deep, skewering two men on the end
of their lances. One pole shattered just back of the tip.
The other man managed to back his lance out, then
clubbed at another Ymirish with it, striking him just
over one ear and knocking him senseless to the ground
before the lance was yanked from his grip.

Spurring forward, sabers rose and fell, rose and fell;
hacking at faces and shoulders and upraised arms.
Blood splattered, and men cried out in pain. A few
Callaughnan warriors ran forward, into the wound in-
flicted on Grimnir's line, their own large swords working incredible damage.

It stalled the northerners' charge. For a moment.

The men of the wolves wasted no time, dragging
down several raiders at the fore while the northerners'
line was a shambles. Wallach Graybeard and Garret
both drove their broadswords into the chest of one of
the saber-tooths, which died slowly, spitting and
snarling and still trying to claw its way toward the
Cimmerians.

Kern and Reave charged forward together, followed
quickly by the others. Their weapons scissored at a
Vanir who had joined Grimnir's charge. Striking him
from both sides. Cutting deep, deep wounds.

Then Grimnir, with a banshee howl like the fury of
a blizzard, leaped into the air, hammer raised. The
frost-giant brought the maul's flat head down between
the eyes of one horse, shattering its skull into bits of
bone and brain. The animal dropped without a whinny
or a whimper.

Kern saw the Aquilonian rider kick free of his stir-
rups, landing in a crouch with his saber held at the
ready. Not that it mattered. Kern was too far away to
help, laying to on all sides in an attempt to gain some
room.

Grimnir smashed around with his battle-axe, the
heavy head catching the saber against the flat, cleaving

through the thin blade and embedding itself halfway through the horseman's conical helm and skull.

Using his foot to shove the man free, Grimnir roared in triumph and turned in search of his next victim. In time to see Kern strike down a Ymirish from behind with two short, stabbing thrusts into the back. Kern's third thrust ran the man through, blade exiting through his gut as Kern held him on his feet a few heartbeats longer with fingers gripping at a heavy shank of bone blond hair.

Blood poured back over Kern's hand, warm and slick. He let the man drop, now standing in the shadow of the northern war leader.

Grimnir towered over Kern by a good arm's length and ten stones' weight. The giant-kin's hide was thick and gnarled with dense, heavy muscles shifting under pebblelike skin. He smelled of old, rotten ice. His hair was coarse and ropy, like the mammoth's, and a dull, dark red the color of clotting blood. It swept back in a tangle, with strips of leather cord and short lengths of silver chain braided into it.

His eyes were fury-bright and the same cold amber of the Ymirish. The same that Kern shared with Frostpaw.

He bared a mouth full of sharp, canine teeth at Kern, growling in a savage, animal way.

Then Grimnir struck.

Kern nearly missed the attack, not believing something so large could move so fast. The battle-axe ripped through the air, sidelong, and Kern barely managed to set his shield in the way before the smashing blow crashed off it, hammering Kern back several steps.

He jumped back farther when the warhammer came thundering overhead, letting it smash the ground instead. Feeling the strength of the blow through his feet.

His return slash had barely the reach of his old arming sword, and was too slow. The giant leader batted it aside with casual strength, spinning Kern around. The

Cimmerian ducked beneath another wild slash and took the warhammer against his shield the next time, feeling it all the way into his chest as the heavy maul drove him back, leaving his shield arm numb and nearly useless.

Kern shuffled back, searching for strong footing beneath the snow and slush.

Grimnir followed, his savage face split into a toothy grin now that he had Kern's measure.

It was as if the two of them stood in an isolated pocket. Kern's pack struggled alongside Callaughnan and Cruaidhi. Taking the best the northern army could throw at them, then shoving the invaders back on their heels, they held off the tide of northerners sweeping to this side of the battlefield. Clansmen fell, wounded, dying, or dead, but in every place they did so they took two or even three enemy to their one.

But Kern had not been fighting to best the monstrous northerner. Only to survive. Waiting for his pack to gather for the chance to pull down the frost-giant with their combined strength. Reave came at the frost-giant from the left, greatsword lunging forward with strong muscles driving it. Ossian and Nahud'r from behind.

It was their best and possibly only moment. Kern leaped forward now, into the monster's embrace. His broadsword sweeping up in a hard, overhead arc and hammering down at Grimnir's guard. Once. Twice.

Battering the terrible war leader in a fury of strength.

Buying time for Reave and the others.

Not enough. Grimnir nearly knocked Kern's blade from his hand with a hard, glancing blow from his warhammer, then he kicked back like a mule, catching Ossian in the gut and folding the man over like a greenstick branch. Nahud'r sliced his scimitar at the side of Grimnir's leg and twice across his wide back, so fast that his arm was a blur of motion. Cutting deeply each time. But the giant-kin hardly seemed to notice.

A half turn and another sidelong blow with the giant

maul. Nahud'r tumbled sideways, rolling into the feet of two Vanir who had rushed forward to the aid of their legendary war leader.

Which left two of the pack. A tangle of arms, legs, and blades. Men against monster, but an intelligent one. A vicious, thinking creature with two years of legend riding at his shoulder.

But they would not give up. Reave bashed greatsword against battle-axe, steel ringing out in violent tones. His second lunge nearly took Grimnir in the throat, but the giant warrior ducked low and forward.

Into Kern's broadsword, which struck him through the breastbone.

Driving deep into the giant's chest.

Grimnir bellowed in pain. His battle-axe dropped to the ground as the frost-giant stiffened, rising up, and for an instant Kern hung from the end of his blade. Then the northern leader planted the head of his warhammer into Kern's chest and *shoved*. Throwing him sideways into Reave and a small drift of snow.

The warriors quickly rolled back up to hands and knees, thinking the fight over.

In fact, the entire battle seemed to hang on an edge, holding its breath. There were a few premature Cimmerian cheers, and shouts of dismay among the Vanir horde. Nearby struggles broke apart as warriors turned toward the legendary leader. Drawn by a kind of terrible magnetism. Waiting.

Only to watch him reach up for Kern's broadsword, take a firm grip, and pull it from his chest with slow deliberation and a savage, toothy smile.

Kern's hopes sank low into the pit of his stomach as Grimnir the Undefeatable, the Immortal, threw back his head for a strong, commanding roar of challenge.

A single word, drawn out in Cimmeria's own tongue. "KILL!"

29

"KILL!"

Then, also in the flat Nordheimir tongue, "To me! TO ME!"

Brig Tall-Wood winced as the challenging shouts roared out, the frost-giant's dark, commanding voice driving daggers into the back of his skull. And again when horns rose from the far end of the battlefield, echoing the call. Glancing back, he saw Grimnir's forces rallying near Kern's position, the legendary leader standing over several fallen warriors with a large hammer in one hand and a Cimmerian broadsword in the other.

No sign of Kern. Or Nahud'r, whose dark skin was also obvious at a distance.

Daol was nothing more than another warrior nearly lost among the tangle of men, mastiffs, and the chaos of battle. Brig picked him out of the tangles only because he was one of very few Cimmerians charging to Kern's side.

No help for them now, Brig saw. The best he could still do was prevent the mammoth and the second sorcerer from leading a new charge to the giant's aid. Stop them. Slow them down. Somehow.

Dodging around several struggles where Vanir and Cimmerian matched themselves in sword strokes and shields, Brig pumped his legs harder. His breathing turned ragged and raw in his throat.

He nearly raced past a struggling knot of Vanir who bashed repeatedly at a trio of Cimmerians, leaving them in his wake as well, until he noticed the tall man at their center with a large pike that flashed around in sharp, violent arcs. The javelin's head jabbed through one throat, then reversed to skewer a raider rushing up from behind. The other two Cimmerians fell to the raiders, though each took a man with them into death. Leaving three more against the pike-bearer's one.

Gard Foehammer was good. No denying that. But still stood to be overwhelmed.

No time to decide. Brig simply acted. Whether out of that measure of respect he himself had felt back in Cruaidh, or because Kern would have stopped to help. Or both. He damned Kern again for invading his thoughts.

But even as he did, it was his own voice echoing back inside his head *chieftain . . . chieftain . . .*

Too far away to challenge one of the northerners directly, Brig shouted a long, angry cry as he sprinted forward, raising his broadsword overhead. Holding the length of blade downward, directly in line with his spine. One of the raiders turned his way, looking for the new challenge, and Brig ducked forward, whipping his blade overhead and giving it a good end-over-end throw.

Not at the warrior who faced him, though. The broadsword tumbled past the Vanir, cutting heavily at the air, and struck hard into the back of one of the men advancing on Gard. The strength of the blow knocked the man off his feet, tumbling the Vanir to the ground with life already ebbing from his body.

Gard lost no time. He battered aside the sword of his remaining opponent with stafflike blows against the arm and shoulder, then punched the blue-iron head of his pike into the raider's chest. Yanking it free again, he turned and threw the pike javelin-style.

It caught the raider charging forward at an unarmed Brig square in the small of the back. Losing his broadsword from nerveless fingers, the man tumbled forward and flopped facedown into the snow and bloody muck. His cry of pain was cut short as Brig raced up to drop a knee hard against the back of the raider's neck, breaking it easily with a loud crunch.

"With Crom's own eye," Foehammer thanked Brig, returning the thrown sword and paying high respect for the savage attack that had brought down the first man.

"We're not done," Brig gasped, with barely time to draw new breath. The taste of blood sat on his tongue and filled his nose with a warm, copperish scent. Seeing an arrow stuck in the ground nearby, he sheathed the broadsword and took the hunting bow from around his shoulder. "The mammoth."

Gard looked, saw how the beast was making a shambles of the Cimmerian force as it pounded back toward its master, and nodded. Helping Brig up with a hand beneath his arm, the valleymen raced back into the fray. Gard the faster of the two. Brig grabbed at the arrow along the way, wrenching it up from the ground. Still good, with no cracks and a broadhead tip with sharp edges.

Overall, it seemed, the mixed band of Cimmerian warriors were holding their own where Ymirish swordsmen and the braying pack of mastiffs loosed among them did not interfere. Fighting for their land, striking back for several years of violent raids, they had nothing left to lose. But the greater numbers of the northerners began to tell as they pushed the battle into scattered clumps all across the bluff's small plateau.

The heaviest fighting was centered around Grimnir, where the legendary warrior drew more forces to him like metal shavings to a lodestone. As the frost-giant drove forward with weapons striking to either side, he pushed men ahead of him, toward the edge of the bluff.

Closer, though, the mammoth tore into a small band of Callaughnan, scattering them with great, swinging blows from its head, trampling them underfoot. Where a man raced up too close, a dark swirl of mist and smoke lashed out like barbed whips. Blinded men screamed and reeled away, and became easy meat for a raider's sword if they did not simply die of the dark, hateful magic.

"Ros-Crana!" Gard Foehammer shouted.

He had pulled several lengths ahead of Brig. Now he thrust his pike at an angle to one side, pointing out the Callaughnan war leader where she rallied her spear-carrying guard in the face of a strong Vanir position. They were right in the path of the war mammoth, falling back on Kern's position, but slowly. If they saw the danger, they did not react to it.

"No," Brig called out, as Gard veered away, not seeing the need to involve the Callaughnan. He slowed, and it cost him another dozen strides as Gard redoubled his own efforts.

The Callaugnan war leader might not notice the approaching mammoth, but she somehow heard Gard's shout and glanced over. She waved her spear overhead.

Brig watched as Gard sprinted forward, pike laid along his arm as he reached back, then skipped forward on one foot a moment, building his momentum into the throw. His body tightened, then snapped forward. He released the pike, which hurtled up into the air on a long, graceful arc that never wavered. Not once. It slowed, then turned back toward the earth building speed again. Brig had thought the throw too far forward of the mammoth, but Gard had taken into account the beast's trundling speed, and when the pike's hard iron point bit down, it was right into the side of the great beast.

The mammoth trumpeted shrilly in fresh pain, warning Ros-Crana how close it was to her position. She spun around a trio of her own men, leaving the rest to drive against the Vanir as she led the smaller group toward the mammoth.

Gard joined them, still several dozen strides ahead of Brig, who watched with growing awe the reckless charge.

By accident or design, the clansfolk ended up on the far side of the beast from most of the Ymirish, including the sorcerer. It bought them time—heartbeats only—before the dark mist could be sent at them. One man was beaten aside and trampled, but Gard had his sword out, slicing deep wounds, and the rest of Ros-Crana's spear-carriers thrust deep into the mammoth's side, turning the creature away from its stampede toward Grimnir and Kern.

Right into the path of Brig Tall-Wood!

The beast had hardly suffered a mortal wound, but perhaps Gard and Ros-Crana had bought Kern's wolves time. They would pay for that, though. And so would Brig, who nocked his arrow and drew back to his cheek. For the first time, he wished he had picked up one of the northerner's war bows, with their heavier draw and flatter arc. It was a fleeting desire. One he dismissed along with the likelihood of ever seeing the other side to this battle.

Calm breath. Eyes both open and unblinking. Brig tracked the point of his arrow across the struggle, and there he froze. Unable to move. Caught between heartbeats. He saw it all laid out before him as he stared past the mammoth's thundering pace. The ground shook. He saw Ymirish set upon by a pack of Cruaidhi in their dark red kilts. Saw the dark, oily mist seeped through the last of the fog, lashing out at Foehammer, who ducked away, shouting in pain, hands guarding his eyes.

Followed the trail of dark, sooty fog back to the sorcerer, who hunched just beyond the mammoth's flank, gaze intent on the spear-carrying Callaughnan, Ros Crana, and Foehammer.

In these last two, Brig saw something he desired. A selflessness, and single-minded pursuit of what was best for clan and for chieftain. But what had finally decided him was not any question on their part for their chieftain's orders. Instead, it was more the idea that they would never have to question them, as he had questioned Cul ever since being set after Kern Wolf-Eye.

Cul had seen Kern's actions as an affront to the Gaudic leader's honor. But rather than meet it himself, he had sent another. An assassin! He had sent Brig Tall-Wood, who would sacrifice his own honor no matter which way he favored.

For Cul, his rightful chieftain who should never have asked this of him, or for Kern, outcast, who never would have.

For Kern, then, who had earned the respect Cul took for granted!

Large legs like sturdy trunks hammered at the ground as the mammoth bore down on Brig, trumpeting in pain and anger, but the archer never flinched. Arrow drawn back until the feather tickled his cheek, he drew in one final, calm breath. Loosed his shaft with smooth release.

Watched it slip easily past the woolly mammoth's hairy shoulder.

Sinking into the sorcerer's chest, right through one of the yellow, tattooed eyes. Spinning the Ymirish to the ground. Dead.

Brig Tall-Wood barely noticed Grimnir's outraged roar as the giant felt his sorcerer's death. It registered in the back of his mind, just as did the last of Foehammer's cries and the oily mist, which dissipated as if swept away on a strong breeze.

Brief glimpses of the battle, as the mammoth ran Brig Tall-Wood down.

KERN HELD OUT little hope for himself, now that Grimnir had focused his giant strength against him.

No tricks would save him.

There were few left to come to his aid.

He read raw fury in Grimnir's eyes as the legendary warrior set Burok's sword against the ground and shattered it with one strong blow of the warhammer. Searching for his dropped battle-axe, he'd batted Reave aside as if the large man had been a child's plaything. The sidehand blow with the hammer had picked Reave up and thrown Kern's friend into a cluster of Vanir and Cimmerians raining blows against each other.

Kern didn't think to see him again.

The ragged cheer of Nordheim voices when their leader pulled the broadsword from his heart had nearly sapped the last of the Cimmerians' flagging strength. Several men fell during the next few moments, unable to rally against the fresh arms streaming to Grimnir's side. Garret was one of those, dragged beneath the claws of Grimnir's second snow-cat.

Many of Kern's warriors were down, in fact, though he counted most still alive as comrades fought to protect them. Aodh and Wallach looked over Nahud'r, the Shemite dazed and bloodied but still moving. Ossian had been picked up and dragged to one side by Old Finn and Ashul, and dour Mogh continued to fight at Desa's back. Even Daol had returned, putting his last arrow into the eye of a nearby Ymirish. But too many warriors stood in the way. Too many.

The ripe smell of blood and opened bowels swam

over the battlefield, and Kern's feet slipped in gore as often as they found good purchase beneath the snow-laden ground. He'd yanked his arming sword free, managing to stab Grimnir once in the arm and again in the chest, but it hardly mattered. Not when blood continued to pump from the deep wound in the giant-kin's chest, yet he seemed barely to notice.

Sword slashing for his head, battering across Kern's shield, driving him ahead. Hammer smashing down, forcing Kern to jump back.

He gave ground slowly, backing up along the edge of the bluff as some Callaughnan and Cruaidhi rushed to his aid. Sensing, perhaps, that Grimnir had to fall before the Vanir could ever be defeated. But too little, too late.

Grimnir turned and dealt them savage blows, driving them back until his Ymirish or Vanir raiders fell at them as well. He also rolled to one side and grabbed up his battle-axe again. And hacked it down through a Cimmerian's chest.

Giving Kern a look at his broad, muscular back. The Gaudic warrior ran forward, thinking he had another chance, and nearly lost an arm to one of the snow-white saber-tooths, which charged in at his side with a snarl and snapping jaws.

It cost Kern several long heartbeats, backing away from its savage attack. Reeling as claws shredded through the shoulder of his tattered poncho, ripping long bloody furrows down his arm.

It might have been worse had not Frostpaw charged in after the large cat, driven to a bloodlust of his own in the presence of so much violence. Bleeding scars and angry, open wounds promised that the large dire wolf had not been still all this time. Hunting mastiffs or tangling with swordsmen, hard to say.

But the saber-tooth—that creature the wolf obviously remembered. It charged in from the side, teeth ripping at the creature's exposed flanks, working with

Kern as it might have fought alongside a member of its long-lost pack.

And when the cat turned to gash the wolf's shoulder with long fangs, Kern lunged forward to put the point of his arming sword into its throat.

That was when Frostpaw turned on him, snarling and leaping at Kern. He did not even think to raise his sword, caught so completely by surprise by the wolf's sudden ferocity.

A good thing, as the husky canine brushed past Kern to leap at Grimnir, sinking teeth into the giant's wrist, just below the hand that held the warhammer. Grimnir's bellow was more anger than pain, though he lost the great maul as he tried to shake the wolf loose. But Frostpaw held on, dragging at the arm as it waited for Kern to rush in beside it to jab the arming sword home, into the giant's side.

Twice . . . Three times . . . Four.

More pain this time, but hardly a dying call. Grimnir slashed his battle-axe overhead at Kern, ripping the Cimmerian's shield away as the mighty blow completely numbed his arm and his fingers.

Then the frost-giant slung his other arm sideways, whipping the wolf side to side as its teeth finally tore loose, throwing the wolf into a nearby pile of boulders, where it struck hard and fell into a stunned pile.

Grimnir advanced on Kern, battle-axe raised overhead.

Then he was spinning about, bellowing. Not in rage or challenge, but in fresh agony as he searched the battlefield behind them. Something . . . ?

From the yell of victory on the far side of the field, Kern thought that the giant-kin's other sorcerer had been taken down. Regardless, he knew to take advantage of it. Kern jumped in beneath the frost-giant's terrible reach, arming sword striking with a viper's speed as he punched it over and over into Grimnir's side and chest.

Not that it did any better than the deep wound he had punched through the beast-leader's heart. Grimnir batted Kern aside with his open hand. It was like being struck with a log across his head and shoulders, throwing him back into a shallow drift of snow and dropping him into an ungainly pile. Kern tasted blood in his mouth, and spit it out as he rolled back to his hands and feet, squatting in a ready crouch as the great leader of the north roared and leaped for him one last time, axe already slashing down.

Kern acted without thought, letting instinct take over. Against such terrifying strength and greater reach, he knew he had to come up close. He shuffled forward quickly, ducking beneath the battle-axe and slamming body to body against the giant. His arming sword rammed deep between two rocklike ribs, burying itself in Grimnir's flesh. Then he lost his grip as the full force of Grimnir's charge bowled him back toward the bluff's nearby edge.

Kern knew then he was lost, and had one last service to pay for his friends' lives. To give them any chance of salvaging the battle, or simply escaping with their lives.

To give Ehmish the chance to fight for his life. To let Daol find Reave, and hopefully Desa.

To give Cimmeria a chance before the Vanir raiders ran over the entire land.

Kern grabbed at his sword and Grimnir's wrist, falling back, and pulling the giant-kin with him. Stumbling up to the edge of the bluff, and hanging there, over the fog that still swam through the glen far, far below.

Then he simply threw himself back, adding a bit more momentum as he hauled the frost-giant back over the cliff face.

Dragging Grimnir the Invulnerable with him into death.

EPILOGUE

DARKNESS SMOTHERED KERN, weighing down his arms, his legs. Making it hard to breathe without tasting the blood that clogged his nose. It pushed his face against the cold, unyielding rock, and winter's touch shivered deep inside in the places where Kern was never warm.

Not even in death, it seemed.

There were eyes on him. He felt their cold touch. And he heard voices that whispered beneath the howl of banshees riding the darkness. Friends, he decided, who had preceded him into death. Wolves of the pack. They scuffled and scratched around him in the dark and the cold. Their fingers were cold as the dead rock on which he lay. And painful. Clawing at his soul and his sanity as they struggled to rip both away from his flesh.

"Broken?" one of the rasping voices asked.

"Nay that I can tell." That one hawked and spit into the howling calls of the winds and distant creatures of the night.

Familiar.

A large, rough hand grabbed him by the chin, shifting his head back and forth. His neck spasmed with pain, and even in the dark he sensed sparks lighting off behind his eyes. The strong fingers did not burn with cold or pain there. Only the ones pressing at his arms, his side, where his skin had been flayed from his body.

"Looked better."

Kern began to suspect that he might not be dead after all.

He forced open one eye. The broad face hanging blurrily before him sharpened into focus only slowly. Oval shaped, with dark hair matted with blood and dirt sticking to the sides of his face. Glacial blue eyes staring at him, an open window into the exhaustion and concern Reave had to be feeling. Mouth set in a grim line, and upper lip clotted with blood that had run from a broken nose.

"Mus' be dead," Kern said. His voice croaked out with rusty strength. "All a' us. Too ugly to let live, this one."

He tried to close his eyes again, but rough hands fastened on to his shoulders and his poncho and hauled him upright. Fire washed over Kern's back and down his side, crisping the flesh of his legs and arms and across his chest. Basically everywhere. He winced in pain, drawing in a sharp breath, and pushed their hands away as he struggled forward on his own.

His friends slammed him back against the rock wall.

"Not so fast," Daol warned. "It is quite a step from here."

Opening his eyes more carefully this time, giving his tired brain time to think about what he was seeing, Kern saw that the three of them perched on a narrow ledge against the side of the cliff face he'd thrown himself down. From his seated position, he could stare up and back along the way he must have come. Steep, but not a straight drop. Lots of handholds and broken alpines that must have claimed their share of skin on the way down. Given the raw pain covering his body, and the bloody swatches he could see on his chest and arms, he changed his mind.

More than their share.

The banshees continued to wail for him, but the darkness had retreated into the back corners of his mind. Kern allowed his friends to help him up, standing on shaky legs as the three rested back against the rock, away from the long drop that continued on toward the floor of the glen. Late afternoon. The fog had all burned away, though a slight haze of smoke remained as a few trees and many of the unprotected homes surrounding Conarch continued to burn. The soot and acrid scent mixed with the taste of blood in his mouth.

Past a low ringing in his ears, Kern listened as the banshee's call changed to the distant, mournful dirges of Vanir horns and the much closer howls of a large wolf. With effort, he shook the last of the cobwebs from his mind and grabbed Daol by the shoulder.

"The Vanir? The northern war host? Grimnir?" No, he didn't care as much about them. If his friends were there, much of that had solved itself, one way or another. "Our warriors?" he asked, voice stronger. "Who made it through?"

"You seem to be fine," Daol said, glancing at their large friend. "Told you," was all he said to Reave in a brief aside.

"And we might have been very lucky. Wallach Graybeard will lose his hand—near severed anyway. Nahud'r has some broken ribs. Old Finn might not walk again, and Garret is clawed up something fierce. But other than a bunch of cuts and bruises, and lots of blood lost, we came through alive." He must have seen the disbelief. "All of us, Kern. You saw us through."

Another long, savage howl. Reave cursed into the cold winds that continued to blow along the cliff face, sweeping the hair in front of his eyes. "Even that damned wolf will see another day. Been howling up a storm ever since it recovered, pacing the cliff edge with its nose to the ground. Stayed up there even when most of the war host cleared out to chase down Vanir survivors."

As it turned out, seeing their legendary warrior and infallible leader pulled over the cliff had dispirited the Vanir force so much that several had broken and run on the spot. As if a spell had washed over them. And perhaps that wasn't far from the case, Kern decided later, hearing tales of the way Grimnir had been very much aware of his sorcerers' deaths, and they his needs.

He waited to ask about the frost-giant warrior until safely back atop the cliff face. It was a long climb, especially considering his rough treatment on the way down, but Kern didn't suffer anything worse than a lot of skin loss and a wrenched neck.

It took more than that to keep a Cimmerian from such a short climb.

Funeral piles heaped up in several places as the northerners' dead were thrown atop each other with no ceremony other than a quick few sword chops and a head stuck up on a freshly cut pole. There was a special row for Ymirish. Seventeen of them in all, with blood matting their long, frost blond beards and yellow eyes permanently staring in death.

They found Brig Tall-Wood there with Gard Foehammer and Sláine Longtooth. Brig looked about as battered as Kern, with deep bruises purpling under the skin on his chest and arms. Gard's eyes were bandaged over, and welts the size of sickness blisters stood out as painful red splotches on his face.

"Still alive, Kern Wolf-Eye." Longtooth had one

arm in a sling, but otherwise looked hale. In his other hand he held a bearing spear for Clan Cruaidh, with its fox's tail tied near the top.

"Still alive," Kern admitted. Though he hardly felt as if he should be.

The sun had driven away all sign of fog and frost. It stood deep in the western sky now, glinting off the snow that still covered the plateau country. But maybe, Kern thought, the end of winter was near.

Though not the threat of Grimnir.

"Tracks was all we found," Ossian told him when he led back an armed party from the base of the cliffs. "Tracks from the war leader hisself and at least fifty men. They staggered south, away from Conarch." A quick glance at Longtooth. "Ros-Crana has already left, to see to the safety of Callaugh."

"Not Narach Chieftain?" Kern asked, sensing that Ossian held something back.

"Dead," Gard said, his voice filled with pain but fighting to remain even. "She will return her brother's body to the village and prepare him for the Field of the Chiefs."

"After she is named chieftain, I don't doubt." This from Reave, who sounded a bit admiring. Desa cuffed him sharply against the side of the head. "Damn, woman!"

There was no laughter. Wounds and the loss of so many good warriors were still too raw for that. But there might have been a grim smile or two. For his part, Kern simply nodded his farewell to Longtooth and staggered back to the bluff's edge to stare down the long drop he had made with Grimnir in tow.

Better they both had died in that fall. Better for Cimmeria, anyway.

Daol and Hydallan joined him first. Reave and Desa and Ossian. They came limping up singly or in pairs after that, like rogues called back to the pack. Only Wallach Graybeard was missing, taken to the shaman who watched over the other wounded. And Ehmish.

But they were all alive. Crom had truly favored Kern's warriors with strength and their will to live.

"Now?" Reave asked. A simple question, but one that limped out under the weight of so many weeks' travel and fighting.

Now. That was the decision Kern had to make. "We are not done," Kern said. "Not while Grimnir lives and the Vanir raid Cimmeria. He'll come at us again. And again. I've no doubt."

"So we chase after and bring the fight to him," Desa said. Her voice was little more than a savage growl. There were nods of assent around the small circle.

"No." Kern looked about until he found what he needed. A broken spear, with half its shaft and the tip still in place. It was bloodied several times over, with the blood of Cimmerians or Vanir—it didn't matter. Very much like the one Gard Foehammer had used to summon help from the valley clans. A symbol every chieftain of Cimmeria would have to consider. "We carry this to other clans," he said. "They have to know that the danger is getting worse. That it is time to rally against Vanaheim."

"How many?" Brig asked. He stared at the bloody spear, and at Kern Wolf-Eye. "How many clans?"

But Kern only had eyes for the northern horizon. And the passes into Nordheim. "All of them," he finally said.

"Starting with home."